ALTERED MASHUP

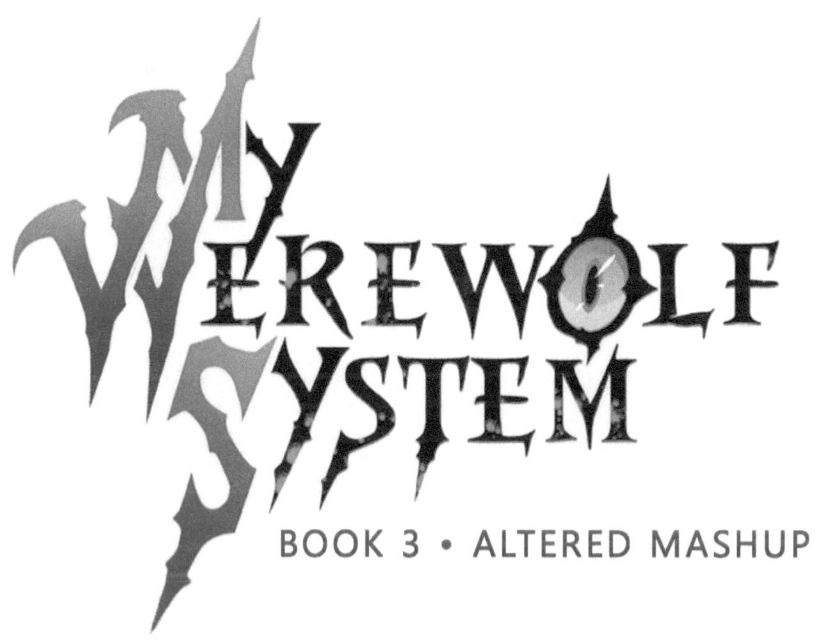

JKSMANGA

Podium

ALTERED MASHUP

CHAPTER 1

GETTING STRONGER (PART 1)

The sun had barely risen, leaving the town of Slough covered in a gray mist. It was an unusual sight for three students in particular because they had never woken up this early in their lives, much less come to school at such an hour.

Innu was groggily walking up the stairs to Westbridge's roof; he saw the door just a little ahead. The teenager was still in the middle of a stretch, yawning so wide that he could have fit his fist inside his mouth. As he opened the door, he was surprised to see that he was apparently the last one to arrive.

"You're late," Kai stated, not even turning around as he continued to look out from the roof's fence. The blond teenager was staring into the distance. As to where exactly, only he seemed to know, for all Marie and Austin could see was the school field, which was currently empty, as well as the shapes of a few buildings. They had seen Kai do this several times in the short amount of time they had known him.

"Late?" Innu checked his phone, which revealed that it was five past six in the morning. "Oh come on, it's only by five minutes."

Under normal circumstances, he would have still been asleep. At this hour, the only person one might expect to see at school was its caretaker. However, Innu lacked the energy to argue right now, so he silently moved over to his fellow Howlers members. Marie and Austin looked just as tired as he did, their bodies slumped over.

How did Austin manage to get here before me? He doesn't even live in this area or go to the same school, Innu thought.

"Aren't you worried you might be late for classes?" he eventually asked Austin, who was fixing his hair.

"Worried about the classes I never go to? At a school that will never get me anywhere in life? I thought joining this gang made it pretty clear that I have nowhere better to go." Austin gave Innu a look that made him feel like an idiot.

Just as Innu was about to say something back, Kai stopped staring outside and turned to look at his fellow gang members.

"Enough with the chitchat. After our fight with the gray color gang, each one of you came up to me individually. You all told me how useless you felt when faced against those freakish twins . . . Well, I felt the same way. Which is why we can't stay the same. If we do, then there is no hope for us.

"Our gang is small and has only just started, but I hope that soon enough it will be the Howlers instead of the Underdogs that people associate with the town of Slough. Once we have achieved that, we can go for the county, then the country, and finally the whole world."

It should have sounded crazy, that type of talk coming from a teenager, yet somehow, when Kai spoke about his ambition, none of the other three felt like laughing, or that it was unrealistic. They might not yet know how, but he seemed determined enough that he would come up with a way to achieve that goal.

"Of course, if it was that easy, anyone could have done that already. Along the way, we will face countless enemies who will make the gray color gang look like a bunch of clowns in comparison. I won't sugarcoat it, we'll eventually have to deal with Altered, and I mean real ones, not whatever those twins turned into!

"So I want you to never forget the fear that you felt that day. How it was mostly luck that we even made it out alive . . .

"Now, I've come up with a strict training regimen for all of us. We'll be practicing two hours each day before school starts," Kai explained with a sadistic smile.

Everyone had their fists clenched tightly, and it looked like they were ready. The little pep talk had almost gotten rid of their tiredness, and everyone was put into action.

Innu and Austin were told to start with some warm-up activities. The idea was to build up their basic stats. The two of them were talented and although Innu trained, he had nearly always done so alone. Austin was the opposite, never having attempted to push his body to the limit but always getting in fights.

The two teenage boys began running around the roof a few times, increasing their basic strength with push-up workouts and more, and eventually they finished up with a few spars here and there. They were learning a lot from each other, and their competitive nature made each one try to outdo the other.

"Forty-five!" Innu loudly announced how many push-ups he had already done, sweat dripping down his forehead, falling on his chiseled abs, as he had long since taken his shirt off, same as Austin.

"Bullshit, you call that a push-up?" Austin sneered, as he demonstrated how to do it correctly. "If you can't do it with proper form, then that means you're done, don't try to force it!"

"Talk to me about form once your bum isn't all the way in the air!" Innu argued back.

Next it looked like the two were moving on to squats; however, they weren't regular squats—at least for Innu, who placed one of his legs straight out and was going down using only the other leg. Seeing this, Austin attempted to do the same, but his balance was horrible.

When he got down to the bottom, he attempted to push off but he had never done this before; his whole body was shaking, and just when he was about to fall over he felt Innu grab him to steady him.

"It's harder than it looks," Innu said. Austin was expecting a smile but Innu didn't give him one as he lifted him up. "You're a strong hitter, and I'm surprised you have punches that strong while having such weak legs. If you strengthen your legs, then your punches will have even more power in them."

As he walked back to do his exercises, Austin studied the sheer size of Innu's legs. His thighs were thick like tree trunks, and it looked like there was no space in his trousers for them to breathe.

I thought Innu was just naturally strong like me, but it looks like he put in a lot of hard work, Austin thought.

CHAPTER 2

GETTING STRONGER (PART 2)

Kai didn't care that the two boys were bickering; as long as they were working hard, they could do whatever they wanted. Meanwhile, he had come over to Marie to give her special training. She had never been much of a fighter, so doing the same as the boys wouldn't help her enough.

When she came to him with her request, Kai had been reluctant. In the past, he had always been there to take care of any problems she might have. However, he couldn't argue much, once Marie had confessed that she was worried she might get kidnapped again.

Coming toward her, Kai opened a small suitcase that contained two four-inch knives.

"Wait, you want me to use these? How did you even manage to get your hands on weapons?" Marie exclaimed, a little shocked, pushing the box back. Immediately she regretted it, because Kai obviously had jumped through some hoops to acquire them.

"Yes, I want you to use them," Kai answered, annoyed. If anyone understood what he was proposing, it should have been her.

"You want to fight like the others, right? Let's not kid ourselves, we both know that you're no fighter, Marie. You neither have the body to compete with fighters around our age, much less adult men, nor do you have the experience or skills to make up for such a deficit.

"There are only two ways for you to catch up quickly. Either you use weapons . . . or you become an Altered. The latter option is pretty much impossible for us, so we can only go with the former. Trust me, there are psychos out there who will use weapons against you without giving it a second thought. We're talking about your life here. Forget about holding on to some stupid pride, thinking that using weapons is wrong. Don't die because of that."

Marie looked at the two weapons again, and this time she took them out of the box and held them in her hands. It felt natural to hold them by the handle, similar to how one would use them in the kitchen.

But the knives weren't like kitchen knives, as there was a guard to keep her hand from touching the blade, but they weren't like daggers either, as the ends were rounded, not pointed.

"It's not pride," Marie finally replied, looking into Kai's eyes. "I just don't want to kill anyone. I know what you're saying, and maybe one day if it's their life against mine I will fight to the death, but these weapons could kill someone."

Kai grabbed both the knives from Marie and stood a distance away from her, so she wouldn't get hurt. He then held the two knives in a combat position, so the blades were sticking out from the backs of his hands rather than from his palms like a pair of daggers.

He looked like one of those secret agents on TV who fought in the jungle.

"You don't have to use the weapons to kill. You will be using them to cut, not to stab," Kai explained. He started to move about with the blades, spinning his body as if he were going up against an opponent. As Marie watched, he seemed to be shadow fighting against more than a single opponent.

Kai's display was so impressive that Innu and Austin couldn't help but stop their warm-up to observe him. He was smooth and quick, but most of all, he was confident as well. When the demonstration was over, the two boys felt motivated to work even harder.

"When you stab an opponent, you risk losing your weapon. You might be unable to pull it out from their body, or worse, they might use it against you. Either scenario gives them a chance to retaliate. Doing it the way I've just shown you is far better for you, especially given your current strength."

Marie took the blades back and nodded. Kai went on to slowly show her the movements one by one, explaining in great detail the best thing to do, step by step. He even had a pair of fake wooden blades as well. Of course, Marie was finding it difficult, but she had never expected things to be easy; she knew that it would take time.

After an hour and a half passed the group decided to take a break, all but Kai huffing and panting, meeting up in the middle. Marie had brought some sandwiches she and her mother had made, and the group happily dug into them.

They ate silently, although all of them had questions they wanted to ask. After seeing what Kai had done, the two boys were interested in knowing more about who he was. But they were more interested in learning what exactly Gary was, since their vice leader seemed to know. But they continued to eat until Marie eventually broke the silence.

"You really like it up here, don't you, Kai? We could have trained somewhere else, but this is still your favorite spot." She smiled.

"'My' spot." Kai chuckled. "Well, I guess it is mine now . . . but I used to come up here in the past and there was always someone else up here looking out at the field; I wonder where that person is now."

The others looked at each other strangely as he was reminiscing, but in the end, Austin was the first to speak up, unable to hold it in any more.

"Kai, I want to know more about who you are. I think after all we've been through, we deserve to know!"

CHAPTER 3

A TEAM UPGRADE

The group had been sitting on the floor with Marie's basket of sandwiches in the middle. They were nearly gone, and Marie thought that training would soon start up again—until Austin asked his question.

As soon as Austin had finished speaking, Marie gave Kai a look. It was clear that she knew something and was wondering whether Kai would tell them.

"I guess you guys got curious after seeing me fight and use the knives back there, huh?" Kai smiled, unfazed by the question. On the other hand, Innu's face was a little red, though he wasn't exactly sure why he felt embarrassed; they had only been caught peeping.

"You're right, you do deserve to know more about me. I don't explicitly want to hide who I am from you guys . . . but now's not the time. I promise I will tell you everything once we've taken over Slough. Just trust me when I say it would do you more harm than good right now." Kai sighed. "Besides, our great leader isn't here, and I don't want to have to repeat it. When I do tell you, I'll tell all of you at once."

Of course, Kai's cryptic answer just made them more curious, but by now he had earned their trust. The bond between all of them had grown greatly after the events at the gray color gang's hideout.

"Speaking of which, why didn't you invite Gary here? As our leader, shouldn't he like, you know, lead by example?" Innu asked. "Also, why did you send me a message telling me not to pry into his matters? I assume you told the others as well, but . . . when he went in there with those twins . . . you saw what he did with them. How's that even possible?"

Another fair question, even though half of them knew the answer to this, though Marie had come to the wrong conclusion.

"If you're really curious, you can ask him yourself, but he'll more than likely lie to you." Kai shrugged. "Besides, does it matter? He saved us back there, risking his own life. Just like any of you, he has his own secrets. I feel that it's best to let him choose to tell it to us on his own.

"As for the reason I didn't call him . . . well, you saw what he did to those twins. Do you really think the kind of training we do will be effective for him? He doesn't need to take part in things like this."

The others agreed, especially if Gary was keeping something from them. Just one of those twins had been too much for all four of them to take down, yet their leader had taken them both on, at the same time no less. What's more, he had spent suspiciously little time . . . not to mention the state they had been left in . . .

"About the things you said to Marie." Austin spoke up. "This training is great and all, and I think we will improve . . . but I don't think it will be enough. Sure, we can get stronger, so that we can be on par with those highly skilled real gang members and not the color gangs—maybe even to the point where even the real gang members will be scared of us, but it's nothing in front of Altered. From what I've been told, only one gang in Slough has one . . . but if that's enough to take over this town, what will we do if someone else comes along?

"I don't know about you, but I don't like just relying on Gary. He might have been able to deal with those twins, but we don't even know if he can do the same against an actual Altered."

Austin was looking Kai straight in the eyes as he posed his question. Surely, their vice leader must have realized this problem as well, so he was hoping Kai had already prepared an answer to this.

"You're right, Altered aren't called superhumans for nothing. While I have a solution . . . it's unfortunately not something we'll be able to get anytime soon." Kai stood up and walked toward the corner of the roof. He opened his school bag and took out a laptop before coming back over.

"Initially, I had believed that we'd only have to deal with Kirk when taking over Slough. However, that was before we fought the twins. Now, I'm honestly afraid that the Gray Elephants gang might have more of that strange solution that turned them into those beasts. If they start to target us, we'll seriously be in trouble . . .

"Just another reason to take this training seriously. If possible, we should also try to team up so we don't get attacked when we're on our own." When Kai said that, he couldn't help but look at Innu, unaware that the Billy issue had already been solved.

After typing a few things on his computer, Kai spun it around. The others saw a mostly black screen with a name at the top, and a date underneath it. The name was *Dark Guild Auction House*.

"What is this?" Innu asked. The date was two weeks from now, but there was no other information. "What's with the name 'Dark Guild'; did an eighth-grader come up with that?"

Kai closed the laptop as he got ready to explain.

"As stupid as the name might sound, those guys are legit. They're one of the biggest gangs in our country, and what's more they're led by one of the Kings. They're one of the richest gangs there are, if not *the* richest. The sums that change hands at their auctions are rumored to be enough to upgrade all Tier 3 towns and below to Tier 1 cities.

"Pretty much every major gang in the country knows about these auctions. They all attend, and from what I've heard, it's not even rare for the Kings to come and bid as well. Those auctions are announced on the website. They don't have them all the time, but it's a big deal whenever they do.

"Unfortunately, with our current funds, we wouldn't even be able to pay the entrance fee for a single member. Even if we had the funds, they might deny us access, simply because we're too small-time at the moment.

"I want us to keep this in mind for the future. We will expand our business and bring in more money, and when we finally have enough we can head to the auction house. Their merchandise appears to change each time, but . . . from what I heard they're most famous for one thing . . . Altered DNA!

"And I'm not talking about regular Altered, but quite exotic Altered. Ones the public doesn't even know about. *That* will be our key to rise to the top! With enough money, we could literally buy ourselves the power to rule the current world," Kai explained with grandeur.

CHAPTER 4

A SECOND CHANCE

Not much happened that day. The news had announced the death of Billy Bruntin and had reported that it was due to the Altered Hunters. Nothing big had happened with Gary since then, and even when he saw Blake the two of them seemed to act normal with each other.

There was one change, though; after Amy had returned to school, Stacy was nowhere to be found. When Amy had asked their homeroom teacher about it, she didn't know any of the specifics, having been told that Stacy had transferred somewhere else.

Whether Stacy had told her parents about everything or insisted on moving, who knew? Perhaps she was even still in Slough, just in a different school. In the end, Gary was happy that at least it was a problem Amy didn't need to deal with, but now there was no one close to watch her over at school.

Still, although there were no worries with how things were progressing, one annoying thing remained in front of Gary.

16 days until the next full moon

Gary stared at the message the next morning as he leaned back on his chair during class, balancing on two legs as he went forward and back.

This month has gone by quickly. I'll soon have to start deal-ing with the "blessing" of the full moon again, and my bloodlust will increase. However, if my theory is correct, as long as I burn through most of my Energy beforehand, to the point that I won't have enough to transform, I should be good. I might be irritable the entire day because of hunger, but if it's just one day, I'll be able to hold out.

Gary suddenly felt a vibration from within his pocket. Pulling out his phone, he read through the message, which put a smile on his face.

"What's the good news?" Tom asked. He had been less involved in his friend's life. For now, Gary had been in a good mood, so Tom decided he would stay in a good one as well and not put a damper on things.

"The repairs are done. It looks like I'll be able to work again starting today," Gary whispered. "Do you wanna come to our grand reopening?"

"Sorry." Tom sighed as he stuck his head back in his books. "For once, I'll be the one who will take the rain check. These days, my parents want me to brush up and help with some of their research. You know how they want me to follow in their footsteps. I think my dad plans to bring me along to their lab during the holidays to help out, and I really don't want to embarrass them. Apparently, he can bring me on as some type of intern. Oh, and don't worry, I'll ask him that question you want to ask as well, about those beasts."

Nodding along, Gary was happy that things were getting back to normal. At least, as normal as they could get, anyway.

"All right, everyone, I know that you're all eager to go home to-day, but I'm reminding you that even though it's Saturday tomorrow, Westbridge's talent show is a mandatory event. Now, I don't want to have to send any of you to detention." Mr. Grey said, standing at the front of the class. "Xin, as the new class representative, would you kindly pass out the flyers?"

Xin did so, and nearly all the boys had a huge grin on their face when she came to them. It had only been this morning that she had been announced to be their class's representative.

As the new girl, she hadn't expected to be elected. It was a mostly unimportant role, and the only reason she had even thrown her name into the ring was to follow her father's suggestion. According to the mayor, it would look good on her future résumé, though she suspected he also saw it as a chance to brag about her accomplishments to his associates.

She had run against Tiffany, and she had won thanks to the major support she had received from the male half of her class. Many of the girls had been split between her and Tiffany, who at this moment was biting her nails as she stared at Xin.

As pretty as Tiffany was, the boys just didn't like her attitude. On the other hand, Xin treated them nicely and it was easy enough to talk to her because of her interest in fighting, especially Altered fights. Unlike the class diva, Xin didn't just assume everyone who was talking to her was hitting on her.

After everyone received a flyer, she began to assign different tasks to her classmates, as they were also supposed to help out with the event, by creating things or setting up the room, among other duties.

Xin . . . she still looks gorgeous. I haven't really talked to her . . . well, since she kicked my butt, Gary realized. He wasn't really listening to her instructions; he was just happy to hear her voice after so long. Now that he didn't have to worry about a bloodthirsty monster, his brain had time to focus on more important things. *Come to think of it, didn't she say that she would date whoever could beat her? I've gotten a lot stronger . . . should I give it a try?*

Although . . . would it be fair? Me, a werewolf, beating her as a human? . . . No, the important thing is getting that date! Then we can get to know each other! I'll finally have the chance to enjoy my life like a normal high school boy! I can't just think about fighting forever, Gary thought as he hyped himself up, ready to ask Xin for a rematch.

The after-school club classes had been canceled for the day because of the talent show tomorrow. Tom was heading home as he said he would.

"Are you ready to head to the Wolf's Pool Club?" Innu asked, since he too had received the news.

"Errrr . . ." Gary hesitated, as he looked out of the corner of his eye and saw that Xin was already leaving the room.

"Oh! I see! You horny dog, you!" Innu punched him on his shoulder. As he did that, Innu realized just how solid Gary's body was, which honestly surprised him.

"All right, go ahead! I'll tell the others you might be late. Afterward, I'll be the one to swoop in after she gets frightened that a broccoli head asked her out."

With that said, it was time for Gary to make a move to advance his love life.

CHAPTER 5

WHY ARE THEY HERE?

Since Innu had volunteered to inform the others, it was time for Gary to initiate his plan. Right now, he was waiting for the right moment to talk to Xin. First, he had to catch up to her, and she had a bit of a head start.

While following Xin, he found it a little strange that she wasn't heading toward the school's front gate but toward the back of the school. The more he thought about it, the worse the feeling in his stomach became.

Eventually, she went past the school athletic field and headed straight to the back fence. This fence went around the whole school, with gates here and there along the perimeter.

Gary had stayed quite far behind, because the two of them were the only ones going toward the back of the school. He felt that it would be strange if she spotted him; he worried that she might mistake him for some type of stalker.

Still, he had come this far, so it seemed stupid to turn around now. He assumed that she might head to a main street from the back. In that case, he could pretend that it was a coincidence that they met. After going through one of the gates, Xin continued on into some trees on the other side.

Meanwhile, Gary ran across the field and went through the gate after her, then quickly hid behind one of the trees. His eyesight and sense of smell allowed him to keep track of her.

Nice going, Gary, hiding behind a tree . . . why would anyone ever think of you as a stalker? he thought, chastising himself. Looking ahead, he saw a parking lot behind the school.

The area was close to several giant trash containers, just one of the "perks" one had to accept when living in a Tier 3 town, and they had been set up in a very strange way. They placed in certain parking spots, almost as if they were blocking the way to the nearby shops.

Now what are the chances she's just come here to enjoy the scenery? Gary thought as he carefully kept watch, curious about her reason for going there.

"Come on!" Xin shouted, tapping her foot impatiently. "I followed the instructions in your stupid note. I came here alone, so just tell me what you want. Just give me back my stuff, and I'll be out of here."

Earlier in the day, after Xin had been called to the teacher's lounge to be introduced to her new job as class representative, she had come back only to find her school bag missing. It wasn't just that; someone had cleared out her school locker, taking everything including the special kit that she used for karate.

Although it wasn't really much trouble for her to just get a new bag and clothes, it would be a pain. At the same time, it didn't take a genius to figure out who was behind all of this, and why. Xin found it hard to believe that Tiffany would actually care about such a stupid thing.

But instead of the class diva, four young adults came out from around the bins. They didn't look friendly, and at a glance she could tell exactly who they were. Each one wore a different item of clothing with one very prominent color: red.

Xin was a little taken aback, and her calm demeanor was gone.

I was expecting her to be with her goons, maybe some people from our school, but other gang members? she thought.

"Thank you for confirming that you are the one we were looking for," one of the men said; he wore a sleeveless shirt and had two large caterpillar-like eyebrows.

"Why would you do her bidding? Who cares; if she sent you, then I guess I won't have to feel so bad about hurting you." Xin got into a fighting stance and hopped forward to get within range.

Immediately throwing out her leg, she kicked the bushy-browed gang member in the head. Seeing this, the other color gang members rushed in, and Xin attempted to kick one of them in the stomach, throwing her other foot sideways.

Unfortunately, the man's reaction was quick; he caught her foot just in time, but Xin was expecting it. She spun her body around to free herself and kick the man in the head once again.

Before she could deal her kick, a green-haired teenager came out of nowhere and planted a heavy fist right into her attacker's head. It was a strong hit that chucked his body into one of the metal trash containers, and he fell to the ground.

When Xin looked for the other two attackers, she found that they had been knocked out as well.

Did Gary do all of this? But how? I saw his skill. Sure, he's resilient, but to take them out so quickly? He must have beaten them all with one hit.

"Come on, let's get out of here; clearly they don't have your stuff." Gary hurried her along as they turned around and headed back toward the school. Eventually they reached the main building, and they took a second to try to figure out what had just happened.

"Thanks for your help back there," Xin said to Gary, to show him that she appreciated his help. "What were you even doing back there? You must have been watching me for a while, if you heard about my missing stuff."

Right now, Xin was suspicious of everyone who was trying to get close to her. Could it be that for once Tiffany was innocent, and this boy had set up everything? Given his green hair, maybe he was one of their members, and he had asked his buddies to create this scenario so he could swoop in and play hero? She wouldn't put it past him since she hardly knew him.

"I'm sorry, I didn't mean to pry," Gary said, rubbing the back of his head. He saw no way to lie his way out of this one, at least not without making it sound too weird. He thought the truth would actually be the best option. "I was actually going to . . . ermm . . . ask you about that duel from before. Last time you said that . . . you would go on a date with me . . . if I could beat you in a match . . . and . . . well, I've been kinda working out . . ." Gary stammered, his face turning beet red, and judging by Xin's face, she hadn't quite expected this type of explanation.

"Oh, okay. Sure, I'll go on a date with you," Xin replied.

CHAPTER 6

THE CULPRIT

For a while, Gary had been playing out scenarios in which he would ask Xin out. How to make it sound casual and cool, and not at all desperate, needy, or obsessive. Unable to find a solution, he had been lagging behind as he followed her.

However, when he saw that she was faced with four men belonging to the red color gang, he just had to act. Afterward, Xin had demanded an explanation as to why he had been there . . . so he had admitted to the truth.

Time seemed to have slowed down, his heart beating faster as he nervously awaited her answer. Still, he had finally done it. He had asked her out . . . well, technically, he had asked her to fight him again. In his head he had convinced himself he was just asking her to a fight and that was how he had finally said those words.

What he didn't expect, though, was the fast reply.

"Oh, okay. Sure, I'll go on a date with you," Xin had replied, after only a few moments of thinking things over. Gary's brain was unable to process the words. If he had been a robot, he would have surely short-circuited. Shaking his head, he just had to ask for clarification.

"I'm sorry, are you saying yes to a date? Don't we have to have a match first?" Gary asked.

"Given your little performance, I think we can skip the duel. You helped me out back there, and it doesn't seem like you were lying about the liking me part. Besides, I have taken a bit of an interest in you myself ever since your rugby match performance.

"I don't see any harm in getting to know each other better. But, errr, let's schedule things another time, all right?" Xin said, looking behind Gary, as she could see that her father's after-school escorts were getting a bit restless.

After what had happened in Cipen, her father had sent out more guards to look after her, and considering how long she had been gone, they might start a manhunt any second now. It looked like Xin was about to set off, but before she did, Gary wanted to know one more thing.

"Wait!" Gary called out. "Why were they after you? The red color gang, I mean!"

She would like to know that as well. Unable to answer, she just continued running off toward the black cars.

I guess the life of a mayor's daughter is tough. Did someone send them after her? But then who took her bag that she was talking about? Gary wondered.

He had knocked out the red color members so fast, he was hoping they hadn't seen him. After all, he was already having trouble with the Gray Elephants as well as the Underdogs; no reason to add another color gang on top of that. With them working with the gray color gang that night, he was sure they had some tie-in with the Gray Elephants, which was why he wanted to get out of there as quickly as possible.

A date . . . I really got a date! This has to be my luckiest day ever! But . . . I don't have her number! I guess I'll just get it tomorrow, Gary thought, smiling to himself as he headed to the Wolf's Pool Club.

A little while later, the embarrassed red color gang members were getting up. They looked at each other and wondered what had happened.

For three of them, their jaws hurt like hell and they wouldn't be surprised if something was broken.

They had all been so focused on the girl that they hadn't seen the other person coming. None of them had any memory of what the person looked like.

"Man, how the hell are we going to explain to Riv that we couldn't even get one girl?" the bushy-browed leader wondered aloud, rubbing the side of his head where he had been kicked.

"You're right, how are you going to explain this to me?"

They didn't need to turn around to know who it was. They all recognized the voice of their leader. Straightaway, they got on their knees to apologize, although they were already on the ground.

"We're sorry, we came out when she appeared to be alone, but she had a guard nearby," Bushy Eyebrows started to explain.

"I thought you were going to get someone reliable," a female voice pouted as the girl appeared behind one of the other trash containers and immediately grabbed Riv's arm. "I took her bag, and we even told you guys to set up this place. She's not an idiot; something like this is not going to work again."

She stomped her foot several times, and it was clear she was annoyed.

"Hey, don't worry, Tiffy, we will have plenty of chances, trust me. I'm not just anyone. You're talking to the leader of the red color gang as well as the newest senior member of the Gray Elephants gang! A few guards won't be a problem, we just have to wait," Riv said, trying to appease her.

It was a strange sight to behold, and the rest of the gang members honestly found it a little disgusting; they had never seen their leader act so lovey-dovey. Not only that, but he was being apologetic, and why did it seem like she was actually the one in charge?

All four of the gang members shared a common thought about their leader: *whipped*.

"No!" Tiffany shouted back like a spoiled princess. "Every day I have to see her, I want to claw that girl's eyes out. She embarrassed me not once but three times! You keep bragging about how great you are, but I have yet to see any of that! I don't want to date a loser!"

Once again, Riv started to pull a sad baby face, which churned the other gang members' stomachs. It seemed as if their leader had forgotten that they were still present.

"You have my word that she'll pay, my little pumpkin. I promise I will do whatever's necessary." Riv then turned to his subordinates on the ground, his face changing to the cruel one they were more used to.

"Gather the red color gang! Tomorrow, we're going to cause quite a mess. Bring whoever you can; it will be a great opportunity to prove that we're not the same losers as the gray color gang." Riv smiled.

"Trust me, Tiffy, I will keep my word. If you want her dealt with as soon as possible, then I will get her in the one place she can't get away from! For you, I'll take down the whole school if I have to."

CHAPTER 7

THE NEXT STEP

Walking down the streets of Slough, one particular teenage boy was getting strange looks from the passersby. All because of the look on his face. Right now, Gary was sporting a grin so wide that his eyes were almost closed, and one couldn't help but look and wonder if he was actually okay.

Funnily enough, Gary didn't notice any of that. Right now, he was in his own world, feeling better than ever before. As he entered the Wolf's Pool Club, the first thing Gary did, without even looking inside, was to announce, "Today's a great day!"

The other Howlers had opened the place a while ago, and a few customers were already inside playing pool and eating snacks, though the majority were from Austin's school. They glanced at Gary, then quickly carried on doing what they were doing before.

One person, though, noticed the smile and almost dropped the tray in his hands.

"No, it can't be . . . she actually said yes?" Innu's mouth was wide open.

Gary didn't say anything, but just put on an apron as he went to ask people if they wanted anything, making sure to praise the club's membership program, trying to win them over as loyal customers.

Meanwhile, Innu needed to sit down for a bit, and he chose a seat on the stool by the counter. Although he didn't know Xin very well, she was a pretty girl, and, as mean as it might sound, he had actually made a few plans for what he would do after she rejected Gary.

Sitting with his head down, the last thing Innu expected was to be pulled by the hem of his shirt, nearly getting dragged across the counter.

"Would you elaborate on that bit about someone saying yes?" Marie requested with a smile. Innu felt like he was staring death straight in the eyes. Peeking down, he saw the two concealed blades that she was training with and he was afraid that she might use them on him.

"Hey, what's the big deal? What exactly do you plan on doing once I tell you, Marie?" Innu asked nervously, unsure where this sudden anger had come from. But she let go as Gary walked past to grab a drink from the fridge.

She smiled at Gary and gave him a light wave, and as he walked back, Gary return the gesture. For the second time today, Innu's mouth was wide open, as he looked back and forth between Marie and Gary.

"Yo-you-yo-you li—"

"Shut up!" Marie hissed at him, quickly placing her hand over Innu's mouth. It was impossible to tell what she planned to do, but luckily for him, a customer came over, saving him from impending doom. He couldn't believe Marie's complete change in behavior as the customer placed his order.

Why the hell are all the cute girls after Gary? And I bet he doesn't even know about Marie's feelings! Seeing it in person is even more annoying than in those drama shows. Innu would have loved to vent his frustration, but now was neither the place nor the time. *Damn, is it his green hair? Should I dye mine as well?*

The day continued on and when the sky started to turn dark, business hours were over. They weren't risking another incident like before, although they assumed it wouldn't happen again . . . not anytime soon, at least.

Today, though, was a bit more special than usual. Kai wore a serious expression. He informed them all that there was something he wanted to talk about now that the place was open for business again. The Howlers were all sitting on the sofa on the other side of the counter, behind the pool tables.

Kai was the only one standing. The tension in the room was high, and even Gary finally snapped out of his daze to focus on what Kai was about to say.

"First of all, great job, everyone. Now that the Wolf's Pool Club is back in business again, we can finally start making some money as a gang," Kai said. "Thankfully, with the money the gray color gang 'generously donated,' we were able to pay for the repairs. After a few more days like this, profit will be no problem, but there is a reason why businesses don't last long in Slough, and that's because what happened to us could happen again.

"The good news is, now that the gray color gang is gone, we don't have to worry about them coming after us. In the meantime, the red color gang is scrapping around doing the Gray Elephants' bidding, and it looks like a fight between the Underdogs and the Gray Elephants is on the horizon."

Innu and Austin were shocked. The gang war between two color gangs had caused the police to quarantine the entire Chavley area, simply because they had lacked the personnel to do anything about it. What would happen if two big-time gangs had a go at each other?

"Now I don't yet know when it will happen, but if I were to make a careful estimate, probably in one week at the earliest, one to two months at the latest. Either way, no matter which gang wins, they'll have suffered serious losses, to the point they won't have the manpower to claim the territory that they have won.

"At that point, the smaller gangs will come in and swoop in on the loser's business. Now here's where the problems begin. As a small-time gang ourselves, we'll be dragged into that mess, whether we like it or not. While the rumors about us causing the gray color gang's disbandment are great for keeping other gangs in line, it will also get us targeted in the upcoming war.

"I, for one, don't want to be caught with my pants down, which is why I called this meeting. Right now, we need to do a few things. The Howlers need to grow our gang reputation to protect this place, our people, and our money. Now what if I told you there was a way to achieve all of that at once?" Kai smiled mischievously.

As expected, the blond teenager already had a plan.

"In addition to the color gangs, which are now down to black and red, there are five small-time gangs that have made a bit of a name for themselves. Their territory isn't really worth mentioning, and the color gangs have used them as sort of buffer zones.

"What we'll do, before everyone starts fighting for scraps, is pay each one of them a visit. While the color gangs may not have cared about them, for the Howlers they'll serve as perfect stepping-stones. We'll take over their territory and spread our name.

"If our leader agrees, of course!" Kai looked over to Gary. Now the others did so too, waiting for an answer.

A war between the Underdogs and the Gray Elephants. Both gangs had a reason to go after Gary, and if the Howlers needed to face them head on, if this was what Kai thought was the best for them, then Gary would gladly lead them.

"Of course," he answered.

CHAPTER 8

A NEW TRANSPORTER

Inside the Basement, which had yet to open, a muscular teenage boy who had seen better days was busy walking through. Dragging his feet across the floor, he approached one of the workers in the club, who wore a suit.

"I finished my delivery," the boy reported.

"Good, just sit at the back and wait for the others. When they're done, you can leave," the man instructed him.

The boy walked through a set of double doors and took a left turn, entering what looked like a break room for the staff, which was completely empty.

Over the last few days, the nightclub had been emptier and emptier. Fewer people were coming in, and he could only assume it was because something was going on outside. The boy sat down on the sofa, leaned back, and suddenly kicked the table.

"Shit! How did I even get myself in this situation! It all happened at that damn supermarket!" He cursed in frustration. After a strange turn of events, Gil had found himself working as a transporter for the Underdogs.

As had become the norm for him, he was thinking back to everything that had happened that day. One person had changed everything: Kirk, the Underdog's Altered. He and his Cheetah Squad had managed to completely overpower the gray color gang members. They all had been beaten badly, Gil especially, and after he woke up, he had found himself in the nightclub.

He wasn't the only one who had been abducted, though. Most of the victims were from the gray color gang, though some red color gang members had been there also. Honestly, Gil was regretting his choice to drop school and join a gang.

They had been warned that they would be attacking Underdog territory, but the original plan had been to get out of there long before the Underdogs arrived on the scene. Unfortunately, nobody had expected the Underdogs to send out their elite forces so quickly, just because the black color gang got their butts kicked.

Around twenty of them had been spread out on the dance floor, surrounded by the Underdogs with Kirk watching over them.

One had tried to make a run for it, but before he could get far, his face had met the Altered's foot; he ended up on the floor, and no one else had tried anything after that. After a while, the leader of the Underdogs, Damion Hawk, finally arrived.

He walked in with great confidence and smiled at them all.

"Welcome to our humble home!" Damion shouted with his arms open wide. "Get all of these wretched souls a change of clothes and some food. They must be hungry, and make sure their wounds are patched up."

Everyone had looked at each other in confusion, including Gil, but the members of the Underdogs didn't need to be told twice. They immediately started taking care of their charges and bringing them hot food.

Most of them had been cautious at first, afraid the food might have been poisoned, but Gil had dug straight in. If the Underdogs were going to kill them, there would be no reason to do it in such a roundabout way. No, Damion had something else planned, Gil could tell.

For one week, they had been trapped there, getting food twice a day, taking bathroom breaks under the supervision of the Underdogs gang members. On the eighth day, Damion came in again.

"Well, I hope you've enjoyed our hospitality for the past week. As you might have noticed, no one has come for you. Not the other gray color gang members, nor the red color gang members, and not even the Gray Elephants themselves.

"You've been used, and now that there's nothing more you can do for them, you've been discarded . . . But you see, here at the Underdogs we're different! Loyalty is number one! As long as you wag your tail like a good dog, you'll get rewarded," Damion explained with a grin.

"Now I'm going to give you all a choice. Most of you are still young. High school and university students with families who must be sick and worried about you. They may even think you are dead after what happened that night.

"We all make mistakes in our youth, and it's important we learn from them, which is why I will give you a choice. Those of you who wish to leave, raise your hand, and those of you who wish to join us, sit still. Those are your two options, no questions allowed!"

They exchanged glances, obviously wanting to ask questions, but the crazy look in Damion's eyes made them afraid to do so. They had learned that whatever he said was the law in this place, so they would have to give him an answer.

Finally, a few of them raised their hands. This experience had revealed that the life of a gang member wasn't for them. In the past, color gangs were experts on real gang warfare. But they would just be used as pawns, and nobody would care.

However, for Gil, something just didn't feel right; if he was let go, what would he even do? Go back to the gray color gang, who had lost in this fight? No, that wasn't a place for him. He had dropped out of Westbridge to rise up in the ranks, to get somewhere in life.

In the end, Gil didn't put his hand up, but around one third of them did. Damion turned around; one of the men in suits had handed him two small axes.

Immediately he leapt forward and struck at the first person who had raised his hand. This caused a panic and many people tried to flee, but like a possessed demon Damion cut them down. He seemingly remembered each one who had raised their hand, leaving everyone else alone.

The scene was ingrained in the minds of all the survivors, and they understood why Damion talked about loyalty. They were now part of the Underdogs, whether they liked it or not, and if they even thought about betraying him, they all knew what fate they would suffer.

Gil didn't care; this was life for him . . . the only thing he hadn't imagined was that the next day he would be told to work as a transporter.

Eventually the doors opened, and several teenagers entered the room. Gil had seen them a few times; they were the other transporters who would be working for the Underdogs.

Damn it, I have to get out of this job somehow, Gil thought.

Suddenly he heard shouting from one of the other rooms.

"You still can't find him?" This was followed by a loud crash.

"I'm sorry, sir, but we really are doing our best! There are thousands of kids in Slough. We have nothing to go by other than his green hair. He must have dyed it a long time ago; maybe he cut it off," someone said.

"Even if he hasn't, there are countless punks that fit his description! It's impossible, sir, we've been going around everywhere looking for him!" Another person tried to explain their failure.

"What's that all about?" Gil asked.

"The boss is pissed because they can't find one of the old transporters," one of them said. "The kid with green hair came before you, and apparently he stole one of the packages he was delivering. It seems pretty important because they've been looking for him ever since. He was a strange guy, that Greeny G. He would always try to talk to us."

"Greeny G?" Gil replied.

"Ah, his nickname. You know how no one knows each other's real name here? He went by G, but because of his green hair, the boss kept calling him Greeny, so Greeny G."

As Gil heard this description, an image appeared in his mind. It reminded him of a boy that he had gone to school with.

G . . . for Gary? No, it couldn't . . . A smile appeared across Gil's face as he remembered the look Gary had given him in the hallway that one time; it was a stare as if he wanted to hit him. *Ha, does it even matter if it's really him or not? I think I just found my way out of these stupid deliveries!*

CHAPTER 9

BAD NEWS

A delightful hum had woken up Amy Dem, and she wondered if the next-door neighbor had left the TV on again as she headed to the toilet. However, to her surprise, the sound was actually coming from their apartment's kitchen, more specifically from Gary, who was cooking his usual breakfast.

He was now able to cook an omelet, flipping it at just the right time, catching it in the pan before placing it cleanly on a plate.

"Who are you? And what did you do with my brother?" Amy stood in the hallway, still in her pajamas.

"What do you mean?" Gary asked, adding a pinch of salt before slicing the omelet in half and grabbing Amy a plate. "Come on, eat up. Remember, I told you yesterday that I have to go to school today, because of the talent show."

Leaving the food on the kitchen table, Gary headed into the hallway, looked at himself in the mirror, and started to fix the individual spikes in his hair one by one.

"I'sss a guurrl!" Amy shouted with her mouth full. She had just taken a bite of her toast and was pointing toward her brother like a detective who had unveiled the culprit of a crime. She could practically hear the saxophones and more playing behind her.

"What . . . Can't I care about my outer appearance?" Gary replied, his face slightly red. "Do I look good . . . for the talent show, I mean?"

Amy's face was filled with skepticism, and she made it clear that she wouldn't answer his question unless Gary came clean.

"I don't want to be an aunt at this age," Amy said, startling Gary with the unexpected statement. "Please don't do something stupid, like you did when you came home with that green hair. Honestly, I'm a bit worried about the girl who is brave enough to walk side by side with someone who . . . stands out as much as you. And remember there could be others after you."

"Don't you think you're pushing things a bit? We haven't even gone on a date yet! No need to imagine me getting married . . . or you becoming an aunt." Gary sighed as he shook his head. "Anyway, I really gotta go. Text me if you need anything! And don't worry about me."

With that, he put his breakfast into a Tupperware box and rushed off. As soon as he left the apartment, Gary covered his face with his hood, then started to run toward school. If anyone spotted him, they would be unable to stop him for questions. Since the attack on the Chavley area, it had been filled with Underdogs members. However, they seemed to be just checking the area.

Today, though, Gary noticed something different. His route took him mostly through alleyways, allowing his good hearing to catch bits and pieces here and there.

"Is it this one? I'm not sure. Take a photo and send it back to the others to see if they recognize him," one voice said.

Peeking around the corner, Gary saw the Underdogs members doing something different; they were questioning every student who walked past and asking to take their photo.

In broad daylight, and this early as well. It was easy enough to understand why they were doing it.

Ah, come on, all this for a stupid package. I didn't even do anything! Gary grumbled to himself. *I had hoped that they might have let it go by now, but I guess this Werewolf System is really important to them.*

Fortunately, Gary had his own way to get around them. He used Controlled Transformation to change his nails into claws, and then, like a professional rock climber, he snuck over a wall, using every crevice and crack to get a grip and heave himself over, then continued making his way to school.

Seeing the Underdogs members on patrol, Gary thought back to what Kai had suggested in the Wolf's Pool Club yesterday. The Howlers would soon be making a move of their own. Today and tomorrow, the group was going to head into the territories of those other small-time gangs.

They would scout out their businesses, verify their numbers, and then make a plan. Apparently it wasn't as easy as just marching in and taking out the leader. Although that would increase their reputation, they lacked the manpower to take over the businesses on their own.

This was a major problem for the Howlers; there were only five of them who were loyal and could do the job that was needed. Truthfully, Gary didn't know how they were going to solve this one.

For now, I should just enjoy my day. After all, I get to see Xin again and plan that date. The thing is, where would we even go? Should I still take her to the park? I mean, I have a bit of money left over now. Should I take her to the pool club? No, I don't really want the others to interfere . . .

As Gary arrived at school, there was a certain excitement in the air. Maybe it was because the students weren't in uniform, or just because of the talent show.

Either way, this excitement was rubbing off on Gary. He didn't want to go to class just yet in case he found the person he was looking for, and that was when he spotted Xin's gray hair in the distance.

Gary hurried along, hoping to catch up and speak to her or walk her to class, but before he could, a certain upperclassman blocked his way.

"Kai," Gary exclaimed, surprised, but also trying to peek over his shoulder to see where Xin was headed.

"Gary, we need to talk. *Now*," Kai insisted.

From Kai's tone, Gary wondered what it could be, and he was already imagining the worst-case scenario. Kai led Gary away from the main entrance of the school and around the side of the building.

Since it was early morning and everyone was heading to class, the place was relatively empty, so no one would hear what Kai was going to say.

"What's wrong? You're starting to scare me by not saying anything." Gary looked at Kai struggling to speak; his face looked pained.

"I'm sorry, Gary, I really don't know how, but it looks like the Underdogs found out that you go to school here," Kai said.

Gary felt like his whole head was spinning, but before he could have a breakdown, Kai grabbed him firmly by both shoulders.

"It's not all bad; they don't know where you live, and they don't know about your family. I made sure to alter all of your information. I even changed your school records, so there's no way they can get to Amy or your mom. I'm sorry, I really don't know how it got to this. You might have seen them outside; you need to be extremely careful. I'll try my best to keep them off your tail," Kai continued.

Of course, just when things were starting to look up, the world was kicking Gary back down.

CHAPTER 10

THE TALENT SHOW STARTS!

Gary had been expecting to hear this from Kai every day, but when nothing had happened, and for so long, Gary had stopped worrying about it. So now he felt unprepared.

They talked a little further; Gary wanted to know the exact details that they knew about him, but Kai had to admit that he didn't know much. Someone seemed to have convinced the Underdogs that a teenager who matched Gary's description went to this school, and they had gotten his name as well.

They were looking for Gary Dem. The silver lining was that they only knew what school he went to and nothing about his family.

"So, what do we do?" Gary asked, hoping Kai had the perfect answer as always.

It took a while for Kai to respond.

"We can't do anything, not quickly at least. Transferring you somewhere else will only make it suspicious, and if they find you, it might also put me at risk. We can only hope that changing your appearance will make them ignore you for a while, so you should probably dye your hair black or something.

"I know before that I said it was fine, but now that they have narrowed you down to this school, they might pick you out first, but that won't stop the other students from knowing who you are . . . We are just going to have to deal with this head-on."

The one thing Gary was happy about in all this was the fact that Kai had not abandoned him. It would have been easy for Kai to ditch all of his plans because Gary was a big risk. But Kai was also a member of the Underdogs, and if they found Gary at the same school, Kai would surely get into trouble for not reporting him earlier.

The school bell rang, which was their signal to get out of there. Gary's happy mood had completely disappeared; now there was only one thing he could think about. When he arrived late to class, the teacher started to give him a warning, but Gary replied with only a few words:

"Yes, sir."

"I'm sorry, sir."

"It won't happen again, sir."

It was clear something was up, so his homeroom teacher decided to let it go. Besides, today was meant to be a joyous and happy event. Still, many of Gary's classmates noticed his soft demeanor.

Xin thought it might not be the best idea to approach Gary today. No one knew what other people were dealing with in their lives, and when someone was like this, even good friends might have a hard time cheering that person up—and Xin was basically a stranger to Gary.

"Hey, man, is everything okay, is Amy sick or something?" Tom asked straightaway. He wasn't shy. If his best friend seemed worried, he would ask him about it.

"Yeah, Amy's fine . . . my mom is doing okay too, slight improvement but no clear signs of waking up yet. I'm the one with the problem," Gary replied.

With that reply, Tom decided to back off a little. He knew that asking anything now would get him nowhere, so he would wait for Gary to open up to him as the day went on. The class began making little supporting fans and stickers, while those who would be taking part in the talent show were practicing.

Of course, no one Gary was close to was taking part in the show, nor was he. He didn't exactly have a talent. After an hour of what seemed like an arts and crafts lesson, it was finally time for them to head to the main hall.

The gigantic main hall of the school could hold six hundred students, with a large stage at the end of the room. During an assembly they used seats, but because of the number of people invited, students from every class and their families, everyone would be required to stand for the event. The hall didn't have fancy lighting or props like other schools had because it was a normal school in a Tier 3 town, but it would do.

Eventually, all of the students had entered. Tom stuck by Gary's side. He still looked unenergetic and hadn't said a word, and Innu was staying by his side as well.

I got that message from Kai to keep an eye on Gary and report to him. Something is definitely up. I wonder what happened? Innu thought.

Unfortunately, he just wasn't good with this type of situation— what to say or do. He knew that if it were him, he would eventually sort out his own troubles.

The show was about to begin, and the teachers entered and closed the four doors into the hall—two at the back and two at the front, close to the stage. Gary and Tom sat in the center so they could see everything.

"Hey, it looks like we found you," a voice said from the side.

Turning around, they saw Kai, and with him was Marie. Kai headed over and stopped in front of Tom.

"I haven't seen you since that day at the Wolf's Club. Thank you for looking after Marie's mother," Kai said in a soft voice.

Marie also thanked Tom for the help, taking his hands in hers.

A . . . a girl is touching my hands, Tom thought, as he realized that this was the first time he had made contact with the opposite sex, other than his mother. At the same time, he thought that Marie resembled Gary's sister, at least the older version that he had imagined in his head.

"You're welcome . . . if you need help with classes, please ask me as well!" Tom replied. It was a strange and stupid response, but Marie was kind enough to reply with a nod and a smile.

"Gary!" Kai shouted to get him to snap out of his daze. The students were talking excitedly, so they all needed to speak louder than they usually would.

"Enjoy today, watch the show. Deal with the situation as it comes. We've taken all the precautions we can, and besides . . . you're special, right? If it comes down to it, just show them all how special you are and we'll deal with the aftermath somehow."

The house lights started to dim, and the stage lights came up. Everyone was expecting one of the teachers to come out to host the event.

Yet there was silence, no sound, nothing. The students were quiet at first, but gradually they looked at each other and at the teachers standing by the side, but they looked just as confused . . . until a young man no one recognized eventually came onstage.

However, Kai and his gang immediately noticed a red bandana wrapped around his arm.

Walking up to the mic, he leaned in and said, "Thank you all for assembling. Without further ado, let's get this show started!"

Suddenly loud bangs erupted as red color gang members stormed into the hall from all four doors simultaneously.

CHAPTER 11

THE STORM OF THE RED GANG (PART 1)

As soon as the red color gang had burst through the doors, the last person to enter secured the double doors with chains and a lock, sealing them in.

"What are you doing? You're not meant to be in this school!" Mr. Grey shouted at the intruder, reaching for the lock. The gang member turned around and threw his fist right into the teacher's face.

The middle-aged man fell on his backside. The punch wasn't enough to knock him out, but it shook him up. The other teachers concluded that trying to physically stop them was not the best choice.

From how the intruders were dressed and the stunts they were pulling with their makeshift weapons, the teachers had some idea of who they were. It was impossible in this day and age to not know about the several gangs who proudly displayed themselves in the streets of Slough.

Nevertheless, a gang storming into a high school, even though it was just a color gang, had never happened before in the history of the town. There were about sixty red color gang members, and while the students outnumbered them roughly ten to one, they were too scared to do anything, especially since the gang members were armed.

Many of the students attempted to make a call on their phones. The police were usually useless and failed to respond because they were too busy, but in a situation like this, what else could they do?

"Huh . . . that's strange! I'm sure I had a signal in here earlier!" one student muttered, shaking his phone in hopes of getting at least one bar.

"I can't connect to the Wi-Fi either!" another shouted in a panic. Not a single person in the room could use their phone, and with the Wi-Fi down there was no way for them to contact the outside. The locks and chains ensured that they were all trapped.

"Ha ha ha!" The man on the stage laughed into the microphone, watching their reactions. "If you don't want anything to happen, it would be best if you all went into the center and sat down. That includes you teachers as well!"

Of course, the man on the stage was none other than the colored gang leader himself, Riv.

With no choice, most of the students followed his instructions, especially since the teachers had been first to act. They all headed toward the center of the main hall.

> *New Quest received*
> *You're locked in here with me!*
> *You might be surrounded, but as an apex predator, they have only cut off their own path of escape!*
> *Escape or defeat the red color gang who have invaded your school!*
> *Quest reward: Will depend on the number of people hurt by the gang before completion (3/624)*

A quest had appeared now of all times, which just made Gary aware that the situation was worse than he had imagined. When he got in small fights, he sometimes gained Exp, but the system wouldn't always give him a Quest.

This was also the first time the system had based his rewards on another condition. Three people had already been hurt: Mr. Grey and the two students who had tried to make a run for the doors. It appeared that the lower the number remained, the better the quest reward would be, but did he really have time to be thinking about these things?

Why are they here? Gary wondered. *The red color gang teamed up with the gray color gang in that attack on Chavley, which means they should be working for the Gray Elephants.*

Are these guys here because of me? Is it because of what I did . . . and because Stacy told them about me? If Hawk's brother could find out what school she and Amy attended, he definitely could have found mine. It's either that or . . .

"I'm not sure," Kai said when Gary looked over at him. It was the answer to the question he knew Gary wanted to ask. Kai didn't know if this was in any way connected to the Underdogs, or if they had coincidentally decided to act on their own.

In the first place, color gangs were pawns that could easily be influenced by the bigger gangs without knowing it. At the same time, they could even just be pretending to be part of a gang to cause trouble for others, though the appearance of Riv suggested that this was the real red color gang.

"Don't take out your weapons," Kai whispered to Marie. "Not unless you're in serious trouble."

Even in this situation, pulling out two small knives to attack others while in school was a big no.

"Hey, should we try to fight or get out of this or something?" Innu whispered to the other two, as he saw a startled Marie inching her way toward Gary.

Of course, she goes toward him. Innu inwardly shook his head.

Tom, who had overheard this, spoke up. "Are you guys crazy?" he whispered. "There are dozens of them, and most have some type of weapon. I don't care how good you guys might be at fighting, it's impossible for you to take on that many. Don't tell me you're planning to fight!"

CHAPTER 12

THE STORM OF THE RED GANG (PART 2)

There was a slight pause, and then Kai spoke.

"Tom's right. Let's just sit back and see what they want to do first. Depending on what it is, we may have a chance to try to resist them."

Although Gary and his gang were complying with the red color gang's orders, the same couldn't be said for a few of the other students. Members of the rugby club as well as the karate, boxing, and other fighting clubs had gathered.

"There's more of us than them," whispered John, a light heavyweight boxer who was an up-and-coming prospect for the school team. There weren't many talented people in Westbridge, so teenagers like him stood out. His confidence made him shine a bit more and people naturally followed him, both those in his club and others. "We have to act now, and together, while they aren't suspecting it."

Those around him agreed and waited to make their move. The red color gang members were moving in closer, making the circle smaller and pushing them back. The gang members closest to John and his group consisted of five guys, and one of them held a baseball bat, hitting it into the palm of his other hand.

"Hey, you, step back! I said step back!" he shouted at one of John's allies, who wasn't complying. With this distraction, the boxer saw an opportunity to make his move.

"Now!" he shouted, charging forward quickly and grabbing the bat with one hand as he pushed it down, and then he threw a right cross into the gang member's jaw, knocking him out.

The boys behind him charged, trying to bombard the rest. After knocking out his first opponent, John was ready to go for the next one. He assumed a boxing stance, using his arms to protect his head, and punched another gang member. It was a quick one-two, hitting him with both fists, but the gang member didn't fall.

Damn it, these guys are well-built. I'll have to catch them by surprise with a clean hit, John realized.

As he analyzed the situation, from the corner of his eye he saw a bat swinging toward him. It wasn't aimed at his head or body, though; no, it was going for his legs.

It was too late to dodge, and the bat slammed into him, causing instant pain and knocking him to the ground. John wondered if his shin was broken. As he fell, his attacker punched him in the face, and soon he was being battered by a rush of punches and kicks. The only thing he could do was turtle up on the floor, covering his head.

No . . . it hurts . . . it hurts so much . . . I thought we could do it . . . I thought maybe more would come help us once they saw what we were doing . . . where are the others? As he peeked through his arms, he saw a few people knocked out on the ground.

"Enough!" a voice shouted, and the beating abruptly stopped.

John lifted his head slowly, hoping not to get hit again. He was injured, but he could still move thanks to the adrenaline rushing through his body. Behind him, he saw eight students rolling on the floor in pain.

Standing above them were the red color gang members, but the one he had seen onstage seemed to have descended to the main floor at some point.

"Look at this! This is what happens when you pathetic bunch try to rebel against us! Did you really think none of us knew how to fight?" Riv asked the crowd.

By now, the rest of the students and teachers had huddled toward the center of the hall and were sitting quietly, shocked and scared. That was when John noticed something—why only eight of them were injured, despite there having been a few dozen who had tried to chase off the intruders.

"It would have been a good plan if everyone had acted at the same time," Kai whispered. "Too bad, not everyone is as brave as him. It looks like they got scared and backed down at the last second. With how many gang members there are, it's still best to sit and wait."

A color gang attack on a school just didn't make sense to Kai. There was nothing to gain from this, unless it was for personal reasons. Sure, they might cause some chaos, after achieving whatever goal they might have, but most of them would come out of the situation just fine.

If their goal was to get to Gary, Kai believed that he would have a better chance to escape at a later time, away from the eyes of the others. He was willing to bet that not even Damion knew what had been in the package . . . otherwise the gang leader would surely have kept it to himself.

Those that who attacked with John were dragged to the center of the stage, displayed for all the others to see the consequences of their foolishness. Everyone could see the nine students whose faces were beaten and bruised; they were concussed and groggy.

Each student had two members of the red color gang behind them. Riv walked to the first person on the end and squeezed his mouth together, pushing his lips forward.

"Tell me, who planned this little stunt of yours!" Riv demanded to know.

It was hard for the student to speak, but his eyes looked toward his left, at another student, which gave it away. Letting him go, Riv stormed to the next person, who flinched as he approached them.

"Was it this one?" Riv pointed at the next person in line.

The student shook his head, and Riv continued down the line until eventually he pointed toward John, and after a brief moment of hesitation the student under interrogation nodded.

"Hahaha, this is great. Not a shred of loyalty among you all. I knew who it was anyway; he was the only one who could actually fight a little." Riv started to laugh. "During my time at school, I met plenty of people like you. It was a different era back then, but now it's guys like me who reign at the top."

Riv glanced behind him, as if looking for someone among the crowd, before turning back toward John.

"Pull his hands out." Riv smiled, his eyes filled with some sort of strange anger.

CHAPTER 13

THE STORM OF THE RED GANG (PART 3)

At Riv's command, the gang members behind John went in front of him and pulled his arms down by the wrists so his palms were flat on the floor.

"From your form, I can tell that you're a boxer. You had a good stance and your punches seemed to pack some power. Well, you hit one of my guys, so this is only right. Say goodbye to your hands." Riv lifted his foot.

"Wait!" a deep voice bellowed from the crowd. The students to see Mr. Root, their PE teacher and rugby coach, who was as big as a tree in his red tracksuit.

"I was the one who planned that attack. Don't hurt the students because of me!" Mr. Root shouted. Riv's foot hovered over John's hands as he looked at the students one more time before making a decision.

"Fine, then. Bring him up!"

The other gang members stepped into the crowd and grabbed Mr. Root by the arms. Their heads only came midway up his body because he was so tall. However, the coach willingly came to the front.

All the students, including those that were beaten, knew that Mr. Root had taken no part in John's plan. He just couldn't bear to see his students hurt when it was the adults' job to protect them.

The red color gang members threw the others who were injured back into the seated crowd. Some of them looked at those who hadn't stuck to the plan with disgust, while others thought that if they hadn't attacked, their teacher wouldn't be in this situation right now.

They forced Mr. Root to get down on his knees in front of everyone. Four people now held on to Mr. Root just in case he tried anything. Most of the students believed that if Mr. Root tried to defend himself, he might even take down the four gang members holding him. Alas, Mr. Root knew it was useless, as there were far more of the gang members than he could take. Besides, there was also the risk that they would involve the other students if he did anything.

"You see, we need to teach you all a lesson, so you don't try to act out just like those idiots did! If you had just all listened, then this would have been a lot easier." Riv smiled, seemingly enjoying the justification to hurt another human being.

The red color gang members were holding Mr. Root steady so his head and chest were out slightly, and large gang member who was as big as Mr. Root himself stood in front of him. He kicked Mr. Root in the stomach as hard as he could, and a loud grunt resounded throughout the main hall.

Then he delivered another punch to Mr. Root's face, and blood from his mouth splattered on the floor.

"Oh, he looks like a tough guy, it might take a lot to hurt this one." Riv smiled.

The punches kept coming, all over his body. They had stopped hitting his head, as if they just wanted to do as much damage to Mr. Root as possible.

No . . . no, it's my fault . . . this is all my fault, but then why . . . John thought with tears running down his face, gritting his teeth hard. *Why can't I say anything?*

"Hey . . . if they keep hitting Mr. Root like that, they're going to kill him!" Tom whispered, unsure what they could do.

"No." Kai shook his head. "Their punches are just aimed to hurt him. He might end up with a few broken bones, but since he doesn't show any sign of resisting, Riv should become bored soon. They won't kill him in front of us all. We can see his face. I hate to say this, but the best thing to do now is just to stand ba—"

Suddenly someone next to Kai stood up.

"Hey, you . . . sit back down!" one of the gang members shouted, but the student ignored him as he walked past the rest of the seated students.

So you've decided to act, thought Blake, who had stayed at the back of the room, looking at the exits and windows.

"Do you want to get hit as well? I said stay back!" another gang member shouted as the student stood in front of the whole group—only one person who had stood up out of everyone there. One person couldn't make a difference in a situation like this, so nobody felt hopeful.

Mr. Root lifted his head and looked at the solitary student.

"Gary . . ." he muttered. "Don't worry about me. I'll be okay . . . you stay back . . . you're our star player . . . don't let these guys hurt you and ruin your future." Mr. Root smiled, his mouth and teeth stained red with his own blood.

Gary clenched his fist.

"I don't think I can," Gary replied. "You see, I kind of like you as a teacher and our coach."

The red color gang member had lost his patience. He stepped forward, picking up his bat, and swung it toward Gary's head. Gary threw his fist right toward the bat; it connected, breaking the bat in half, and continued forward.

"*Arghh!*" Gary screamed as he planted his fist into the attacker's face. Everyone heard a cracking noise as the gang member's face was pushed into itself; a tooth flew through the air and landed on the ground.

"Get the f*ck out of my school!" Gary shouted.

CHAPTER 14

BLAME HIM!

Gary stood there with his fists by his sides, his knuckles slightly bleeding from hitting the bat. In his current form, his body was still human. He might no longer have human strength and speed, but his skin was still fragile. He knew it based on the amount of times he had been stabbed.

The students sat there in disbelief, that out of all people, Gary had been the one to stand up and knock out a gang member. Hardly anyone had known about him until his contribution at the rugby match against Eton High. Although he had briefly exchanged some friendly greetings here and there, he had quickly gone back to being "that kid who had dyed his hair green."

At that moment, the students all had the same thought: he was brave . . . or stupid. None of them had had the courage to do what he did, but it was also an idiotic thing to do. As impressive as it was, he would face the same problem as John: there were more gang members than he alone could ever take.

The other red color gang members understood this and were coming to surround him. They were a bit cautious after seeing him smash a wooden bat with brute strength. But there were also still plenty of them between Gary and Mr. Root and Riv.

"*Gary!*" a female voice shrieked loudly. Everyone turned their heads to see who had let out this banshee cry. It was another teacher, Mrs. Bedford, a pear-shaped older woman with glasses.

"Why did you do that? Don't you understand that the rest of us might get punished for what you just did!" she continued to shout. "Don't fight them! Just let them have whatever they want, and they will be gone!

"Please, you're not going to hurt us because of what he did, right?" she begged Riv. "Just hurt him! Please don't hurt us!" she cried again, looking at the other gang members.

Tom forced himself to hold his tongue. Gary was the only one who had stepped up to stop them from hurting Mr. Root any further. He'd risked his own hide to protect everyone.

But another voice suddenly sounded out. "She's right, please don't hurt us! We aren't his friends. We don't even know him that well." It was Steven, one of the students John had asked to fight off the invaders, but at the last moment he had decided not to join in. "He's just another one of those troublemakers and delinquents. We had no part in it, just take them!"

Soon more students were chiming in out of fear. Riv couldn't help but laugh deviously. He found it deeply satisfying to see humans reveal their true nature as beings who cared about nothing else but themselves.

"How are they all so stupid?" Innu whispered in frustration as he angrily clenched his fists. It was one thing for the other students and teachers to be cowering in fear, hoping to get out of this situation, but actively distancing themselves from Gary . . .

"What do they think is going to happen? That they'll just beat some of us up and call it a day? What if they've come to take all the girls away, or take all of us? Would they still be so willing to sit back and do nothing?

"I bet if they were the ones getting hit, they'd be crying and begging for Gary to help them."

In reality, more than a few students agreed with Gary's approach. Unfortunately, just like John, they were too afraid of the consequences to voice their opinion now, much less act.

"Shut up!" Gary shouted back at Mrs. Bedford and his schoolmates. "I'm not fighting them for any of you. Why the hell should I give two shits about you guys and what you think? I have people I care about, and people I don't care about, so I'm getting out of here!"

Gary ran forward, heading straight for Mr. Root. One of the red gang members jumped out in front of him. Not slowing down his momentum, the green-haired teenager rugby-tackled him, lifting him up into the air, and slammed him down before the others could do anything.

The back of the gang member's head hit the hall floor, and he was in such great pain that he wasn't going to get up any time soon. Seeing this, the other gang members switched to a more aggressive approach, intending to attack Gary from the back with their weapons.

But before they could reach him, one of them felt his shirt being pulled back, while another received an elbow to his face. Two others were kicked in the back of the knee, knocking them to the floor. Before they could turn around to see who had done it, they were finished off with another kick to the head.

None of the red color gang members had come close to touching Gary.

"Let's get out of here. I'm with you!" Innu shouted.

"I hope we're among those people you care about," Kai smirked.

"I hope you don't mind me tagging along. I think I have better chances with you than all those backstabbers over there," Blake said.

Since Gary had decided to act, the three of them couldn't sit back any longer and do nothing. This was their best chance to get out of the situation.

"Damn, look at all those guys showing off." Marie sighed.

CHAPTER 15

STAMPEDE

One person was worried about Marie, after seeing the strange look on her face.

"Don't worry, Marie, I know you must be scared, but I'll figure out a way for us to get out of here while they're fighting," Tom exclaimed, trying his best to sound confident. Marie just gave him a sad smile, because she wasn't scared. No, she was just upset because she understood that she wasn't strong enough to openly join the others, and revealing that she had brought blades into school would cause a problem down the line.

Meanwhile, Innu, Kai, Blake, and Gary had formed a circle to deal with the red color gang members who were charging toward them. The four teenage boys were skillful enough to deal with them and not get hurt. The students were baffled at the sight; it looked like a scene out of a movie.

They couldn't understand how John and the other members from the fighting clubs had failed so miserably against the gang members, and yet these four made it look easy. At the same time, it appeared as if the gang members were getting concerned about what was happening in front of them, to the point that they had kept their eyes off everyone else who was sitting down.

However, one person stood out. Gary didn't care if he got hit, he just continued to fight nonstop like a machine. He even lifted one of the gang members by the neck, throwing him toward another wave of attackers.

Then another baseball bat was heading toward him, but he grabbed it with his bare hands and swung it, hitting another gang member and breaking it at the same time.

"Gary, you have to do something. Unlike you, we don't have unlimited stamina! They don't care about Mr. Root, so let's cause some chaos. Go open the door!" Kai shouted.

Gary understood Kai's logic. He covered his head with his arms and charged forward, running as fast as he could toward the back door, since there were less red color gang members there.

The others tried to get in his way, but with his speed and strength he was like a bull. He rushed into people, knocking them over, but just before he reached the double door, a large figure lumbered in front of it.

It was the one red color gang member who was nearly as large as Mr. Root. The giant took on a sumo-like stance as he got ready to stop Gary from advancing any farther.

He's a big guy, and he looks to be tough, but I need to get past him now!

3 Points have been allocated into Strength
Your base Strength is now at 18
Skill activated: Controlled Transformation
Current Agility: 15 (+3)

Gary placed all of his available stat points into Strength, while also boosting his speed via Controlled Transformation to transform the bottom half of his legs.

He had only changed them ever so slightly, in order to gain a boost in speed at the last second. Using his power to springboard himself off the floor, Gary flew up like a rocket, and the large gang member was unprepared for what he was about to face.

The giant man could hardly resist Gary's power, and his body was pushed back, slamming into the metal door. The chains and the door gave way, opening up a gap as the door dug into the man's back.

"Get out of my way!" Gary shouted as he threw out a kick, hitting the man on the side of the head, causing him to fly to the side and fall to the floor.

The door had caved in, but it wasn't completely done yet. Gary grabbed the chains and pulled. As a result of Controlled Transformation, his forearms grew slightly bigger and the chains eventually snapped. He kicked the door open, and the escape route was now open to everybody.

The students and teachers still couldn't believe it. The large man who had terrified all of them had just been defeated, and not only that, Gary had secured a way to freedom. Strangely, for some reason he wasn't going through it; instead he seemed to be making his way back toward the stage.

"Everyone, what are you waiting for?" John screamed at the top of his lungs. "Let's get out of here!"

The scream woke everyone up from their stupor. One would think the teachers and students were being chased by a zombie horde as they all shoved each other to be the first to run through the small exit. The power of more than six hundred people pushing in one direction was too much for even the red color gang members to take.

None of them could stop it; they were simply overwhelmed by the suddenness of their action. The large group that had been so frightened and scared one second had suddenly transformed into something akin to a wildebeest stampede.

As the crowd stormed toward the exit, Gary didn't expect to be swept up along with them. No one stopped to thank him, and for a moment he was afraid of getting trampled.

"Gary!" He heard a familiar voice and immediately pushed past the people, shoving them out of the way, and saw that Tom had fallen down. The others were stepping on him, not even caring what they were doing, and Tom seemed to be covering another person as well.

Gary picked Tom up and saw that he had shielded Marie from the mass of people. He then stood in front of them, like a solid wall, making sure that no one else could hurt them. Eventually everyone had escaped, and the only ones left were Gary, Tom, and the three friends who had stood up with him.

"Those people . . . what is wrong with them?" Gary asked as he made sure Tom and Marie were okay. Tom had suffered a few bruises, but he seemed okay otherwise. What surprised Gary was that his weak little friend, who had never gotten into a single fight in his life, had selflessly protected someone.

"Hey!" Kai shouted, trying to grab Gary's attention.

Turning around, Gary saw that the others were checking on Mr. Root. They didn't want to move him, in case he was seriously injured. But something else was shocking.

"The red color gang, where are they?" Gary looked around, only to see that the other door had also been unlocked. The dozen or so gang members that they had beaten were still on the floor rolling about in pain, but the rest had seemingly escaped in the panic.

"I think they used some type of jammer in this hall. When you opened that door, it allowed everyone to escape, so they should be able to use their phones again. They were probably afraid that the police would come soon. That's what I was hoping for, but I didn't expect everyone else to act the way they did," Kai explained, before he let out a sigh.

Gary went over to see Mr. Root's condition for himself. The teacher's face didn't look too bad because they had mainly focused on other areas, but he seemed to be hurt everywhere else.

"Hey, broccoli head . . . you were . . . amazing back there," Mr. Root coughed out, and it sounded like he was choking on something. "You know . . . ever since you joined, I was . . . I was always watching you . . . I saw what you did. How you were able to analyze everyone's movements."

"Stop." Gary worried that Mr. Root had to be in pain just from speaking.

"No . . . I want you . . . you . . . to know that you were always special. I was just waiting for you to shine . . . and I'm so happy that I . . . you . . . you got to . . ."

It was at that moment that Gary realized something.

"His heart rate is slowing down!" he shouted in a panic. "Some-body call an ambulance!"

CHAPTER 16

NO MORE OF THIS!

An ambulance left the school a little while later, yet the only students who seemed to care were those on the rugby team, as well as those like John who felt guilty about Mr. Root's sacrifice. Gary had watched the ambulance drive off into the distance until he couldn't see it any more, worried about his teacher.

Is it my fault that everyone I care about ends up being hurt? Why didn't I act sooner? I should have stood up when Mr. Root took the blame . . . not after *they had beaten him up so badly . . .*

"It's not your fault." Kai spoke up to comfort his friend. Gary turned and saw the other members of the Howlers next to Kai, along with Tom. "We should have acted from the beginning. I wasn't much better than the rest of those scared sheeple. I was too worried about that . . ." He let out a frustrated sigh.

Kai seemed to understand how Gary was feeling and blamed himself for his earlier advice to just observe the situation first. Nevertheless, Gary understood what Kai was really worried about . . . whether the Underdogs or the Gray Elephants might have been behind the entire attack.

They still had no idea why the red color gang would do something so daring in the first place.

"Kai . . . I want to put a stop to all of this mess. I don't want anything like this to ever occur again, be it in our school, our town . . . or my home," Gary said.

"So do I." Innu stepped forward, and so did the rest, standing by Gary's side.

Although Riv had escaped with most of his men, Gary had not only saved his schoolmates, he had also completed his quest.

Quest reward: Instant Level Up + Bonus Exp
Congratulations, you have now reached: Level 13
A stat point has been granted

Aside from the Instant Level Up, which had earned Gary the obligatory stat point, he had further received 2 Exp for each person who had gotten out of the situation unharmed. Unfortunately, the number had dropped a bit, which suggested that Tom wasn't the only one who had been hurt when everyone stormed out of the main hall.

That, coupled with Gary having defeated a few gang members, meant that he was currently sitting on 1,546 experience points out of 2,346.

Gary had noticed that after getting stronger, especially after he had chosen the Warrior Class, the amount of Exp he gained for people he could easily defeat had lessened. So he wasn't too disappointed that his rewards had only been in the form of an Instant Level Up and extra Exp, rather than a new skill.

The group turned around and went back to the others. All the students had gathered on the field. Principal Young, who hadn't been at school at the time of the attack, rushed over as soon as she was contacted. Right now, she and the other teachers were busy doing a head count.

The police had arrived a few minutes before the ambulance and were investigating the scene, while some officers had asked the teachers and students for testimony about what happened. They were confident that they would catch the criminals, since they were able to apprehend the red color gang members that Gary and the others had knocked out.

"Hey, that's them, right? They're the ones who fought off those gangsters," one of the students whispered while pointing at Gary's group.

"Yeah, I mean, we all saw the green-haired kid, but I couldn't see the others well. I'm not surprised Blake stood up for us!"

"They were kinda cool when they were fighting. I didn't know they were that strong."

Gary might have enjoyed the compliments from his fellow students in the past, but not today, especially not after the vocal majority had tried to make him into a straw man. For a second, he caught Mrs. Bedford glancing his way, and Gary stared back at her. She turned her head, unable to look him in the eyes.

Eventually, after waiting outside for some time, Gary and his group were approached by two police officers. One of them wore a long brown coat, while the other one, who looked quite young, wore a blue shirt with suspenders.

"Nice to meet you, kids. I'm Chief of Police Anton Millstun, and this is my assistant, Roo Game," the older man said, introducing them both.

"We just got the reports from your teachers and fellow students about what had happened. Unless you want to add anything, I believe we have heard enough about your 'courageous act'." Millstun sighed, seemingly unwilling to say what came next.

"What you guys did back there was a very dangerous thing. While it might have worked out in your favor this time, you shouldn't forget that those were gang members.

"Most color gang members might be low-ranking and not very different from a regular delinquent, but you never know what someone might do when pushed into a desperate situation. Of course, none of you will get into trouble for what you did. It was self-defense, after all!

Millstun sighed. "Personally, I think all of you did the right thing. You acted when no one else did, and while it was reckless of you, I'm glad that things turned out well. I hope to have more people like you on our police force. Still, the next time you find yourself in a tough situation . . . Please, just run and call us!"

After saying what he wanted to say, the police chief started to leave, but then he turned around and looked at the kids.

"This school . . . it's the same one that deceased kid went to, if I'm not mistaken. We only ever found his fingerprints on the knife, making it clear that he had been the aggressor. According to the testimony of his peers and lack of any criminal history, it must have been a crime of passion . . .

"Which means most likely it was someone he knew. We checked all those that were close to him, but maybe the murderer is here? Is the person we are looking for in this school? Come to think of it, isn't this school also the one White Rose visited because of a suspected unregistered Altered?"

Anton started to scratch his head, contemplating whether all of this was coincidence or if there might be some sort of connection. It was a bit of a reach, but he had learned never to ignore any hunches. However, he's have to consider this idea some other time. Right now, the most important thing was to find out why the red color gang had gone so far against this school.

"Sir!" One of the other officers came running toward the two of them. They hadn't moved far from their spot, and with his enhanced hearing, Gary was able to listen in on everything they said.

"I have a report to make. All the students have been accounted for, apart from one. The teachers checked and checked again. The missing student is a Xin Clove. She's the mayor's daughter!"

CHAPTER 17

THE LONE WOLF

After Anton heard this crucial bit of information, everything seemed to have fallen into place. He had never thought a color gang would try to abduct someone in such a crazy manner, but if their target had been the mayor's daughter, It might have been their best shot.

Aside from a few officers who stayed behind to gather more evidence, the rest of the police force promptly left the school. One of them had informed Principal Young, but she made no announcement about the missing student.

Instead, a different announcement was made.

"All of you must have been looking forward to watching your fellow students display their talents, but given today's tragic turn of events, I believe it's for the best to postpone the talent show. Your parents have already been made aware of the situation and will be here to pick you up. For the rest of you, please stay safe and if possible go home in groups."

Honestly, Gary thought the whole thing to be a bad joke. Who cared about the stupid talent show? If coming in hadn't been mandatory, barely anyone would have shown up on a Saturday. However, based on how the teachers had acted, he wasn't too surprised that Principal Young wanted to just dismiss everyone.

"It looks like our day ended early, so what do you want to do?" Kai asked, turning toward Gary.

He wasn't sure why Kai was asking him; didn't they already have plans? Or was it because Kai was worried about whether Gary was in the mood to continue. In the end, he had only one thought on his mind at the moment: Xin.

The police are useless . . . they won't be able to find her and even if they do, they will be too scared to retrieve her from wherever the red color gang might have taken her, Gary thought. *They were here today, but were they really here for her? Or were they here for me and decided just to take her for a substitute? Somehow, I have a feeling that what happened to her today is my fault.* He clenched his fist as he decided what to do.

"Is it okay for me to take a rain check on today's plan? I don't think I'll be able to work either," Gary finally said.

Blake had gone home, but Tom was still with the group. Seeing the look in Gary's eyes, he was naturally worried what Gary might have in mind. Perhaps tomorrow he would find out on the dark web that another color gang had gone missing in Slough. But what could he do to stop his friend? It wasn't like he could follow him home.

Just then, Tom received a text from his parents, who must have heard about what had happened.

"It looks like my parents are on their way here to pick me up. Gary . . . whatever you plan to do . . . promise me to stay safe," Tom said, only to receive a slight nod after some hesitation. He sighed but understood this response to be the best he could have hoped for, so he left the Howlers to discuss things without him.

"It's all right, we don't necessarily need you to come in today." Kai patted Gary on the shoulder. "Today was supposed to be a simple scouting job. I can head off with the others and bring back the information and fill you in later. Don't worry about your job, either.

"Since we were going to be away, I've asked Austin to prepare some replacements for us this weekend." Kai smiled. "Since they're Austin's friends, their wages are on the cheap side. He sent over the three he trusts the most. With them and Miss Degrace, they will be able to look after the club.

"Honestly, what I'm more concerned about is you. It's clear you don't just plan to go home . . . Nobody doubts your strength, but are you sure you want to go at it alone?"

Gary looked at the faces of the others, and he could see that they were all determined. Wherever he went, they would follow. If he asked them, for the first time in his life he felt like there were people who would agree no matter what . . . at the same time, exactly because they had put their trust into him, he couldn't ask them to come along.

Unlike him, they didn't have a reason to save Xin, except for Innu, perhaps. Besides, if anyone could get her out of that situation unhurt, it would be him. As harsh as it sounded, the rest might actually hold him back, if he were to go wild.

"Thank you, guys. We all have a job to do, and this gang needs to move fast. If you guys still feel the same way you did when we saw those red color gang members here today, then we better get a move on. Let's become big enough that no gang would ever dare to pull off such a stunt in our time!" Gary smiled.

"It looks like someone has gotten into your head!" Innu commented, as he wrapped his arm around Gary's head and started to rub his knuckles in his hair. "Eww, is this gel? How much did—" Innu was about to ask how much he'd used when Gary gave him a mean look that shut him up.

With everyone gone, Gary decided to head back into school for a while. The teachers weren't supposed to let them in, but none of them had the gall to stop Gary after what had happened. He needed something that smelled like Xin to be able to follow where she was.

It wasn't like her scent was all around; it would only help when he was close. After that, Gary would visit the places where the red color gang had been seen frequently, and Kai had already texted him all the information he required for that.

As Gary entered their empty classroom, he started to think back to something, and that was Mr. Root. Back in the main hall, when Mr. Root's heart rate had started dropping, he had been worried he might not make it.

It had been impossible to tell how long the ambulance would take to reach them. For one, it was Slough, and ambulances were in demand at all times of the day. Seeing someone he cared about close to death, he wanted to save him, and there was actually something he could do about it.

What if I bite him? Gary had thought.

If he were to bite Mr. Root, he might turn him. Given a werewolf's vitality, his teacher would surely recover. Unlike what had happened with Billy, if he were to turn his teacher into a beta wolf, he wouldn't have to worry about an adult trying to usurp his position.

However . . . What kind of life would Mr. Root have to lead if he made him into a werewolf? Would he hate Gary for turning him into a monster? Perhaps he would even become another monster like Billy, forcing Gary to do what Blake had done to Billy . . .

Since he hadn't been there, there was no telling how long it took for one to become an omega wolf. Heck, he didn't even know if there was a guarantee. What if Billy had simply been a unlucky coincidence?

Even if it would work, what about the bloodlust? He still remembered that the first thing he had read after becoming a werewolf was a system message that read:

Your bloodlust has been lowered

Also, Billy had said something that Gary remembered at that moment. *I'd killed them both. I didn't do it on purpose. It was as if the hunger and bloodlust took over me!* What if he hadn't lied? What if it was the natural instinct of a werewolf to attack and feast on the first thing it saw?

In the end, while he had been contemplating this option, the ambulance had arrived, making him abandon his idea. Still, it made

Gary wonder whether he could help others by turning them. After all, everyone wanted to become Altered these days, and with a simple bite he could make them become something that was close enough . . . maybe even better?

That's a crazy idea, Gary thought. *Or is it?*

CHAPTER 18

THE WRONG GIRL

Away from the busy parts of Slough, out in the sticks where there were more open fields and greenery, stood a large house behind a gated driveway. Inside that luxury home, not too long ago, Mayor Clove had been informed about the sudden absence of his daughter.

"What the hell do I even pay you for, huh? You've not only failed to properly protect her, *now you've allowed her to get abducted?*" The mayor shouted and banged his hands on the table in front of him like a toddler throwing a tantrum.

He was breathing heavily because of all the shouting he had done. Ben Clove reached into the breast pocket of the suit that barely fit him these days. The middle-aged man had been gaining a lot of weight ever since he had taken on this job. Bringing out some pills, he took three of them at once and waited for them to do their job.

"Sir, please understand that we are doing the best we can; you blaming us is not helping the situation," the man dressed in black replied. One would expect some worry when being shouted at by the mayor, but the man with the dragon tattoo crawling up his neck was taking things nonchalantly.

The man sitting opposite the mayor wasn't just anybody. D was the head of the Rising Dragon gang, one of Slough's five small-time gangs. Ever since the mayor's election, they had been cooperating with Ben Clove. In fact, it was mostly because of them that the mayor was able to keep his promise of protecting the main street of Slough, as it was part of their territory.

"One, it was a school day; we were waiting to pick her up at her usual time, the time that she should have been leaving. In fact, we always come an hour early to search the area and make sure nothing suspicious is seen during that time.

"Yet this happened little after lunch, and in school of all things. We aren't allowed to bring guards inside, and we thought that perhaps the students being in school would be adequate to stop gang members from attacking. Not that we ever imagined that somebody would do this. I admit this was a fault on my part," D replied, neither bowing nor sounding apologetic.

"I don't want to keep hearing your excuses!" Ben shouted. "I want solutions to the problem. Why have you not acted yet? It doesn't take a genius to know that it could only have been the red color gang who took her, so just get in there and pull her out!"

D simply shook his head. "We would have a hard time against the red color gang on their own, much less now that they have fused with the remnants of the gray color gang. Attacking the color gang is the same as offending the Gray Elephants. As one of the biggest gangs in Slough, they could crush our gang if they wanted to.

"Please relax, sir, your daughter will be safe. She's too valuable as a hostage. I've already put in a request to the Gray Elephants' leader. Once I get a reply, I will let you know."

Ben couldn't take it any more. He leaned over the desk and attempted to pull on D's shirt, but the gang leader simply leaned back to avoid the middle-aged man's grab, until he felt his back hit something solid.

Turning around, he saw a young man staring back at him. He wore a tight sports shirt and he towered over D.

"Don't worry, I'll do it for you, Dad," the young man spoke up. He was none other than Jayden Clove, Ben's firstborn son and one of the country's top fifty Altered fighters. He casually lifted D by the scruff of his shirt with one hand.

For the first time, D looked panicked and grabbed Jayden's hand, trying to release his grip, but it wouldn't budge at all. Jayden threw the man against the wall so hard that it left a dent.

"You guys had one job, yet you *failed* to protect my sister. I should wipe out your whole gang for that alone! Dad, let me deal with the situation," Jayden said with his hand on his chest. "I promise to find Xin. There is not a gang in Slough or anyone I might come across that I can't handle."

The sound of dripping water was the first thing Xin heard as she slowly regained consciousness. Her body felt sore all over. When she tried to move her hands, she discovered that she could not. The same held true for her legs; only her head had been spared, not that she could do much with that alone.

They tied me to a chair. It feels like one of those interrogation scenes in the movies, Xin thought, trying her best to keep her mind away from the bleakness of her current situation. She might be a strong fighter, but that was in a normal situation, not when she had been abducted. Right now, she was beginning to feel very scared.

Looking around, she could hardly make out anything. There was barely any light, only a little that shone in through the cracks of the roof above her. The flooring was crooked, with wooden panels sticking out and more. Judging by the fact that they hadn't gagged her, she imagined that wherever she was, it would be far enough away from anybody willing to help her.

"*Help!*" Xin shouted as loud as she could. There wasn't much else she could do, and it was at least worth a shot. Indeed, it did achieve one thing. Soon she heard footsteps approaching her in the dark . . . followed by an annoying giggle.

"Ah, it's so nice to see you like this." As the person stepped into a patch of light, Xin could make out a familiar face, though she had already recognized who it was by the annoying sound. The red color gang leader Riv was standing by Tiffany's side, his smile just as big as hers.

"I wish I could say the same," Xin replied sarcastically. "You know, I wasn't too sure who'd set things up for me. For a moment, I even gave you the benefit of the doubt. But now I just gotta ask . . . Are you really this stupid?"

The taunt might have gotten to Tiffany another time, but seeing Xin unable to do anything but taunt her made the class diva cackle.

"You seem to have yet to realize your own situation. Why don't you cry for help again, see how that works for you?" Tiffany smirked, making fun of the abducted girl. "I told you, Xin, you chose the wrong girl to mess with! And today you're finally going to pay for everything you did to me! Not just you, but your whole family as well!"

"I wonder how much the mayor will pay for his sweet little daughter. With a large sum, we'll even be able to get out of this place," Riv said. "It will be nice to live with you in a Tier 2 city, Tiffy!"

"Of course, darling, that's the plan!" Tiffany held on to Riv's arm.

Xin started to laugh.

"Haha, you did all of this for money? No wonder you never accepted my apology. I actually felt bad for the things I did to you, even though it was an honest mistake. If you just wanted revenge, you could have tried to get me back at school, but you're asking for money and trying to involve my family.

"You said I messed with the wrong girl . . . you have no idea."

CHAPTER 19

ONE OF THE FIVE

After Principal Young had dismissed everyone, Kai, Marie, and Innu headed to the bus stop. Austin was already waiting there, since he had been informed over the group chat that they had been let out early.

Right now, the whole gang was riding the bus, heading to an area called Burnham. On the way there, it was obvious that it wasn't as busy as the rest of Slough, most likely because it wasn't a residential area. Nevertheless, the area still had someone controlling it, and they made their money by catering to a certain clientele.

"I can't believe the red color gang would not only come to your doorstep but try to hold your whole school hostage," Austin said after getting the full story on the mostly empty bus. The news about the event had spread like wildfire, but with everyone exaggerating, it had been hard to find out how much of it had been true.

"It's a good thing they didn't enter my school, otherwise there would have been an outright brawl between the students and the red color gang. We would have pounded them and taught them a lesson."

"You mean like the time when Billy entered the school?" Innu interjected. He was sure that Austin would have acted just like Gary, and he didn't doubt his fellow gang member's strength . . . yet he had a feeling it would have turned out no different from John's resistance. Austin's stare made Innu quickly change the topic. "Anyway, Kai, you said there were five small-time gangs in Slough, so why did you pick this one? It's really far away, so are they easy or something?"

The second Innu said those words, it was Kai's turn to give him a glare, and he instantly understood the mistake he had made. Innu couldn't help it, he was just someone who spoke his mind before thinking. No one should ever call any gang "easy"; underestimating them would be a big mistake.

"We'll have to see about them being an easy target, but them being so far away is actually a good thing," Kai eventually replied after letting out a sigh. "We take over this place, the chance of anyone interfering will be less than in any other location. At the same time, if we leave it alone for a bit, it will be okay as well.

"We still really haven't solved the problem with helping people run the territories we take over. We can't just ask Austin to send over his guys every time. If possible, we'll have to persuade some members from the gang we take over to work for us.

"Putting them on a payroll isn't a problem, but we still need trustworthy people at the top keeping them in check. Otherwise, other gangs can always swoop in and convince them to stab us in the back while we're small.

"Once we get bigger and control this place completely like the Gray Elephants or the Underdogs, we'll be okay. At that point, the others won't even try to mess with us."

"Does this place have a school?" Austin suddenly asked. It seemed to be a weird question, yet Kai didn't outright dismiss it, seemingly understanding what the tall teenager was referring to.

"It does, but it's not a school full of delinquents. It doesn't look like the gang uses them as a recruitment base, but I have to admit that I haven't looked into them too much, so what I have is probably just some surface information. They might have someone like you on the top, since they don't seem to be as disorganized as Eton High was," Kai answered. "Your guys might actually know more about it."

Austin's idea was to pay the school a visit, to challenge its top dog. The delinquents at each school cared about the hierarchy a lot. In a way, it was a more harmless version of gang wars. If the large teenager could take down the school leaders, then the school delinquents would willingly do the Howlers' bidding.

As long as they were put on the payroll, they should stay fairly loyal. Even a little money looked like a gold mine to those types of students. In a way, this made delinquent students far easier to deal with than gang members, simply because the former had yet to experience the real world.

"Are we really just going to continue ignoring the issue?" Marie finally said. "We all saw that look on Gary's face. He has clearly gone off to fight the red color gang. It's probably for revenge because of what they did to Mr. Root . . . I know how strong he is, but what if he gets into trouble? "He's our leader, so shouldn't we help him?"

The group descended into silence at this question. Surprisingly, Innu was the one to break it.

"You heard Kai offer him our help. He didn't want it. While I don't like him wanting to do things alone, he's our leader, so we should respect his wishes," Innu said. "He took care of those monstrous twins, so he should be fine . . . as long as they don't have more of them . . ."

At the end, Innu's voice started to shake a bit, and Marie noticed that his knee was bouncing up and down and he was fiddling with his hands. It was clear that thinking about Gary made him restless.

When the hell did this group get so close with each other? she wondered, looking down and smiling at the floor.

The group had finally arrived at in Burnham. There seemed to be fewer people here, but the bus had stopped at the main area. It was a Saturday, so quite a lot of families were in this area.

"Wow, I didn't even know Slough had a place like this . . . I think this is better than Cipen," Innu said as they walked down the street, where every second shop was a restaurant of some kind.

"Depends on what you're looking for. Cipen has the nightlife, whereas this place is just filled with restaurants." Kai shrugged.

The group continued walking down the street, passing various Chinese restaurants, pizza places, Japanese sushi places, Korean barbecues. It all looked so delicious and there were multiple families inside, but there was one thing that Innu noticed more than the others.

"There are a lot of beautiful girls here. The workers here are stunning; look at her!" As they walked past yet another Chinese restaurant, Innu pointed at a girl wearing a traditional red Chinese dress with a slit in the skirt that showed off her long legs.

"Wait, now that you mention it, there are an awful lot of girls who work here," Marie agreed. That was a signal for Kai to stop in the middle of the street.

"Remember, we are here on a scouting mission, but while we are here, why don't we grab a bite?"

It took a long time for the group to decide where they wanted to eat. There were far too many choices, and discovering that everyone's favorite food was something different didn't make things easier. Ultimately, they agreed to settle for an all-you-can-eat restaurant that had a little of everything.

They headed inside, and Kai paid as they waited for the waiter to bring over their plates and drinks. Even in this place, all they could see were female workers.

"So tell me, these places aren't really restaurants, right?" Austin eventually asked. The other two turned around, wondering what he meant by this, but judging by Kai's smile, he was right.

"In some ways, you are right. Of course, restaurants can be a lucrative business, but a gang wouldn't take control of a whole area just for that," Kai explained. "At night this place is completely different. All the restaurants have a double front. You noticed a lot of girls, right? And all of them being pretty . . . well, that's because the gang brings in a lot of trafficking and prostitution.

"The reason this place is on the edge of Slough is because their clientele don't choose those from Slough. It's a crucial point for us if we want to go beyond Slough at some point, besides all the other reasons."

Innu couldn't quite believe it as he looked around, but as he noticed the skimpy dresses they wore, the tired look on their faces and in their eyes . . . it was starting to make sense.

There was a look on the other members' faces as Kai casually discussed the topic. This was the real gang life . . . everything was suddenly becoming a little too real for them, and they wondered how Gary would feel about taking over such a place.

Innu looked like he was about to say something, but just then the waitress approached.

"Hi there, here are your drinks, and the table is for the four of you, correct?" The girl smiled at them all.

Looking at her up close, Innu felt like there was something off about her. Sure, she was pretty, but she seemed to be wearing a lot of makeup. He was starting to feel . . . bad for her. If she was working here out of choice, then so be it, but judging from her eyes, that didn't seem to be the case at all.

"Do you like working here?" Innu suddenly asked her. She was startled by the question as she raised the empty tray over her body. She looked out of the corner of her eye at the one man who was in the room with them, one of the very few.

"Please ignore our nosy friend here, he just wanted to say that this here's a great place . . . that's all. Yes, just four of us will be fine." Kai smiled at the girl, who placed the tray down before taking her leave. Kai had paid close attention to the girl, noticing that her name tag read *Stacy*.

CHAPTER 20

TWO THE SAME

After searching around for a while, the only things Gary found of Xin's were a few of her school books, as well as her pencil case. He had been hoping for something more tangible like an item of clothing. He felt quite strange sniffing her belongings, but he was trying to save her life, after all. Luckily, there wasn't anyone in the classroom either . . . However, the smell was too faint.

It was easier tracking Tom's shirt . . . then again, I was following the smell of his blood. I guess a werewolf's nose is just extra sensitive to that, Gary mused.

For a brief moment, he contemplated trying his luck with her locker, but seeing as someone had just stolen her stuff yesterday, he wasn't too optimistic. Instead, he checked his phone. Kai had sent him a list of known hangout spots for red color gang members, as well as some supposed bases of operations.

Kai had added a suggested order for him to check things out. At the end, he had even attached his personal analysis.

I doubt the red color gang that attacked today have fled far from the school. Riv himself might have returned to one of their bases, but I bet that a good chunk of those involved in the attack live close by.

I know you didn't want us to come along, and knowing your strength I can't argue, but since you seem to be planning to attack them, you should at least wear the gang uniform. Don't forget your mask either.

Gary couldn't help but smile when he read how Kai cared for and trusted him.

A short while later, he found himself in an alleyway that was wider than most. He stopped just around the corner, as he could hear people talking on the other side. Having taken Kai's advice, he was wearing his new black and gold blazer as well as the mask he had been given.

The red color gang came to our school just after Kai told me the Underdogs know about me going to school there. The Gray Elephants should also know my real name by now, so they must be looking for me as well. Either way, right now showing my face isn't the best idea.

Around the same time, a tall handsome figure in a tight sports shirt was walking around what looked like a fish marketplace. There were countless stalls with different types of fish. Most of them were alive in containers, while others were being freshly cut up. The whole place had a distinctive smell, which was hitting Jayden in the nose.

Still, he ignored it, as he was looking for something in particular. Turning his head countless times, he finally found what he had been looking for. Along one side of the market with stalls, there were also a few storefronts.

Heading inside a particular one, Jayden triggered the bell on top of the door.

"I'll be with you as a second," the owner said from behind the counter. He appeared to be talking to three people in the back of the shop. Jayden could clearly make out the red clothing they all shared. Walking up to them confidently, Jayden stood right behind them, close to the countertop, which held countless fish on ice and a chopping board where the large man did his work.

"It's okay, I'm not here for you." Jayden smiled. "I'm here for them."

Without hesitation, the Altered grabbed one of the gang members by the scruff of his neck and slammed him right into the pile of fish, twisting and turning his head into the ice, creating crunching sounds.

The other two gang members were shocked at the sudden brutality, but at least they understood that they were being targeted. The one on the right was ready to make a move, but Jayden kicked him in the side of his leg. With a loud snap, the man's leg was now bent inward.

The terrifying thing was that it had looked like just a casual kick without much power, but it had been enough to cripple the man. Still holding on to the neck of the first gang member, Jayden lifted his body out of the ice and slammed him down again. He lifted him one more time and slammed him into the ice a third time while looking the other person in the eyes.

Blood was pooling in the ice, and it was hard to tell if it was from the red color gang member or one of the fish. The owner was shaking behind the counter, and seeing that Jayden wasn't interested in him, he ran into the freezer and shut the door behind him.

"Today, your gang attacked Westbridge High School. During the attack, your guys happened to kidnap a girl. Where is she?" Jayden asked as he stared down the remaining gang member.

"I don't know, I wasn't part of the attack!" The twentysomething had peed his pants in fright, and he hastily tried to back off, only to stumble over the passed-out body of the crippled gang member.

"Well, you seem to at least know about the attack, and something's telling me, you're going to remember more about it in a second," Jayden said, walking toward him as he let go of the first guy's head. His body just slid down until it eventually fell to the floor.

Desperate to get out of the situation, the gang member searched for something to throw at Jayden. He found the knife that the owner had dropped during his escape, yet the Altered easily evaded the weapon. Jayden let out a sigh before grabbing the last gang member's head and dragging him behind the counter.

He then punched the man lightly in the head before grabbing his arm and placing it on the chopping board. Next, he picked up the knife that had just been thrown at him.

"Wait! I'll tell you!" the man cried out in a panic.

Not reacting in any way, Jayden swung the knife down, striking the board and slicing the man's little finger off.

"Get talking, unless you want to lose them all today," Jayden demanded, lifting the knife once again. "Don't try to bullshit me, either, or I *will* be back for you! You should know something about me . . . I hate gangs!"

In the alleyway, Gary had found a total of five red color gang members who seemed to be having a good time together. However, less than a minute later, only one of them was still left standing.

The group had made a bonfire, and Gary had yet to get an answer from a single one of them. Currently, he had the last one held by the back of his neck, already beaten quite a bit.

He started to drag the man's body closer to the fire, making him intensify his struggle.

"Tell me where she is! Tell me where I can find the girl you abducted!" Gary demanded, as he pushed the man's head closer to the flames, now only inches away.

"*Stop! I'll tell you, I'll tell you everything!*" The man pleaded to be let go.

Once Gary had gotten the information he needed to find Xin, he chucked the man against the wall, knocking him out like the others. As he walked away, he had a single thought in his mind.

I hate gangs . . .

CHAPTER 21

COLLISION

Stepping outside an old, beaten-down cabin, Riv raised his arm to shield his eyes. The light was quite bright outside since it was still the afternoon. He stretched a few times and made sure that everyone was still waiting outside in their positions.

There were about twenty gang members total. Most of them had been part of the attack on Westbridge High School, following his orders, and now they were standing guard in the middle of the woods. Of course, he couldn't use the entire red gang for this, otherwise it would catch the eye of those above him, which was something he didn't want. Still, he needed a few here for safety. Not that he was expecting any trouble.

"Looks like everything is going smoothly." Riv smiled. His trouser pocket was vibrating; taking out his phone, he saw the name *Brandon* on the screen. He placed it back in his pocket, ignoring the call.

"With the amount of money we'll get from this, I won't need to rely on the Gray Elephants any more. My work has only doubled ever since that idiot Buffin got his ass kicked by some nobodies and I had to take in his stragglers, yet they still treat me like trash!" Riv mumbled in frustration.

One of the members turned around, and the red color gang leader realized that he needed to keep his lips sealed a while longer.

Shit, I have to be careful. The others still think that we've kidnapped the mayor's daughter, following the Gray Elephants' orders. I can't have any of them inform Brandon now. Once we get the money, Tiffany and I will have to leave Slough ASAP. Then we can live a happy and long life together. I really do have the best girl.

"Riv, get in here!" a voice screamed from inside. Quickly, Riv turned around and headed back into the cabin to see what exactly was going on. The others turned back toward the cabin and smirked, agreeing that their leader was completely whipped.

"What a simp," one of them mumbled, making those close to him who had heard his remark snicker.

The area around the cabin was quite open; the guards were standing around it in all directions, just where the edge of the forest began.

Man, I wonder how long it's going to take, one of the guards thought as he let out a big yawn. The next thing he saw was a fist directly coming toward his face. It was a clean hit that nearly flipped him around, and it was safe to say he wouldn't be getting up anytime soon.

"Hey, who is that?" one of the gang members shouted, as some of them pulled out their weapons: pocketknives, brass knuckles, and more.

"Get that masked freak!" another shouted.

Two of them ran quickly toward Gary, throwing out a punch each, but he easily avoided them. Charging in, he grabbed the backs of their necks and pulled their heads down while jumping up, slamming his knees into their faces.

Another gang member had taken out a chain and, not caring about his comrades, had swung it out like a whip. One of the men that Gary had just been attacked was merely concussed, and he instinctively grabbed his assailant's leg, preventing him from going anywhere.

The chains hit Gary's back, hurting him quite a bit.

–6 HP

Something like that will never kill me. Before the chain fell to the ground or the person could use it again, Gary grabbed it and pulled. The red color gang member believed that he would win in a tug-of-war, but he was unaware that Gary had used Controlled Transformation on his biceps, adding to his already great strength.

The chain was ripped from his hands in seconds, and with the others getting closer, Gary knew exactly how to use it. First he kicked the gang member who was holding on to his leg, while swinging the chain at the original user, hitting him in the leg. With Gary's speed and strength, the heavy chain snapped his leg, causing him to fall to the ground.

I have no reason to go easy on any of you! Gary thought, as he continued to swing the chain, hitting anyone else who got close. Eventually he swung it around another person and the chain snapped in half.

It was old and rusty, but that didn't matter; Gary was strong enough to deal with them all using just his fists and legs. All the fighting matches he had watched, all the moves he had ingrained in his head from a young age, he was now able to use thanks to his improved body.

Another gang member came running toward Gary, but he spun around on one leg and kicked his attacker with the side of his foot. The gang member fell and slid across the ground, kicking up the leaves on the ground.

This new uniform is great. What material is it made out of? It seems to not rip as easily, even if I use Controlled Transformation. Like it can expand with my body as well. Did Kai get this specially made for me? Gary wondered.

Five gang members on one side had already been defeated, and there were still a lot left. Now they were cautious about attacking Gary after seeing what he was capable of.

"This guy is dangerous. We need backup. Why aren't the other guys coming over to help us? What are they doing?" One of the gang members had informed those on the other side about the intruder, but he had yet to receive a reply. Just then they saw another intruder coming in from the side. He was walking calmly, approaching the cabin, and the whole group turned to look at him.

"Looks like I'm in the right place," the man in a sports shirt said, cracking his knuckles as he got into a fighting stance at the same time that Gary recognized him. How could he not? Not only had Gary seen him on TV multiple times before, he had even been saved by him.

It was none other than Jayden Tiger, one of the top fifty Altered fighters in the country.

What is he doing here? Gary wondered. *It can't be . . . is he working with the red color gang? No, that's impossible. They're too small for that . . . Shit, could it be that the Gray Elephants are his sponsors like the Underdogs are for Kirk?*

The next second, Jayden had run across the clearing and thrown a fist, but it wasn't aimed toward the red color gang members; instead it was coming straight for Gary.

"I have a good sense for these things. You look like the strongest, so it's best to deal with you first!" Jayden shouted.

CHAPTER 22

FIGHTING AN ALTERED

The fist coming toward Gary was fast, a little too fast, but thankfully there was some space between the two of them that allowed him to at least do something. He quickly lifted his arms into a cross-shaped position; the only thing he could do in time was block.

Jayden threw the punch a bit wide; there was no technique involved, he had just run and thrown a punch. After he hit Gary, he skidded along the ground before stopping. His arms were heavy and sore, throbbing like a heartbeat, and each time the pain got worse.

You have incurred a grave injury
–15 HP
79/100 HP
Bones in your arms have been broken
Energy points will be used to perform emergency healing
–10 Energy

*Holy f*ck* was Gary's first thought. A few moments later, he felt a rush of pain in his forearms. *I know he's one of the top fifty Altered fighters, but my endurance isn't a joke . . . what's more, he hasn't even transformed yet! You're telling me a single punch did that much damage?*

Emergency healing now in progress

"Hey, isn't that guy Jayden Tiger? I swear it looks just like him," one of the gang members exclaimed.

"Are you crazy? What would someone like him be doing here? Did someone hire him?" another replied.

Unlike Gary, Jayden wasn't wearing a mask or hiding his identity in any other way, simply because he wasn't worried about some gang members recognizing him. He would happily deal with anything that was to come after this event. At the same time, there were plenty of people who would happily stay clear of him as well.

Wait a minute, something's wrong, Gary thought. *If Jayden was really working for them . . . then wouldn't they already know who he is? . . . But then why is he here? And why did he decide to beat me into a pulp?*

"Hang on, I think there's a mis—" Unfortunately, the teenager didn't get a chance to explain himself.

"I told you my instincts were always right." Jayden smiled. "You are the strongest out of all of them. It looks like your arms are in pretty good condition still, so let's do this."

For whatever reason, the Altered started to take off his sports shirt and threw it on the ground, revealing his six-pack abs and his chiseled body. This wasn't simply the body of an athlete, but one of an Altered. It looked like a human body that had been enhanced by performance drugs and then further Photoshopped, but it was right here in the flesh.

What do I do? How do I get myself out of this one? . . . and why the hell did he take off his shirt? Gary had trouble comprehending the absurdity of the situation. He had come here to save Xin, yet he had somehow ended up fighting one of his idols.

Identifying Jayden as the larger threat, the red color gang members ignored Gary for the time being and charged forward, yet the Altered didn't even look away from the masked teenager. He was like a beast that had found its prey, and it wasn't going to let Gary go.

Once the first two gang members were close enough, the Altered fighter swung his arms, and the next moment the two grown men were on the ground, knocked out cold. Gary barely saw the punches. What's more, he had heard the impact on their faces, and he was sure they had broken noses or missing teeth.

"I'm surprised to find someone like you in a place like this. Why would you work for a gang?" Jayden asked, charging forward again.

"Listen, I'm n—" Once again, Gary failed to correct him. It was as if the Altered had already made up his mind about Gary being part of the color gang, even though his outfit should have been a dead giveaway . . .

Damn it, I'll use Controlled Transformation, buy enough time for him to notice. I can't leave now, I have to save Xin . . . even if that means I have to defeat him first!

Gary expanded his biceps, and through his shirt he could feel that they were now like two small cannonballs. He got into a boxing-like stance and waited for the right time. Instead of joining in the fight, the remaining gang members had decided to run back into the cabin, leaving only the two Altered to duke it out outside.

"See, some loyal gang members you have there!" Jayden shouted, to the frustration of the masked high schooler.

Gary threw out a punch, a perfect jab like Kirk had shown him. It was clean and smooth, and most importantly it was fast. Unfortunately, the punch was also telegraphed, allowing Jayden to predict his actions from a mile away.

He moved his head down slightly and to the right, avoiding the punch. He heard the way it *swished* through the air, and could tell it would have been strong.

"Your body . . . it's not normal," Jayden commented, but surprisingly he could see that the masked guy's face seemed calm rather than panicked.

"I never thought my punch was going to hit you in the first place. Besides, I know more than just boxing."

His hand wrapped around Jayden's neck, and Gary was ready to perform his favorite move. He had clinched him, holding him tightly, ready to knee him. The only thing was, Jayden's strength was overwhelming.

Even with a base Strength of 18 as well as the addition from Controlled Transformation, he was finding it hard to hold on to Jayden's head. When he lifted his knee for the attack, instead of aiming at the head, he chose to go for the stomach instead. It was a solid hit, and Gary could feel the impact. With this strength, his opponent should have been down for the count. Alas . . .

"A strong blow, but I've taken thousands of hits to the stomach stronger than this. You're not bad . . . but you can't compare to an Altered!" Jayden shouted, as he lifted his head and broke free from Gary's grasp, pushing him back. The high schooler lost his balance, and before he had a chance to regain it, the Altered threw a punch deep into his side, aiming for his liver.

−16 HP

This attack hurts more than the last time! He must have been holding back!

Before Gary could recover, a kick was already coming in from the other side. He lifted his arm, but it was useless and he was knocked to the ground. The kick was too heavy and strong.

−8 HP

I can't beat him, I can't beat him with just Controlled Transformation. I'll have to either use more of it . . . or use a kick again, Gary thought, but just as he was about to get up, he was kicked in the face, flinging his head back to land spread-eagle.

"You have a good body and good power, you're fast, and you can somewhat see my moves. All of that potential, yet you *waste* it by working as some gang's lackey!" Jayden sounded really annoyed as he lifted Gary by the scruff of his shirt.

"Streaker boy?" Jayden exclaimed in surprise as he let go.

CHAPTER 23

BEAST'S POWER

With the barrage of attacks, Gary hadn't even had the chance to register that his mask had flown off from that last kick. It wasn't until Jayden had called him "streaker boy" that he touched his face and noticed that there was nothing hiding his identity.

"I can't believe a kid like you stimulated my Altered instincts!" Jayden shook his head in disbelief, yet he also looked somewhat troubled about how to deal with Gary. "If I had known that you were in the red color gang, then I wou—"

"*I'm not!*" Gary quickly interrupted him, finally seeing a chance to clear up the misunderstanding. "That's what I've been trying to tell you this whole time!"

Based on Jayden's earlier actions, as well as his apparent dislike for the red color gang, the Altered fighter was clearly here on his own. Given their brief interaction on the night of the full moon, Gary hoped that Jayden would at least hear him out now. That unique nickname proved that he hadn't forgotten about him . . . for better or for worse.

"You honestly want me to believe that?" Jayden said as he lifted Gary up by his shirt—and Gary didn't resist. "In that case, why would somebody like you be here, huh?"

"Does my uniform look like I'm part of their gang?" Gary retorted, making sure to avoid sounding sarcastic.

When Jayden took a closer look at "streaker boy," he saw that his uniform, as well as his mask, were black and golden, rather than red. Holding him up, Jayden faced the forest, and behind Gary several red color gang members lay knocked out on the ground or rolling about in pain.

Turning around, he saw his own path of havoc, meaning that someone else had fought with the color gang. Slowly, the puzzle pieces fit together to form a clearer picture. Jayden eased his grip on Gary's shirt and allowed him to speak.

"It might be hard to believe, but the red color gang attacked my school earlier today. We resisted, but they managed to kidnap my classmate. I'm just here . . . I'm just here to bring her back," Gary explained.

"So you're not part of the red color gang . . . and you're here for Xin?" Jayden said. For a moment, Gary was shocked that the Altered knew who was inside, yet he quickly nodded. With that, Jayden let go of his shirt, and Gary quickly walked over to pick up his mask.

Phew, he finally let go of me. However . . . how does he know about Xin? . . . Could it be . . . Is he her . . . Gary snapped around and looked at Jayden, who still had his shirt off. He was a good-looking young man. The age gap wasn't too big, and maybe she was into older guys.

If she already has a boyfriend, then why would she have agreed to a date?

"What's with the mask?" Jayden asked, now feeling guilty and awkward for wrongfully attacking Gary. Putting the mask in his inner blazer pocket for safekeeping, Gary felt a little too embarrassed to put it on again.

"I'm not like you. I understand that what I'm doing is borderline suicidal. I mean, it's not like I expected to encounter you here. No matter if I failed or succeeded, I didn't want them to know who I was," Gary answered, earning an approving nod from Jayden, who could get behind that reasoning.

"Say, now that we know that we're on the same side, how about . . . we cooperate?"

Now that Gary had gotten a break, his passive healing had kicked in, and it was already beginning to heal him, consuming his Energy. He doubted he would find anyone as strong as Jayden inside. Since he had already come all the way out here, he didn't want his idol to get all the credit . . . especially if he turned out to be his rival in love.

"There's no need. I'm going inside, and I'll handle everything. If you want to make yourself useful, feel free to call the police," Jayden said, as Gary started heading toward the entrance of the cabin.

"No . . . I have to see who did this and why," Gary insisted. "They . . . they hurt someone I care about!"

From the look in Gary's eyes, Jayden could tell he was serious. Having just fought him, although only briefly, he could tell that the kid was capable enough to not end up as a burden.

"Fine, but listen to what I have to say. Also, don't even think about disappearing afterward. I still have a bone to pick with you for all the food you stole. Don't think I forgot. You made me very late that day for a photo shoot," Jayden said as he walked ahead.

Ironically, Gary would probably never forget the raided fridge, since it was thanks to Jayden's endless supply of meat that he managed to survive that horrible night. Besides, it was one of the best meals of his life, something he would forever treasure after being forced to hunt wild creatures and spend large amounts of money to fill up his Energy reserves.

When Gary reached the cabin steps, something hit his nose.

"That smell . . . it's blood!"

The smell of blood from the members outside was consistent, but this was coming from another direction; it was coming from inside, but neither of them had gone into the cabin yet. Aware of the implication, Gary rushed past Jayden.

"Hey, wait! They already know we're outside! They're most likely waiting for us already!" Jayden shouted. He had planned to enter the second floor and take them all out from above.

However, Gary had already barged through the door, breaking it off. It was a weak door, but Gary had used force that would have broken a normal door as well. Quickly catching up, Jayden stood next to Gary, who was frozen in place.

At the very back of the room, they saw the gang members who had scurried inside. They all turned to look toward the door. Xin was being held up on her feet while Tiffany held a little knife to her neck. Xin's face was bruised, and blood was dripping slightly from her nose.

Standing by Tiffany's side was Riv, who nervously smiled at the situation.

"Shit, those reports weren't exaggerated. Of all people, why is Jayden Tiger here? Tell me, did the mayor hire you to rescue her? How much is he paying you? You know the amount of money that he would pay for his daughter, right? I can give you half if you just look the other way." The red color gang leader tried to bargain with the Altered, aware that their chances of standing up to him were slim to none.

Looking at who had busted through the door, Xin had known Jayden would come, but as for the person standing beside him . . . why was Gary here? Why did someone she barely knew come all the way here for her? It was the first time in her life someone other than her family came looking for her.

Seeing Xin in such a desperate state, Gary clenched his fists so hard that his nails dug into the palms of his hands. Veins were popping at the top of his head.

"You . . . you . . ." Gary was so angry he was stuttering, and he was a little worried that Jayden might accept Riv's offer.

Little did he know, Jayden's blood was boiling even more.

"*Get your filthy hands off my sister!*" Jayden demanded as his body started to transform.

CHAPTER 24

NO CHANCE

Being the Altered fight fanatic that he was, Gary knew quite a lot about Altered. After the change, an Altered would first have to get used to their new body, as well as the capabilities it held. One of the most important skills was changing their body from human to Altered form.

According to some documentaries, that wasn't an easy thing to do, at all. The first time was apparently the hardest. Some could only fully transform into their beast selves; others often mistakenly transformed the wrong parts of their body, changing their feet when they wanted to change their hands, for example.

So it was essential for an Altered fighter to master this skill. In Gary and Jayden's case, they competed in regard to the time it would take them to transform. This was crucial, since both fighters were required to start out in their human forms.

Fortunately, Gary didn't have that problem . . . at least not anymore. Thanks to his acquiring the Controlled Transformation skill, the system took care of it for him. He just had to imagine which part of his body he wanted to transform and to what degree. If he wanted to, he could also use Full Transformation to become a complete werewolf.

Regardless, he knew that Jayden was a strong Altered, a professional who was on top of his game, and his body was already turning in a fraction of a second. The first thing that was noticeable was that his skin had started to turn whiter, almost pale, till it looked like snow itself.

A light layer of fur appeared across his skin; it wasn't thick like Gary's. This fur also was white and looked soft. Still, there were some similarities between the two, as his hands had turned into deadly claws, yet the most noticeable change was on his face.

It now had black marking patterns coming from his forehead and down the side of his cheeks. His eyes narrowed like those of a beast and his black ash-gray hair started to grow down his back. Soon it began to turn completely white as well.

All of this had taken less than half a second, but Gary couldn't help but be bewitched by this majestic beauty. It certainly was one of the most beautiful Altered the world had ever seen, and it was why Jayden had become popular not just as an Altered fighter but a model and celebrity as well, known as the White Tiger.

"That's . . . so cool." Gary couldn't help but stare. He soon snapped out of his reverie as he remembered the situation he was in, and the words that had come out of Jayden's mouth a second ago. *Did he just say that Xin . . . is his sister? But their names, Xin Clove . . . Jayden Tiger.*

Gary was ready to facepalm. It wasn't rare for an Altered fighter to use a stage name. There were many reasons why. Most did it to pick a more menacing-sounding name that would easily catch on. Jayden had naturally chosen Tiger as his last name because of his Altered form.

Despite his public appearances, the Altered fighter's real name had been kept a secret, yet it wasn't hard for Gary to guess that it had to be Clove. Now, it made sense why Jayden had come all the way out here to Slough, and why he had come to this cabin. He wasn't here for the pay, but because he genuinely cared for his sister.

Unfortunately, Gary failed to see how transforming at this point and time would help Xin, who was being held at knifepoint. If not for that, he would have already stormed in.

What . . . is she doing here? Gary thought.

"Don't move!" Tiffany screeched; her hands were visibly shaking, leaving a small cut on the hostage's neck. It was clear she was scared; seeing an Altered on TV and in real life were two different things.

They were so rare in the world that to normal people they seemed like something straight out of a fairy tale. Not moving from his spot, Jayden tilted his head back and opened his mouth wide, revealing sharp teeth. The next second, flinging his head forward, he emitted a loud roar.

The whole cabin began shaking, and Gary, who had been standing next to him, suffered the brunt of it because of his sensitive ears. He fell to his knees, covering his ears as he rolled on the floor with pain, though he wasn't the only one.

What Jayden had let out wasn't a regular roar. An invisible, strong force had traveled through the air and hit Riv, on the other side of the room. The red color gang leader was chucked into the wall behind him, where the wooden panels snapped in half. One second later, he fell to the floor in pain.

What was that? From a roar? Gary wondered as he opened one eye to look up.

"Riv!" Tiffany cried out. Seeing her opportunity, Xin bit down hard on Tiffany's hand. Her arms were tied, but the ropes tied around her legs looked like they had been sliced apart.

Believing this to have been her brother's doing, she kicked her tormentor's leg, and Tiffany fell over.

"You had this coming!" Xin shouted as she kicked the class diva in the side of the head, knocking her out.

Riv had gotten up, his body aching, only to see that his sweetheart was being hurt.

"What are you guys doing? Get him!" the red color gang leader shouted.

The others were about to make their move from their position by the door. But Jayden swung both his hands out fast with a whip-like sound as they cut through the air.

Gary wasn't sure if he was imagining things, but it appeared as if giant claw marks were flying through the air. Seconds later, there was no doubt that those claw marks had been very real. They hit the men who were standing by the door, cutting through their clothes and skin. Some of the weapons they held were also cut in half and fell to the floor.

The cuts weren't shallow either, going quite deep, and blood was spilling everywhere as the men fell to the floor. Those farther away might have been lucky, but they were too afraid to get up again.

Gary was still trying to figure out what had happened. Jayden hadn't moved from his spot, yet he had somehow hurt Riv, who was on the other side of the room, and dealt damage to the others as well.

He had seen hundreds of Altered fights, yet not a single one had been this devastating.

"There are some things that aren't shown on TV." Jayden said, seemingly aware of Gary's confusion while he walked toward his sister.

Staring at him, Gary could only think one thing.

I stood no chance.

CHAPTER 25

THE TURN

Gary stared at Jayden's back in disbelief; his transformation had ended but the memory of what he had just done was burned into Gary's mind, possibly forever.

No wonder the system didn't issue a quest. Even if I used a Full Transformation, it would have been impossible to defeat him. Jayden hasn't even fully transformed, so this was just a fraction of his power . . . Do all Altered have these kinds of powers, or is he just special? Gary was still shocked.

Jayden saw that his sister was okay, and after checking her over, he found just a little dried blood by her nose from being hit. Her nose wasn't broken, and the cut on her neck was shallow and small enough that it wouldn't leave a scar. He would have paid for the best medical care in the world if his sister had come out of this with any permanent damage.

At that moment, Riv saw an opening and started to make a run for it. He fled toward the exit, abandoning Tiffany. Having seen how Jayden had dealt with his subordinates, he knew that the Altered wouldn't shy away from killing him.

"Jayden, he's getting away!" Xin called out. After everything he had done to her, even if it was because of his psycho girlfriend, she wanted him to pay. "What are you doing? Aren't you going to go after him?"

"Don't worry, streaker boy can handle it." Jayden smiled, to Xin's confusion.

Gary stood up as Riv ran toward him.

"Get the f*ck out of my way!" Riv shouted, recognizing Gary as the guy who had ruined their plans back in Westbridge. He didn't have time to care what he was doing here, he just needed to get out of the place.

Riv threw a punch, and at the same time Gary stepped forward, moving his hand to the side. He swung his arm out, clenching his fist as he used Controlled Transformation to increase its power before he whacked Riv right in the face, aiming right between his upper teeth and his nose.

Riv's nose broke with a loud crack, and his front teeth shattered. The red color gang leader slid across the floor, banging his head into the wall.

"Mr. Root . . . didn't deserve that," Gary said. He hoped Riv hadn't passed out from the single hit, yet he had received a system message informing him that Riv had been defeated. Still, he wanted to hurt him more for all the pain he had inflicted on his coach.

"Hey," Jayden called out as he saw Gary's unwillingness to let it go. "That was a good hit, but you should stop there. Trust me, it's taking every cell in my body to not rip all of these guys apart. I can see that it's the same for you, but don't become worse than them. Otherwise, one day I might have to come for you."

Gary took a deep breath and tried to calm down. As if on cue, a system screen appeared in front of him and gave Gary even more to smile about.

Secret achievement unlocked: Color Gang Destroyer II
Two color gangs down.
Are you trying to collect a rainbow?
Something good might happen if you take out all three.
Reward: 25% Level Up

Congratulations, you have now reached: Level 14
A stat point has been granted
Exp 232/2578

From the fighting Gary had done so far, he had been getting Exp for every single gang member he had beaten, and with this unexpected reward, he had accumulated enough to reach Level 14. Still, after seeing Jayden in action, he felt like there was a long way ahead of him before he would catch up.

Jayden was busy untying his sister, and while doing so he leaned in closer.

"Nice choice for a boyfriend. Setting aside his strange hobbies, I wouldn't let him go if I was you."

Immediately, Xin's face lit up red, and she kicked her brother in the shin.

"Hey! Is that what I get for saving you?" Jayden complained as he rubbed his leg. Xin would have felt bad for him . . . if it weren't for the teasing smile on his face.

The three of them had a lot to talk about. Xin had a lot of questions, starting with how Gary had even found her and why he was with her brother, but all of that would have to wait. First, they needed to get out of here. Quite a few people were worrying about Xin. Gary was also sure that some people were worrying about him as well.

"Hey, pick that one up." Jayden pointed toward Riv, who was still on the floor, while he himself had Tiffany over his shoulder. "These people aren't going to just get away with this. We'll take them to the police station ourselves, so no gang member can get involved."

Picking up Riv, Gary took pleasure in knowing that for once the judicial system would punish these people, but it was only because the mayor was involved. If it had been a normal family, the red color gang probably would have been able to buy their way out of trouble.

With Riv over Gary's shoulder, the three of them walked outside, but they stopped on the deck outside. About fifty people were standing at the edge of the forest. They were clearly not police or regular citizens, and they weren't members of the red color gang either.

A large man stood in the center; next to him was a man wearing a leather jacket and shades, and finally there was a third man with a dragon tattoo up his neck.

Why are there so many people here? Didn't the system say that the red color gang was out? What are they doing? Gary wondered.

It was obvious from their clothes that they weren't with the red color gang, but Gary sensed that the main battle was still ahead.

"I see, so you finally managed to call the Gray Elephants over? Well, it's a little late, don't you think?" Jayden shouted.

The words were aimed at the man with the dragon tattoo. The gang leader was too afraid to do what Jayden had done, but at least it looked like the goons that the mayor had hired hadn't been completely useless. The question remained whether that was a good or a bad thing.

Gary stood next to Jayden, his hands shaking.

Did he just say . . . Gray Elephants?

These weren't just any ordinary members of the Gray Elephants gang. Standing at the front was their leader, Brandon Trunk. A bit behind him was D, leader of the Rising Dragons, and finally, to the right of Brandon, was Raven, the other leader of the Gray Elephants.

CHAPTER 26

THREE VS. FIFTY

Gary had heard quite a lot about the Gray Elephants gang during his time as a transporter. After all, they were the second-largest gang in Slough, though it wasn't as if anybody had ever shown him a picture of the leaders' faces. Nevertheless, the presence of these people made it clear that they were high-ranking members of the gang.

These people are the ones that captured Amy . . . who made her go through all that crap.

Despite how much Gary wanted to get out of here and deal with them, he knew now was not the time. Not with how many there were, and not while involving others. Fortunately, the Gray Elephants had yet to make a move.

If they're here now, does that mean they were the ones who ordered the attack on the school? I still have no clue why Tiffany was with them. Seriously, this whole thing seems to be more complicated than it looks.

Unsure about the full scope of the situation, Gary decided to keep his mouth shut and just let things play out. He was also regretting that he hadn't put on his mask again, though it was too late for it now. His best course of action seemed to be to let Jayden do the talking and try to appear as unimportant as a green-haired teenager in the middle of the woods could be.

"We don't want to mess with you, Mr. Tiger!" Brandon shouted out. "That was not why we came. You see, D here informed me that one of my subordinates took matters into his own hands and captured the young miss over there.

"Once the matter came to my attention, we got to work. As soon as we learned about Riv having fled here, I gathered my men to rescue the young miss. It appears that you've managed to locate them before us, though.

"Let me assure you again that we played no part in this plan, and I apologize for not keeping my people in check. I hope you can hand over the culprits, and I promise that we will give them the appropriate punishment."

Jayden stood there for a while, not saying anything as he thought about what to do. It was clear he wasn't afraid of the Gray Elephants. At the same time, going against them or getting on their bad side would likely prove to be a major annoyance to his father and sister, who had chosen to live in this town.

Jayden was smart enough to know that the big gangs would never act this flashy, nor would they involve the public to this degree. Besides, they wouldn't have gone after Xin to blackmail the mayor; instead they would have gone directly after her father, forcing him to submit to them.

Xin was now safe. Jayden was also sure that now that they knew that he was associated with the mayor and his daughter, they wouldn't dare to act against them anytime soon.

Jayden made the first move, walking down the cabin's old steps, and now they stood fifty feet apart. He looked toward Gary and nodded. Taking this as a sign, Gary walked forward and placed Riv on the ground in front of the Altered.

He looked Brandon in the eye for a second, and Raven, who seemed to be staring at him, before quickly going back to Xin's side. Jayden did the same, placing Tiffany on the ground as well.

"Who's this wench?" Brandon asked, since this was the first time he had seen her. He then kicked Riv on the ground a couple of times, which managed to jolt him awake.

"Where am I?" Riv looked around, confused. Getting up fast, the red color gang leader touched his face and looked at Gary and Jayden angrily.

"You bastards!" Riv shouted, but before he could do anything, he was lifted off the ground. His own shirt was starting to choke him around the neck. Turning around, he started to sweat as he recognized the Gray Elephants leader.

"Boss!" Riv let out a choked gasp.

"Oh, so suddenly you remember that I'm your boss, hm?" Brandon sounded very annoyed. He threw Riv back to the ground so hard that he bounced slightly and blood spewed from his mouth. Before Riv could do anything else, Brandon stomped on the back of his head, crushing part of his skull.

Everything had happened so fast, and although it was clear that Brandon wasn't stronger than Jayden, his actions were terrifying. Riv no longer had a heartbeat; he was dead.

But Brandon wasn't done just yet. He soon picked up Tiffany by the mouth; his hand was so big it was able to grab her entire head. She suddenly came to and grabbed Brandon's forearm, kicking and screaming.

"Wait!" Xin shouted. "Please, she's just a high school student . . . let her go! She's not part of the red color gang."

Xin could tell that Tiffany wasn't really a part of their gang. In fact, she had complained about Riv whenever he left the room. To Xin it appeared as if Tiffany had begun dating him just for fun, but when she got in too deep, there was no way she could leave.

Riv was a dangerous person, but the people he had associated with were even more dangerous and more unscrupulous than he was.

"This little girl could get us in a lot of trouble," Raven said, stepping forward. "It looks like she was one of the people who kidnapped you, yet you want to save her? We have a relationship with the Rising Dragons, and this could have ruined it. Other gangs might even use this situation against us. We can't let her go, not someone who was so close to the matter."

It looked like Xin's plea wasn't going to work and she tugged on Jayden's arm. Did Xin hate Tiffany? Of course she did, but not so much that she wanted her dead. For some reason, she knew that not for a second did Tiffany want to truly hurt her.

From what Xin had overheard, the plan to get her family involved, the ransom and taking her away, and even the attack on the school had not been something Tiffany ever intended. The plan kept getting deeper and Tiffany didn't know how to deal with it.

Jayden sighed. "You heard my sister, let her go," he demanded, looking up at Brandon.

Is a fight going to break out? Right now? Gary wondered, as he prepared to be ready at any second.

CHAPTER 27

BREAKTHROUGH

Seeing Jayden so close to the Gray Elephants leader sent shivers down Gary's spine. He didn't know how Jayden could just walk up to him after what he'd done, unless he was planning to do something.

If a fight breaks out, I know whose side I'm going to be on. The question is, will I have to fully transform?

"I said, *let her go!*" Jayden repeated, and Brandon let go of Tiffany, letting her fall to the ground, close to her now deceased boyfriend.

"As I said, we don't want to get on your bad side, Mr. Tiger. If that is your wish, then so be it. However, we'll have to ask you to make sure that she doesn't tell anyone about what happened here." Brandon turned and pointed toward the forest. The rest of the Gray Elephants members immediately moved to the side, making way.

Honestly, Gary was at a loss for words. He couldn't believe what had just happened. Did one of the biggest gangs in Slough really submit to a single person . . . simply because they had been told to?

This wasn't the ruthless behavior that Gary expected from being in a gang.

Is this what it means to have power? So much power that not even a top gang can mess with him?

The simple truth was that the Gray Elephants didn't dare to go up against Jayden. It was a fight that Brandon wasn't sure they would win, nor did they have anything to gain from it.

It was better to just let the Altered get his way.

Seeing this, Xin ran over to Tiffany's side and offered her a shoulder. Her former tormentor's legs were wet; Tiffany must have peed herself in fear when Brandon picked her up.

After losing consciousness and being held up like that by an unknown brute, Xin couldn't blame her. And Tiffany didn't seem to mind that her captive was helping her out of this situation, as she accepted her assistance.

Gary rushed over and gave his other shoulder to Tiffany. The two girls were walking slowly, and quite frankly he didn't want to stay here for long. A part of him felt like the gang would turn around in seconds, but thankfully they never did.

"Interesting, huh? Who would have thought that the mayor was keeping someone like that kid by his side," Brandon said. "Do you remember the reports we got from the color gang that day, about how the Underdogs had acted quicker than usual, and that they had asked each of the members about a green-haired boy. Do you know who that was?"

"I have no idea." D shrugged. "He seems a little too young to be a friend of Jayden's. Perhaps he's an associate of the young miss. However, I don't remember seeing him in the mayor's family."

"Raven, it might be a long shot, but if you have time after dealing with that personal project of yours, check him out. See if he has any relation to the Underdogs or the underworld in general," Brandon ordered as he walked off.

"And someone clean up this mess!"

Eventually, the group came to a road just outside the forest that led to a more residential area. Looking behind him, Gary couldn't see any of the Gray Elephants following them.

"What do we do now?" he asked. Since he had been following Jayden this whole time, it just felt natural to ask the Altered.

"We?" Jayden stopped for a moment, before he turned around. "Since D was here, I'm sure his goons will be here soon as well. So 'we,' as in me and my little sister, will take that girl with us and knock some sense into her, so she knows how lucky she was to make it out today."

Tiffany looked like she had completely lost it. Her eyelids were open wide like she was awake but not really registering what the others were saying.

"Gary," Xin eventually said, as she helped Tiffany slowly stand on her own two feet. She looked down the road as if she was looking for something and then quickly turned back. "Why are you with my brother?"

Gary nervously scratched the back of his head as he tried to think of a good way to explain himself.

But then Jayden spoke up. "Haha, I think you've got it wrong. Food thief here was already at the cabin before me. Like a knight in shining armor, he seemed to have been looking out for you, Xin. Who knows, if it's him, maybe you could convince Dad to hire him as your guard." Jayden clapped his hands together as he had a lightbulb moment.

"Come to think of it, you should come over some time," he said to Gary. "Not today, that won't be the best with everything that has happened, but I'm sure our father would like to thank you for what you did. If not, I might have something for you."

Gary didn't know how to reply. Getting invited to the mayor's house seemed more like a reward for an honor student, not a nobody like him. At the same time, it felt like meeting the parents before a first date was also skipping a few too many steps.

Just then, three black luxury cars pulled up. Xin and the others headed toward them, leaving Gary on his own.

"Wait!" Gary shouted to Xin. "Before you go, what about our . . . you know, date?" Being honest about his feelings was becoming a lot easier after everything he had been through.

"Ah." Xin turned around and reached her hand toward him, palm up. It took a moment for Gary to figure out she was asking for his phone. A few seconds later she returned it. "It's my number, if you haven't guessed. I'm sorry, but I have no idea what my dad will decide to do after everything that has happened today. I know it might be awkward, but I'm afraid my brother's idea will have to count as our first date. I'll keep you updated."

The car door closed, and for a brief second Gary had seen an expression on Xin's face he had never seen before; it was one of sadness, pure sadness.

She looked so happy just a second ago . . . but she changed only after she said those words, Gary thought as he looked after the disappearing cars. Letting out a sigh, Gary finally had a free moment to check his phone, only to see that Kai had left him a message.

Let us know when you're done on your end. We'll be staying here until late in the evening, and we wouldn't mind having an extra pair of eyes.

Although Kai and the others were doing scouting work for the gang, for once he just wanted to relax a little with his friends.

Before that . . . I need to do something that's long overdue . . . Should I maybe try out red or blue this time?

CHAPTER 28

SORRY MEANS NOTHING

Three black sedans were driving down the road, single file, equal distances apart, and each one was filled with guards from the Rising Dragon gang.

However, the person who had orchestrated this wasn't their gang leader, but the mayor. In the back seat of the center sedan, Xin sat in the middle, while Tiffany sat on one side and her brother Jayden on the other.

They had been riding for quite a while. The Clove family lived close to the outskirts of Slough, but Jayden told the driver to stop by the hospital first. He wanted to drop Tiffany off there, so she could get checked out before getting picked up by her guardian.

For the most part, the class diva had been out of it, still coming to terms with what had happened today, her role in this entire mess, and how close she had come to her own death. All the while, she had been holding the side of her head where Xin had kicked her.

"I'm sorry," Tiffany blurted out as she turned to Xin. "I'm really sorry . . . for everything."

She didn't break eye contact with Xin for even a second, as if waiting for an answer. It made an already awkward situation even more awkward, especially since the girls were only inches apart. However, Xin didn't accept her apology.

Xin clenched her fists around the shirt she was wearing, scrunching it up tightly. With all the anger inside her, the frustration built up had to be released somehow.

"You think a simple 'sorry' is going to cut it?" Xin yelled, her eyes narrowed to slits. "All I ever wanted was the opportunity to enjoy a normal high school life! Was that really too much to ask for?"

Honestly, although Tiffany was sorry for what Xin had been through, since they had all gotten out of it relatively okay she thought things would be fine. As long as she didn't tell anyone what she had seen today, and didn't get involved with the gang mess again, everything would be okay.

"Why are you so upset? I don't understand. We're okay, right? Please, is there anything I can do to fix it?" Tiffany asked, trying to be more sincere this time. She wasn't used to apologizing; usually she just got whatever she wanted. Nevertheless, she knew that she had screwed up royally today.

"*Why?*" Xin shouted, raising her voice, and the man behind the wheel glanced at her in the rearview mirror. "Tell me, why did you have to take things this far? Why couldn't you have just kept it between the two of us?

"I've tried apologizing to you for more than a week in which you tortured me, only for your goons to prevent me from so much as talking to you . . . Why couldn't you have called it quits after that?

"All of this . . . because I accidentally threw you into a pile of vomit? I apologized to you straightaway, didn't I? And I really meant it, because I knew what I had done was wrong, but do you? Do you even have a whiff of an idea how much could have gone wrong today?

"Everyone at school suffered this morning, because of you! Worse, you've gotten my entire family involved!" Xin was tearing up, which she rarely did, but she couldn't hold in her frustration any more.

"You wanted to make my life miserable, didn't you? Well, congratulations, you've actually managed to do it. You have no idea how long I had to plead and beg my father to give me a chance to come to a normal high school like Westbridge. After today, it's safe to say, he'll have me transfer somewhere else!

"I want you to know this, and I want you to carry this weight with you for the rest of your life. You've ruined my life. My one chance at freedom and a normal school life has vanished." Even though saying the words was painful, and her throat felt heavy when she said them, when she looked at Tiffany she smiled, her face teary-eyed.

Tiffany didn't understand, but seeing Xin force a smile like that, even though she didn't know why she was sad, hurt her a lot.

What . . . did I do? Tiffany thought. It was hard for her to self-reflect at this moment, because she really didn't understand why she had done the things she did. Why did she want to hurt Xin so bad? Was it the environment, or the people around her, or did she just want to show what she was capable of because someone hadn't listened to her . . . or was Xin a threat?

Either way, all those reasons seemed stupid now.

The only silver lining was that the car was approaching the hospital. Since Xin was obviously no longer in the mood to talk, Jayden decided to do the talking instead. He informed Tiffany about what she should say to the hospital.

One of the Rising Dragon gang members would accompany her to pay for everything. At the same time, he would be there to make sure she didn't blab about anything that had happened today, and that included the fact that Jayden Tiger was actually Xin Clove's brother.

After Jayden explained everything, Tiffany and her guard got out of the car and were left standing in front of the hospital. She looked up toward the sky but could see only the roof of the hospital's carport.

"*Ahhhhhh!*" Tiffany screamed at the top of her lungs, releasing all of her frustration and worry.

Back in the car, Jayden was trying to think of a way to cheer Xin up. He was smart enough not to attempt small talk after her breakdown. However, he got a sudden inspiration when he looked outside and spotted a strange green plant that reminded him of someone.

"Soooo, do you need a new outfit for that upcoming date?" Jayden asked, which worked wonders in catching Xin's attention, but she was speechless. "Care to tell me what the hell you did that would make a guy be willing to fight an entire color gang for you? You've been here for barely a month . . . did you cast a magic spell on him or something?"

Xin's face was turning red as usual. However, her brother's words did make her wonder about how she had gotten Gary to like her. She hadn't done much, and if it was just simple physical attraction, she could understand.

And now he's saved me twice, Xin thought.

Meanwhile, Jayden's thoughts also revolved around Gary.

How could a kid the same age as Xin be so strong? Food thief, what exactly are you hiding? That date is certainly something I'll be looking forward to . . .

CHAPTER 29

LIFE WORTH LIVING

As the gates to her grand estate opened up, Xin felt more nervous than ever before. She noticed that there were more men in suits than usual outside the gates, and even more standing outside the house itself.

Was Dad worried that they would come after him as well after finding out about me? she wondered.

She also thought that having all these guards was useless. When Xin was kidnapped, they weren't the ones who came to rescue her. In her opinion, her father was just wasting his money and time with them.

Still, she understood a lot of the gang business and government politics that went on. How they all worked together in nearly every city to do what they needed to do.

Unfortunately, it had become abundantly clear that although her father had joined hands with the Rising Dragon gang, it meant nothing in to any of Slough's big-time gangs. Despite anything Mayor Clove might have promised during his election, the ones really in charge of the town were still the gangs . . . just like everywhere else.

After exiting of the car, the two siblings walked up the wide stairs that led to the large front doors. The closer Xin came to those doors, the heavier her legs felt, as if they were about to buckle.

"Jayden," Xin said to her brother, stopping at the top of the stairs. "You'll back me up, right?"

Jayden glanced at her for a second before letting out a small sigh and continuing up the stairs. It wasn't a good sign, as it indicated that he wouldn't be able to shield her from what would come next.

Inside the double doors, Xin's mother paced back and forth, biting her fingernails. As soon as she saw her children came in, she ran right up to Xin and gave her a huge hug.

"My baby!" she exclaimed, holding her tightly as if she was unwilling to ever let go again. "I can't believe those guys did that to you! I knew we shouldn't have moved to this town. I've been worried about you since day one, and now this."

"Mom, you're starting to hurt me," Xin said softly, and her mother let go for a moment. The middle-aged woman stood up and gave Jayden a kiss on the forehead. Although she knew that it should be nearly impossible for normal gangsters to hurt her son, a mother would always worry about her children.

Alas, there was still someone else Xin had to meet. "Come on, your father is waiting for you. Don't worry, darling, your father and I have already been making preparations to prevent something like this from ever happening again."

Xin took a deep breath and gulped down hard. She couldn't avoid this. The three of them walked toward a large black door, which opened into an office with bookshelves lining the walls and a large desk in the center.

The person sitting behind the desk was naturally Ben Clove, Slough's mayor. He even had a little plaque on the desk to make sure that any potential guest would know who he was. Her father didn't rise from his chair and see if she was okay, as her mother had done. He remained seated.

Meanwhile, her mother went to stand behind the mayor's chair. There was a chair opposite him, and Xin understood that her father wanted her to take the seat. She did so and was happy that her brother was in the room with her.

"First, I know this whole event must have been scary for you, and it's my fault. We knew that you might become a target because you are my daughter. I thought that perhaps the gang would use you to leverage my position and get me to help the other gangs, but I never imagined that the only thing they would want was money," Ben explained.

"Wait," Xin interrupted. "Dad, I don't want you to get the wrong idea. They didn't kidnap me for money. Well, they did, but that was just the secondary reason. All of this was just because I had a falling-out with one of the girls at school and—"

Her father pounded his fist on the desk with a loud bang.

"Xin, whatever reason they might have had, it doesn't matter. We want to keep you safe. We tried it your way, and it didn't work out. We even had guards taking you to and from school, yet this still happened. Even if their target wasn't really me, it can still happen, and I just can't take that risk.

"I admit that I was selfish when I listened to my advisors. 'A mayor who is so trusting that he sends his own daughter to a public school' . . . it sounded good for my public image, but I should have never risked your well-being . . . I've made a mistake, Xin. Your life is far more important than what the voters think of me.

"That's why your mother and I have agreed that we'll be sending you to a boarding school in a Tier 2 city under a fake name. You can come back to see us on the weekends."

This was what she had been afraid of when she heard her mother say those few words by the doorway.

I have to fight back . . . I don't want to live like that.

"Dad!" Xin shouted back. "You just said that my life is more important. This is *my* life you are talking about. I might not be an adult yet, but I'm sixteen, so shouldn't I get some say? Come on, Jayden, you didn't have to go through this stuff. Please!"

Her parents were often stubborn when it came to decisions, having already made up their mind, but they did listen to their firstborn son.

"I'm sorry, Xin, but I actually kind of agree with them." Jayden looked down. "I know it's not fair for you to suffer like this when I didn't have to. However, when I was younger, our parents weren't important figures yet. Barely anybody cared about our family, but after what happened today . . . Slough isn't safe right now. I won't always be there to protect you."

Xin felt defeated; not even her brother was on her side. Her parents would never trust her, not even when she was an adult. She knew that her father would constantly be putting guards on her. When would it end? She couldn't see any light in sight.

"Still, I have to agree that this is your life. That's why I do have a suggestion. None of us would have to worry if Xin was . . . like me, right?" Jayden asked, and from her parents' reaction it was clear that this was the first time they had even entertained such a possibility.

"If she could protect herself, you wouldn't have to worry. Xin, this is completely up to you, okay, but what do you think about joining the Altered Fighting Academy like I did?"

Her parents looked at each other; they didn't really know what to say, and it wasn't really a suggestion they were expecting.

"Don't get me wrong, I'm not telling Xin to become a professional fighter or anything like that, but it's a two-year course, and we do have the money. So why not make her into an Altered so she can protect herself? We'll keep her identity away from the public and change her name. After two years of training, there won't be any thugs in the street that will be able to take her on."

Xin had never even considered it. She liked fighting because of her brother but never thought about it as a profession. Even though her brother said she didn't have to make it a job, going to the AFA meant no longer going to a regular school.

"I'll do it!" She had made up her mind. "If that's what it takes, so I can live the way I want, I'll gladly become an Altered!"

CHAPTER 30

A CHANGED PERSON

Describing the way Gary currently felt as annoyed would be a vast understatement. He was jogging back to Chavley, and running—fortunately—wasn't really a problem for him because of his improved stamina. He had a lot of time until it was evening in Burnham, so there were a few things he could do before then.

He wouldn't have minded the jog, but after seeing those three nice cars with so many empty seats in them, he thought the others could have at least offered him a lift back home. Of course, there was also the option to take the bus, but that would cost him a bit of money. The bus fares in Slough seemed like a rip-off no matter how much money he had, so he preferred the free method.

I think I might just run to Burnham at this rate. I wonder what that look was on Xin's face when she got in the car. Maybe she's still shaken up by everything that happened.

Soon enough, Gary's frown turned upside down as he thought about the progress he had made in his relationship with Xin. A date, a visit to her house, and he had managed to rescue her, which surely would win him some brownie points.

Along the way, Gary stopped by the convenience store, where he picked up two boxes of hair dye and some food. As usual, Gary intended to eat some raw meat in an alleyway to quickly restore his Energy on the way back.

"Is that everything for you, kid? You sure do eat a lot of meat, but looking at your body, I can see where all that protein is going," the clerk joked. His name tag read *Tyler*. The bespectacled university student was the hardworking type. He also seemed to always be on duty whenever Gary came in. Ever since he had become a werewolf the teenager had come here regularly, and he and Tyler enjoyed occasional small talk, especially when the store was as empty as it was now.

"Ah yeah, do you have the bag that I gave you from before?" Gary asked.

Tyler handed Gary a sports bag from under the counter, and he quickly changed out of his gang uniform. There was no one else in the shop, and honestly it was just putting his blazer away and putting on a hoodie instead. Because he lived in Chavley, Gary would always wore a hoodie near his home.

However, he couldn't carry a bag around with him while fighting. That would only make things harder. So he'd decided to leave several bags containing a change of clothes in certain spots. Tyler had happily agreed to it, once Gary had offered him twenty dollars. As much as Gary needed to save his money, he regarded this as an investment. It still pained him to do so, and it was something that had taken him a long time to decide.

The school and this convenience store were two of the many places where Gary had stashed a bag. However, now that Kai had gotten him stretchy clothes, perhaps he wouldn't have to go through so many.

Do I have to worry that once the Howlers gang becomes famous, people will start noticing our uniform? Will it be a problem that I go around in these colors? At least I don't think Tyler knows I'm in a gang yet.

Just then, the electric door made a sound to inform them that a new customer had entered. It was a man in a suit who looked to be . . . quite drunk, as he could barely keep his balance.

It's not even five p.m. yet . . . Did he just finish work and start drinking straightaway? Or maybe he's still in the middle of a binge.

Gary didn't need werewolf senses to smell the alcohol on him. However, his poor nose was practically being assaulted by the stench. He just wanted to get out of there as soon as possible. He got out of the man's way; he had actually managed to make it to the counter.

Gary was getting ready to leave to enjoy his nice meal. He was getting used to the taste of raw meat and was actually looking forward to eating it before heading home.

"Hey, get me some Leaf Blacks!" the drunk man yelled.

"Here you go, sir, that will be eight fifty!" Tyler smiled politely, placing the cigarette pack on the counter.

The man then pulled out his card and stuck it into the reader, but then he slapped his head.

"Damn it, what's my PIN?" he grumbled loudly, then proceeded to push the buttons. Unsurprisingly, an error message appeared on the screen. The man tried this two more times, until the machine informed him that his card was now blocked.

"Shit! Your damn machine is broken!" the man yelled drunkenly as he tried to pull apart the machine. "Just give me my damn cigs." He reached over to snatch the cigarettes away, but Tyler quickly pulled them back and put them away.

"I'm sorry, sir, but your card has been declined. If you happen to have some cash, I would be happy to give them to you." Tyler smiled nervously.

"Why the hell do you care? You're just a poor sod working for this shop. You don't own them, so might as well give them to me!" the man demanded as he stretched out his arm and opened his palm. However, when nothing happened, he became even angrier.

"Do you think I won't do anything because this place is protected by the Underdogs? You think I'm scared of those guys?"

The man then leaned over the counter and grabbed Tyler's shirt, pulling him over the counter. Tyler could smell his alcoholic breath, and the next second, the man spat on his head.

"Sir, what are you doing!" Tyler shouted.

"You think I'm stupid, huh? That I didn't notice the way you looked at me? Screw you, and my superiors. All of you look at me like I'm scum. Where are your gang members to help you out now, huh?" It looked like the man was about to spit on Tyler once again, but before he could do so, a hand reached out and grabbed him, intercepting the glob of spit.

"What is wrong with you, old man? How is it his fault that your superiors treat you badly? I'm pretty sure if a gang member were in this shop right now, you would be shaking in your boots." Gary, having heard the commotion from outside, had come back in.

Perhaps it was because of the events of today, with his teacher being hurt, Xin being taken away, and more, but Gary just couldn't look the other way.

CHAPTER 31

GOING DOWN A TIER

The drunken man looked the teenager up and down. Given his new appearance, Gary looked like someone who often visited the local gym, yet the drunken man didn't fear him just yet.

"Haha, this is brilliant! Now even kids these days are acting like gangsters," the man said as he got a big one ready in his throat and spat it out, hitting Gary right in the cheek. Gary let it drip down his face for a few seconds, then smiled back at the drunken man.

"I'm not acting like one," Gary said as he clenched his fist, then shoved his other hand, which was covered with the man's spit, back in his face, rubbing it in. When the startled man stepped back, Gary whacked him in the face, and he fell to the floor. The teenager's hot-headedness had taken over, and he just couldn't deal with it any more.

Tyler was so amazed that he leaned over the counter to look at the old man.

"Sorry . . . I couldn't control myself," Gary said, apologizing to the university student.

"Nah, he definitely deserved it. I would have done the same if I didn't really need this job." Tyler tensed his biceps, but there was nothing to see.

A few seconds later, the man came to, rubbing his face. Gary had held back a little, but the man's legs were still wobbly as he fell backward.

"You . . . you! You will pay for this. I'll remember you, you green-haired kid!" And with that, the man stumbled out the door.

Still annoyed at the man's attitude, Gary picked up a chocolate bar from the counter and, aiming carefully, threw it, hitting the man in the back of the head.

"Have a Bickers if you're annoyed!" Gary shouted, then turned around to pay for the chocolate bar, but Tyler refused payment, as a way of saying thanks.

Before this, Gary would have been worried that the man would remember his face and hair color, especially with gang members looking for him. However, Gary couldn't care less . . . for after today, he would no longer have green hair.

As Gary left the shop, Tyler thanked him and promised that he wouldn't mention to anyone what had happened. Given the slip of his tongue, he had expected Tyler to ask questions, but the university student didn't mention it. Either he chose to keep it to himself . . . or he simply mistook the truth for a bluff. Either scenario worked for Gary.

With his hood now up, Gary entered the Chavley area, where members of the Underdogs would still be keeping up their patrols. Using his enhanced senses and following his personal route, he managed to avoid all gang members on his way home.

As he approached his apartment block, Gary could see that many of the residents had gathered outside, near the bulletin board. However, they didn't seem interested in the notices that were posted there; instead they were talking to an old man whose face resembled a nutsack. It was a crude image, sure, but Gary couldn't deny the resemblance.

The man was the landlord of the apartment building, Mr. Morten. Gary was interested to hear what all the commotion was about. He remained at the back of the crowd, which was filled with families, students, and others.

"This is crazy, you have to say something to them, Morten!" an older woman yelled. "If this continues, then soon we won't even be able to afford to live here! And then we'll . . . have to . . ."

She didn't dare to finish the sentence, but everyone was aware that if she couldn't stay here, her only choice would be to move to a Tier 4 town. Living in a Tier 3 town like Slough was already bad enough, but at least the Underdogs and Gray Elephants ensured a certain level of peace.

A Tier 4 town, on the other hand, had no such thing. Multiple small-time gangs were constantly vying for a piece of the already small cake. There was next to no order in a place like that, and no one wanted to end up there.

Progression from a Tier 4 town often spiraled downward badly In the first place, there weren't many jobs in such an area. Moving from a Tier 3 town probably meant you didn't have sufficient skills for a decent job, and it was a slippery slope that might force you to move to a Tier 5 town.

The crime rate would be similar to that of a Tier 4 town, yet the living conditions were far worse. In a way, it was similar to living in a dumpster. A junkyard with scraps here and there. No jobs, just people searching through junk and living in shacks they built themselves. Honestly, though, all this information was based on what Gary had seen on TV.

"It isn't his fault. You really think old Morten can stand up to them? He's just one man. A wrinkly old man." Another person tried to calm down the bitter woman.

"Still, he should at least try to talk to them! That's all we ask . . . that's all."

Eventually, after listening for a while, Gary understood the gist of what had happened. Everyone's rent had gone up. The letter didn't name the concrete reason, but the residents didn't care; in their eyes it was a sudden and sharp increase. All those who lived here were like the Dems, families that barely lived from paycheck to paycheck.

Gary didn't think he needed to worry too much about an increase, but he knew how the other people felt, because he had been there not too long ago. Eventually, when everyone had left, Morten had nearly collapsed from exhaustion, and he sat down on a nearby bench.

"Is it the Underdogs?" Gary asked as he sat down next to the landlord.

The man sighed, which only confirmed Gary's suspicions.

CHAPTER 32

A NEW LOOK

"What has happened to this world that even a brat like you can so easily figure out the reason behind the rent increase?" Morten shook his head. "You're correct. After what happened recently, those parasites have been patrolling the area . . . so now that they're actually doing the job we've already been paying them to do, they're suddenly demanding more. It's not just me either; all the landlords will have to pay higher fees in this area.

"Unfortunately, I'm not as wealthy as my residents believe me to be. Although I own this place, I've never once made a profit. There are countless repairs that need to be done everywhere, and everything I get is just enough to allow me to live by myself while improving the place. Do you know how many things get broken around here? Especially after that attack.

"I wanted to make a change, give people another chance, but because of my already low prices . . . Since the Underdogs ask for more, I have no choice but to increase rent . . . it's the first time in ten years I had to make a decision that I was uncomfortable with."

Adam Morten was a good man. Gary knew that his mother had been late paying the rent a few times, yet he had never pressured her. Now, hearing the regret in the old man's voice, Gary was even more convinced that their landlord was a decent man.

He couldn't believe that just moments ago he had met a drunken scumbag who would pester a retail worker because he was frustrated with his own job, when there were people like Mr. Morten in the world.

"I'm getting old and tired, Gary." Morten sighed. "If things continue like this, I might have to sell this place. The only thing holding me back are people like you. If I sell this place . . . what are the chances that the next landlord will keep the rent the same?"

The answer to that question was obvious.

"I'm sorry, Gary. I didn't want to burden you with all of this. Just take it as the ramblings of an old man. Say, now that you're here, I haven't seen your mother much lately. Is everything all right?"

Gary stood up from the bench and looked at his fist; he felt more useless than ever. The question was, could he do something to help these people? The fist he was looking at now was the only thing he had. He wasn't good academically at school, nor was he strong before, but he was strong now.

Some people say violence isn't the answer, but in the world we live in at the moment I can't agree. The Underdogs are the problem, and they are still after me . . . If only I had power like Jayden. How great would it be, if I could change things around? Gary thought, before he shook his head to wake himself up from his daydream.

"Thanks for asking. Mom is doing fine, she's just a little unwell from all the overtime she puts in. You must have just missed her. And Mr. Morten, I'm sure things will look up at some point." Gary smiled at the man as he headed to his apartment.

Seeing a young teenager like Gary still believe in the good of humankind, Mr. Morten felt refreshed, and he stood up from the bench. "He's right. It's too early to give up. Maybe I should have a talk with Damion."

Finally back home, Gary made sure that Amy was okay. Ironically, it was his sister who had a million questions about what had happened at his school, since it had been all over the news.

With the whole school having been involved in the red color gang attack, it had been impossible to cover up the entire incident. Gary didn't want Amy to worry too much about him, so he lied about how John's call to arms had been successful, and told her that the red color gang had quickly fled the school.

He made them both a meal for dinner, then headed to the bathroom. He placed both boxes of dye he had purchased on the sink. One was black and the other gold.

I guess if I'm starting to take this gang stuff seriously, I might as well use our gang colors. Gary grinned at the thought.

Originally, Kai had told him that it would be fine for him to keep his hair green. At the time, the Underdogs had lacked any real information for finding Gary, so doing the "stupid" thing of not changing his hair color was supposed to throw them off.

Unfortunately, they had somehow discovered what school he went to, changing the entire situation. So Gary chose to dye his hair black, which was a common hair color among his classmates.

A hairdresser had dyed his hair last time, but he was too paranoid that he might be spotted by a gang member in the middle of changing it, so he had opted for the DIY version. He carefully read the instructions and went through the process step by step. When he was finally done, he washed the dye out a couple of times, then lifted his head to in the mirror.

Staring back at him, he saw a teenager with a full head of black hair.

I'll have to get used to this new look. Hope Xin wasn't too fond of my green hair, Gary thought.

Next, he picked up the other hair dye—the "gold," which was technically just a variation of blond. It was just to add a few nice touches since he was curious how it would look. If he didn't like it, he planned to change his hair back to black afterward . . .

However, before he had a chance, a system message sprang up.

Your hair has been damaged
Energy points will be used to perform emergency healing
Emergency healing will be used to restore the user to its original self

Huh?
It only took a few seconds, but strand by strand, Gary watched his black hair turn back to green.
What the hell?

CHAPTER 33

PAWN POINT

Gary's hands were tense as he gripped the sink top. He had tried the process a few times already. It didn't matter if he used the black dye or the gold one. He only got to enjoy his new look for a few seconds.

Every time, Gary got the same message from the system. In the end, he gave up, because it was consuming Energy to restore him to his "original self," and there just seemed to be no hope.

You damn system, this isn't my original self! Have you ever encountered anyone who had green as their natural color? Should I just go bald? Just shave it all off? Or will the system just regrow my hair back using Energy to bring me back to my natural self again?

When he thought about it, it wasn't the strangest thing. Even Jayden's hair had grown when transforming, and when he reverted to his human form, his hair did as well.

But this . . . am I really going to have green hair for the rest of my life?

Gary wondered when exactly the system had decided that this was his natural hair color. Was it back when he had received the system . . . or did it perhaps tamper with his body when his grade had gone from Pawn to Knight? He had grown taller and his muscle mass had increased, so would it be really unbelievable if it had changed his hair color?

Aware that dwelling on it wouldn't help him in any way, Gary decided to leave it for now and get ready to head over to Burnham. It was getting late, and if he didn't head over soon, the others might just head back.

In fact, based on the group chat, they all wanted to ask him questions about what had happened. News of the red color gang's demise hadn't spread just yet. Today he wouldn't be wearing his gang clothes. It would bring too much attention, and as Kai had explained, today's job scope was simply scouting.

So he picked out a set of normal clothes, and once again a hoodie. Gary was nearly ready to leave. He had been looking forward to seeing the reaction of the Howlers when he showed up with a brand-new look, but unfortunately it was not to be.

Before he left, though, Gary made a decision after seeing Jayden.

I don't know if it's just him, or Altered in general, but Jayden was clearly stronger than me. If Kirk is also that strong, I'll have no chance against him. So far, I've kept my stat points ready for my opponents, just in case I need them. However, if all fights will be this hectic, I won't be able to use that point.

Unlike his stat point, the Pawn point he had received after consuming Billy had many uses.

Would you like to convert your Pawn point into skill point(s)?

Gary wasn't sure he was doing the right thing. According to the message he had received when he gained the Pawn point, he could use it to upgrade his body to the next grade, upgrade his skills with it, or convert it to stat points. So far, he hadn't seen the benefit in doing that.

Stat points he could always gain from leveling up or consuming people . . . well, as a Knight-grade werewolf, he would apparently have to eat beasts, as the system claimed.

Beasts might no longer exist in the world, but he could still level up in other ways, as the system had shown him. The most useful thing therefore seemed to be to convert the Pawn point into a skill point, so he could strengthen his Claw Drain to the next level.

Yes

3 skill points have been obtained
Skill points can be used to upgrade certain existing skills or to purchase new ones
New tab has been added: Skill Shop

Gary was baffled at this sudden development. He would have been happy to simply upgrade his Claw Drain skill to Level 2, but his system had blessed him with a new tab. What's more, his one Pawn point had been converted into three skill points, instead of one. He was curious about whether he could change them back, yet he received no option to do so.

If this were a game, then I would usually get a worse deal when converting... Does that mean the Pawn point would have been better used to upgrade that Grade thingy? Gary wondered, but the Werewolf System simply kept him guessing. Unfortunately, it wasn't as if there was another werewolf around for him to gain another point.

Curious, Gary checked out the new Skill Shop . . . only to be vastly underwhelmed.

Claw Drain—Forced Level Up: 1 Point
Berserker: 1 Skill Point
Magnetic Howl: 2 Skill Points
Last Stand—Cost: 3 Skill Points

Seeing that the Claw Drain claimed to be a Forced Level Up, Gary felt reassured that just like games, it should be possible to level it up naturally, most likely by using it more.

Seriously? What kind of shop doesn't say anything about its own skills? Gary wondered. *This seems more like a back-alley deal with some rough-looking tattooed man with a bad attitude who simply tells me "Take it or leave it."*

Alas, not even this accusation of foul play earned him any reaction from the system. There was no information at all, which made him think that this system seriously sucked. If it were a game developer, Gary would have already been making a complaint.

He might have even understood it for the two new skills, but hadn't he already been told what Berserker could do? What was the point of playing coy now?

With three skill points, Gary could theoretically purchase Berserker and Magnetic Howl. Two skills should be better than one, allowing him to be more flexible . . . this might have been the logical choice. Alas, Gary wasn't the most logical person, and something drew him to the third skill.

Perhaps it was the fact that it cost the most skill points. Surely the higher the cost, the better skill he would get. Maybe it would give him something that would let him deal with an Altered or an Altered Hunter.

Are you sure you would like to select the skill "Last Stand"?
Yes / No

Screw it, Gary thought as he selected *Yes* on the menu.

CHAPTER 34

A RED PLACE

Just like when he had selected Claw Drain and Controlled Transformation, he felt a flood of information enter his head, and his body's muscles twitched a few times. It was as if his body was learning how to activate the skill for him. After that, a strange energy entered his body, and it was gone a second later.

Gary had done his utmost to pay attention to every little detail this time, since he was still trying to figure out what exactly this system was and how it worked. Unfortunately, it didn't really amount to much. It was similar to seeing a bullet train pass by for a moment. Just because he had seen it didn't give him any expertise on how it worked.

Let's see what this skill can do. Gary happily smiled to himself, opening up the system and checking his skill list. Though he instinctively knew how it would work, he wasn't yet too familiar with all the intricacies.

Last Stand

When activated, the user's Health cannot fall below 1 HP
The skill will take 0 points of Energy to use
Warning: While Last Stand is active, you'll continue to take damage as normal

Skill duration: 60 secs

Skill reset time: This skill can only be used once a day

After reading about the skill, Gary immediately gulped. This wasn't what he had imagined. Sure, it might be useful in a game, allowing him to charge in without worrying while brazenly attacking and allowing his teammates to help out. Unfortunately, this was real life, and there was no respawn mechanic.

If all the Werewolf Warriors' skills worked like this, he wasn't too surprised that the description of the Warrior Class had claimed that they boasted the highest fatality rate. If Gary used this type of skill while fighting, it would have to be in a situation in which he was able to defeat whoever was around him within that minute. If he failed to do so, well, 1 HP meant he would be as good as dead.

The thought itself was scary, if it ever needed to come to that.

Come on, Gary, let's try to find the silver lining. For one, the skill doesn't consume any Energy. It can also be used as a sort of lifeline in a situation that would have killed me, like a second chance . . . Yeah, in a way, this skill gives me a lease on life. If I can't beat someone, I can at least try to run away.

This skill would have been so cool if it could have made me invulnerable for that one minute . . . but if I still take damage it's pretty much just an increased Health pool, isn't it? I guess I really should have figured out what type of skill it would be.

Why didn't I ask Tom before making a choice? I could have just told him that it was part of that game . . . although if I do that too often, he'll probably get suspicious, if he hasn't already . . . Should I just tell him about the whole Werewolf System thing?

Gary ran his fingers through his hair, as he was stressed out. He felt like he had made the wrong decision. He had been hoping for a power-up to bridge the gap between him and Jayden, but the skill just made him aware that some situations that he might have to face could end up very deadly . . .

At the same time, touching his hair reminded him of the other stupid things the system had done.

Wasting no more time on the system, Gary sent a message in the Howlers group chat, informing his friends that he was on his way. However, he naturally didn't take the bus, and just as planned, he jogged there.

He ran through the streets, although those who saw him would describe him as sprinting. If only they knew how long the boy had been running for. Eventually, Gary arrived at the street where the others had told him to meet them.

He couldn't believe his eyes. It was dark out, nearly eight p.m. When the sun went down, this place looked completely different. Glowing neon signs were flashing, and the street was filled with people walking up and down, exploring the place.

Even the people here seemed different from those Gary saw in Slough. They carried confidence in their steps.

It looked so pretty; Gary had never seen so many neon signs in his life, but looking around, he realized what this place was. The streets were filled with pretty girls standing outside the restaurants. They wore skimpy dresses such as air hostess outfits little red devil costumes, and all of them wore extra short skirts.

The girls frequently whistled at those who passed them, holding up signs stating what their rates were. Of course, a few restaurants were still operating as restaurants, but the street had undeniably turned into a red-light district.

Above Gary's head was a large sign marking the entrance: *Burnham Street.*

"Hey, you made it!" Marie shouted, with a big wave and a smile on her face. The rest of the group were behind her as well.

"Yeah," Gary said, still taking in what he was seeing. As a sixteen-year-old teenager, he had never visited a place quite like this one.

"So did everything go okay?" Kai asked casually, but Gary wasn't in the mood to answer him; he had a question of his own to ask.

"Are you . . . planning for us to take over this place, Kai? I mean, if we take out the gang here, it means that we would then run this place, right? Do you intend for people to still do . . . all of this?"

The others looked at Kai nervously because based on what they knew about Gary, they had assumed that this would be his reaction. Kai was the brain, whereas Gary was the muscle. Without one, the other couldn't work. For the Howlers to work, they needed both.

CHAPTER 35

TAKE OVER! (PART 1)

Kai didn't reply outright; instead he sighed. Not too long ago, the others had asked him the exact same question.

"Tell me, Gary, do you see yourself as a savior?" Kai replied, but Gary just raised his eyebrows as if he didn't understand the question. "I selected this place for several reasons. First, it's far away from the other gangs. Second, it's ideal to serve as our link to outside of Slough.

"Third, a good chunk of the clientele who come here are from big companies, which could be the true kick-start that the Howlers need. Last, and perhaps most important, it's making serious cash. Think about how much we grabbed from the gray color gang. That on a daily basis . . . for each of us."

Although all the things Kai said were true, they still annoyed Gary somewhat.

"I need the cash . . . you know that. Still . . . to go this far?"

Once again, Kai let out a sigh, this time bigger.

"I get why you would want to put an end to this. Sure, morally speaking, this place is a travesty. However . . . have you taken a moment to consider the consequences of such an action? Let's say we take over, and you close down this place . . . What do you think will happen then?

"Do you really believe that those guys who have come here for their entertainment will stop? Best-case scenario, they migrate to another town; more likely, though, the Gray Elephants or Underdogs will just offer these services in their own areas.

"Not all the girls have been forced into this. Sure, some have, and if you wish to let them go, I wouldn't mind agreeing with you there. However, for a lot of these girls, it's a way for them to earn money to live in a city like this. We might not like it, but to them, it's just like a real job.

"You close down this place, it might make you feel better, but you'll rob them of their means to make money to support their family. Need me to tell you what happens then? No job means no way to pay their bills. They will be forced down to a Tier 4 town . . . or worse.

"Do you think living like this is really worse than living like that? As gang members, we will always cross a line with the law, but we can still be a gang with our own ethics. Look, at the end of the day, you're our gang leader, so I will go with your decision no matter what.

"However, as a good leader you need to be aware of the consequences. For that, you should also listen to the voices of the people your choices will affect before making such a decision."

The world wasn't as black and white as police officers, TV, and such liked to make it out to be. Gary, having been in a position that had made him join a gang, understood. Who knew, maybe if his family's situation had gotten worse, he might have ended up becoming a boy toy for some of those older women.

Gary shivered, imagining something resembling Jabba the Hutt asking him to do strange deeds.

"You're right . . . Let's talk about it more once we've actually taken over," Gary said, with a change in attitude. Meanwhile, Innu was looking around, wondering if that cute waitress was also out on the streets.

The group walked down the street, turning their heads constantly left and right. For those who had been here earlier in the day, it was just as much of a shock as it was for Gary. It seemed as if they had stepped through a portal transporting them to an alternate reality.

They noticed a few other things that hadn't been there during the day. Outside nearly every establishment stood a pair of male guards with their arms crossed. They all gave off an intimidating look. A place like this, serving a particular clientele and doing what they were doing, would need the help.

In fact, walking down this street, they had seen the need for the guards to get involved a few times. However, those fights stopped as soon as one of these men stepped forward. Still, twice they had watched them use stun guns on some drunken men who didn't understand that *no* actually meant *no*. A stun gun was quick at shocking the person unexpectedly, and then the guards took them inside. For what, the others could only imagine.

While they were walking through, Kai explained a few more details about what they were trying to do.

"As I've already told the others, the gang in charge of this area is called the Pincers. They're one of the five small-time gangs we'll have to take care of before the Underdogs and the Gray Elephants fall out," Kai explained.

"Every one of those men in suits that you have seen is a part of their gang, and as you can tell, controlling a busy street like this, there are a lot of them. Shouldn't be too surprising, though, given the type of their business, yet it also means that their gang is heavily concentrated in one place and reliant on that one place.

"There are some unwritten rules here. We've already seen 'No pestering the women' in action. Aside from that, you should keep your phones to yourself. While they won't stop you from making a call, if they suspect you're trying to take a picture, or worse, film anything . . . things will turn out bad.

"This is a rule that is set up to keep their clientele out of trouble, and most people will follow that rule. Sure, some try to test it, but they all pay the price. Those guys work under the assumption that it's better to grab one too many than to let one slip."

There certainly were a lot of people, and even Innu, who was a good fighter, was starting to worry that the Howlers were out-matched by this large force. If this could be called small-time, then what were they, mini-time?

"So, what's the plan? Surely, you don't expect us to just raid this place like with the gray color gang?" Innu asked.

CHAPTER 36

TAKE OVER! (PART 2)

The others were waiting to hear Kai's plan, hoping he wouldn't send them into the lions' den.

"Of course not. Did you already forget that we're just here to scout out the area today?" Kai looked at Innu, who sheepishly rubbed the back of his head. "The quickest way to take down a gang or to make it collapse is to take out the head. Still, that will leave us with the problem I mentioned earlier about running the place, but we can worry about that later.

"The issue is . . . finding the location of the Pincers' base. The information I received only helped me narrow it down. It should be located on this street. As to where exactly . . . well, that's why we're here."

The others attempted to look around for clues. Perhaps it was the place that was busiest, the one with the most workers, or maybe even the one that had the most guards outside. Alas, it wasn't like after entering, they would instantly recognize the leader.

"I can't sniff him out," Gary mumbled, thinking that Kai was expecting him to do something. The others had heard what their leader said, and they were confused, but Kai smirked.

"I never expected you to. Remember what I said about willing workers? It will be impossible to get information out of anyone who has been working for them for a while. However, there will also be some who have been forced to work here. We'll focus on the workers who aren't afraid of the Pincers just yet. Our goal is to try to find one of these workers to . . . help us out."

Strange, wild thoughts started to run through everyone's head as soon as Kai mentioned this. If they needed to talk to the workers, and they were here, did that mean they needed to partake in . . . that?

Kai handed Austin and Gary a large pile of cash each.

"You two look the oldest out of all of us. I'm afraid it's too risky for the rest of us to try our luck. They probably wouldn't even let us past the door if we requested a worker. You know what to do, try to get the girls to confess something. Oh, and if you want to have some fun . . . at least give us a heads-up." Kai grinned.

"Hey, Gary!" Marie immediately went up to him. "You're not actually going to listen to that idiot, right? Just go into the room with them, ask some questions, and head out." Her face was red, aware that she had no right to tell the green-haired teenager what to do. "Since they think you will be doing . . . doing that, they most likely won't have cameras or that in the rooms, in order to protect their important clientele."

Gary just nodded, as he was left a bit speechless. Out of everything he had done, maybe this would be the hardest thing after all.

BPM is rising
BPM 95

"Shut up!"

One person seemed a bit bummed out about the whole thing, though, and that was Innu. He was cursing his small frame that made him appear young to others. He could understand Austin, but seeing Gary, who had only recently enjoyed his growth spurt, pass him on their way to adulthood was a nasty pill to swallow.

After Kai made it clear what they needed to do, the real question was where would they start.

"I have a suggestion," Innu said. "Why don't we head to where we had the meal today? It's as good a starting point as any other, right?"

Still curious about the girl who had acted strangely, Innu wanted to know whether she was a willing or a forced worker; he felt a little bad for her. For once, he was talking a surprising amount of sense.

When Gary and Austin walked through the door, they were led in by a businesswoman who had a walkie-talkie attached to her hip.

She was wearing a silk blouse and a tight skirt, and she herself didn't look bad as she led the two of them to the reception room. The restaurant wasn't even open for business. The tables had all been cleared, and now they were sitting on one sofa out of several. There were other clients here as well.

"Please, what service would you like to select from our menu?" the woman asked as she handed them a sheet of paper.

Reading the items on the list made Gary's heart beat even faster, imagining each scene in his head. As a young teenager who had done nothing like this before, he was worried that any second now he might stain the inside of his trousers.

What the hell is wrong with me . . . think Jabba the Hutt . . . Jabba the Hutt . . .

"Austin, handle this one, please," Gary whispered.

Since the large teenager seemed less affected, the gang leader left the talking to him.

"It's hard to order from the menu's description alone. Would it be possible to see all the girls here?" Austin asked. Gary was quite impressed that he had said those words so calmly, without stuttering. It all felt so . . . natural. *Could it be this isn't his first time in a place like this?*

The businesswoman got on her walkie-talkie, and a few moments later several girls walked out in a row, each with a number on a large badge pinned at her right shoulder. They were wearing the same flashy red Chinese dresses that the others had seen today, only the slit seemed to go up the thigh, revealing more.

"Please, tell me which number you like the best, and what service you would like to get," the woman told them.

Fourteen beautiful girls came to stand before the two teenage boys. Having somewhat calmed himself down, Gary lifted his head to take a look at the girls. That was when his eyes locked onto a certain individual.

Stacy! What is she doing here?

CHAPTER 37

A "HAPPY" ENDING

Inside the dark venue, some of the girls were doing their best to be chosen by the customers: throwing kisses toward the men in the room and lifting their dresses to show off more than just their legs.

"Sirs, while we do abide by the principle that the customer is king, I'll have to ask you to hurry up your decision. We can't keep the girls out here forever, especially not when we have other customers they could attend to." The businesswoman had her arms crossed in front of her, her right foot impatiently tapping up and down.

On another sofa, some older men were already mumbling, and Gary could hear a few of them mentioning numbers here and there. Everyone had a menu, but not everyone had asked to see all the girls as Austin had done.

Looking at the girls, Gary immediately noticed a few things. While many of them tried to present themselves to the two teenagers, some of them were standing in a defensive position, rubbing their arms and covering themselves from the gazes of others. It was clear that they didn't want to be there.

I was right; sure, there are some who are willing, but not all of them want to be here. This realization calmed Gary down a bit. He looked over all the girls before he announced, "Number thirteen."

Her head held low, Stacy stepped forward. The businesswoman cleared her throat, making her flinch before she looked up and put on a nervous smile for her suitor. Gary still had his hood up, even in the establishment. The workers didn't seem to mind, indicating that he wasn't the only one who had come without wanting anyone to recognize him.

That was the girl that Innu kept trying to talk to as well, Austin thought. *Man, those two are into the same girl. That's going to cause a problem, that's for sure. Should I stir the pot with Innu for a bit?* Austin smirked as he finally made a decision.

"Do any of you have a kid?" Austin asked loudly with his arms crossed. The atmosphere immediately changed, and Gary almost fell out of his chair. Even the girls who had been vying for attention stopped and looked at each other strangely. It wasn't a request they often got, that was for sure.

A kid? Gary wondered. *Why is he asking if any of the girls have a kid . . . unless he is just here for fun. Does that mean he has a thing for older women? Man, I'm learning too many things I don't want to know about people who are close to me today. I'm afraid that if Innu were here, he would be asking for the girls to show off their feet or something.*

The truth was that Austin had asked this question not because of some personal preference, but because he believed that those with children might be more willing to talk. Since they had more on the line, they might be more frightened of the Pincers. Potentially, they might agree to share information in exchange for money.

"Apologies, sir, but that is private information our workers don't feel comfortable revealing. Please just select the one you like. If she feels comfortable, perhaps she will answer your question then." The businesswoman was clearly frustrated, since the teenage boys had already wasted so much time. She was even second-guessing whether she shouldn't have just thrown them out immediately.

"Okay, number eight," Austin declared, and a small, young-looking girl stepped forward. If Gary were a betting man, that one would have been the last person he had picked, especially after his question. Honestly, he couldn't comprehend his fellow gang member's way of thinking.

The rest of the girls walked away, and the workers showed them where to go next. The two pairs took an elevator to the second floor, exiting into a long hallway with several rooms on either side. Each room had a corresponding number above the door. They followed the girls, and it was finally time.

I can't believe I'm in a place like this . . . what the hell happened to my life? Gary asked himself when Stacy opened the door with the number *13* on it. Meanwhile, on the opposite side of the hallway, Austin casually entered the door with the number *8* on it.

"Thank you," Gary said, heading inside. His legs felt like they were going to buckle at any second, and he was wondering just how Austin was dealing so nonchalantly with all of it.

As he entered the room, Gary didn't know what he had imagined, but it wasn't . . . this. There was a large bed with all kinds of fancy pillows on it. He could just imagine how soft they were.

Then there was a closed-off bath and a separate shower with marble flooring. Gary ran inside excitedly. "Hey, this is like a hotel, right? Meaning all these small shampoo bottles and stuff are free?"

"Y-yeah, I guess," Stacy answered in a stutter.

Shoving them into his pocket, Gary felt elated, believing he had just obtained the perfect gift for Amy's upcoming birthday. Hotel shampoo was a luxury . . . at least from where they were from. He would just have to keep quiet as to where exactly he had procured it from.

"This . . . is like a dream place. I've never even been in a hotel before." He couldn't stop smiling.

Emerging from the bathroom, Gary ran into the main room with the same enthusiasm as a little boy in a candy shop. The first thing he did was jump on the bed and lie on his back. It bounced a little, yet soon enough his body started to sink in. It was, as expected, the softest sensation he had ever experienced.

He could only imagine how nice it would be to fall asleep in such a place. Not just that, but on his own. Without having to share a room. After a few seconds of bliss, he remembered that he was actually here to do a job.

He wasn't alone, but he soon got distracted again. Several items were laid out on the table. The toys stood up hard and long and there were all sorts of different colors. Some had unusual designs: rigid, big and small, all shapes and sizes. He had seen these items in videos. It made him gulp.

Gary went over to the table and picked up one of the strange objects. The one he chose was pink. He started to shake it to the left and right, and surprisingly it had some give as it flopped about. His thumb rubbed against the bottom, and he noticed there was a button. Curious, he pressed it, and the object started to shake violently.

Whoa, I nearly dropped the thing! Gary thought. *That's really violent. Do they really like these things?*

As he was about to put the pink object down on the table, he heard the sound of sobbing and realized it was coming from the girl.

"I can't do it . . . please, I don't want to do it . . ." Stacy was in tears, hardly able to stand up.

"I'm sorry, sir, but please . . . it's my first day, and . . . I haven't had time to adjust myself . . . I-if you could . . . just pick someone else," Stacy continued to plead amid her sobs.

Gary walked over, not realizing he still had the object in his hand, which was only frightening Stacy more, wondering what this person planned to do to her. He said gently, "It's okay. I'm not going to do anything like that. I'm just here to ask you a few questions."

He lowered his hood, showing that he was the last person Stacy had ever expected to see in a place like this. Recognizing the green hair, she loudly exclaimed: "Gary!"

CHAPTER 38

THE TRUTH

If Stacy hadn't been so worried about her situation, she might have recognized Gary by his face alone. However, he had changed quite a bit since the last time she saw him.

Now, seeing his green hair, Stacy instantly recognized him. After yelling out his name, it seemed like she was about to say something else, but the words were stuck in her throat. Gary quickly placed his finger on his lips, silencing her.

He also looked behind her, making sure the door was still shut.

"Look, I'm not here to do . . . *that* with you, I promise. So you'll be okay, all right?" Gary said, trying to calm her down by using a gentle voice. However, he noticed that her eyes were looking in a particular direction—at the object in his hand.

Of course, if I'm still holding this thing, she'll be scared. Gary nervously smiled and put the pink object back down on the table. Showing his open palms, he called Stacy over. His sister's former best friend still seemed a bit shocked by the whole thing.

"Gary . . . why are you in a place like this? And why did you pick me . . . Since you knew it was me, you could have picked someone else. I . . . I . . . You haven't always had a thing for me, have you?" Stacy asked, as she either hadn't heard or didn't believe the boy's claims.

"Please." Gary scoffed. "Don't flatter yourself. Let me make something crystal clear. I'm not here as your friend. Amy told me everything that happened that day. I understand your situation at the time; it must have been scary, especially as a girl, but that doesn't change that you left Amy behind! I don't even care that you told them about me . . . but I'll never forgive you for what you did to her!"

Looking into Gary's eyes caused Stacy to swallow nervously. His tone of voice was severe, and she was beginning to believe that if he was in a place like this, he wasn't the ordinary boy his sister thought him to be.

"Now that we have cleared that up, can you tell me how you ended up in a place like this? I might have understood it if it had been the Gray Elephants, but this area is controlled by the Pincers."

When Stacy heard the two gang names, her eyes widened, as she realized that her suspicions were correct.

I guess he isn't here just to see some girls . . .

She hesitated, wondering if she should tell Gary or not. Even if he might have some knowledge in that area, what could he even do if she did tell him? Nevertheless, the whole situation was too much for a young girl like her, and it had been eating her up inside. Nearly breaking down again, she sat up straight to stop herself.

"My situation . . . has nothing to do with Amy or the Gray Elephants, if that's what you were worried about. I've done enough to Amy, but she's safe from this life. All of this was because of my parents," Stacy explained.

"I bet Amy thinks that I changed schools because of what happened, but that's not true at all. My parents have been having money troubles for a while now. If you didn't know, they own their own auto repair business. We weren't wealthy by any means but better off than many people in Slough. Many workers relied on our shop for their income.

"However, apparently, one day, my parents had a client who refused to pay. To make matters worse, it was a big job as well. Usually, they keep the car as compensation, until they're paid. They did the same in that case, even though the guy claimed he was a gang member.

"Eventually he came back with others. They beat my parents and all their workers as well. It might have been fine if it had just stopped there, but they kept coming back and disrupting the business. From what they told me, some time later they got approached by someone who had heard about their troubles.

"My parents took out a loan with them, even though they knew the loan shark belonged to a gang, but with so many people relying on them, what choice did they have? The situation at home was stressful. So . . . I spent my time on some dubious sites, pretending to be someone I wasn't . . .

"Coincidentally, I eventually ended up chatting with Hawk. Maybe I just wanted some escape. Whatever . . . I'm sorry I got you and Amy mixed up in all of it . . ."

Stacy stopped her story there, but Gary had already gotten the gist of it. The loan must have come from the Pincers. They must have charged her parents criminally high interest rates, the type that would be impossible to pay off.

Then, in the end, they forced Stacy to do this, moved her and her family to this area. The loan was illegal, so the police wouldn't do anything about it, and it's not like they would act even if her parents explained the situation.

He wasn't sure if Stacy knew it, but her family had most likely been targeted from the beginning. Even if the Pincers had not been the ones harassing them, it wouldn't surprise Gary to learn that the small-time gang had paid off another gang to create the ruckus.

"Wasn't your dad's business in the Gray Elephants' area? Why didn't they do anything to protect you?" Gary asked.

She shook her head.

"I have no idea, Gary. I don't understand most of this stuff in the first place. Everything is so scary to me. They told my parents I would just be working off their debt as a waitress for a restaurant.

As soon as they had me here, though, they told me that if I don't do as they tell me, my parents would have their organs sold. These guys are scary . . . they're terrifying people, Gary. What do I do?"

It was clear that Stacy was beginning to panic again. He was wondering if he should help her or not. Hearing her story, as much as he didn't like her, he realized it wasn't her fault she had gotten into this situation, and he imagined there were others in the same boat.

"Stacy, I need you to help me. We might be able to get you out of here, but to do that, I require some information. Have you met the boss of the Pincers, by any chance? If not, do you at least know what he or she looks like and where they are located?"

According to Kai, Stacy was the perfect target to get information from. She didn't want to be here, and she hadn't been here long enough to know just how scary the Pincers were.

Wiping her tears from her face, she looked at Gary once more. Her thick, heavy makeup was halfway down her cheeks.

"I can't . . . there's a rule. When we first came here, they said we'd be done for if anyone speaks about the Pincers. If anyone even tries to talk to us, then we need to get out of there and inform them immediately.

"I've put you and Amy through too much already, so I won't do that. Honestly, Gary, I'm just happy to see someone from my normal life. I couldn't tell anyone about any of this, not even Amy! Thank you . . . for listening to me."

Ironically, Gary had tuned out what Stacy was saying, so he was completely surprised to feel her hand pressed up against his thigh.

"Say . . . if it's you, Gary . . . I think it would be okay . . . you could be my . . . first."

"Austin!" Gary shot up like a bamboo shoot. He hadn't heard the last few words because he was thinking about what he had just been told, how it could mean trouble for their group.

"*Ahhhhh!*" A scream came from the hallway.

"Someone asked about the Pincers! Help, help!" a female voice cried out.

CHAPTER 39

HOW STRONG ARE YOU?

Austin was large for his age, a little over six feet tall, and he had quite the wide body as well. It was a solid natural body that he did little work to maintain. On top of this, his outdated pompadour hairstyle made him seem like he was older than he was.

The girl he had selected came up to just below his chest. She sat down on the bed, swinging her feet, smiling away. Austin walked over, casting a shadow over her face.

"You seem awfully calm," Austin said.

"Is there a reason for me to be scared? You know, just because you are big, doesn't exactly mean that all of you is big. You might be surprised how often the package doesn't match the cover." The girl started to chuckle.

Austin walked over to sit on the single sofa that was next to a table. Leaning over with his elbows on his knees, he gave her a serious look.

"What's your name?" Austin asked.

"Nini!" the girl answered, still smiling away as she played with her hair.

"All right, Nini, tell me . . . what school do you go to?" After he asked this question, her legs stopped swinging. Before she could say anything else, Austin continued.

"I know you're not old enough to work in this place, and you're not the only one. So how did they get to you?" Austin said, doubling down.

For a second, it looked like Nini was worried, but she lifted her head.

"I promise I'm over eighteen, so you have nothing to worry about, old man."

"Old man?" Austin chuckled. "Well, if I'm really an old man, it will be quite the surprise when this old man pays a visit to the school in this area. While I might not find a Nini, I bet I'll be able to find you. Look, if it makes you feel better, I'm underage myself, so if you really are as old as you say you are, we can see who would get in trouble for all this mess."

Austin thought he had her where he wanted her, but she started to laugh.

"You really think you have everything figured out?"

Austin pulled out his phone and started to play a recording.

Shortly after they had gotten off the bus, Austin had messaged the guys from his school to gather some information about the school in the area. It turned out that Kai had indeed just scratched the surface.

While it didn't have a big problem with delinquents like Eton High, there was still a small delinquent circle. Sure, they weren't part of any gangs themselves, but according to what Austin's guys found out, they seemed to be working with the Pincers. They apparently targeted some of the pretty high school girls, trying to get them to walk down the wrong path.

After being harassed for a while, these girls would undergo a drastic change. It wasn't hard to connect the dots. Many of these "shy" girls would suddenly appear in school wearing heavy makeup.

From what Austin gathered, every girl those delinquents introduced to the Pincers would earn them a commission.

Playing the recording of one of her schoolmates admitting to the delinquent circle's doing, Nini finally realized that Austin actually wasn't just making wild guesses.

"I may be unfamiliar with this gang business, but I happen to run the delinquent circle in my area. Anything that happens at the schools, I will know about it," Austin proudly admitted.

Since Nini now knew this wasn't a real customer, she stood up and headed toward the door.

"Okay, you're right, I lied. However, despite how I look, I'm actually seventeen. Now, unless you want me and you to still have a bit of fun, assuming you have the cash for that, I'm afraid I have to try to earn my keep with someone else."

Austin stood up and walked over toward her, but then he stopped, not wanting to get too close and scare her. She was already practically out the door, and he didn't want that.

"I'm here to find out information about the Pincers. You guys don't have to lead this life; just tell us where their base is and what their boss looks like."

Nini let out a big sigh as she pulled down the door handle.

"It's cute that you want to be some vigilante when you're just the head of a group of delinquents, but let me tell you, the Pincers don't play around. They're actual gangsters, and they're in a completely different ballpark from what you're used to.

"Unfortunately, I don't think telling you will change anything," she replied, sticking out her tongue. "I'd probably be in deep trouble if I told you . . . well, let's see how strong you really are." Nini opened the door and quickly rushed out.

"Someone asked about the Pincers! Help, help!" she cried out.

Austin chased after her, but she was already down the hallway. Unfortunately, some of the countless guards they had seen in the area came flooding in. Five of them blocked the hallway at the front, and another five did the same from behind.

A second later, Gary opened the door to see nearly a dozen guards, ready to take out Austin.

"I guess . . . you didn't have any luck, then?" Gary asked.

"Nope, but it seems you've made a new friend," Austin replied, seeing that Stacy had left the room with him and was holding on to his arm tightly.

"Stand down!" one of the guards shouted. "This area is under control of the Pincers. Come with us peacefully and there won't be any trouble."

Despite the man's proclamation, the guards behind him had pulled out a few stun guns and knives, and so had the ones opposite them.

"Well, boss, your call." Austin looked at Gary.

"You see them. Peace was never an option. We need to get out of here ASAP. The others must have already left the area, so it's just me and you," Gary replied.

Looking past the guards, Austin saw Nini peeking at them, waiting to see what they would do.

"Perfect!" Austin grinned as he charged toward the girl who had sold him out. Gary was quick to follow his lead, hoping they could take them out quickly and leave this place, when he felt Stacy grab his arm, refusing to let go.

"Gary, don't! They'll kill you," she called out.

Seeing Austin charge forward, the guards trapped them from either side. With his strong fists, Austin whacked the first one in the face, causing him to fall into the others, but another got through and Tased him.

"Stacy, get off, I have to help him!" Gary shouted.

Trying to pull her off him, he managed to push her away, but he had done so with a little too much strength, causing her to fall in the other direction. She felt a sharp pain in her stomach and saw one of the Pincers' guards with blood all over his arms and a knife in his hands.

CHAPTER 40

TWENTY MINUTES

Stacy was slowly staggering back toward Gary. Because of this he couldn't see anything, but he didn't need to see because he could already smell the blood.

Eventually, she stumbled, falling into Gary's arms. He saw the wound in her stomach, and, though he wasn't a professional, it looked quite bad.

Shit . . . she was stabbed! . . . and the knife is in that guy's hand. You're not supposed to take it out, right? Gary tried to think back to any form of training or movies he had watched for some knowledge.

"Stacy!" Gary shouted at her. "You need to put pressure on the wound! Hang on, I'll take you to a hospital. It will all be okay!"

The man who was responsible for Stacy's injury showed no signs of remorse; instead he charged in again. Quickly, pulling her so she was behind him, Gary kicked the man in the stomach, causing the gangster to fly into his colleagues.

He placed Stacy over his shoulder and turned around to leave, but there was a problem. Austin still hadn't managed to take on his five guys. The stun guns were disrupting his flow, and he needed to be careful of the knives so he didn't get a serious wound like Stacy's.

There were cuts across his chest and forearms, and he was bleeding, but there were no serious wounds. Thankfully, he had taken out two people already, but just then reinforcements appeared at the front door.

"Gary . . . it . . . really . . . I don't even know if it hurts," Stacy whispered, her face ghostly white.

> *New Quest received*
> *Who wants to live forever?*
> *Should have let her pop your cherry, boy.*
> *A girl is dying in your arms, yet you wish to save her life.*
> *While the wound isn't too deep, you lack the expertise to treat her.*
> *If you don't do something, she'll die from blood loss (~20 minutes)*
> *Warning: External circumstances can worsen her condition!*
> *Quest reward: ???*
> *Time limit: 20 minutes*
> *Failure: Death of Stacy Turnhell*
> *Optional complete condition: Bite her*

As he read the last line, a wave of thoughts came into his head. Mainly that when Mr. Root had been in critical condition, Gary had contemplated this way of saving him, and now it looked like his system was subtly pushing him toward it.

When Gary read the consequences for failing the quest, he understood that things were very serious. He himself had been stabbed multiple times, but Stacy was just a normal high school girl. She didn't have the same vitality he had . . .

No . . . I still have time! I can still consider this possibility if we can't get out, Gary decided as he turned around.

"Austin, get back here, I need you to carry her!" Gary yelled down the hallway. After delivering a punch and knocking a guy's shades off, Austin returned to where his friend was. Without asking any questions, he placed Stacy on his back.

Although they had taken out a few of the gangsters, more had arrived. There were more than a dozen in front of them, and half that number behind them. The men were being cautious after seeing the strength that the intruders had displayed. Fortunately, the hallway was narrow, limiting the gangsters' movement.

"I'll open a path, just stay behind me!" Gary ordered, and looked to his left, toward the door to the room he had been in.

Austin was wondering what Gary's plan was. Honestly, even he couldn't see a way to get out of here; the number of opponents was endless, but Gary had saved them from those two monsters, so he could do the same again.

Skill activated: Controlled Transformation
Transformation has begun

Gary chose to just transform his nails lightly, which he then used to rip into the side of the wall. Once they were in, he transformed his biceps, granting him not just regular super strength, but werewolf super strength. He could feel the clothes tightening around his biceps.

He grabbed the door and pulled it off its hinges.

"Now!" Gary shouted, as he charged forward while holding the door as an impromptu shield. Austin followed right behind him, but he quickly noticed something.

Gary was too fast.

The teenager had used his skill on his legs to give him an edge as he pushed forward. The gangsters had already seen him do something inhuman, yet he didn't want to give any other clear indication that he was an Altered. He had transformed just enough to give him extra strength in stats and speed without any change in his outward appearance.

The men tried to move out of the way of what was coming toward them, but their large number proved to be a detriment in that regard. Gary slammed the door into the first man, knocking him back. He continued to run forward, not slowing down, and pushed through like a bulldozer.

Eventually they emerged from the hallway and were now in the open area by the elevators.

"Go!" Gary shouted.

Austin pushed the elevator button. He suddenly felt something warm on his shoulder and as he touched it, he saw that it was Stacy's blood dripping down.

The men that Gary had knocked down were getting back up, and now that they were out of the hallway, the door was pretty useless. Since it was already falling apart, he threw it toward those who were still on the floor and stood there waiting for the elevator.

That was when Austin noticed the small girl in the corner: Nini. She was clearly trying to avoid trouble by hiding behind a large plant.

"You see this?" Austin said as he pointed at Stacy. "This is how 'valuable' you are to them. Today, it's the girl on my shoulder, but tomorrow it could easily be you . . . I'll be paying you a visit at school soon. You're scared of the Pincers . . . but trust me, you should be more scared of us!"

Suddenly they heard a cry of pain. They turned to see Gary taking care of all the gangsters. He dodged a punch and threw an overhand right into the face of another. He had been hit with a stun gun but powered through it.

Still, after kicking another gangster, he lifted one above his head, and another stabbed him in the stomach, not just once but a few times. Seeing this, Austin prepared to put Stacy down to protect his leader.

"Arghh!" Gary screamed, hurling the man toward the others; he then grabbed the one attacking him with the knife with his bare hand and punched him in the face three times quickly, then kicked him to the ground.

"You tried to kill me!" Gary screamed as he continued to punch the unconscious man's face, until he was eventually rugby-tackled to the ground, but seconds later the green-haired teenager had flung the other gangster off. He threw his assailant across the room before getting back up again.

It was the first time that Austin had seen Gary fight so wildly. He understood that it was both of their lives on the line, and he genuinely wanted to help . . . only, how was he even supposed to get in there, in the middle of all that mess?

Finally, the elevator dinged, but there were even more men inside.

CHAPTER 41

SIXTEEN MINUTES

With one hand, Austin grabbed the closest gangster's head and quickly slammed it into the side of the wall before throwing him down. Then he kicked another one right in the balls. Now wasn't the time to fight like gentlemen, not when the gangsters were using weapons.

A third man was about to hit Austin, but a hand grabbed the man's arm and pulled him out of the elevator, and suddenly Gary was by his side. The group got in and pressed the button to go down to the first floor.

No words were spoken, and Gary's frantic breathing was the only sound. Naturally, Austin couldn't help but look at his friend's stomach, where he had received multiple stab wounds. Blood covered his shirt and was dripping onto the elevator floor.

"Are you—"

"I'm fine," Gary interrupted in a pained voice. "We need to get her to a hospital!"

The elevator opened once again. Unsurprisingly, there were people waiting for the trio.

16 minutes remaining
Energy points will be used to perform emergency healing

–30 Energy
173/300 Energy
64/100 HP
Passive healing will not take effect until you are no longer in combat

While the elevator was still on its way down, Gary had been checking out his stats. Once he no longer fought for a certain amount of time, his body would consume Energy and naturally start to heal himself.

Despite its name, emergency healing was only useful to seal his wounds and mend his bones; it didn't actually bring his Health back up. So Gary was currently in rough shape, and he'd used up a lot of Energy healing the cuts on his body.

Since becoming a Warrior-Class Werewolf, other than the fight with Billy, this is the first time I've had to worry about my Energy. I haven't been using Controlled Transformation a lot, but still, if it comes down to it, I might have to use the new skill. Yet for some reason . . . I'm not scared.

When Gary acquired the Last Stand skill, he'd imagined that if he ever had to use it, it would be in a situation where he would be frightened out of his mind, but instead he was filled with anger. He was angry about the way the gang treated people, and he was angry that they had hurt Stacy, who was just an innocent schoolgirl caught in the middle of all of this.

There were about twenty gang members on the ground floor now. After the earlier scuffles, Gary was aware that these attackers were hard to deal with, and it was quite possible that there were more of them as well.

Gary quickly took Stacy off Austin's shoulder.

"Run!" Gary shouted, and took off toward the exit.

The guards here seemed relaxed, most likely assuming that those who had been sent down would have dealt with Gary and Austin by now. They were only two people, after all, and they couldn't imagine how they would beat ten times their number.

Using the surprise factor to their advantage, the trio made a break for the door. Now that Austin no longer had Stacy over his shoulder, it was easy for him to catch up with Gary, whose legs were still strengthened.

A single person stood in their way, but Austin and Gary threw their fists right in his face, knocking him out cold, and bursting through the doors they were finally out of the establishment.

The two high school boys saw Kai and the others, who had come back to wait for them. They made eye contact for a second, and Kai instantly understood that something must have gone horribly wrong. Then again, the blood on Austin's shirt and the girl over Gary's shoulder would have been a natural giveaway.

"Hey! Who are you filming?" Kai shouted. "Careful, these guys have been filming you!"

Keeping it vague on purpose, Kai had ensured that everyone who had something to hide would assume that the gang members had filmed them. It was a perfect way to cause a commotion in the area, making people disregard Gary and Austin. Thankfully, with the busy street, many people got in the attacker's way and demanded that they delete their footage.

14 minutes remaining

Damn it, I have to get there faster, an ambulance isn't going to be quick enough.

"Look at them, is that blood?" a passerby commented as they entered another area.

"Maybe something happened, getting a little too frisky."

"Just leave it, the Pincers will probably deal with it."

Hearing the comments of the others as Gary went by them, he could tell that to the public who went here, this was quite a normal scene. Nobody was panicking, nor did anyone show signs of wanting to call the police. There were a few frightened voices here and there, but others quickly calmed them down. Gary thought that there was something deeply wrong with this place.

"Austin," Gary shouted back at his friend, who was struggling to keep up with him. "I'm sorry, but I'm going to have to leave you. Tell the others I'm going to the hospital I saw nearby when I was running here."

By now, Austin was so out of breath that he could only give his friend a thumbs-up. Gary picked up the pace, almost doubling his speed as he continued running.

How can he run that fast while carrying somebody? He even fought more than me . . . how is that possible? Austin wondered, but more than anything he was worried about Gary's wounds.

Gary was running as fast as he could, yet the timer was brutally ticking down. He needed to get Stacy to a hospital. He had just gotten rid of a huge problem, and he had no desire to trade one werewolf for another. Sure, she might not be as bad as Billy, but . . . what if she would be worse?

"Stacy, you can hear me, right? Answer me!" Gary shouted as he rushed along.

"Amy, I miss . . . you . . . Sorry . . ." Stacy mumbled.

ZERO MINUTES

Austin had managed to get away. Not long after he left Burnham Street, the Pincers members had given up their chase.

It seems they can't really afford to leave the area unattended since they need to look after it in case anything else comes up. Smart move, since it would be a good way to distract them and get their leader. These guys are definitely not as simple as delinquents, and they don't even care to use weapons. I think Kai might have chosen the wrong gang.

The fact was the gang wasn't afraid of doing these things so openly, and it made Austin wonder. The police had to be aware of this place, same with the mayor, yet no one was doing anything about it. They either were on a high payroll or had chosen to look the other way because there was nothing they could do about it.

Austin was waiting at the bus stop where they had arrived, which was a ten-minute walk from Burnham Street. Eventually, the rest of the Howlers showed up, just as a bus appeared.

"I know you must have a million questions you want to ask, but I'll explain on the way, all right? Right now, we have to get to the hospital and check to see if Gary is okay," Austin said.

With that the group was off, and just as he had promised, Austin explained the details of what had occurred while he and Gary were inside. Of course, he had no clue what Gary had or hadn't done with the girl; he just knew that she had gotten seriously hurt afterward.

After learning all of this, the group had eventually reached a small local hospital. It didn't usually deal with big emergencies, but given that it was the closest one, they were sure Gary had taken Stacy here.

As they went inside they looked around the small reception area; about ten people were waiting, and one person with green hair stuck out like a sore thumb. Austin ran over to where Gary was staring off into space, blood on his shoulder.

"Gary, what are you doing here? They couldn't have seen to you so fast!" Austin said, as he went to take a look. But Gary wasn't bleeding. The holes were still in his shirt, and as Austin lifted it in shock, he saw that there was no blood, no wounds.

"I told you I'm fine," Gary insisted as he pushed Austin's hand away.

Austin stared at him in pure disbelief. He had seen Gary bleed; he had seen his friend get stabbed multiple times, over and over. How could someone not only survive all those wounds but heal this fast?

There was only one explanation. Putting this together with the other event with the twins, he could only think one thing . . . their leader had to be an Altered.

Is that why Kai didn't want to say anything? Did he not want us to snoop around as to how a kid like Gary could have chosen to become an Altered?

"Hey, why don't we just sit down and relax for a bit? When you're ready, Gary, you can explain what happened. Meanwhile, let's just pray that the girl will be okay," Kai suggested in an attempt to calm everyone down.

Innu, after hearing what girl Gary had selected, was a little worried as well.

Meanwhile, Gary was in the middle of his own thoughts.

What . . . have I done?

Congratulations! You have endured a lot and have successfully brought the girl to the hospital within 20 minutes.
Endurance +1
Your base Endurance is now at 16
Quest reward: Instant Level Up
Congratulations, you have now reached: Level 15
A stat point has been granted

Is it my fault Stacy got hurt? If we had never gone there, would she be fine?

As if reading his mind, Kai went to sit next to him. The situation felt familiar, and it made Gary uncomfortable. He would like to avoid ever having to be in a hospital again. It was horrible, having to wait to hear whether a person would live.

"I'm sure you saw it when you were running through those crowds of people. Their reaction wasn't what you were expecting because that type of thing happens there frequently," Kai explained. "Like you said, when people are doing things against their will, these types of things are bound to occur. It was unfortunate, but you have done your best by bringing her here."

"I . . . I know her," Gary finally revealed. "She's a friend of my sister's . . . well, former friend . . . not that it matters anyway. You know, for a long time I thought this underworld stuff was only surrounding me, because I was the one who decided to get involved in it.

"But when I see a regular person who hardly knows me get involved like that, I realize the truth is quite different. Someone who just goes to school every day could suddenly get wrapped up in all of this crap.

"Guys, I want to tell you all something," Gary said, looking at them all. He waited as the others gathered around him. Some were nervous; Marie and Austin believed that he was going to come clean about his secret.

"I think if we are going to be serious about this gang stuff, then you guys should know the truth about me. If you don't want to get involved further, I guess this is your chance to leave." The others said nothing, waiting for Gary to explain.

"I used to be a transporter for the Underdogs, but I'm no longer part of them. Because I failed to deliver a very important package, they're still looking for me. Since I'm the leader of this gang, you guys are involved too, but I promise I don't plan to just sit back and let things happen. I'll fight back."

Before the others could respond, they were interrupted.

"Excuse me!" a woman in a white lab coat said as she came over.

"You are the boy who came in with the girl, correct? Do you know her, or do you have her emergency contact information?"

"How is she?" Gary replied, ignoring the doctor's question. There was a strange look on her face when he asked her that.

"How is she?" he asked again, and when there was no answer, he pushed past the doctor. The Howlers tried to stop him, but Gary was already running ahead, following the scent of the blood that was on his clothes.

Eventually he reached a cubicle and shoved the curtain aside . . . and saw Stacy. The line on the heart monitor was flat, and Gary could hear no heartbeat.

CHAPTER 43

SYSTEM ERROR

The flat line on the monitor, Stacy motionless on the gurney, and the fact that Gary couldn't hear a heartbeat confirmed everything. He couldn't believe it. Just then the hospital workers rushed in to get him out of the room.

Gary didn't resist; he lacked the energy to do so. Despite the system telling him he had energy, he certainly didn't feel like it. The security guards easily pulled him away, but because he didn't make a scene, they just returned him back to the reception area. They had experienced this with others before, and Gary was no exception.

A nurse came to ask Gary questions about the deceased girl. The hospital didn't know her name yet. She had been carrying no identification, perhaps a condition of the Pincers gang for working in a place like that. However, seeing the state Gary was in, Kai took over.

He subtly motioned for the rest of the group to take Gary out and let him handle things. Because Stacy had died as a result of blood loss from her knife injuries, police were bound to get on the case. Whether someone from the Pincers would cover it up or not was another thing.

Marie and the others were extremely worried about Gary. He had yet to say a single word, simply following behind his friends as if on autopilot. All three of them tried to reach out to him a couple of times, but there was no response.

The Howlers ended up returning to the Wolf's Pool Club to discuss what to do next. However, they agreed to wait for Gary to be back to his usual self.

Gary sat on one of the sofas in the club; he was starting to come back a bit.

When did we get back to the pool club? he wondered as he touched his head. He was so out of it that he hadn't even registered what his body had been doing. His mind wasn't even thinking straight, but now that he had some time, he could think clearly.

How did this happen? I don't understand . . . the system gave me a quest to get her to the hospital within twenty minutes. Why didn't it work? I even made it with a few minutes to spare!

Did the timer include operation time? No, that makes no sense! I brought her back and even got a reward, so then why did Stacy still die?

Gary angrily waited for an answer, yet there was nothing. The system remained eerily silent as always. Looking over the system's log, he still saw the notification congratulating him, which made him think back to the other option the quest had given him.

I guess in the end . . . the system can't change what actually happens in real life . . . this is entirely my fault. I shouldn't have put my trust into a damn game screen! Gary got up from his seat and angrily swiped the screen interface he had opened, but to the others he looked like a madman throwing a fit.

"Gary, are you with us?" Kai asked, since he had finally moved and there was life in his eyes for the first time.

"Huh? Oh, yeah," Gary replied, noticing the strange looks the others were giving him.

"Good. I was just explaining to everyone that for now, if anyone comes to us and asks, we didn't have anything to do with that girl at the hospital. We can't afford to get in trouble with the police, not at this stage. Not that I think it will go that far.

"Unless you've had better luck, we don't have any information on the Pincers' base or their boss's whereabouts. So we will have to try to do some more digging."

In the middle of Kai summing things up, Gary got up and headed to the door.

"Sorry, Kai. I won't tell anyone, but I don't think I'm in the right mindset to talk about taking over their gang right now. Also . . . she's not 'that girl,' Her name is . . . was Stacy," Gary said as he closed the door behind him.

The others exchanged glances.

"Let's give him some time," Austin finally said. "He said he knew the gi— Stacy. I saw how he acted in that place . . . he really gave it his all to save her."

Although Austin was somewhat right, it was troubling Gary even more because one, he had trusted the system, and two, if he had chosen differently, he might have saved her. Eventually, Gary ended up going home.

His sister rushed to the door when she saw him, but she could immediately tell something was up by the way he was dragging his feet. He looked like he needed to cry, yet for some reason no tears were coming out.

"Gary?" Amy called out.

Seeing her brother in such a state, Amy wrapped her arms around him in a big hug.

"You have a lot on your plate, huh?" Amy said softly. "Whatever's troubling you, I know you won't just let it build up. You'll deal with it. And if you want to talk about it, I'm here for you."

Amy patted her brother's head, leading him to hug her a bit tighter. "Remember what Mom used to say. 'We can't keep thinking about the past, it's already happened. If you think too much about the future, you'll miss what's happening now. We need to treasure the present, treasure the now, and that's why it's a gift.'"

"That wasn't Mom, I'm pretty sure that was that old turtle from that panda movie? Master Genbu or something?" Gary chuckled as he lifted his head.

He hadn't expected it, but his sister had managed to cheer him up and bring him back to his senses.

"I wanted to ask you something . . . do you hate Stacy for what she did to you that day?"

It took a while for Amy to respond; it seemed like she was really considering the question, and Gary was a little afraid of the answer. He didn't want his sister to speak ill of the dead.

"You know, if you had asked me that question the day when she left me on my own in that café, I wouldn't have hesitated to say yes," Amy replied. "But now . . . after not seeing her for a bit . . . I've realized how good a friend she was, not counting that day . . . or with Hawk . . .

"As far back as I can remember, Stacy was always a bit of a scaredy-cat and a pushover. Even though she began playing tough after we came to Bayles, her façade would always break at the smallest sign of trouble.

"Honestly, it's impressive that she managed to keep everything about you a secret for so long. I didn't even have to ask her to. She knew I didn't want her to tell that psycho a word about you. It wasn't until the situation had gotten desperate that she confessed to everything.

"I often wonder if the roles were reversed, would I have done the same thing? What if I had a family . . . or what if you were sick. I dunno . . . maybe I'm just being stupid and looking for reasons to forgive her. I tried staying mad at her, but after the first day at school without her, I realized that I missed her.

"It's lonely not having her greet me in the morning, having her there to talk to during our breaks. I feel like an outcast now, being the only girl to eat my homemade packed lunch. As stupid as she was in recent times, she always did her best to cheer me up, especially after what happened to Mom . . .

"I even tried to reach out to her, but she never replied. The most frustrating thing is that I never got the chance to tell her off for what she did back then. Maybe then I could have forgiven her . . . but now she's gone."

Those words at the end pained Gary more than his sister could have realized. He put his hand softly on her shoulder.

"Stacy really was a good friend to you . . . right?"

Amy didn't know why, but hearing her brother say that made her start to cry. She rubbed her eyes, not quite understanding where these emotions were coming from. Now it was Gary's turn to hold her for a bit, before she excused herself and went into their room.

Still, talking to his sister had allowed Gary to make up his mind. He took out his phone and entered the Howlers' group chat, typing away. The others, who were still at the Wolf's Pool Club, received the message and shared a smile as they read it.

I've decided I'm going to take out the whole of that damned Pincers gang tomorrow!
Let me know if you are in or out.

In less than half a minute, he got replies from the other four.

In!
In!
In!
In!

CHAPTER 44

BAIT

13 Days until the next full moon.
Your bloodlust is increasing.
40 Exp has been gained from current Bond Marks (4)
Exp 596/2876

When Gary woke up that Sunday morning, the weather was quite dull with a gray sky, perfectly matching his mood. There wasn't much sunshine to enjoy, not that it often came through the thick smog that seemed to cover Slough.

Maybe I'm feeling this way because it's getting closer to the full moon, Gary thought after seeing the message. *Either way . . . the Pincers took something away from me, so it's time I take something from them.*

Gary filled a backpack with all the things he would need, and just as he was about to head out the door, Amy came rushing out of their bedroom, tears rolling down her face.

"Gary . . . Gary, did you hear?" His sister could barely say the words Her throat was too choked up. "I . . . I just got a me-message from Sta-Stacy's parents . . . the-they found her in so-some hospital . . . a-and Stacy didn't make it . . . sh-she's dead . . ."

Gary stopped just before opening the door. This morning he had read a news article about a local girl who had apparently overdosed on drugs. As expected, the Pincers had covered up Stacy's death, so it wouldn't link her back to them.

Everything in that article had been utterly false: the name of the hospital, the way she had died, and where she had died. Just thinking about it, Gary clenched the doorknob. For a moment, he considered staying and comforting his sister through this tough time.

Unfortunately, staying here with Amy wouldn't change things with the Pincers. The longer they were allowed to remain operating, the more the girls working for them would suffer.

"Amy, I'm so sorry to hear that . . . she was your best friend . . . but I'm sure the people who did this to her will receive their karma." And with that, Gary opened the door and quickly closed it behind him.

Letting out a big breath, he headed to the pool club. On the way there, he saw Mr. Morten outside the apartment building, sitting on a bench and looking troubled. When he saw Gary, the old man smiled.

"The people here, they're struggling as well," Gary said.

A short while later, Gary had reached the Wolf's Pool Club. It wasn't open to the public yet, but everyone was there, including Austin's three friends who had essentially become employees of the place. It had been getting a good flow of customers lately, enough to cover the teens' income while also making profit for Gary and the others. They took over the primary duties at the club, giving the Howlers more free time.

Miss Degrace was in charge of scheduling the employees and assigning their duties; why they were here so early with the others, Gary didn't know.

"Let's get straight down to business," Kai stated with a smile, now that they were all here.

"We had trouble gathering information about the Pincers yesterday, but we still have a lead. Austin's friends did a good job finding out that those who are working in the school area are linked to the Pincers.

"Apparently, they don't just deal with school kids; they also scout the streets trying to entice pretty girls into an easy way of making a living. Sometimes they even trick them by saying it's a modeling job, and things progressively worsen.

"Seeing that these guys deliver the girls, they must have some idea who and where the real Pincers leader is. Even if they don't personally, finding the contact person should help us uncover their leader.

"We know the general area they work in, and because it's the weekend, they will be busy on the streets as usual. All of this information was gathered by our three friends here." Kai gave the credit that was due to the three students from Austin's school.

Innu already knew them, since they were the delinquent trio from his former class. They had also gone up against Billy when he came to their school, and they had suffered more than just a few broken bones doing so.

Honestly, Gary didn't know how reliable or strong they were because it was hard to compare a normal human to an omega wolf. Still, if the stories he heard in the shop were true, they were strong fighters when they were up against normal delinquent students.

There was Bo, who wore his hair in an Afro and was relatively thin but tall. Then there was Felix, who was the polar opposite, short and on the wide side. He always had a scrunched-up look on his face as if he was constantly angry about something. Last but not least was Alfie, who was mostly silent. Alfie's hair covered his face and he usually went around with his hands in his pockets.

According to Austin, they were his trustworthy men who would always help him, no matter the cause. For example, they didn't even ask to be paid for working at the club because Austin had asked them to do it. However, Kai had insisted that they couldn't work for free; the club had to pay them even if only to gain their trust and loyalty in the long run.

"All right," Bo began, nodding. "It's, like, hard to explain, but these guys, like, don't, like, come out all the time. Like, they sometimes act like pussies, so like, if they see us, then it might, like, you know, scare them."

It was clear to Gary that Afro boy wasn't the best of speakers, but quite a few people in his own class talked like Bo.

"What he's trying to say is, if those guys see us all together approaching them, there's a good chance they'll run away," Austin explained. "At the same time, they don't exactly make it obvious what they're trying to do. They work in groups but approach girls on their own, so it's hard to tell who is working for the Pincers and who is just trying to hit on pretty girls."

"So we need bait?" Kai summed it up nicely.

The group was thought about it for a while, until eventually they all looked toward Marie, the only girl in the room.

"Is she . . . good enough?" Kai asked, raising his eyebrow.

When Marie heard this, her whole body shook with anger. She raised her hand and slapped Kai across the face. It was so loud that the others could feel the power behind the strike, which left a big red mark on Kai's cheek.

Innu shook his head. As much as Kai seemed like a playboy, he certainly didn't know how to speak to girls like one.

Then Marie took the two scrunchies out of her hair, releasing the two large pigtails, and now her hair went halfway down her back. She straightened it with her fingers a few times, and the others couldn't quite believe it.

Just with the change of hairstyle, Marie looked like a completely different girl. The delinquent trio all gave her a thumbs-up, which caused her face to go red.

"It's a good start, but if you could put on some more makeup, I think it could work even better," Austin suggested excitedly.

"I think Marie will make the perfect bait; she is a really pretty girl," Gary agreed as he got up and walked over to her. Suddenly he noticed her heartbeat thumping louder and faster as he got closer.

"Are you okay?" he asked her, worried.

"Yeah . . . I-I'm fine . . . just a bit nervous." Marie smiled back. "I'll happily play the bait. Finally, I'll be able to do more than just watch from the sidelines."

Smiling back, Gary wanted her to know something.

"Marie . . . don't worry, I'll be watching you the whole time. I promise you, I won't let you end up like Stacy."

Gary continued to be blissfully unaware of why her heartbeat had increased once again. Marie just nodded, and a small smile appeared on her face.

We will take out the Pincers today . . . they will get their karma as promised, Amy, Gary thought.

CHAPTER 45

AN UNBREAKABLE PROMISE

Before the group set off toward Burnham, all the boys had agreed on wearing their gang clothes. The black-and-gold blazers. Although it made them stand out, giving them the appearance of a group looking for trouble, that was exactly what they were going to do.

Still, as long as they split up and watched over Marie in Burnham, they shouldn't attract too much attention. According to Kai, it would help spread awareness of the Howlers, because if everything went right, after today they would be all set for their future operation in Slough.

Just in case, Gary also brought along his mask. Fortunately, it hadn't been destroyed in his fight with Jayden; it was currently tucked away inside his blazer. Wearing it in public would just attract a lot of unwanted attention, but it might prove useful later on.

The group decided to go to Burnham by bus, rejecting their leader's suggestion of walking over. Instead of the street with all the restaurants, their destination was the school.

They sat at the back of the bus in a row of four seats. With Austin's size he took up two seats, which meant Marie and Gary were sitting next to each other. She looked forward, hardly turning her head.

"Aw man, this is kinda lame, don't you think?" Innu complained as he looked out the window. "Aren't we meant to be some hotshot gang? Why're we taking the bus? Don't gangsters usually have those expensive black cars and crap? Even a taxi would have even been better than this."

"A taxi is expensive," Gary said. "And with all of us, we would have had to take two taxis. You could buy ten loaves of bread, jam, and ketchup instead."

Gary's quick reply had Innu a little worried for their leader's mental well-being. They already knew that he was tight with money, even before he had suggested walking over to Burnham, but what was up with the supermarket calculations?

"Please tell me that's not all you eat . . . Seriously, ketchup sandwiches? Remind me to never go to the toilet after you," Innu teased, wafting his hand in front of his face.

Gary let out an awkward laugh. *If only they knew how much money I actually have to spend to avoid hunting rats . . .*

"Unless you've managed to purchase one of those fancy cars with your cut and are willing to let us use it, that's not happening. Gary's right, there's no need to spend money like that when there are cheaper alternatives," Kai said. "However, I'm open to revisit this topic at a later time. Hopefully by then all of you will be able to drive on your own, because I'm not up for being a chauffeur," he added with his usual smirk. Being seventeen, Kai already had a driver's license, whereas the rest of the boys would have to wait until their next birthday.

The journey to Burnham was long, so they spent a lot of time on the bus twiddling their thumbs, reviewing the plan.

"Marie, are you okay? Your face is a little red, and you look a bit nervous," Gary said; he could practically feel the heat coming off the girl's cheeks. She was that red, even though it was a bit hard to see through the makeup she had applied.

With her hair down and her makeup done in a natural look, she certainly did look like a different person. She also looked older than her seventeen years, more like a young university student.

Makeup is really a dangerous thing, Gary thought

"Yeah, the bus is just a bit hot, and I'm a little worried about what will happen if I mess up," Marie replied. "Or that they won't approach me."

There was a lot riding on Marie's shoulders, but Gary wasn't worrying too much. As long as the delinquents were up and about, he believed he might be able to pick up a few things just from walking the streets and listening in on conversations.

Still, the best-case scenario would be if they were to approach Marie, but after what happened with Stacy, she had a right to be worried, because even he was.

The others can handle themselves quite well. I wanted to save my Marks in case I needed them in the future . . . but I don't want to have any more regrets. As long as I mark her, I'll be able to find her, no matter what happens.

"Marie," Gary said, hesitating about what promise to extract. "Can you promise me not to die?"

"Huh?" Marie looked at him strangely, and her expression sank. "Are you trying to jinx me? Don't even mention that possibility after what happened yesterday!"

Seeing the range of emotions on Gary's face as he searched for the right words to explain that he didn't mean it like that, Marie scratched the back of her head.

"Argh, fine . . . If it makes you feel better, I promise you not to die."

Error: Spoken deal is too vague

What the . . . what do you mean, "too vague"?

Placing a Bond Mark on someone was very useful, allowing the werewolf to find that person, while also granting him 10 Exp each day, yet there was always the risk that the person could become a hunting target. So Gary had tried to come up with ways to make unbreakable promises.

Unfortunately, the system didn't allow him to outsmart it. He was seriously racking his brain, trying to come up with one that wasn't too vague before Marie went into the Pincers' territory.

"Thanks, I . . . I was just worried about you. I'm not used to you being in on the action yet. Say, do you think you'll be in this gang forever? Or do you think this gang will last forever?" Gary honestly didn't know where these words had come from, but he did notice one thing.

Before answering, Marie looked over at Kai.

"As long as it's still his dream, then of course I will stay with the Howlers. Although I also have my own reasons to stay now," she said, staring back at Gary. "I honestly can't think of following anyone else, or think of anyone else that is better for this gang."

"All right . . . as long as you're one of the Howlers, I promise I'll protect you. So don't leave us, okay?" Gary asked, putting out his pinky finger.

Marie thought that Gary might be thinking a bit more of her. As far as she knew, he hadn't asked any of the other members about staying in the gang forever.

Is this his way of saying he wants to be with me forever?

"Of course, I promise." Marie smiled, intertwining his finger with her own.

A spoken deal has been made, would you like to mark "Marie Degrace"?

Just in time, as the bus had arrived at their stop and it was time for them to get to work.

CHAPTER 46

NOT JUST A GIRL

Every area in Slough had its own little shopping street, where retailers sold all sorts of different things. When the Howlers reached Burnham's main street, though, they realized that this area wasn't as affluent as the street they had seen yesterday.

There were a few clothing shops, shoe stores, and hardware stores, among other things, but the shops looked a little worn down, and there was graffiti on the walls. Many of the shops were boarded up. A Tier 3 town wasn't a place where people could afford the luxury of buying things, which was why there were so many factories and manual-labor jobs in the area.

"Now this is more like the Slough I know." Innu sounded happy. It was an awkward reaction, but honestly, the others also felt it. Lately they had been visiting areas in Slough that felt foreign to them, that they would have never set foot in before. It seemed like all the money in the town was being funneled toward the big gangs.

Off in the distance, not too far away, they could see the upper floors of the high school, which was why they were here in the first place.

"All right, let's stick to the plan. Keep your phones on you at all times," Kai reminded them. The group nodded and split up.

Although they hadn't seen anyone who even vaguely resembled a high school recruiter, they thought that if they did run into one, the recruiter might immediately start running. Still, everyone made sure to keep an eye on Marie while pretending to window-shop.

Walking down the main street, Marie wore black boots that went up to her thigh, along with a fitted coat, and she had tucked her hair back, revealing a pair of nice earrings.

None of them had ever seen her dress so girly; the other thing they noticed was that she stood out in a place like this. There were other girls, but none of them were dressed in such expensive, high-quality clothes.

I guess that's all that blond boy's money, huh? Innu thought, staring at her. *I'm starting to suspect that he gave her and her mom a bigger cut from the gray color gang money than he let on.*

He also had something else on his mind: what Gary had said at the hospital. He had mentioned the Underdogs being after him. Unfortunately, a doctor had interrupted them at that moment, leaving them no time to discuss what he meant.

The Pincers were just a small-time gang, and they were proving to be difficult to deal with . . . how the hell were five teenagers supposed to deal with a big gang like the Underdogs? Still, Innu couldn't help but smile as he imagined what the Howlers could be like if they ever got to that level.

"Hey, I bet you hear this every day, but you look really stunning. You look familiar; have you done any modeling, by chance?" A voice called out from the middle of the street, and suddenly everyone's head turned to Marie.

The voice belonged to a teenage boy who was dressed quite hip and was carrying a professional camera. It wasn't cheap, that was for sure, and out of everyone on the street he had chosen to approach Marie.

"Um, no, I've never even thought about it," Marie answered, fluttering her eyes at him.

"Well, you really have the right look for it from head to toe, and you obviously have a great fashion sense," the boy said appreciatively, giving Marie a thumbs-up. "If you're free, want to give it a shot? I actually work for a modeling agency, and we're looking for young university students like you.

"I feel like you have the perfect look that we're going for with our next campaign. Of course, you'll be compensated, and if my boss likes you, your pictures could be in all the Tier 2 cities and Tier 3 towns. Wait . . ." The boy suddenly paused his excitement and started to look her up and down, as if he was judging her.

"Since you said you haven't modeled before . . . do you mind if I take some practice photos of you? We have a studio that's not too far away from here."

Marie made it seem like she was trying to make up her mind for a bit before answering, because she really didn't know what to do. The plan was to try to see if there were others as well. After all, perhaps one person wouldn't know, and she was surprised to hear they had a physical shop.

"You know what, that sounds great . . . Thank you so much." Marie smiled, not wanting to disappoint the others.

Marie and the boy started walking together toward his special shop. They left the main street, going down an alleyway to another area that was close by.

This is getting too dangerous, I have to stop her, Gary thought.

A text message appeared in the group chat. Surprisingly, it was from Kai.

Don't intervene just yet. Let's first check where he is taking her.

However, with what had happened to Stacy still fresh on his mind, it was hard for Gary to just take a back seat.

Don't worry, that guy was just a delinquent. Remember, they're high school students like us, and they need to present the girls intact. They will take us to the right place.

The message calmed Gary down a bit, but he would still try to stick close to her. Unlike the others, he was following Marie more directly; he went down the alleyway and observed them from about thirty yards away.

"How far is your shop?" Marie asked.

The boy had been pretty chatty initially, but for some reason he suddenly stopped, and that was when Marie noticed that he was glancing behind him. At the next alleyway, he suddenly grabbed Marie's hand and shoved her down it.

"You . . . you're following us! Who are you? One of the girl's friends to get revenge? Who put you up to this?" the boy asked, trying to intimidate her, but Marie said nothing.

"Oh well, I'm sure that my other friends will be dealing with yours pretty soon. So why don't I have some fun with you myself? You will become damaged goods soon anyway!" he sneered, reaching for her.

At that moment, Marie lifted the hem of her short coat. She wore a strap around her thigh that held two knives. Pulling them out, she quickly delivered two slashes, cutting the boy's hand.

"I'm not just some pushover girl! Thanks for not making me feel guilty about hurting you. I wonder how many lives you have ruined!" Marie shouted.

CHAPTER 47

ANSWERS

"You bitch!" the teenage boy shouted. Blood was dripping from his hand. The slashes weren't too deep, but they were painful. "You damn whore, how dare you use weapons like that?"

Honestly, Marie had dreaded the day when she would have to use her knives on someone. Still, she had started getting up early to join the training with Kai, Innu, and Austin, without Gary knowing anything about it. Not only that, but without the others knowing as well, she practiced during any spare time she had afterward.

It was undeniable that most boys would be physically stronger than her, and that was why Kai had procured weapons to make up for the difference. Marie had absorbed everything she had learned during Kai's lessons. One of the most important concepts was that she had to prevent the other person from grabbing her.

The boy was pissed off and tried to come after her again to get his revenge, but Marie swiftly avoided the punch while slashing upward with one of her knives, adding another big injury across his forearm.

She was nimble and flexible, whereas the boy was relying on raw power. Having been hit twice, he was seriously getting angry.

Where the hell are the others? How have they still not dealt with those guys yet? he wondered, as he scanned the alleyway to see where his reinforcements were. While doing so, he spotted a plank of wood with a nail in it, possibly part of a broken chair.

Picking it up off the ground, the boy smirked again.

"Blame yourself for what's gonna happen next, you bitch!"

Seeing the boy pick up a weapon of his own, Marie recalled what Kai had told her to do in such a situation. A wooden plank or stick would give the other person the advantage through extra range. However, an inexperienced fighter tended to overcommit with each hit, leaving themself quite open. She needed to capitalize on this.

Without any sort of technique the boy swung wide with strong conviction. Marie knew that if he hit her with the makeshift weapon, she wouldn't be getting back up.

This was her first fight, and it was beyond terrifying.

After avoiding the first couple of swings, Marie felt something hit her back, something solid. The next time the boy attacked, Marie ducked under the plank, making it connect with the wall. This was the break she needed; rushing in, she slashed twice along his chest, slicing an X into his clothes.

He screamed as the knife reached his skin, and honestly it was completely different from how Marie imagined it would be. With these sharp knives, cutting through skin was far easier than she thought, and it gave her goose bumps.

The boy's hands were in pain from hitting the wall with the plank, his chest and arm were bleeding, and it was all because of the girl behind him. Just then he heard footsteps, followed by applause.

"You've done a great job, Marie." A male voice congratulated her.

The delinquent boy had expected to see his friends, but instead he saw four unfamiliar boys standing there. All of them were dressed in black-and-gold clothing, and one wore a wolf mask.

"Now, we already asked your friends 'kindly' about the location of the Pincers' base and their leader, but unfortunately none of them seemed to know the answer. Then again, most of them were unable to answer because we knocked them out. I'm just glad our friend here didn't do the same to you."

The truth was, when Gary was following Marie down the alleyway, his path had been blocked off by a large person. It seemed like the delinquents weren't as stupid as they had thought. He must have deliberately gone through this alleyway to shake off any would-be pursuers.

It wasn't just one person who blocked his way either; others had been hiding nearby. Unfortunately for them, the Howlers weren't as weak as the delinquents they were used to dealing with. Against all four boys they never stood a chance.

As soon as they took care of them, Gary wanted to go help Marie. However, Kai stopped him once again, telling him to let her handle it herself. Honestly, when Kai saw Marie fighting like that, he wondered how it was possible for her to be this good. It had only been a few days, so she had to be a natural at it.

Still, Gary noticed that Kai's heart rate increased when he saw the delinquent grab the plank, not holding back in strength. He wasn't the only one, though. Gary couldn't take it any longer, and he put his mask on as the Howlers advanced.

The boy still had the wooden plank in his hand, and as the group come toward him, he panicked, unsure what to do. Slowly he backed away.

"Ahhh!" the boy shouted, charging not toward Gary and the others, but toward Marie. She had let her guard down when the boys showed themselves, which had left the delinquent an opening.

The boy intended to take the girl hostage, but just a few steps in, a hand gripped his throat. In seconds, Gary was squeezing his throat tightly.

3 Points have been allocated into Dexterity
Your base Dexterity is now at 18

Skill activated: Controlled Transformation
Agility 18 (+3)

"What do you think you're doing? You bastard, you could have killed her!" Gary shouted as he slammed the boy against the wall, still holding him with one hand. "Let's see how you like it when someone tries to kill you!" Gary tightened his grip, slowly lifting him off his feet and into the air. The boy's face was turning red, and his eyes looked like they were going to pop.

"Stop!" Marie shouted as she grabbed his arm.

"Let him go! We need him alive to find the others!" Kai shouted as well.

Snapping out of his rage, Gary let go and allowed the delinquent to fall to the ground. The boy started coughing and gasping for air; he had already seen his life flash before him.

Kai turned his attention to the boy and grabbed him by the back of his hair, forcing him to look up.

"If you don't want my friend over here to finish what he started, you better get talking. Tell us, where's the Pincers' main base? Where do you take the girls after introducing them? Who's their boss?"

The boy was still afraid for his life, so he didn't put up any struggle. "Burnham Street! I bring them to a place called the Kraken. I've never seen the boss, only his right-hand man. They're definitely in that place, though!"

"Let's go," Gary ordered, already walking off and heading toward Burnham Street.

CHAPTER 48

KEEPING SECRETS

On the weekends, Amy often found herself doing nothing these days. She was too afraid to go out on her own ever since Raven had abducted her and Stacy. Even if she did want to go somewhere . . . who could she go with? When she thought about this, her heart just sank deeper.

Today was just one of those days when Amy felt like her life was cursed. Even more than usual. Her eyes were puffy and slightly sore because she had been rubbing them so much, and she had nearly emptied the box of tissues on the table.

Ah damn . . . Gary is going to get annoyed at me for wasting this many tissues, Amy thought, looking at the box. Imagining his angry reaction, she couldn't help but chuckle. Thinking about her brother was the only thing that cheered her up these days.

Where did Gary even go? Was it just a coincidence that he asked me about Stacy yesterday? Did he somehow already know that she's . . . dead? Unwilling to keep thinking about her former best friend, who was now deceased, Amy tried to focus on something else.

Unfortunately, her mind jumped from one bad thing to another, in this case the bloody clothes she had found. As much as she tried not to think about them, whenever she went into her wardrobe, she ended up looking at her brother's, where the clothes had been left.

Why hasn't he buried them or burned them by now? Is he keep-ing them here because he wants me to know? She sulked, feeling the heavy burden of having to keep such an important secret. Usually it was bearable, but with today's news, it felt far heavier than before.

Amy got up and grabbed her phone. Perhaps it was because she was trying to keep her mind off Stacy's death, but her mind was now filled with Gary. She wanted to know what had happened that day.

Amy didn't plan to get involved in whatever he was doing, but she wanted to learn the truth. No matter what he had done, she knew that her brother must have done it for her, but she wanted to share that burden with him . . . even if he might never learn that she did.

Besides, knowing him, he might be out doing something crazy to try to cover this all up . . . Yeah, if I leave him on his own, he's just go-ing to get in more trouble. I have to help my brother out! she thought, trying to justify her behavior.

She scrolled through her contacts list, looking for the one per-son she believed would have an idea of what Gary had been up to. If she was lucky, then he might even know the truth! Someone who was as close to Gary as she was.

She wasn't in a waiting mood, though, so rather than send a text, she decided to call him instead. After a few rings, he picked up.

"Amy! What's wrong? Did something happen to Gary? Is he okay? Oh no, he didn't try to hurt you or anything, did he? Amy, talk to me!"

With the storm of questions, Amy was forced to pull the phone away from her ear. She switched over to speaker mode, which Tom had seemingly already done on his side, judging by the way he had shouted.

"What are you talking about, Tom?" Amy replied. "Gary came back fine yesterday . . . And why would he ever hurt me?"

There was silence on the other end, which gave Amy time to think about what Tom just had said. Clearly, he was acting strange and pan-icked for a reason. *It looks like he really does know something.*

The reason Tom was over-the-top worried was that he had not received any news from Gary. After the strange events at school, he had seen the look on Gary's face. He had known his best friend long enough to understand that he planned to do something crazy, such as raiding the red color gang.

Tom already had his suspicions that Gary was behind the attack on the gray color gang, and with the approaching full moon, he was worried that his best friend might allow a certain side to take over again.

"Sorry, I didn't want to startle you. I guess you must have heard about it by now. How the red color gang gathered us all in school. It's all still fresh in my head, and I was worried about that hotheaded brother of yours.

"Anyway, how are you holding up? I heard about what happened to your mother. My condolences." Tom tried to come up with an explanation for his behavior. However, suddenly he realized that he was talking to his best friend's sister . . . and *she* had been the one to call *him*!

Meanwhile, Amy thought, *Damn it, he's changing the subject. How do I get him to talk about Gary again?*

"Oh, he told you about that? Unfortunately, she's yet to show any signs of waking up. She's not doing any worse, though, so I guess there's that. I'm as okay as I can be. But Gary has been acting weird ever since.

"He's been going out a lot and coming back late. Not sure if it's connected to that, or if something else has happened. I was wondering . . . as his best friend, do you know anything about it? Something that he might be hiding, perhaps?" Amy asked, but when she said the last few words, her tone of voice indicated that she already knew what he was hiding.

How much does she know? . . . She clearly knows at least something . . . could Gary have told her about him being a werewolf? Tom panicked and didn't say anything. Of course, this just made Amy all the more suspicious.

"So it looks like you do know," Amy finally said. "Look, Tom, I found . . . some things . . . and I really don't know how to deal with it. Gary doesn't know that I know . . . but I just don't know what to do about it."

Suddenly Amy started sobbing on the other end of the phone, and Tom tried to think of something to make her stop. He knew that Amy was a pure person, someone who always helped Gary no matter what. As his best friend, Tom knew that the Dem family lived a troubled life, and now Amy carried the secret that her brother was a werewolf . . . it must be crushing her inside. Tom thought of an idea to help her get over this problem.

"Why don't we go see Gary and ask him?" Tom suggested. "If you already know about it, then there is no need for him to hide it from you, right? He should be the one to tell you. It's best if you both get all those things sorted out; it will probably make you both feel a lot better. Besides, if you hear it from him, there won't be a chance for any misunderstandings."

The truth was, Tom also wanted to ask Gary some questions: whether he was the one behind the attack on the gray color gang, and what exactly he had done after school yesterday. Unfortunately, ever since he had become a werewolf, Gary could be scary at times. Tom hoped that with his little sister present, she could serve as the backup that he would need.

"Okay." Amy sniffled. "But Gary isn't even here, and I don't know when he will be back."

"I have a good idea where he might be. He's been working at a place called the Wolf's Pool Club. Even if he's not there, his co-workers should know where we might be able to find him. How about I pick you up and we go there together?"

With a plan agreed between the two of them, the call ended. Tom held his phone for a second, as his face started to feel a little hot. Looking in the mirror, he saw his cheeks blushing.

I'm going out, with just me and Amy . . . I mean, she's only one year younger than me, no problem there, right? But then again, her brother is Gary . . . if I did something to upset her . . .

An image appeared in Tom's head of Gary transforming and biting his head off . . . Shaking off that thought, he reminded himself that it wasn't a date, just two teenagers of the opposite sex looking for Gary.

Right . . . even though it's not a date, it can't hurt if I wear my best clothes, right?

When Tom turned up at Amy's house, she looked through the peephole to confirm that was him.

"What are you wearing?" was Amy's first question as she opened the door. Tom wore something that resembled a suit, and he even had a tie on. "You look like you're going for a job interview."

Embarrassed, Tom quickly undid his tie and placed it in his pocket. "Ah, my bad. I just came from an intern interview at my dad's place . . . Since you sounded so serious, I kinda hurried here, without a chance to change," Tom explained, scratching his head in embarrassment.

Closing the door behind them, they set off, and it wasn't long until they stood in front of the place known as the Wolf's Pool Club.

"So this is where Gary has been working and earning money?" Amy asked.

"Yeah . . . Let's go find out what secrets your brother has been keeping."

CHAPTER 49

THE KRAKEN

The Kraken was at on the far end of Burnham Street, right on the corner. The building was black on the outside and had been made to look like an old ship, with fake broken wooden panels. On top of the building, just by its name, was what looked like a giant octopus intertwined with the letters.

It wasn't only unique on the outside, though. Inside the restaurant, the floor was under a few inches of water, with large wooden panels above the water forming pathways that branched off to little seating areas designed to look like boats, where the customers would enjoy their meal with a nautical feel.

This unique setting ensured that the Kraken was a popular restaurant. In fact, it was one of the few places in Burnham that remained in operation as a restaurant even when nighttime came, instead of indulging in the other side of business. Only a few people knew that all of it was just a front for the gang known as the Pincers.

There was a grand office on the third floor, a place where no customer was allowed to enter. That room itself was as big as the dining area below.

The office went on and on, and at the very end was a large desk where the leader of the Pincers sat, in a chair that faced the other way. The room was currently filled with men on either side lined up still like statues. In the center of the room, not too far from the desk, stood more men in suits, along with a few women.

"Boss!" one of the men in the center of the room shouted at the top of his lungs. "Let me show you our newest products. We defer to your judgment as to where we should send them!"

The chair slowly turned around, revealing a middle-aged woman with long black hair wearing a tight-fitting leopard print dress. The center part of the dress opened up in a large V shape, revealing generous cleavage. If it weren't for the large fur piece she had over her shoulders, one might even be able to see more.

This person, whom they referred to as "Boss," was in charge of the trafficking in Slough's red-light district area. Her name was Olivia Pearl. She stood up, revealing that her height reached nearly six feet.

As she walked toward the others, some of the men couldn't help but stare at her long legs and nice figure. However, there was one place that nobody dared to look at for too long . . . and that was Olivia's face.

Not because the large woman was ugly, in fact the opposite was true, but even without her height, she had a menacing aura and her eyes seemed to have the ability to pierce right through whoever she was looking at.

Not to mention, she had quite the temperament. If she caught someone staring at her, she snapped at them . . . however, this treatment was only given to a particular type of person.

Olivia stood in front of the row of girls and inspected the four of them. However, she didn't seem to regard them as fellow humans; more like livestock.

"Hmm, you look a little young. Let's send you to the Yangs for the time being." Going down the line, she then looked at the next girl and after a few moments she declared, "Birchwood House."

As each girl's future workplace was decided, one of the men took her away. There, she would be introduced to the full scope of her duties.

Finally, she stopped at the last girl, studying her for longer than the others. This girl was a snow-white beauty. She had clear skin, and there wasn't a mark on her, but she was visibly shaking. Scared, as if she knew what was going to happen to her.

"As for you . . . you'll stay at the Kraken." For the first time Olivia showed a change of emotion as a small smile appeared on her face. "For now, just come and stand by my desk over there."

The girl was reluctant to move, so the man by her side gave her a little nudge. Immediately Olivia looked his way, and the man turned his head, careful not to make eye contact.

"I apologize . . . please, young miss, listen to the Lady Boss's orders. It will be the best for us all," the man pleaded.

Hearing this, the young snow-white beauty walked over to the desk and waited patiently there.

"I heard there was a disturbance yesterday. Someone asking about the Pincers . . . and one of our girls died?" Olivia asked as she returned to her seat.

"Yes, Boss," replied the man who had been doing all the speaking so far. "They were two young men who pretended to be clients. One of the girls ran out and informed the guards. Unfortunately, while we were trying to capture them, one of the workers got injured.

"The intruders managed to flee with that girl, however, you don't have to worry, Boss. They tried saving her by bringing her to the nearby hospital. We had one of the nurses ensure that she won't be talking to anyone."

Olivia lit her pipe, then inhaled before letting out some smoke.

"In other words, you not only failed to apprehend two intruders, but you've also had one of our girls killed . . . to silence her before she could reveal any of our secrets? Who was it? Any of our top earners?"

The man quickly shook his head. "No, Boss, she just had her first day. She's one of the girls whose parents borrowed money from us."

"You really are lucky that you managed to procure such a good one today. Otherwise, I would have been in a terrible mood." Olivia smiled as she looked at the remaining girl

The man let out a sigh of relief. He hadn't told her everything yet. If the woman knew just how many of the Pincers gang members had been injured during their escape, there would be no helping them. The man was just hoping that they would never see those two ever again.

It was unlikely that any gang would try to start trouble so openly in their area, not so soon after what had happened yesterday.

"All right, everyone out!" Olivia shouted. The men in the room immediately started to leave, and as the door was closing, they turned back to see their Lady Boss licking her lips as she beckoned with her finger, instructing the girl to come to her.

She opened her mouth and slowly forced her tongue into the younger girl's mouth.

"Relax and enjoy this moment," Olivia said as she caressed the girl's face. "I will make you experience things you've never experienced before."

A group of people dressed in black-and-gold blazers were walking down Burnham Street at a fast pace. At the center was a figure with a black wolf mask covering his face from the top of his head to his nose.

It was the middle of the day, so there weren't as many people as usual. Still, it certainly caught the attention of the guards who were standing outside each place.

Inside, watching commotion through the window, Nini recognized the large man with them.

They came back . . . after what they did yesterday? Are these guys suicidal?

Nini had heard about what happened to Stacy. The workers often talked to each other, and before Stacy had arrived, Nini had been the newest girl. Coincidentally, she had been the one to show Stacy the ropes and how things worked here.

Hearing of her death had affected Nini more than she cared to admit.

Please, just leave this place. You're only going to make it worse for yourselves, Nini thought as she continued to watch them walk down the street.

Eventually, they stopped outside the Kraken and pushed past the two outside guards.

"Get out of the way," Gary demanded before they even tried to stop them. They entered the establishment, and were now in the main hall. The customers were enjoying their food, eating peacefully, but a few stopped as they noticed the strange group.

"Everyone!" Gary shouted. "The Howlers gang will be taking over this place! You have two minutes to leave. Anyone who is still here after two minutes will be considered an enemy!"

Most of the customers were shocked by this surprise proclamation. A gang daring enough to attack in broad daylight? However, those who were part of the Underworld had never heard of this gang. So they waited for the guards to kick them out.

A few moments later, a group of four guards rushed in. "Hey, if you know what this place is, then you need to get out of here!" one of them said, and tried to grab Gary.

But Gary grabbed his wrist and twisted it with his full strength, until everyone heard a crack. Pulling his arm forward, the masked teenager slammed his fist into the man's face, causing him to fall to the ground.

"One minute!" Gary shouted.

CHAPTER 50

THE HOWLERS TAKE OVER

The strange person wearing the wolf mask no longer looked like a nobody to them. The fact that this group of people knew where they were and who they were dealing with meant that it was serious business.

On top of that, there was something intimidating about them: the fact that the group decided to stay a little ahead of the entrance and still weren't moving. It gave the sense that these people could do what they wanted, even in enemy territory.

At the same time, the others could see that not only was the guard's wrist broken, but he wasn't going to be getting up any time soon. He just lay flat, with his mouth full of blood.

"Hey, we better get out of here, it looks like a real gang fight is about to start," one of the customers said to his partner, and they immediately stood up to leave. But they hesitated, worried that the intruders might attack them as well.

"You guys better hurry and get out of here, you've only got thirty seconds left," Kai told the couple, who had been the first pair to make a run for it. When he brought out his phone as if he was timing the whole thing, they ran straight past the Howlers.

The other customers, seeing that the group hadn't attacked them, quickly followed suit. A few still didn't want to move, thinking that maybe the matter could still be dealt with. They soon changed their minds when a person who looked like the leader of the current group of the Pincers, who had a large scar on his chin, gave an order.

"You heard them, everyone get out. We're closed for business for now, but don't worry, come back in a couple of hours and everything will be sorted out." He smirked, and the remaining customers also left.

After the last customer was out the door, Gary heard it close behind them, but not only that, he heard the click of a lock.

"They're locking us in?" Innu said, looking back. "Well, that's good in a way, I guess. At least we won't have to worry about one of them returning and stabbing us in the back. Besides, it wasn't like we were planning to run away."

"Time," Kai announced, putting his phone away just as a few dozen gang members came rushing down the stairs at the very back of the establishment. "I'm getting a little nervous with how many people there are," Marie confessed in a low voice, staying close to Kai. Eventually the onslaught stopped and the men smiled. There were around thirty of them.

"This is why I decided to go straight for their base rather than take out the whole street," Kai explained to his fellow gang members. "They may just be a small-time gang compared to the Underdogs and Gray Elephants, but they have many people working for them.

"For our small group, it would have been impossible to fight off all of them. This is the easier option . . . but we still will have to deal with at least this many."

"This is the easy option?" Marie gulped.

"We saw how well you did against that boy, Marie. Come on, this is not that much different. Besides, this time, all of us are with you. Each one of us just has to take care of like six of them." Innu smiled as he encouraged her.

Their opponents started to pull out the same weapons they had used yesterday: mostly stun guns and knives.

"Put that shit away!" Gary shouted as he advanced toward them. One of the men charged forward, thrusting his knife at the masked teenager. Once again, though, Gary moved out of the way and grabbed his attacker's arm, just as he had done before.

"Using a weapon like this can kill someone," Gary pointed out. He had used Controlled Transformation to further boost his Strength as he pushed the man's arm back at an unnatural angle. He was using so much force that everyone heard the elbow joint popping.

The man screamed in pain, but Gary didn't care, and he continued to move the arm in the other direction, bending it like a V toward the man, the knife pointing at his chest.

"If you shits use weapons like this, then you have to be prepared to die yourself!"

The man wasn't so sure if he was seeing things correctly, but through the mask he saw strange glowing yellow eyes that weren't shaped like a human's . . . these were the eyes of a beast. His human instincts were telling him that he really was going to die.

"Get them!" the leader shouted.

Gary kicked the man in the stomach, causing him to lean forward, and the top of his shoulder now fell into his own blade. Then he threw him aside into the shallow water. He ran forward as the Pincers all rushed toward the masked intruder.

Joining in, Innu was the fastest of the group. He leapt on top of one of the gang members and repeatedly elbowed the top of his head. He didn't let up until the man fell back and splashed into the water.

Another gangster swung a bat down toward him, and he barely rolled away, avoiding the strike. It ended up hitting nothing but water, causing it to rise up. Quickly getting up, Innu kneed the man in the face, knocking him back, but the first man Innu had attacked came back and punched him just underneath the ribs.

The blow was surprisingly heavy, but Innu stayed firm and continued to fight back. "For an adult, your punches sure are weaker than a high school student's," he said, taunting his opponent.

The man didn't understand what Innu was saying, but before he could attack again, a large fist hit him in the face, knocking him out cold.

"I've warned you, these guys are more resilient than the guys you're used to fighting!" Austin said. "You're a small guy in the first place, so they're going to take a few more hits than usual."

Innu saw the second guy he had kneed in the face getting up. At only sixteen years old, with a weight disadvantage, he saw that Austin was right. This wasn't a typical fight that Innu was used to, and not just because it wasn't one on one.

"Still, I don't think anyone can beat us both. Not unless they are some type of Altered." Austin let out a grin.

Not too far from where they were, Marie had her two knives out. She was worried because these men were clearly more used to fighting than the delinquent who had attacked her. So far, though, she was doing well, following Kai's advice while he stayed next to her.

He had instructed her not to go in for the attack, only to defend. So when one of the gang members came at her, she just watched carefully, avoiding the punches and knife attacks and using her own knives to slash away. In the meantime, Kai would be the one to finish them off.

One person had tried to attack Marie, and, turning to avoid the strike, she had slashed, cutting his arm a little. The man looked like he was about to do more, but before he could, Kai spun around and delivered a spinning side kick right into his stomach, sending the man flying back.

As he brought his leg up for another attack, he kicked water into the air, blinding the person who was charging forward. It looked like a rising waterfall, but what came up was soon to come down, and hammering his leg down like an axe, Kai smashed the bottom of his heel into another gangster, shattering the man's collar bone.

"Leader!" Kai shouted. "Your job isn't here. These guys aren't worth your time. Leave this to us, we can handle it, I promise you that."

Most of the men were targeting Gary, because it looked like he was heading toward the staircase. If he left, the others would have to deal with more, yet they couldn't just let him pass, either.

"Trust me . . . I know whether we can handle it or not, and we can definitely handle this!" Kai shouted before switching to a normal voice, so that only Marie could hear it, and hopefully Gary.

"Once they find out that we're strong enough to take all these guys down, their leader might make a run for it. You'll have to stop them! Just go straight for the Pincers' leader. That's your job!"

Turning around, Gary saw the confident smiles on their faces.

"All right," Gary replied, looking toward the staircase. "You heard him, move!"

CHAPTER 51

BLACKMAIL

Regardless of how strong Gary was, the Pincers gang members were not going to jump out of his way willingly. Although he could attempt to take them out, it would take up too much time and maybe too much Energy.

This might not be the whole gang. There could be more on the upper floors. I can't use all my Energy here, not unless I plan to eat some of them on the way.

Thinking about this, and with the staircase in sight, Gary ran backward a bit before quickly turning around and sprinting forward. He had never attempted this before, but if he went at full speed as fast as possible, there was a good chance that he could make it.

Skill activated: Controlled Transformation
Transformation has begun

His calf muscles expanded in size, and so did his thighs. Because he was wearing his gang uniform, specially made and given to him by Kai, the material was able to withstand the stretching and would revert to normal. He didn't have to worry about suddenly showing his hairy legs. Not that it mattered much anyway when he wore the mask.

Before he reached the first person, Gary pushed off and leapt into the air. He had never achieved such height before; it seemed impossible for a human to do. His feet were a good head above all the gang members. He landed on the other side, clearing them all and landing at the base of the stairs.

If you keep doing crazy crap like that, how am I supposed to keep your secret from everyone, Kai thought, smiling. "Head toward the stairs, let's make sure they can't follow him!" Kai shouted.

Before running up the stairs, Gary turned around to look at all the gangsters. He grabbed the closest one, lifted him over his head, and chucked him toward the others like a barrel.

Being picked up and thrown into a crowd would have been painful enough, but Gary's strength added speed and weight to the throw. When the man crashed into the group, it looked like a bowling ball hitting a set of pins.

"Well . . . I guess you just made our job that much easier. Good luck, Gary!" Kai said, reaching the staircase and seeing the injured Pincer gang members.

215/300 Energy
92/100 HP

Am I getting stronger? I've used up a lot of Energy for Controlled Transformation, but I was hardly hit in those scuffles back there. I even have a lot of Health as well.

With the increased stats, without a doubt, Gary was getting stronger, and he was able to think about the amount of Controlled Transformation he wanted to use. No longer did he have to adjust the slider, because he had been using it so much that he could control how much he wanted to transform one part of the body with just a thought.

Meanwhile, Gary had reached the second floor. He looked to his left and heard the sound of plates crashing. So the kitchen area was on the second floor.

There are more stairs. The leader wouldn't be here, would they? Gary thought.

As he took the first step up the staircase, he heard a scream.

"Stop . . . please stop! I don't want to do this!"

He ran toward the sound. It was clearly a girl's voice, and remembering the pain his sister had gone through, and the trouble that Stacy had gone through as well, he rushed to the door.

"You wanted to leave this work, right? Well, this is all you have to do. You've done it a hundred times before, so what's the problem?" a man's voice said.

It was locked, but kicking it open was easy, and Gary didn't care. But what he saw was worse than he had expected. In front of him stood a naked man, and a girl spread out on the bed, but they had also set up a camera in the room.

The girl was crying, her eyes full of tears, and there were more girls in the back of the room.

It sounded like the girls wanted to leave, and in order to leave they had to be filmed having sex with one of the gang members. A way to blackmail them if the gang ever needed something from them again, or needed them to keep secrets.

"Who the f*ck are you?" the man shouted, and ran toward Gary, throwing out a fist. Gary kicked him in the knee, knocking him down, and grabbed his head just before it touched the floor. He raised him up to his full height.

"The more I'm learning about this damned Pincers gang, the more I'm really starting to hate you all!" Gary shouted.

Skill activated: Controlled Transformation

Gary's hand turned into a claw with long, sharp fingernails. He swiped his hand low on the naked man's body, and everyone heard a small thud as a body part fell on the floor and blood splattered from it.

"You won't be needing that any more!" Gary yelled as he let go of the man. "If you want to live, go to the hospital. Everyone else, you are free to go! Get out of this place. The Howlers are taking over."

Gary didn't stay to see if the women were okay. He also didn't care to watch what the women might do to the man after he had left. Whatever it was, he felt like the man had it coming to him. There were no more distractions as the werewolf ascended the final staircase.

He entered a large wide hallway, and up ahead was a large double black door, bearing a picture of a crab and its two pincers. If Gary needed a sign telling him that he was in the right place, that certainly was it.

No one was guarding the door, but Gary heard voices on the other side. He slashed at the locks on the handles and pushed the heavy doors open to enter the main office.

On each side stood ten guards who all looked his way as soon as he entered, and at the very end was the Pincers gang's leader: a woman.

"Oh . . . we have an unexpected guest, I see," she said, smiling. Gary didn't know what he had expected to see, but it certainly wasn't a woman as the gang's boss. After all, her business involved mainly forcing women to do terrible things, but gangsters came in all different shapes and sizes.

"I guess our invader isn't very smart. I heard that someone had asked about us, so I was expecting an attack from one of the other gangs, but I've never seen you before, and you entered this room all on your own. In front of all these people?" the gang leader asked, thinking, of course, there was no way that a single person could survive what was about to happen.

All the men in the room pulled out knives. None of them had mere stun guns. Every single one had a weapon that could easily cause death.

Gary saw another woman in the room, shivering and frightened. Her skin was snow white, and she had bruises all over her body and cuts on her hands.

I think for the first time in a while . . . I've met someone who doesn't deserve to live.

Bloodlust has been detected
Forced Bond has been activated
7/8 Marks have been assigned

The red mist started to form in front of Gary's face, and it was leading straight to the Pincers' leader. She had become a hunting target, and there was only one way to remove the Mark . . .

CHAPTER 52

POOL OF BLOOD

It was rare for Burnham Street to have commotions during the day. After all, most of the visitors were just there to enjoy some yummy food. A big percentage consisted of families who visited the place unaware of what it really was . . . or at least looked the other way to the street's alternative business during the night.

However, today was a little different. Outside one of the most popular establishments, the Kraken, a crowd had formed, consisting of visitors, curious passersby, and nearby guards. They seemed to be watching the front entrance, while the customers who had just had their meals interrupted explained the situation inside.

Nini had asked to take a break, and given that there was barely anything happening, even less so with the commotion nearby, the shop allowed it. The news was starting to spread through the whole street. Some shops were even closing as the guards continued to flood toward one place. Nini ran down in her Chinese dress and saw the crowd outside the Kraken.

I can't believe it. They really went into that place? Are they just trying to get themselves killed? They barely made it out yesterday, so I thought they had learned their lesson, but they really went in there. It wasn't hard to guess who was inside, especially since she had recognized Austin earlier.

He and Gary had left quite an impression on her, yet she couldn't help but feel like it was impossible to do anything with so few people. Even if they had brought the others with them, they seemed so young, giving her the impression that they were all just delinquent teenagers who were playing with fire.

Still, she joined the crowd, who were all waiting for something to happen, curious who would come out . . . and in what state.

In the main office, Gary had just placed a Forced Bond on the Pincers' boss, and he had his eyes clearly set on the target. The only problem was she wasn't on her own. Around her were twenty-two of her goons, all of whom had knives.

"Screw all of you!"

Skill activated: Controlled Transformation
Strength 18 (+6)

Gary's hands started to change in front of their very eyes. He didn't just go halfway with his arms but all the way. His hands changed to claws, with visible fur. Seeing this, some of the guards stepped back a bit.

"He's an Altered! Be careful!"

"Another gang has an Altered in Slough? When did that happen? Did the Gray Elephants finally gather enough to pay for the operation to have someone to go up against Kirk?"

The gang's leader smiled.

"Now I see why you're so confident, but do you think I'm worried about that?" She reached under her desk, and the next moment she had a whip in her hands.

New Quest received
Into the Pincers' den
You have entered the Pincers' den, and you are trapped
Survive!

Quest reward: ???

Are you joking, system? You should be saying that to her!

Gary charged forward and swiped toward the man closest to him. The man retreated slightly and Gary's nails slashed his chest. Still, the werewolf was quite surprised that the gang member was somewhat able to avoid him.

Another gangster approached, and Gary tried to swipe him as well, but before his claws reached the man's chest, the whip lashed out and wrapped around his arm. It immediately pulled him down and the gangster's knife plunged into his side.

–8 HP
84/100 HP

Gary tried to move his hand, but the whip stayed firmly on him. He didn't understand how it hadn't snapped and how a woman could have enough strength to contend with him. He tried to claw the whip with his free hand . . . to no avail.

That's clearly no ordinary whip.

Using Controlled Transformation on his legs, Gary kicked away the next man with a knife, but the first knife was still in his body. With one of his hands occupied, the teenager decided to use his legs instead. As soon as the next goon came within range, he tried to kick him, but before he could the whip came undone and lashed around his leg, and the man with the knife successfully stabbed him right through his calf.

–7 HP
77/100 HP

Damn it, that whip is ruining my fighting flow! I can't allow them to keep hurting me like this!

As Gary tried to ignore the whip, he punched one of the gangsters in the face, and before he could claw at another the whip stopped him again. His next attacker managed to stab him in the chest.

The pain was immense and blood was dripping from his body.

–10 HP
67/100 HP

"Haha, you seem to have only recently become an Altered. I bet you thought that becoming one would make you king of the world, but you're just a frog in a well! You think I wouldn't have prepared something for the likes of you?

"We might be smaller than the big-time gangs, but we are still one of the wealthiest gangs in Slough. This little whip cost me a small fortune at the auction, but it's perfect to deal with things like you," the gang boss explained, as she went on a rampage with the whip.

Gary had only knocked out four of the men, and there were still plenty more, but they stood to the side as they let the whip do its work. It snapped, each time striking at a fast speed, and ripped across the werewolf's chest.

–4 HP

The whip was even faster than what he was used to, and he had attempted to grab it but failed as it only cut his hand.

–3 HP

Repeated lashes started to come out one after another, and stepping forward, trying to bear the pain, was all that Gary could do.

–4 HP
–5 HP

Why . . . why the hell do people like her get away with this crap? Where the fuck are the police? Where were they when Stacy died? Gary wondered in his fog of pain. Why was it up to him to deal with this mess?

A pool of blood was forming under his feet as his Health dropped lower and lower. The lashes eventually stopped, and all the men who had been patiently waiting charged forward to stab Gary from all directions.

–8 HP
–5 HP
–10 HP
–6 HP
–8 HP
–4 HP

Gary had been stabbed multiple times in multiple areas, and blood was pouring out of his wounds. It was hard to imagine how he was still standing as blood filled his mouth.

"Ah, it's such a shame. Here I thought an Altered would have put up more of a fight. You should have waited a couple of years before trying to challenge us. The men in here aren't like the regular guards that you fought on your way up here. Of course, the most skilled are here to protect me.

"Back in the day they were all the best fighters from their respective schools, and now after joining a gang and participating in fight after fight, well, you know the rest. Too bad, you never stood a chance."

Gary had thought during the fight that the men seemed more skilled. His speed usually would have been enough; it had certainly been the case for those down below. At least this meant that he wouldn't have to worry about Kai and the others.

The gang boss smiled in satisfaction as she approached the injured Altered. She looked at the silly mask on his face, and her men pulled their knives out.

"Let's see what's under that mask." She took it off, revealing Gary's face, his bright green hair, and his glowing yellow eyes.

"It's a shame you were born a boy. If you were a girl, I might have considered sparing you." She patted the side of his face.

What she didn't expect, though, was for Gary to look up and smile. Seeing this, she leapt back, dropping the mask, aware that something was wrong.

1/100 HP
Last Stand is activated (43 seconds remaining)

With all the knives coming toward him, Gary hadn't hesitated to use his newly acquired skill.

140/300 Energy

I guess they hurt me so fast that my body didn't even have time to use my energy for emergency healing, especially with the knives still in me, but it left me with plenty. Looks like picking Last Stand over the other two skills was the right choice after all, Gary muttered to himself, his eyes still on the woman, while the smile never left his face.

Skill activated: Full Transformation
–20 Energy
Transformation has begun

Gary's body started to change, and within seconds he had assumed his full-fledged werewolf form. The edges of his clothes still ripped a little, as they couldn't handle the complete change.

"Kill him!" the woman shouted as she lashed her whip out; it hit Gary, and he started to bleed.

–5 HP
1/100 HP
Last stand is still active (39 seconds remaining)

Alas, it had done nothing.

CHAPTER 53

AN EXPERIMENT

Although Gary was able to use Controlled Transformation to change only parts of his body to full werewolf form, there was a large difference in power between the two skills. His status also clearly showed that the stats gained overall were different.

Perhaps it was because Full Transformation changed his whole body, including his organs, rather than just parts of his body. Unfortunately, this skill not only cost a good bit of Energy, but it was also costly to upkeep, making it less than ideal for prolonged fights.

While Gary changed, the guards positioned themselves to protect their boss, but he wasn't aiming at her anyway. He quickly leapt on one of the gang members at her side and pinned him to the ground.

Skill activated: Claw Drain
–15 Energy

Gary started to rip at the man's chest as quickly as possible. Claw Drain lasted only two seconds, but the more damage he did, the more Health he would recover. The werewolf made the most of his time, managing to claw the man on the ground a total of six times.

+8 HP
+4 HP

+5 HP
+6 HP
+3 HP
+6 HP
33/100 HP
Last Stand is activated (25 seconds remaining)

During his attack, another gangster tried to stab him in the back, but his thick hide only allowed it to shallowly pierce him, causing a small nick. A regular knife wasn't going to do much, unlike an Altered Hunter's weapons.

–2 HP

Turning around, Gary whacked the man and easily sent him flying off in the other direction. He quickly ran through and overpowered the guards. Single hits from his large hands and kicks from his big feet were enough to knock them out in one or two blows.

Gary even activated his Claw Drain a second time, restoring his Health nearly to the halfway mark.

44/100 HP
70/300 Energy

The onslaught continued. As Gary took out the gang members, they tried to stab him, but because there were fewer of them, and the werewolf was faster, he was no longer getting hit.

Charging toward one of the few guards left, Gary leapt into the air, with his knee facing forward. While he was airborne, his body was reverting to human form.

Full Transformation canceled

Still, the speed he had gained while in his full form for a fraction of a second helped him as his knee smashed into the man's face, knocking him out.

Now there were only two guards left and the woman. The room was a complete mess, splattered with blood. The gang boss was frozen for the first time. She had been shaking and hadn't used the whip during the massacre.

"How?" she screamed. "How can you still be alive? They stabbed you over and over again! You were all but dead!"

The reason for her fear wasn't just what she had seen, but the fact that this person in front of her, who should have been dead, was still alive and very much kicking. Not only that, he was moving perfectly fine, to the point that he looked better than he had before.

His wounds were even healing in front of her. She had never heard of this before. It should be impossible for an Altered of this level to appear in a town like Slough.

One of the men dropped his knife out of fear, but Gary didn't let him off. He kneed him in the stomach, and when he doubled over, Gary kneed him in the face, making sure he got the punishment he deserved.

"You're a lot easier to deal with one on one. All of you are guilty . . . You tried to kill me just now, and you didn't even hesitate," Gary growled. "Not just me but the workers on this street, and you even killed Stacy!"

"Is that what this is all about?" The boss let out a mad laugh. "You came here because a whore died? Which one was it? I can give you plenty of other whores! Just take your pick! I can even send them all to you in our best suite!"

Turning his attention to the last remaining guard, Gary whacked the knife out of his hand and grabbed him by the neck, then ran forward toward the woman.

Out of fear she swung the whip, but Gary held up the man's body as a shield and shoved the body into her. She fell over backward next to her desk.

Quickly, Gary stepped on her wrist, twisting and turning his foot, until she finally let go of the whip.

"Do you have anything to say?" Gary asked.

She studied Gary's human face and noticed that he seemed quite young. He couldn't have been older than twenty.

I just can't believe it, my life ending like this because of one of those damned whores. Come on, kill me, get revenge for your damn whore... I used to be one of them, but I've managed to turn things around. You will learn that if you rid of me, your life won't be the same!

In her expression, Gary saw no guilt for what she had done, no fear of death as she had shown just a second ago. She seemed to have accepted it, which caused Gary's blood to boil more. He wanted her to suffer for the death she had caused, as well as for what she had done to girls like Stacy.

"Fine, I was going to kill you anyway."

Just as Gary was about to do so, he heard chattering teeth, and he looked up to see the snow-white girl facing the wall, shaking, with several whip marks on her back.

It was easy to put two and two together; Gary could guess who had done it.

"No, just killing you would be giving you an easy way out," Gary decided. "I doubt this girl was the only one you treated like this. Do you even think of them as human beings at this point? Using them as you wish ... Were you really one of them? Whatever, it just means you only deserve what comes next. I'm going to use you to make up for it!"

The gang boss started to laugh like a madwoman.

"So what, you're going to rape me? Go ahead! It's not like it hasn't happened before!"

"Rape? No, I have no interest in doing that to you."

Skill activated: Controlled Transformation

Gary had activated the Controlled Transformation for a body part he hadn't transformed before; his mouth started to change slightly, and his teeth began to grow.

"You treated the others with no respect, so you're going to become my little experiment!"

Gary lifted her off the ground, and before she realized it, he bit right into the back of her neck.

CHAPTER 54

AN ALPHA WOLF
IS BORN

Recently Gary had occasionally thought about turning others. For example, when Mr. Root was in critical condition, turning him would have saved his life. In the end, his coach's condition had stabilized and he was recovering at the hospital.

Perhaps because of what had happened with Mr. Root, he had believed the same would happen with Stacy. Now, though, he felt like he had made the wrong decision. Turning her to save her might have been the right choice.

At the same time, in this business, they were bound to run into more Altered or creatures like the red-haired twins. Gary wasn't the only one in the gang, and already the others had put their lives on the line.

Which meant that more strength for everyone was a plus; Gary saw it every time he talked to Kai. It was on the tip of his tongue to ask him: why not turn him?

A werewolf and an Altered were different, and because of fantasy books and other resources, many people knew the difference between the two. Gary was a werewolf, not an Altered; the test by the White Rose agents had proved that. Unlike the Altered, Gary could pass on his power to others.

When Gary thought about why he had hesitated in the past, he realized that his main reason was Billy. But Billy was the first, and unstable. He didn't even know he was a werewolf until later.

The real reason why Gary had yet to consider turning others was that he had no information.

He did not know what would happen to anyone that he turned, what it meant to accept them into his pack, and whether he could control them during a full moon. The one thing he didn't want to do was test this idea on people he wanted to save. So Gary had an idea.

A person whose life he didn't care about had fallen right into his lap, and she was the perfect test subject to see just what it actually meant to turn someone.

His teeth sank into the back of her neck, and she screamed in pain. The sound was so piercing that the people on the floor below might have heard her, but it soon stopped. It took all of Gary's willpower to stop biting her because of the Energy he had lost before, but he pulled his mouth away.

The second he let go, her body started shaking on the floor. Her veins were popping all over her neck as something inside felt like it was ripping her apart.

If she proves to be too much trouble, I'll kill her and get the Pawn point anyway. I'll give her until the next full moon. That is . . . if she survives this.

Judging by how much she was wriggling about in pain, how bloodshot her eyes were, Gary wasn't sure if every person could survive such a thing, but eventually the system screen appeared.

You have successfully created a Beta Werewolf (Grade: Pawn)

"A beta werewolf, not an omega werewolf? So it's different from Billy?"

Werewolves created by the user can only be at the same grade as the creator or below

A werewolf created at a lower grade than you will automatically join the pack
Werewolves created at the same grade will turn into omega werewolves

When Gary first bit Billy, he himself had only been a Pawn-grade werewolf, even though he hadn't known that yet. Which meant no matter who he turned they would always become an omega wolf, but this time it was different since he had evolved into Knight grade.

An Omega Werewolf can join the pack by willingly submitting to you, or after you defeat him

Gary knew at least the latter option to be true, since he had received that option after defeating Billy.

Congratulations, your state has changed: Omega Werewolf →
Alpha Werewolf
Alpha Werewolf title will now be applied
Please select a name for your pack

It looked like Gary couldn't do anything else or see information from the system until he picked a name. He wanted to know what benefits this title had; he was sure it had some, as stated the last time he was upgraded.

Looking through the screen, he saw that the woman he'd bitten was passed out on the ground, but she was clearly alive, as he could hear a heartbeat. Which meant he had time to mess around with the system for a little while longer.

The Howlers

Gary chose this name since it was already the name of their current gang. Having two names would just confuse him anyway.

The Howlers pack has successfully been created

Current members
Alpha Werewolf: Gary Dem
Grade: Knight
Beta Werewolf: Olivia Pearl
Grade: Pawn
The Luna position is currently empty
A Luna Werewolf holds the same position as the Alpha Werewolf
Having a Luna Werewolf will create more benefits for the entire pack
There is currently no one suitable for the Luna position
The Luna Werewolf has to be a female werewolf at the same grade as the Alpha Werewolf

So much information about this pack stuff was coming to Gary at once; it seemed like what he thought he knew about the system was only the tip of the whole thing.

"So that means that Olivia should also be able to increase her grade . . . somehow. And if she's the same grade as me, she might fulfill this Luna position. But if I'm reading this correctly, it means she would hold a position similar to mine, kind of like a subcaptain on a team. That I definitely don't want."

For a split second, he pictured the image of another girl who he thought might do well in the position.

Pack members can increase their grades but are unable to grow beyond their Alpha

Only now, Gary was starting to understand how important the Pawn point had been. If he was able to upgrade himself, then all those under him could grow as well. He still was unsure if there were other benefits to going up a grade.

"System, since you seem awfully chatty today, I was wondering, does this mean that pack members can create other werewolves as well?"

Pack members can create other werewolves, but they will only produce werewolves of a lower grade than themselves
All werewolves created this way will automatically become pack members as well
Pawn-grade werewolves are unable to create other werewolves

"Huh, but then what about me?" At least it looked like Olivia wouldn't be able to turn people for now, but then what the system stated made no sense to him.

Gary waited for an answer, but none came. He wondered if increasing the grade did anything else. For now, it looked like it was just a way to control other werewolves and to get strong omega werewolves to join his pack.

What was the benefit of that, though, unless Gary created his own werewolf army—unless that was exactly what the system wanted him to do?

I'm starting to worry a little . . . is there someone else with the same system as me? I did get it from that suitcase, after all. If there are other werewolves, they probably already have people under them, growing their forces.

It's a little scary to think that way. It's almost like if a werewolf belongs to another pack, then that immediately makes you their enemy. Is that why the system is focusing on this so much?

In the middle of his thoughts, the system came up with one more notification.

Beta Werewolves will always follow the order of their Alpha
Once in a pack, they cannot leave unless the Alpha permits it
Pack members are able to challenge the Alpha for his position once a month, regardless of their grade
There is an exception to all rules, and that is on the day when the moon is at its strongest

The last line worried Gary quite a bit. Was it saying that on the day of the full moon, werewolves were just wild beasts? Even if he ordered them to do nothing, they would still hunt anyway?

I guess I really might have to get rid of her before then . . . or lock her up or something? Gary thought.

Please establish the five absolute rules for your pack
These will be the rules all pack members must follow, whether the Alpha is present or not
The rules do not apply to the Alpha Werewolf
The rules may be adjusted through the system whenever the Alpha wishes

A big smile appeared on Gary's face; this was the safety net he needed. He still needed to know just how absolute these rules were, but he could test that. After all, she was his experiment for all of this.

The question is, what should I have as the rules?

PACK RULES

The system had opened up a special screen for Gary. At the top were the words *Howlers Pack Rules* and underneath that were the numbers one to five, waiting to be filled in. The new alpha werewolf was happy to see that he only had to think of a rule to automatically add it to the list. It was just as easy to change their order, though he wasn't yet sure if it made any difference.

Depending on the rule he chose, the system displayed it in red, yellow, or green text. Fortunately, the system was still being helpful, so it explained the colors. Red meant that what he proposed could not be made into a rule, yellow meant it was too vague, and green meant it was acceptable as a rule.

Gary spent a bit of time testing the rules before deciding on them. According to the system, he could adjust the rules as he wished at any point, as long as he stayed the alpha werewolf of the pack. Finally, he had five rules for his pack to follow.

1. No member of the pack is allowed to hurt the members of the Howlers gang, their relatives, or their friends.

Gary had decided to make this the first rule, in case the order actually mattered. This way, he didn't need to worry about Kai and the others getting hurt or his own family getting in trouble. If Olivia was unable to take revenge on him personally, he was sure they would become her next target.

2. No member of the pack may kill another human without the Alpha Werewolf's permission, unless they are in a life-or-death situation.

Gary was proud that he had come up with the idea of adjusting the second half of this rule and that the system allowed it. Being a werewolf meant that others would seek to kill them. As if that weren't bad enough, as gang members, it wouldn't be rare for them to go out and fight.

For this reason, Gary had chosen *kill* rather than *hurt*; but this way it would stop Olivia from hunting down random people or those she had some type of grudge against without permission.

3. No member of the pack is to betray the Howlers gang in any way, shape, or form.

This third rule was essential, and to be honest, Gary was quite surprised that the Werewolf System had actually allowed it to pass. He was hoping, although unsure, that this rule would cover a lot of bases. He was unsure how these rules would be enforced. He could only imagine it as a sort of spell making his members behave a certain way.

If Olivia felt like her actions were betraying the Howlers gang, then she shouldn't be able to do it. That was how he hoped it would work, anyway. Otherwise, after he left her, although she might be unable to do anything herself, she could easily go to the Underdogs or other gangs and inform them about what had happened here.

4. No member of the pack is to create other werewolves without the Alpha Werewolf's permission.

This rule seemed like a no-brainer. There was still so much for Gary to figure out about his system, and there was no reason to add more problems.

5. Every member of the pack must kneel when entering due to the Alpha Werewolf's presence.

The last one wasn't a real rule he intended to keep. It was simply a test to see if the rules truly worked. Once he confirmed that, he was planning to change it into: *No member of the pack is to tell anyone about what they really are, nor to spread word about the existence of werewolves.*

Gary looked over and noticed that Olivia hadn't woken up yet. He went to pick up his mask to cover his face. Even though the Pincers had already seen him without it, for some reason Gary felt more comfortable when he had it on. He noticed that some unconscious guards were twitching in pain, while others had outright been killed, not that he had much sympathy for them.

Heading back to the desk, he approached the snow-white girl, who still faced the other way. She had covered her eyes, not wishing to see the bloodbath . . . which was probably the best choice she could have made.

"Hey, do you mind stepping outside for a moment? I should have taken care of all of those who were outside, but just scream if anything bad happens. I just need some time alone with the person who was responsible for all of it."

The girl was still startled, and the mask didn't really help her calm down. Still, the voice of this stranger was far more inviting than staying here with the Pincers. As she started to leave, her arms wrapped around herself, Gary sighed and took off his blazer, putting it over her shoulders. She flinched at first, but then gladly accepted it.

"I'm sorry it's a little ripped, but it will do for now. I'll try not to be too long." With that, the girl finally left the room, and just in time, as the gangster boss seemed to be getting up from her daze.

Olivia's head was pounding, and she felt way worse than the last time she had an extreme hangover. For a second, she wondered if everything that had happened had just been a dream, a nightmare. Unfortunately, when she looked around her office, she saw the masked boy standing in the bloody room, and all her guards lying on the floor.

"You!" was Olivia's first word as she pointed toward the masked intruder. However, unaware of what came over her, the next moment she found herself on her knees in front of him. It felt like a command had been issued to her head and she was unable to stand up.

And she noticed something else. The burning anger she had been experiencing just seconds ago seemed to be fading. Still, when she looked around the room, it added fuel to the fire.

"Your eyes . . . they're glowing," Gary noted as he approached her.

"So are yours," Olivia replied, staring at him angrily.

Gary touched his mask, unaware that sometimes when he transformed, his eyes would glow yellow. However, now that he was an alpha, the color of his eyes had changed to red, whereas Olivia's eyes had changed to blue, indicating she was a beta in a pack.

He was happy to see her kneeling, especially since she seemed unable to stand up on her own. It made him believe that the rules were really working as intended. He couldn't imagine that Olivia would be doing that willingly, not after everything that had transpired.

He opened the system and went into the new Pack tab to change the fifth rule. As soon as he had saved the change, Olivia could stand once again. Out of the corner of her eye, she noticed the whip, and she immediately made a run for it.

"Stop!" Gary shouted, and midsprint the woman halted.

CHAPTER 56

A CHALLENGE TO THE ALPHA

"What have you done to me? What are you?" Olivia cried, noticing that her body refused to listen to her. She had been confused as to why she had knelt in front of Gary, but this time there was no doubt in her mind that he must have done something to her to make her listen. And whatever it was . . . it seemed to have done a lot more than just make her obedient.

He noticed that while she remained in position, her eyes darted around the surrounding bodies. He also didn't miss her licking her lips as she looked over them. However, she couldn't approach them and do the one thing she obviously wished to do.

"I see . . . you must be weak, tired . . . and hungry, right? I guess I can't blame you when you wake up surrounded by . . . such a sight. All right, go ahead. Eat your own people."

After he said these words, she didn't know what came over her, but Olivia went to the closest dead guard and chomped down on his arm. She had hesitated for only a second, but her thoughts left her head as the taste filled her mouth with desire.

Gary theorized that Olivia must be low on Energy, meaning she desperately needed food. Because of the pack rules, she was unable to kill unless he gave his permission, so this might be the only chance she would get to do such a thing since they were already dead. Allowing her to follow her instincts was also the perfect way to make it clear that she was no longer completely human.

Seeing her in this state further strengthened Gary's theory that a newly turned werewolf was no different from him, when he had starved himself on the night of the full moon. He also remembered that after he had first turned, the Werewolf System had greeted him with a message that his bloodlust had been lowered.

Although Gary had avoided thinking about it, he was sure of it now. The men who had stabbed him when he had the package, the ones who had ended up dead the next day . . . the Underdogs weren't the ones who had killed them.

"You're now like me," Gary explained as he moved in closer and whispered in her ear. "You are a werewolf, and you're under my control. I'm sure you can already tell and feel it." He walked away, allowing that information to settle in.

After satisfying her hunger, Olivia stopped eating. She had regained her Energy and was only now realizing what she had just done.

"I wasn't joking when I said you would be my little experiment. However, we're not done yet. I still have other tests I need to do," Gary told her. "Now tell me, do you have a system of some sort? Are you able to change or use any skills?"

Since Blake had killed Billy before Gary could ask him any questions, he had lost his chance to learn more about other werewolves. It remained a mystery whether the Werewolf System was exclusive to him, or if everyone he had turned might gain something similar to it.

Turning around, though, Olivia stood up, her eyes glowing blue, filled with anger.

The Beta Werewolf (Olivia Pearl) has initiated a challenge for your position as Alpha Werewolf

Oh, I didn't think that would happen this soon.

Gary wasn't surprised at this turn of events; after all he had turned the Pincers' gang leader against her will. He had expected that this challenge would come sooner than later, but all of it was still within his calculations.

As a newly turned werewolf, Olivia had only just gotten her first taste of human flesh. Gary wasn't even sure if it had been enough to fill up her Energy, and even if she did gain a stat point because of it, there was no way she would be as strong as Billy. It would be informative to learn if she even had any clues about the powers of her changed body, or if he would have to teach her.

"Let's get this challenge over and done with, shall we?"

Gary ran toward Olivia; he could see her hands going for him, but only a little faster than before. Without her annoying whip, she didn't pose any challenge whatsoever, and it looked like she was unable to change into her werewolf form.

On the other hand, Gary had used Controlled Transformation on his arms, just in case. He knocked hers out of the way and punched her in her gut. Still, he refrained from using his claws because he didn't want to risk leaving a fatal wound on her . . . not yet, anyway.

As she doubled over from the powerful blow, Gary grabbed her head and slammed it down, leaving a dent in the floor as he covered her mouth.

"Just because you're like me doesn't mean you stand a chance against me. You should be aware that I can still beat you anytime I want. I hope we have our positions clear with each other." Gary smiled.

Congratulations, you have retained your seat as Alpha
Beta Werewolf (Olivia Pearl) will be unable to initiate another
challenge until the next month

Gary let go of Olivia's mouth, and she stood up; her head hurt, but not as much as she had imagined. Since it was clear she didn't quite understand the situation, Gary decided to fill her in. He didn't go into too much detail, refraining from telling her how he himself had become a werewolf. He focused on explaining what a werewolf was, and what would change now that she was one too, such as her having to follow a certain set of rules.

He listed all the rules he had entered into the system, and Olivia nodded along. She had already discovered that something was controlling her mind, and her body was telling her that these were indeed the rules a beta werewolf had to live by.

Gary felt like it was easier this way, if she at least knew what she was now and what rules not to disobey. When he repeated his question about the system, she wasn't aware what he meant, so he described it as a message that floated in midair, similar to a computer program. Olivia found this question quite strange, but she shook her head.

There were a lot of questions the two wanted to ask each other, but Gary decided they would save that for later. He hadn't forgotten that he hadn't come alone, and he was worried about the others.

"Follow me . . . I need you to stop your men downstairs," Gary instructed her, and Olivia started walking behind him like a loyal dog, her head held down. She felt humiliated, defeated, and worst of all, she didn't know if this was because of her having become a beta werewolf or if those were her true feelings. Either way, Olivia felt like she had become Gary's slave.

Exiting the door, Gary saw that the snow-white girl was waiting for him just outside. It didn't seem like anybody else had come in, which he took as a good sign.

At the same time, a message had appeared, informing him that he had completed the quest, but he just closed it and planned to check out the rewards a bit later.

"Come on, we're getting out of here," Gary told the girl, who hesitated when she saw Olivia come out. However, since the woman ignored her, and the girl was scared of being left alone, she followed behind them, though with some distance.

Gary couldn't imagine what the girl had been through. If he hadn't come in, he was sure she might have ended up like Stacy . . . but how many had he failed to save? Thinking about the women he had met on the lower floor, he was getting angrier by the second.

Honestly, he didn't know how much longer he could allow Olivia to stay alive.

CHAPTER 57

SPREADING THE NAME

"You know . . . it wasn't always like thi—"

"Shut up!" Gary grabbed Olivia's mouth before she could say anything else. "I don't care what your reason for joining a gang was. I don't want to know what possible justification you might have come up with. At the end of the day, you're involved in this shitty business!

"You hurt this poor girl behind you, as well as countless others! Because of your scummy ways, Stacy ended up here, and died, and someone I truly care about is devastated at her loss! So don't you dare make any excuses! If I hear so much as a peep from you without my permission, I'll rip out your tongue and see if it regrows!"

Olivia nodded. She wasn't going to say anything else. At first she had believed that the teenage boy might be naive based on his actions. She had taken him for someone who didn't know how the gang world worked, but he surely was acting like a gangster right now. Worst of all, she was convinced that his threat wasn't empty.

Heading down the stairs, Gary saw that at least Marie was safe; her Mark was still fully visible. But when he came down he was surprised at the scene below. Everyone was knocked out . . . including the rest of the Howlers.

"Guys!" Gary shouted, and as if answering his call, the four of them shot up from the water.

"Ah, Gary!" Kai waved at him. "We were just taking a break. The water is nice and cool."

The boys had sustained a few injuries here and there, but apart from some cuts, all of them seemed to be in good condition. None of them had been seriously hurt, and Gary couldn't help but smile.

"Hey, weren't you supposed to defeat the leader? Why have you brought two pretty girls down with you?" Innu complained, as he pointed to Olivia and the woman behind her.

"What do you mean? She is the leader," Gary said with a grin.

The four shared a look of confusion until Olivia went to the closed door and ordered the men behind it to stand down. Still confused, the Howlers were led to a different office on the second floor, away from the unconscious men who might wake up.

Gary didn't explain a lot to Kai and the others, just that Olivia and the gang known as the Pincers were no longer. She would now be part of the Howlers instead. Of course the question came up about how they could trust her, but Kai already had an idea.

Like a devout servant, the former boss simply led them to another office, a small room hidden behind a contraption. She pulled a few books off a shelf, making a safe appear.

"Open it," Gary ordered, and of course Olivia did as she had been told without any resistance. The others couldn't believe it. Just what could their leader have done in such a short amount of time to make Olivia obey his every word? Still, it was the best result that they could hope for out of this whole event.

When they looked in the safe, Innu and Austin were expecting a bunch of cash, but instead it was just a bunch of papers, and by the look on their faces they were clearly disappointed.

"O ye of little faith, this is a lot better than cash. This here is everything that the Pincers owned! We will be taking all of this, and Olivia here will sign it all over to the new company known as the Howlers Ltd.," Kai explained with a giant grin on his face.

"You see, gangs have to operate between the fine line of being legal and illegal, and with several signatures . . . we will legally gain ownership of all the restaurants on Burnham Street!"

When the rest of the Howlers heard these words, dollar signs shone in their eyes. This wasn't just protection money for small businesses like the Wolf's Pool Club. Based on what they could see, the actual shop space was owned by the Pincers. They would make a hefty profit not only through a percentage of the restaurant's earnings, but also from the real estate and rent!

The process would take a few days, but Olivia had agreed to hand everything over.

"The place will still be run by Olivia," Gary pointed out, which shocked a lot of them, but he wasn't finished. "However, we're going to make a few things clear. After today, the Pincers will no longer exist. This entire street belongs to the Howlers, and we are at the top of the gang. The members from before can decide to stay or not, but Olivia will make it clear she is no longer the leader."

The others gulped when Gary said this.

"If anyone asks who owns this street, it's now the Howlers. If someone attacks this place, then it's them making an attack on us! However, we are going to change a few things here. The red-light district can continue running, but I have conditions.

"Anyone who wants to leave is free to leave; they will not be forced to work here. That includes all those whose parents you have tricked into debt! Under no conditions is anyone underage allowed to work here, even if they want to, and we will be breaking all contact with anyone who is looking to traffic girls to this place! I don't want to be involved with them."

"Are you crazy?" Olivia finally spoke up for the first time. "If you do all that, then we'll be lucky if we can retain even half our current earnings! Are you really a gangster? Don't you understand any of this? What about paying all the guards? Half of them will leave if you pay them peanuts!"

Gary gave her a look, and Olivia soon sat back down.

"People like you really make me sick. So what if profits drop? Doesn't that mean we'll still end up with a gain? You know what, just hand everything over to Kai so he can deal with the paperwork. If I contact you or Kai does, you have to answer. You better start making the changes to the place, and make sure everyone knows about it!"

Alas, there was nothing she could do; Olivia had to obey because it was an order from the alpha werewolf. By now, she knew she couldn't fight against it; her body was already rushing her to do the job.

The news that the Pincers gang no longer existed quickly spread throughout Slough. Naturally, all the gangs had learned that there was a new group in town known as the Howlers.

Now everyone was looking forward to how the big-time gangs would react to that . . .

CHAPTER 58

REWARDS FOR THE ALPHA

The crowd around the Kraken had yet to disperse. The people were still curious about what was taking place, and the guards were starting to get concerned themselves. They wondered if they should just barge in, especially since there had been no noise for a while. All fighting had stopped. They had been told that only a handful of teenagers had entered. Those inside should have long since dealt with the troublemakers and resumed business, so what was taking so long?

Eventually the doors opened, and standing in front of them all was Olivia Pearl.

"Oh, I didn't expect there to be such a large crowd of people here. Are all the other restaurants filled to the brim?" Olivia said with a smirk. She was wearing the same outfit as before, and she had cleared up the marks on her body. There had been a lump on the back of her head, but the swelling soon went away, much more quickly than normal.

So those who were seeing her believed that she was the same as she had always been.

Seeing who had come out, though, Nini felt herself sulking.

I knew it . . . those guys couldn't do anything. That damned big guy was just all talk . . . I just hope they didn't . . .

In the middle of her thoughts, Nini saw the group with the black-and-gold blazers leave the establishment. They walked straight past Olivia, and the guards looked at them with menacing glances, confused. Several guards looked like they were ready to jump the intruders.

"Let them go!" Olivia snapped before anyone could move. "Everyone, the show is over. The Kraken will reopen this evening; until then please enjoy yourselves elsewhere. Guards, tell the managers that all of them are to gather at the Kraken in thirty minutes. Spread the news, and apologize to our dear customers."

The guards didn't move at first, until Olivia stomped her foot on the ground.

"Are you deaf? What do I pay you for? Get back to your workplace and do as you've been told!" she shouted, and soon everyone got a move on.

There was blood covering the clothes of those who had left the place. It was hard to imagine what had occurred inside, and the scene left many confused. In the meantime, Olivia had a lot of work to do. There was a lot to clean up, and she had to spread the news that the Pincers had been taken over by the Howlers.

The current workers of the establishment were left in the dark, but they too would soon be informed of the changes, especially to their nighttime activities.

The Howlers had finally reached the bus stop; Gary had removed his mask and slumped onto the bench, while the others did the same.

"Did all of that just really happen? . . . Did we actually just manage to take over a gang?" Marie asked.

Each one of them was looking through the glass above them at the clouds floating by. It had been an hour or so since they had entered the Kraken, and then another hour to clear things up, so it still wasn't evening outside, and the sky was blue.

"We did," Kai answered. "It looks like I created a lot of work for myself, but I thought this would happen, and after today, you might start to hear our name being spread around a lot more."

"Does this mean my money problems are finally over?" Gary asked.

Everyone chuckled, as that seemed to be the only thing on the mind of their leader.

"I'll have to look at our finances after this, but I can safely say you won't have to worry about your personal expenses, at least. However, remember as the gang gets bigger there are more costs, more people to pay, and this is just a Tier 3 town. We are still a ways off from being anywhere near the top of the food chain."

Gary knew that the Underdogs and the Gray Elephants were in control of Slough, and both of them had their reasons to hunt him. Although he couldn't bring Stacy back from the dead, he could focus on protecting others from this mess from now on.

"I couldn't have done it without you, system." Gary smiled as he decided to look at his quest reward.

Congratulations! You have set a new world record for surviving stab wounds.

Keep it up, and you'll be able to hug a cactus without a second thought.

Endurance +2

Quest reward: Instant Level Up

Congratulations, you have now reached: Level 16

A stat point has been granted

Optional Quest (Start your own family): complete

Quest reward: 1 Pawn point

Depending on the grade of the werewolf added to the family, more Pawn points will be given

During the constant notifications, Gary had somehow managed to miss that he had completed the quest that was given to him when he first realized he had turned Billy. It was a new way to gain Pawn points, which seemed to be the most precious of them all.

Still, it wasn't an easy way, but at least easier than killing other werewolves. Gary focused on the other things as well.

Figures, just when I compliment you, you try to put me down. All right, if you really want to keep up this strange relationship, that's fine with me, Gary thought as he inwardly rolled his eyes. *It's a shame that I didn't get the extra stat point for making Olivia a hunting target, but it looks like I got better things.*

The message from the system did put things into perspective. Fighting against a gang, even if it was just small-time, was a far bigger risk than Gary had initially thought. He had believed that with his werewolf form and current skill set, they should have been able to take on the Pincers, but the truth was that without the Last Stand skill, he might have died today.

Fortunately, everything had turned out well and he had received good rewards from the system. His stats had even balanced out once again.

Name: Gary Dem
Class: Warrior
State: Human (Alpha)
Grade: Knight
Level 16
Exp 796/3002
Health 100/100
Energy 42/300
Strength 18
Dexterity 18
Endurance 18
1 stat point unassigned
1 Pawn point available

"Stats, Skills, Health, Energy, I really need to improve them all . . . and then I also might have to look into getting my grade up as well. I have a feeling the system didn't explain all the benefits of going up a grade. I could use some of those from the Pincers that tried to stab me . . . but it still feels wrong to me. For now, let's see what exactly those title benefits include."

Title: Alpha Werewolf of the Howlers Pack

CHAPTER 59

THE ALPHA TITLE

Title: Alpha Werewolf of the Howlers Pack

Howling Force (Alpha skill—Level 1)

When activated, the Alpha lets out a howl to energize nearby members of his pack

Level 1: 10% overall stat boost

The skill will take 0 points of Energy to use.

Skill duration: 15 minutes

Skill reset time: 1 hour

Alpha Bite (Alpha skill)

When activated, the Alpha uses a special bite to attempt to turn a target.

An Alpha's bite has a higher chance of successfully turning a person into a werewolf

The higher the Alpha's grade, the higher the chance of creating a higher-grade werewolf.

The skill will take 0 points of Energy to use.

Skill reset time: 1 week

Wait, "attempt"? "Higher chance"? Do you want to tell me that just biting someone isn't guaranteed to turn them? So what happens if a bite doesn't turn them into a werewolf?"

Although the system didn't answer, based on what he had seen Olivia go through, Gary could predict the answer.

Pack ruler (Alpha passive skill)
The Alpha will gain 10% of the experience his Beta Werewolves earn during their hunts and kills
Should a Beta Werewolf kill a hunting target marked by the Alpha, both werewolves will enjoy the benefits

The skills and effects earned by becoming an Alpha seemed promising, but they only seemed useful if Gary were to create more beta werewolves. In a way, the more betas he gained, the more quickly he would get stronger. It seemed similar to a pyramid scheme, with Gary at the top leeching off all the others below him.

Once again, it looked like the system was incentivizing him to turn as many people as possible into werewolves. However, after finding out that there was no actual guarantee that it would work, Gary was a lot more hesitant to do that.

Given pack rule number four, I don't have to worry about Olivia trying to turn anyone, and maybe now that it's an actual skill I can use my teeth in combat without having to worry too much about the potential consequences.

There were times when the werewolf had wished to use his large mouth. After all, it was yet another natural weapon, yet he had suppressed that desire for fear of creating more Billys.

"Hey, Gary," Innu said as they all observed the scene below. "What shall we do about your girlfriend over there?"

"Girlfriend?" Gary turned around in confusion, wondering how and when Xin had appeared. Although they weren't officially a couple yet, since he had yet to set up a date, he didn't know who else Innu could be referring to.

However, the only person there apart from the Howlers was the young woman with the snow-white skin. She had changed clothes after Olivia had given her something to wear, and Gary had gotten back his blazer.

"Hey, what are you still doing here? You can go home now, there's no need for you to stay in the streets." Gary spoke to her in a gentle voice. She looked fragile and pale, even though he suspected that she must be older than him. Still, after seeing what she had endured, he didn't want to be harsh to the frightened young woman.

"I don't have anywhere to go," she said. "My parents are dead . . . they killed themselves, because they were unable to pay off a large debt they had accrued. One of those guys came to collect, but since there was nothing of value, they brought me here . . . I have nowhere else to go."

The others looked at each other awkwardly, and Gary didn't really know what to do. Was she expecting him to help her out? Wasn't this a situation that the police would usually deal with?

Just then Marie received a text on her phone.

Erghh, Gary, I think we might have a small issue on our hands. My mom just informed me that your bald-headed friend and your sister are at the pool club.

The bus driver had hesitated a bit before he allowed the Howlers to hop in, since their clothes were stained with blood. Only after Kai explained that they had been working on a film project did the driver let them board. However, Gary suspected that the extra twenty Kai had tipped the man might have played a major part in convincing him.

Unlike before, this time there were six of them on the bus. The small, frail young woman sat next to Gary. She had refused to sit next to anybody else, and Marie felt a little annoyed at her behavior, though ultimately she had given up her seat as she looked into the woman's pleading eyes.

Since they were sitting next to each other, and the ride from Burnham back to the Wolf's Pool Club wasn't a short one, Gary had asked her a few questions. The rescued woman introduced herself simply as White, which might just have been her nickname, but it was quite fitting.

Gary also found out that White had only turned twenty a few months ago. She had only recently started to attend university to become a teacher, which coincidentally seemed to have been the reason her parents had borrowed money from the Pincers gang.

"I have answered all your questions. So I think it's fair that you answer one of mine," White replied after a while, as she stared directly into Gary's eyes. "Why didn't you kill her?"

Luckily, the group were at the back of the bus, and it was relatively empty apart from a granny who had entered the bus at some point and was staying at the front. However, the rest of the Howlers certainly heard the question and were just as interested to know what had happened.

Wait a minute? Did White see me bite her? She was too scared to look and turned around, right? Gary tried to remember. *Yeah, that has to be the case, otherwise she wouldn't have asked why I didn't kill her.*

"I heard you say you were going to experiment on her," White continued.

Innu started coughing. He remembered seeing the Pincers' leader's provocative clothing, and when he heard someone saying they would experiment on her, his mind went to dirty places.

"White . . . it seems that you have heard a lot, but let me explain. We're just a small-time gang. In fact, everyone you see here is the entire gang. We might have taken out the ones inside the Kraken, but you've seen how many guards there were outside the other restaurants.

"Without her telling them off, those other members of the Pincers gang would have surely come after us. I needed to . . . get her on our side," Gary explained, and he thought that would be the end of it.

The look on White's face showed that she wasn't pleased with the answer.

"If it had been up to me . . . I would have killed her in a second," White mumbled, looking out the window. Honestly, Gary couldn't blame her . . . especially since part of him still wanted Olivia dead. Alas, right now, it was more beneficial to keep her alive.

Why are there so many troublesome girls? And now I have to deal with my sister as well.

CHAPTER 60

A WORSE SECRET

Eventually, the group arrived at the Wolf's Pool Club. Their clothes were still covered in blood, since none of them had brought along a change of clothes, which worried Gary . . . nearly as much as what he was supposed to do with White.

Taking a deep breath, Gary prepared what he would say as he entered the place. Opening the doors, he saw Amy and Tom at the bar talking to Miss Degrace. They immediately turned their heads.

Hopping down from her barstool, Amy ran over to her brother, yet before giving him a big hug, she stopped, checking him from top to bottom, before asking the obvious.

"Gary . . . is that blood?"

Too many thoughts were going through her head, and the same was true for Tom. Still, his heart settled down somewhat when he saw that the rest also had bloody clothes. Whatever might have happened, at least they made it out alive.

"Ah, don't worry about this," Kai explained with a smile. "We were just making a promo shoot for this place. I know it's a bit early for Halloween, but we'll need time to edit things before we upload it. Hopefully it will get us more customers."

Tom was quite satisfied with the explanation, and Gary was happy that Kai had taken over. He seemed to be better at lying than Gary was, that was for sure.

However, Amy didn't quite buy it, and seeing the blood on Gary's clothes reminded her of the blood she had already seen in his closet. The shady place, what had happened to those people, and now this, especially after hearing Miss Degrace talk: she really didn't know what to think anymore. She looked Gary up and down suspiciously, and studied the rest of them with a wrinkle in her forehead.

"Looks like you guys have some catching up to do," Kai said, patting Gary on the shoulder. "I'll be downstairs looking over a few things. If you need anything you can call me."

"I need to get out of these clothes before someone calls the police," Innu said, making a swift exit.

"What's that, Mum, you need help with counting the stock?" Marie randomly shouted, and walked off.

Austin just walked past the remaining two people without saying anything.

I see now, you've all left me, the only one who has stayed by my side is White, and it would be better if she left. Gary was inwardly slapping his forehead.

"Amy, what are you doing here?" he asked, snapping her out of her thoughts.

Amy and Tom looked at each other before answering. They were planning to learn a bit more about what Gary was doing. For one, Tom wanted his best friend to come clean to his sister about his werewolf tendencies; he thought she already knew about them and had questions. But Tom had something else he wanted to ask him.

However, their earlier curiosity had diminished after their talk with Miss Degrace.

Earlier in the day, they both had sat down near the bar since the place wasn't as busy yet. Tom was expecting to see the others or maybe even Gary himself, but he was nowhere to be seen.

"Oh, you're that boy who took me to the hospital before. It's Tom, right? I'm afraid I didn't yet have time to properly thank you.

Can I make it up to you by offering you and your date free drinks?" Miss Degrace suggested with a friendly smile.

She seemed to have mistaken the relationship between the two teenagers, not that Tom was going to correct her . . . and not that he needed to anyway, because Amy did just that the next moment herself.

"I'm not his girlfriend, I only came here because I wanted to talk to my brother," Amy clarified. She showed no fear even in front of this person who was practically a stranger to her. "You know my brother is only sixteen, right? So why do you have him working in a place like this? I know it's legal, but this place serves alcohol, right? And he's not allowed to handle cash."

"Do you have him doing other things for you as well?" She might not have stated it clearly, but Miss Degrace understood what the teenage girl was accusing her of. Given the location of the Wolf's Pool Club, Amy felt like it was only a question of time until her brother would get into trouble.

Tom wanted to calm Amy down, but thankfully it didn't seem like the bartender was upset; instead she let out a chuckle. "You know, I haven't known Gary for as long as you, but the way you're acting right now, it's almost as if you're the older sister looking out for him. Your brother is really lucky to have such an overprotective sister."

These comments, of course, just made Amy even more angry, but before saying anything else, Miss Degrace poured a glass of Coke and placed it on the table in front of her.

"There you go; as the boss's sister you deserve a free drink, right?" She winked.

The two looked at each other, wondering if they had misheard what the woman had just said.

"Boss? What do you mean, 'boss'? Is he the manager here? How's that possible?" Amy said.

She had only come to find her brother, maybe learn a bit more about what he had been doing to earn the money to pay their moth-er's hospital bills. Of course, she would have liked to discover the truth behind the bloody clothes, but learning that he was living a second life, a life that she wasn't involved in, was worrying her.

"Look, I'm a bit older than all you kids, and I've learned a few things during my time. I can understand why he might want to keep secrets from you, but I've also learned how many problems secrets can cause.

"It's only human to want to know the truth about everything, and it would certainly mean troubling situations like this one could be avoided, but you should ask yourself something first. Are you really ready to learn the truth? Why do you think a person would want to keep something a secret from you in the first place?

"You look like you've drawn your own conclusions and are hoping to get a different answer. I've given you a hint into his world, but do you really want to know everything about Gary?" she asked.

This also wasn't what Tom was expecting either. He knew Gary was spending more time with the people who worked here, but what was she saying about this world? Right now, Tom felt like he was in a red pill, blue pill situation. Learning the truth about Gary might affect both of their lives forever.

I already know about him being a werewolf, and I'm sure Gary hasn't told others about that. He would be insane if he did. So just what could be a worse secret than that? Tom wondered.

CHAPTER 61

WE NEED A LAWYER

Amy stared at her big brother, while Gary's eyes were desperately darting around the room, looking for a way out of this situation. The two people he had most wanted to keep away from all the gang stuff had voluntarily come to seek him out.

Part of him knew that even if he could avoid talking about it today, if they had taken this much initiative they would come and ask him again. But what was the right thing to do? This question was often on Gary's mind these days. His usual gut-instinct approach just wasn't working. He sighed and met his little sister's eyes.

Happy to see that Gary had stopped flinching, Amy finally told him why she had come.

"Gary, what happened to those guys at the Kobo Karaoke Club after Stacy and I left? What are you doing here . . . and what were you doing today that you ignored all my calls?"

She was straightforward and direct, even though it took a lot out of her to ask him these things after everything Gary had done for them. The questions themselves, though, made Tom gasp for air. He realized that Amy didn't know that Gary was a werewolf . . . fortunately, he hadn't revealed that to her.

Tom was now also very curious about the answers to Amy's last two questions. Perhaps learning more about this place and the people Gary had started to associate with would answer his own questions.

After talking to Miss Degrace, Tom and Amy had to make a decision. In the end, they stopped questioning her any further about Gary. Instead, Amy told Tom about Stacy having been found dead, and how much of a strange coincidence all of this was. It reminded Tom of how he felt when he found out that the gray color gang no longer existed.

Having done some research of his own, Tom had a guess. He suspected that Gary was gathering delinquents from Westbridge and other schools to deal with the other troublemaker groups. As a werewolf, Gary would naturally make an excellent fighter.

Although Tom hadn't been wrong, he had been thinking too small-scale, which wasn't surprising given his lack of awareness about Slough's gang structure. He had no clue that the gray color gang was connected to a bigger gang that controlled the whole town.

"Didn't I tell you already?" Gary scratched the back of his head. "After I saw that you made it out, I just ran out and slammed the door. As you can tell, this is just a normal pool club, and I'm sorry that I didn't check my phone . . ." Gary trailed off as Amy got up and headed for the exit. Tom followed her, opening the door for her, and Amy looked back at her brother.

"Fine, if that's what you want me to believe, then I won't bother you any more about it . . . I just want you to know that whatever you do, you'll always be my brother. If you need help, or it gets to be too much, I'll be there to help you."

Tom said, "Don't worry, Gary, I'll make sure she gets home safe." And then they were gone.

Gary didn't get what had just happened, but at least Amy didn't seem angry or upset with him. He would have understood if she was, but even knowing that he had not been honest with her, the outcome wasn't as bad as he had feared.

He headed toward the basement of the club, which was one of the places where he kept extra clothes. He was eager to change into his trusty hoodie. Finally out of his bloody clothes, he saw that Kai was busy in a makeshift office. He had no idea when Kai had found the time to set it up.

A man wearing a fancy blue suit and holding a briefcase sat across from him. He was quite well-built, though in the wrong areas. All show muscles. His dirty-blond hair was neatly trimmed, giving him a professional look. However, something was telling Gary to run away. Not because he feared the man's fighting abilities. No, he had another dangerous air around him.

Is he a member of the Underdogs? No, Kai wouldn't bring one of them here. Gary wondered what was giving off that bad feeling.

Seeing that Gary had survived his ordeal, Kai gave him a smile and waved him over.

"Gary, let me introduce you to Mr. Volkun Vala, lawyer for the Pincers, though now he'll be helping us out. Olivia had already sent him my details, and he's going to help us go through all the paperwork." Volkun looked at Gary and gave him a wink.

"Not just that, kiddo, but if you ever need anything, and I mean *anything*, I'll deal with it. You get in trouble, need someone to clean up your mess for you, no problem, just give your boss a call, and I'll deal with it."

After this introduction, Gary understood his apprehension toward Volkun. The guy was an underworld lawyer. One who not only was familiar with the loopholes in the legal system, but also knew the right people to pay before a case even went to court, or if needed to bribe the jury.

The underworld wasn't only composed of corrupt people. Money could truly solve anyone's problems.

"Hey." Kai interrupted Volkun. "You should be a bit more polite; the person you are talking to right now is the leader of the Howlers."

Volkun started to chuckle, thinking it was some type of joke, but seeing the look on Kai's face, he cleared his throat. He was rarely surprised, but he couldn't fathom how a bunch of teenagers could bring down Olivia Pearl's gang and make her hand everything over.

"Hey, I'm going to call it a night . . . I think I need some rest. Also, I might need another uniform. If possible, a little bigger," Gary told Kai, ignoring the lawyer who was looking him over.

"Don't worry." Kai smiled. "I'll be ordering a lot of them. Soon Burnham Street will be full of our gang colors, and I'll order plenty of spares, so you don't have to worry too much. After all, we should have the funds for that. You let me deal with the paperwork; Olivia's accountant will be coming over soon as well."

It was a good thing that the Howlers had taken over a well-established gang rather than having to build up everything on their own. That hadn't originally been part of Kai's plan. In fact, thanks to Gary being more than he had ever anticipated, they were actually years ahead of his initial plan.

Now they could use all the assets and everything the Pincers already had in place. On top of that, Olivia, who had set up everything before, was happy to do it all.

I have a feeling this is something to do with your powers, Gary . . . I'm dying to know more about that, but I can't exactly ask you to reveal all your secrets while I still keep my own . . . Anyway, I should just finish everything here first, Kai thought.

Sitting back down, He continued to go through the papers with the lawyer. There were deeds to the shops and restaurants, statements for the gang's bank accounts, and so on.

The Pincers had a lot of spare cash lying around and were making some big profits. If we go through with what Gary had planned, we will still be able to make money and have a good bit to spare. Gary was right, these people are sick . . . they were just obsessed with making more. It's hard to believe that this still is not enough for the auction, though.

Still, the best thing is this.

The papers included a list of VIP customers that the gang served quite frequently at night. Some of them were from the higher-tier cities. However, a big surprise was that some clients were members of the Rising Dragon gang.

Why did Olivia keep such a list? Was it some type of blackmail? Maybe the Pincers had bigger plans to use this information. If they spread any information about people from the Tier 2 cities, the whole of Slough would probably end up annihilated . . . Why am I over-thinking things? I can just ask Olivia later.

Kai continued to go through the papers, just in case there were other things he wanted to ask. Maybe there was something that they could use to improve their current position. He had already found some information that could help the Howlers in the future but not right now—until . . .

"Clove? Isn't that . . . well, seems like things are getting very interesting."

CHAPTER 62

BETA TRAINING

After coming back upstairs, Gary was ready to leave the club, but he didn't expect to see that White had changed into a work uniform and was busy serving customers. He didn't even know the place had a work uniform; it was a black dress shirt and black pants, with a gold apron.

Kai really likes those two colors, but how long was I down there? They already have her working?

"I can see the look on your face," Miss Degrace said from across the room. "She said she needed a job, and we are going to need some night staff soon, so I hired her."

"Night staff?" Gary replied.

"Didn't Kai tell you that this place will soon be open as a bar at night?"

Gary remembered that this was part of the initial plan, and judging by the uniform, Kai was going to make it clear that this place was owned by the Howlers. Still, Gary was worried that this would cause trouble down the line.

Would it, though? Kai said that the Pincers were one of the five small-time gangs in the area. At the moment, they don't really know our strength, which has come out of nowhere. For them, it would be a risky move.

While thinking about this, Gary looked over at White, who looked happy doing her job. He also realized now was his chance to sneak out of the club, before anyone else wanted to talk to him.

Once he was outside, he checked his text messages and was happy to read that Amy had gotten home safely. He was also checking for another text, because he had another destination in mind before returning home.

The night sky was darkening, which was perfect, and Gary headed to the wooded area near his school where he and Innu used to train. Eventually he saw someone in the distance, despite the darkness, and she spotted him as well.

"Well, as you can see, I came here as asked, O great leader!" Olivia curtsied, clearly upset about having been called to a forest of all places after dark.

"You should have an idea of why we are here. Have you had time to get familiar with the differences in your body yet? Have you tried to tell someone about those changes?" Gary wasn't sure, but the fact that Olivia froze up made it obvious that she had tried.

The rules seemed to be working, which was good news for the alpha werewolf.

She asked, "Now that it's just us, can you explain what you did to me? When my men were clearing up my office, I . . . I was unable to stay in the room. When I saw the dead bodies . . . the smell that entered my nose . . ."

Gary understood what she was trying to say. Such a bloody scene would make a human want to throw up; for a werewolf it was as appetizing as an all-you-can-eat buffet.

As long as Gary had ample Energy, it was easy to resist the urge, but he had to remind himself that it was actually abnormal behavior.

"Oh, 'your' men? Funny, here I thought that had changed. Anyway, I called you here tonight to help both of us," Gary explained.

"Argh, fine . . . in that case, you should be aware that a good portion of 'your' men have left. Not all of them, but we're down to less than half of what we had after I spread the word that the Howlers had taken over.

"People don't just follow a new gang that came out of nowhere. We had to get rid of people who had specific jobs that are no longer there, and even those who have stayed out of loyalty are afraid of another attack. Since everyone will know that we just lost a fight, it's just a question of when the other gangs will try to claim a piece of us," Olivia complained.

Gary had thought about this as well. Now that the place belonged to him, he needed to look after it.

"Well then, we just need to protect the place, don't we? Lots of genuine workers in that area as well, so if anything happened there, it would just make their lives more complicated. Another good reason for you to take what I have planned seriously.

"I'm going to teach you a few new things. What I am . . . well, what *we* are. At first, I thought it was a curse, but now I'm grateful to have this power.

"Technically, you and I are werewolves, but I think it will make things easier if you just consider us 'special Altered.' I'm not sure who is more powerful, us or actual Altered, but I can promise you that we're far more powerful than normal humans."

Gary had thought a lot before he decided to train Olivia. After all, helping her control her powers meant there was a good chance that she might grow powerful enough to take him on.

However, based on the rules and the way the system was currently set up, it would be impossible for her to grow stronger than him unless he got lazy. Fortunately, he planned to train against her, so he would always be aware how strong she was.

"Okay," Olivia said, still sulking. "I'm in this situation and I don't seem to be able to get out of it. If you can help me, then I might as well take advantage of that."

Having seen the type of person Olivia was, Gary doubted that she would just let it go if anyone tried to attack Burnham Street or the Kraken again. He expected her to put up a fight. In a way, not much had changed for Olivia, except that she had gained a boss she had to answer to.

Apart from the fact that they were taking all her money and assets gained over the years, she was still able to live a lavish life. If Burnham Street was attacked, Gary also hoped that the pack's rule not to betray the Howlers would kick in.

"As we get closer to the full moon, your bloodlust will grow. Although the rules state that you can't hunt humans, you can hunt animals. Usually raw meat will satisfy your hunger, but as the full moon gets closer it feels like your body has to kill instead.

"If you can't control it, or if something feels seriously wrong, call me."

Gary then pulled something from behind his trousers and threw it toward her. It was Olivia's special whip. He had inspected it for a while, trying to use all his strength to break it. It was definitely not a normal whip.

"You're . . . just giving this back to me?" Olivia sounded surprised.

"I can't afford to have you die on me anytime soon. That would just complicate everything. You seemed proficient with the whip, so it's better to return it than just to sell it off. As long as you continue being useful to me, you get to live.

"You should keep that in mind. Since I created you, I can easily replace you. If you start becoming a pain in my backside . . ." Gary left the threat unspoken, his eyes glowing red, and he still had lingering thoughts of what had happened to Stacy.

"Now tell me, what sort of whip is that? It was even able to hurt me."

Olivia stretched the whip out a few times, checking that it was still in good condition and working. She then flung it out once and a smile appeared on her face.

"This was from the special auction house run by the Dark Guild. Although even with my funds I was only able to get this, they sell all sorts of things there. Altered DNA is rare.

"Even if you're rich, sometimes that isn't enough to get your hands on Altered DNA. Imagine a stronger gang bidding on the DNA. No smaller gang will even try to make a higher bid. Anyway, they needed to create weapons to deal with the Altered, and this is one of them."

Auction house . . . sounds interesting, Gary thought, but one thing was putting him off more than anything: the fact that she had said the auction was extremely expensive. If that was the case, Gary didn't want to go there any time soon. Still . . .

Maybe if I went there, I could find out what to do with that suitcase, Gary thought as he got into a fighting stance.

"Come on, attack me at full strength with everything you've got, don't hold back!" he shouted.

With her new body and the whip in her hand, Olivia should be even more dangerous than she was before, but that was exactly what Gary wanted. If he wanted to beat people like Jayden Tiger, then he needed to push himself further.

CHAPTER 63

A MESS

The Pincers gang had always had a unique position in Slough. There was a reason why the other gangs hadn't wanted to touch them, which was the special relationships they had. Not just with those within Slough but also those outside it.

Which is why, even though it had only been a few hours, one afternoon and evening, since their demise, the news had spread like wildfire. The drastic actions the Howlers gang had taken didn't help, and those who left the Pincers had let everyone know why they were disappointed with Olivia Pearl.

The Pincers also told their contacts and their workers involved in trafficking that they would no longer be needed. The whole reason for this . . . was the gang known as the Howlers.

"Ha!" Brandon couldn't help but laugh. The two leaders of the Gray Elephants were once again in the warehouse, in a special office placed in the top corner just for them. They had just been discussing all the rumors about this new gang.

"Have you heard the ridiculous claims that have been coming out of their mouths? They say that it was only five teenagers who took over the entire place. If they want to make it sound believable, they should at least say that Jayden Tiger was with them," Brandon grumbled.

The event was still fresh in his mind. In fact, Raven had been forced to listen to him talk about it nonstop ever since they came back: whether they should have attempted to take out the Altered there and then. However, they both knew what the result would have been.

"However, we don't have time to care about them," Brandon continued. "That bastard from the Phoenix gang contacted me yesterday. He told me that he would come over in a week or so, and if we couldn't show him any results, he would just get rid of the Gray Elephants and Underdogs altogether.

"While I doubt that he can do that without any repercussions from the other Kings, I'm afraid nothing good will come out of antagonizing him." As he took a puff of his large cigar, it was clear that Brandon was quite worried. "So, any bright ideas?"

"Only a skeleton crew is left after the stunt Riv pulled, and the gray color gang isn't faring much better. We put Buffin in charge of what's left of both gangs, but they're just a shadow of their former self. The only silver lining is that the black color gang is in a similar situation, still recovering from the attack that day.

"In other words, it's basically us against the Underdogs . . . who still outnumber us, mind you. Not to mention, they have that Altered on their side." Raven let out a deep sigh. "If we declare war on them, the best we can hope for is to inflict as much damage as possible. That also seems to be the only reason why Damion hasn't come out to attack us himself.

"Our only choice seems to be to get one of the smaller gangs on our side for support. The problem is, they're all on the fence about joining either side . . . and you don't need me to tell you that they just use that as an excuse to gobble up the loser's territory."

"So what? You are suggesting we approach these Howlers to help us?" Brandon scoffed at the idea.

"Rumors or not, Olivia Pearl has started spreading the news that they've been taken over. That woman might be ambitious, but she also understands the pecking order. I can't imagine that this is a ploy. Anyway, unless you have a better idea, we should at least make sure that they won't end up helping the Underdogs." Raven folded his arms across his chest as he leaned back in his chair.

"You seem overly interested in those Howlers. Tell me, is that because you think it's the best for the Gray Elephants . . . or is this somehow related to your personal matter? I thought you would have dealt with it by now."

"No," Raven replied immediately, clearly annoyed. The Howlers were a mysterious gang that seemed to have come out of nowhere, so he knew as little about them as everyone else. "I have a lead, and I'm just biding my time till the lead feels safe, and eventually I will use her again. I only have a name and a school to go on, and after what those red idiots did, it's not like I can just come barging in, now can I?

"All of my actions have reasons behind them, even if others think they are a bit over the top, but at least I get good results. This time I need to make sure I have the right person, and when I do, I'll crush him slowly."

The smile on Raven's face reminded Brandon why he had teamed up with him and Yovan to create the Gray Elephants in the first place. The two of them knew that many people considered Brandon the real leader of the Gray Elephants, even though the three of them were supposed to be equal heads of the gang.

However, all gangs started from somewhere, and Brandon was acting as the brawn to Raven's brain. Unfortunately, Yovan was no longer with them. He had been the glue that held both sides together, acting as the middleman when the two of them butted heads, which wasn't a rare occurrence. They had to use their smarts to rise to the position they were in, and Brandon could tell that Raven had a plan for whoever had messed with him.

"Well, since you seem to have put your personal life on hold, I actually have an idea about how to use the resources that Phoenix bastard gave us without losing more of our own men in the process. That little experiment of yours worked out in our favor. Let's just say it's a good thing we still have plenty of that liquid left."

CHAPTER 64

A BETTER LIFE

It was Sunday evening and the night sky was out. Inside the Black Rock Orphanage, Kevin was helping Suzan tuck in the kids at bedtime.

"Is . . . Big Brother Innu still not coming today?" A small girl yawned as she struggled to keep her eyes open. Usually she would have been asleep by now, and Kevin knew she had stayed up just to see him.

"I'm sorry, Innu seems to be busy this weekend, but I'm sure he will visit us soon. Don't worry, you have a lot of time to see him." Kevin smiled and waited until she fell asleep.

It wasn't something he had to do, but since he was a bit older than the rest, he had volunteered to help out, just like every other night. They all knew that Suzan had a lot on her plate, so Kevin wanted to help her at least a little.

He let out a little sigh.

As they left one of the large communal bedrooms where several young children slept on a mattress, Kevin told Suzan, "Innu asked me to apologize to you that he was unable to come yesterday and to-day. He also wants us to tell the other kids that he promises to make up for it next weekend."

"Innu really has grown up, hasn't he? I can tell he's working hard and really cares for us." Suzan sighed. "As happy as that makes me . . . sometimes I wish that he would concentrate on himself and his own life rather than looking after us."

Just then, they heard a soft knock on the door. Kevin wondered who it could be at such a late hour, but Suzan told him to go to bed. As he watched her run off with her hair in a mess, he could only wryly smile.

Innu and us other kids want the same for you, Suzan; that's why he's trying so hard . . .

Out of curiosity, Kevin decided to see who it was. The orphanage didn't get many visitors, and at this time of night it couldn't have been someone looking to adopt a child. He peeked around the corner and recognized the three men at the door. They had come over a few times already, and he wasn't sure if that was a good or bad thing.

After Suzan let them in, they followed her to the kitchen. Sneaking after them, he waited by the door so he could listen to their conversation.

"Have you considered our offer? You won't be able to survive much longer on your own." said a man with a gruff voice.

"I have . . . I assure you, I have been thinking about it a lot. It's just this place is like a home for everyone. If they had to move out . . ."

"Forgive me for saying this, ma'am," another voice interrupted. "But I think your refusal is quite selfish."

When Kevin heard this strange man call Suzan selfish—the most selfless person he had ever met—he clenched his fists, but if he tried anything he knew he would get her in trouble.

What would Innu do? Kevin wondered. However, he imagined that Innu would tell those men to shove something up their backside and get out of here. He shook his head because he knew that would be a very bad approach.

"With all due respect, but it's obvious that you're lacking the proper funds. Just on the way here, I saw multiple areas where this place is falling apart. The new location would be ten times better.

"If it's a question of money, I can reassure you that you have nothing to worry about. Our boss even allocated some extra funds today. We told you, he is a generous man who was once in the same situation as these kids. That's why he wants to help them out.

"Unfortunately, it just doesn't make any financial sense to give this place a complete overhaul. It would be cheaper to demolish it and rebuild it from scratch. Please, think about the kids and their future."

At this, Kevin relaxed the tension in his fists. What the man said was true; the government's help hadn't increased in over a decade, and with inflation doing its thing, Suzan had been forced to spend her own money to compensate, making next to nothing from the place.

The number of orphans was also steadily increasing, and each new mouth just put additional strain on the funds. Simply put, they lacked money, and now a private organization was willing to take over.

"Suzan," Kevin said, coming into the kitchen and surprising Suzan, who started to tell him to go to his room.

"You should accept the deal. You have already done so much for us. We all know that, so don't worry. It's not like they are going to put us in the worst place, right? If you're worried, I bet you can come and visit us. Nobody will blame you if you decide to rest, and it would stop idiots like Innu from having to worry about you as well."

Suzan was of two minds. It felt wrong for her to stop being involved in these kids' lives and just hand them over to someone else, especially a stranger she had never met. However, hearing these words from one of the oldest and smartest kids she had ever looked after, she was finally willing to agree. Suzan picked up the pen and signed on the dotted line. The deal was done.

"Thank you for being so cooperative. It will be a few days until we can move them, but we will inform you about everything that needs to be done in due time," the man with the gruff voice said, and with that they were on their way.

The moment they walked out the door, the gruff man made a call. "Boss . . . it's done."

On the other end of the line, Brandon placed the phone down and smiled at Raven.

CHAPTER 65

PAWN UPGRADE

When Gary woke up, he felt like he had possibly gone through one of the longest weekends of his life. So much had happened, it was quite unbelievable.

The red color gang had attacked the school. Gary had saved Xin's life and fought against Jayden Tiger, who turned out to be her brother, and the Howlers had taken over the Pincers gang. To top it all off, Gary had created something called a beta wolf and turned himself into an alpha.

12 Days until the next full moon.
Your bloodlust is increasing.
50 Exp has been gained from current Bond Marks (5)
Exp 846/3002

Seeing this message, Gary wasn't too concerned about himself; instead he was more concerned for Olivia. He thought back to what had happened last night in their training session.

Without her guards around, Gary had found it a lot easier to deal with Olivia during their practice fight. It was apparent that she was a lot faster at using the whip than at attacking him head on, and she knew that as well.

However, Olivia wasn't used to fighting, even though she did seem experienced with the whip, though Gary had started to suspect that was for non-fighting-related reasons.

He had used this chance to vary his speed during a fight. Using Controlled Transformation, he benefited from small bursts here and there, making sudden movements so he could reach his opponent more easily and disarm her.

Avoiding her whip made for good practice. It was a fast and painful weapon, despite his high Endurance. Even with his advantage in speed, Olivia managed to surprise him a few times and get a strike in.

Pain was a good way to encourage someone not to make the same mistake twice.

After that, Gary had attempted to train Olivia herself, since he wanted to know what exactly she could do. Her natural strength and skills had improved, but she was nowhere near Gary's level. He estimated her to be around the same level as he had been just after he was turned, making him think that Billy might have been a special case.

Maybe . . . it's because of the person themself before they were turned. Billy was already strong, after all. I struggled to beat him when he was fully human, so no wonder he was such a monster. I should note this down somewhere.

However, he was afraid that if he were to write it down, someone might stumble upon his notes. So Gary decided to just leave it as a mental note. Unfortunately, all their attempts to make Olivia transform failed.

It was already a hard thing to explain, especially since Gary realized that his system actually took care of it for him, but even showing it to her did nothing for Olivia. She was unable to do it, either partially or fully. The only thing that happened was that her eyes changed color briefly, glowing slightly blue when she tried to activate that power.

They faded soon after, though. Gary half expected this, since he had been unable to control his turning initially, and he guessed that Billy had also only succeeded after the first night of the full moon.

Still, they did make some progress. For one, they verified that Olivia still benefited from fast healing. He scratched her skin with his claw and they waited for a while, only to see it heal on its own. Naturally, this consumed Olivia's Energy, making her hungry, but without a system to tell her exactly how hungry she was, she would have to rely on her stomach.

In the end, while trying to figure out a few more things, Gary decided to open the system and see if he could spot anything. Underneath the Pack tab, he could see Olivia's name.

Here he also saw that she had no class and was only at the Pawn grade.

If she has all this information as well, then it should mean she can evolve, right? If she gets stronger, she might also be able to choose a class. Or maybe I'm the one who gets to pick the class? It could also just be automatically assigned, depending on what suits her the most.

There was another issue, which was how to level her up. This was something the system didn't have a stat for. Did she have to just keep fighting, go to the gym like he did? He could only guess.

"Olivia . . . I want you to start going to the gym . . . and also you should be eating two kilograms of meat every day."

As he recalled giving her that order, his face went bright red. Olivia had looked at him like he was some type of freak. He had done his best to keep his composure, reminding himself that she was just an experiment. It really seemed like a game. If only this were a VR situation and not real life, he would be quite pleased.

Gary made a decision while he was putting on his school uniform: what to do with the Pawn point. As tempted as he was to convert it into stat points or more skill points, he wanted to find out more about those grades.

Since those points were so rare, and putting them into his grade appeared to be the natural way to use them, he decided to see what happened. If all went well with Olivia after the full moon, then he might consider turning the others as well.

Hopefully, a higher grade would also increase his chances for successfully creating another beta werewolf. He didn't want to gamble on what would happen if it failed.

1 Pawn point has been assigned to increase your Grade

"What the f*ck?" Gary cursed out loud.

CHAPTER 66

A BAD DAY

"Gary, why are you swearing so early in the morning?" Amy asked as she was rubbed her eyes. She didn't usually sleep in late; her brother tended to start the day incredibly early so he could prepare breakfast for the two of them.

"Ah, I'm sorry, it's just that my uniform is really tight. It seems like I can't delay buying a new one," Gary replied as he flexed his muscles, almost ripping his shirt and popping one of the buttons off, which he didn't expect to happen. This revealed a couple of his abs that his sister was surprised to see. The shirt was indeed too tight for him. Ever since his body had changed, he had yet to order a new set of school clothes, which cost money.

System, don't you think you should have warned me that I needed more to upgrade myself? Gary was fuming as he looked at the message. He could practically see a mischievous grin from whoever had designed it.

1 Pawn point has been assigned to increase your Grade
You need a total of 5 Pawn points to upgrade your body into a Knight-grade werewolf

If he knew it was going to take more than one Pawn point, he would have saved up to use them all at once. After all, what use were they when assigned like this? He could have converted it in case a situation arose where he might need it.

With how useful Last Stand had proven to be, more skills wouldn't hurt, either.

Be honest, system, did you choose five Pawn points as the requirement on purpose? Is this your way of making me try to turn Kai and the others? 'Cause I doubt you expect me to hunt down four more werewolves.

Argh, whatever. If it costs so much, then it better be quite the good upgrade once I get it! And you better let me change my frigging hair back to normal as well! Gary smiled bitterly; however, the next moment he thought about the potential boost in strength.

As a Knight-grade werewolf, maybe he could ask Jayden for a rematch. However, he had no reason to challenge the Altered fighter. Who knew, perhaps one day the two of them could meet in the ring.

Should I try making extra money as an AFC fighter?

As Gary thought about a certain person, his mood became quite pleasant as he headed out with a spring in his step. He hadn't bothered texting Xin; there had been too much going on since her rescue. Besides, he didn't want to appear needy.

Gary had to do everything perfectly. Too many times he had read in webtoons how the guy put in too much effort and only ended up creeping the girl out. That was the last thing he wanted to do.

On the way to school, Gary waved over to old man Morten, the head of the apartment block, as well as Tyler, who was working at the convenience store again, but he also noticed that the Underdogs gang members who had roamed all over the Chavley area had disappeared.

Does this mean they're finally doing something else? Gary wondered. *That guy from the Gray Elephants should know my name and what school I go to, and the same goes for the Underdogs. After the red color gang incident, the school must have at least increased their security, so they shouldn't attack any time soon.*

In a way, their stupid stunt actually helped me get the big gangs off my case for a while. Still, Hawk's brother already knows about Amy's school. I'm a bit worried that he'll come after her again.

Gary decided to text Kai to ask if they could set up some protection for his little sister. Now that they had Olivia's people to use, it should hopefully be possible.

A few minutes later, he got a reply.

Yeah, no problem. I'll pick out someone reliable. BTW I won't be at school today. If you need anything else, just send me a message.

Won't be in school . . . well, I guess there's not much point in us being in school if this is going to be our lives from now on . . . but we only have two more years, right? No, wait, Kai should only have one more year ahead of him.

Isn't he worried about all this gang stuff not working out? What's so important that he's skipping school for it? . . . Must be something to do with that lawyer and the Pincers. Yeah, I should probably thank him for taking care of those things . . .

Thinking about this led Gary to start thinking about money once again. He could only imagine the things he could afford to buy. Perhaps he could get that new phone for his sister after all, and it might relieve his conscience for lying to Amy.

Shouldn't I start to think bigger? If it really is a lot more money, wouldn't it be great to move out of that crummy apartment to a nice place like Cipen? Gary smiled. *Yeah, I can't exactly invite the mayor's daughter to our apartment. But how will I explain it to Mom and Amy? There's no way they'll believe I got enough cash from a measly part-time job as a waiter . . .*

In his first class he saw Tom and Innu, who waved back at him. Innu had his head down on his desk as usual, while Tom seemed as happy as he did for some reason.

"What's up with you?" Gary asked, not used to seeing his best friend in such a good mood.

"It's nothing, I just think I'm in love," Tom replied, which was the last thing Gary had been expecting to hear. And for some reason, seeing the dumb grin on Tom's face, part of him felt the urge to hit it.

"Well, as long as it's not Xin, then I'm happy for you. Not that she would go after you anyway . . . she's already got a date." Gary couldn't help but brag as he pointed his thumb at his own chest. On top of saving her life, he was sure she had fallen for him already.

At that moment, Mr. Grey entered the room, with a bandage around his head from being hit by one of the red color gang members, but the wound didn't seem too bad. If anything, the bandage looked a bit excessive.

"All right, settle down, everyone. Unfortunately, we'll have to start off the week with some disappointing news," Mr. Grey announced, grasping the desk in front of him. "Although she hasn't been with us for long, I'm sorry to inform you that your fellow student Xin Clove will no longer attend Westbridge. I have just been informed that her father has chosen to transfer her out of school."

Gary was in the middle of getting his bag out at that moment, and he dropped it straight on the floor.

CHAPTER 67

NOTHING TO LOSE

Gary hadn't known Xin for long. In fact, he had only been able to talk to her occasionally. Whenever he did, though, it felt so natural to him. Although his heart beat rapidly when he approached her, she was afraid even with his awkward actions and stupid face. Despite all his flaws, she had even agreed to go on a date with him.

My wonderful future days at Westbridge are over?

"Hey, what should we do, bro? He hasn't moved since this morning," Innu said as he waved his hand in front of Gary's eyes

"It's heartbreak. I don't think there's anything we can do." Tom shrugged helplessly. "Gary always had a fragile heart. I remember when he confessed to Lily when we were in third grade, and Betty in fifth grade. Whenever he got rejected, he would be like this for a while. Last year, he even confessed to Yon Lee, but she said she wasn't into nice guys . . . wait a minute, Gary, is that why you came back with green hair?"

"You're not alone, Gary, I understand your pain!" Innu put his hand on his friend's shoulder.

Judging by Innu's reaction, Tom guessed that he had also experienced his fair share of rejections.

"It's different this time." Gary finally spoke up, yet his eyes continued to be lifeless. "This time I wasn't rejected. Xin actually agreed to a date . . . but now she's moved away before we even had a chance to go on one."

After all those years of rejection from countless girls, this hurt even more than that. He felt like fate was telling him that he was destined to end up alone.

It was lunchtime, but Gary had no appetite. Instead, he stared down at his phone, hovering over Xin's number. She had given it to him so they could arrange their date, but he hadn't received a text . . . He thought they might just talk about it in person.

Why am I still hesitating? It's not like I have anything to lose. If she agrees, then I might at least have the chance to see her off.

Tom noticed the change in Gary's face as he started tapping out a text.

Mr. Grey told us that you're transferring. It's a real shame, I was actually looking forward to that date and getting to know you more. I guess your father didn't want you in Westbridge after what happened. I don't know if you're even still in Slough, but if you are, do you think we could meet up?

He had typed the message in one go, not really thinking too much about it. He didn't want to worry about making it perfect; otherwise he felt like he would chicken out. But his thumb hovered over the send button, hesitating to press it.

"I . . ."

"Just hit send, bro!" Innu said, snatching the phone out of his hand. "And let me adjust this a bit for you." He quickly added something before sending the text.

Immediately, Gary grabbed his phone back.

"Ahh! What the f*ck? Why would you add that?" Gary shouted as he read Innu's addition.

From your Romeo, Gary.

"She's going to think I'm so cringy!" Gary complained.

"There's a fine line between cringe and romance. Wheat we think is cringe could be romantic to others. Everyone has different tastes."

"And your tastes are just weird," Gary replied. Just then his phone dinged.

They all looked down and read the message together.

Sorry, Gary, I'm still coming to terms with transferring myself. Thanks to Tiffany, I wasn't really able to get close to anyone at Westbridge, so apart from you, there wasn't really anyone to tell that I was moving. Honestly, it's pretty sad to admit, but you're probably the only person I will miss. I'm still in Slough at the moment. Depending on how my new school life will be, I might come back some weekends, but I'll probably be in another city most of the time.

Anyway, a promise is a promise. While I would have loved to have a classic first date with you, I'm afraid that's not really possible, but do you want to come over to my house for a meal today? It's the only way I think you'll be able to see me. I would like to see you again, so I can explain everything to you in person. Oh, and it will be a meal with my parents, so if you want to make a good impression now would be the time.

From your potential Juliet :)

"Whoa, that text actually worked, and you're skipping right to meeting her parents? I don't know, man, aren't you crapping your pants right now?" Innu asked teasingly, but Gary was all smiles.

"Hey, Gary, just to make things clear, you do remember that her father is Slough's mayor, right?" Tom reminded him. "You're going to have to put on a suit or something, and I know you ain't got one. I would let you borrow mine, but I'm afraid it won't fit you anymore. Also, you might want to change something else about your appearance."

His sudden happiness started to disappear when Tom pointed at his green hair, which thanks to the system might stay this way forever. There was nothing he could do about that, but getting a suit should be easy enough. Unfortunately, he didn't know anything about them, he did know someone who could help him find one, and a good one at that.

Getting back on his phone, he sent two texts, one accepting the date and asking Xin what time he should come over, and another asking his friend to get him a nice suit. The rest of the day couldn't move fast enough for Gary, and the good news was that rugby practice was canceled until Mr. Root was out of the hospital.

This meant he had even more time to prepare himself before the date. As he, Tom, and Innu walked out of the building after school, they heard a bunch of students talking about something.

"Hey, did you see that car that's waiting outside the school gate?"

"Yeah, I saw it from the window. Other than Xin's bodyguards, I've never seen such a nice car in front of this school. Do you think there's a celebrity waiting to pick someone up?"

"Dunno, but I'm pretty sure that was a Bersedez Menz, and those easily cost over a hundred K!"

"What, that's easily more than our house is worth!"

The students' excitement was spreading quickly.

"Who the hell would be stupid enough to buy such an expensive car? If it was me, I'd save that money." Gary scoffed when he heard that.

"I wonder who's here, though? Xin's no longer here, so they must be here for someone else, right?" Innu said.

As they approached the school gate, students were crowded around the car so much that the others couldn't even see it. So Gary and his two friends just kept walking—until someone called out his name.

"Hey, Gary, where are you going?" a familiar voice shouted from the direction of the crowd.

"Hey guys, would you mind moving out of the way?" said a teenager who had just gotten out of the car, and the students quickly complied because a scary-looking man in a suit was standing right next to him.

"Kai!" Gary shouted. The car was clearly his. He knew Kai was rich, but this rich?

"What the? If you had such a nice car from the beginning, why didn't you tell us about it?" Innu complained. As he got closer, he noticed that the car wasn't completely black. The chrome details on the windows and the grille at the front had a golden color. Gary also noticed this, and it gave him a weird feeling.

At that moment, Kai chucked over the keys, and Gary caught them in midair.

"What are you on about? The car isn't mine, it's Gary's."

All the students' heads turned to look toward the green-haired teenager, even Tom. How could a normal kid like Gary ever afford something like this?

CHAPTER 68

SMALL TIME IS OVER

Gary looked down at the keys, then up at the car again. He repeated this process two more times. He was searching for the right words to say, but it was as if they had gotten stuck in his throat. He had heard what Kai had said, yet none of it made any sense to him.

"Hey, were Kai and Gary always this close?" one of the students asked.

"What's with the fancy car? Did he win the lottery or something?"

"I don't think so. Wouldn't they have announced it on the news? Maybe one of those Nigerian prince scams turned out to be actually true?"

"Why . . . why would you do this in front of everyone?" was Gary's only thought, as he clenched the keys and walked forward.

"Kai, you're really a jokester," Gary said as he returned the keys. "I haven't even had driving lessons, so how on earth could this be my car? Does your dad even know that you took his car out?"

Gary had made sure to be extra loud, so everyone would hear him. The car belonging to Kai's father was the only logical explanation. Kai wore an expensive watch, so for his father to have such a car wasn't much of a stretch.

Of course, Tom wasn't buying it; it was clear that his best friend was just trying to deflect the situation.

These people, that business, and now this expensive car . . . that isn't easy money, Gary. Did you get rich by gambling . . . or have you pulled off something even shadier? Tom was worried, still unaware that Gary was the leader of the gang.

Before anyone could ask any questions, Gary quickly got into the car, followed by Innu. They usually went to the Wolf's Pool Club after school anyway. Kai got in the passenger seat while the man in the suit got in on the driver's side and started the ignition.

Rolling down the window, Gary didn't forget his best friend. "I'll see you tomorrow, Tom. Depending on how it goes, I might text you later."

With that the car was on its way. Gary had a lot of questions, but he couldn't stop looking all over the car. There was a screen on the back of the seat. Cup holders down the middle. A digital screen to control the air conditioning. The upholstery was nice, and even the back seats were heated.

It was a luxurious life he could quickly get used to.

"Judging by the smile on your face, you approve of the car. That's nice," Kai commented with a smirk.

The smile on Gary's face dropped.

"Why did you do that, Kai?" Gary asked in a serious tone. "Why did you buy this car, come to school, and tell everyone that it was mine? Are you trying to change my life?"

Unwilling to get in the middle, Innu decided to look out the window and enjoy the ride.

"Because the car is yours . . . well, it's ours." Kai clarified. "Innu kept complaining about how we as a proper gang didn't have a nice vehicle, and I actually agree with him. Besides, we'll need it for when we'll set our sights outside Slough.

"And what do you mean by 'Am I trying to change your life,' Gary? I don't want to tell you any of that 'Once you're in, you're in for life' bullshit, but after everything you've been through, how exactly do you picture returning to your 'normal' life?"

Was it true? Was Gary really thinking that way? He realized that when he was trying to meet up with Xin or playing rugby, he enjoyed these things because they reminded him of his ordinary life . . . but could he really go back to that? Quitting the Howlers would be one thing, but how would he quit being a werewolf? . . . and did he even want to do one or the other?

"Now come on, don't tell me you haven't at least entertained the possibilities of what you could do with the extra income we'll generate from the Pincers gang. It would be weird if you and the others hadn't been daydreaming at least a little. It's not wrong . . . but if you are going to use that money, then you have already crossed to this side, Gary.

"Knowing you, I bet you want to move somewhere nice. However, you'll need to explain to your sister and mother how you were able to obtain all this money. What are you doing to tell them? Right now, having taken over the Pincers, we are a gang that no longer needs to hide.

"We Howlers should not shy away from spreading our name; otherwise it might actually become dangerous for us. Right now, the other gangs are all desperately trying to find information about us, but our mystery factor will quickly cool off if we don't do anything. The other gangs will believe that what we did was just a fluke, so we have to make them afraid of us.

"We want to create the image that saying you are under the Howlers will offer more protection than saying you are not. We aren't any small-time color gang any more, Gary. We are the damn Howlers," Kai said with pride in his voice.

Whenever Kai talked, he was always looking into the future. Every decision he made was one step closer to his grand ambition. Perhaps he had not come to school today because purchasing the car was just another step in that plan.

"In the future, the Howlers will have to deal with corporations, among other things. We are going to be a business, Gary. We have to make a good impression and show that we can look after ourselves, otherwise why would anyone believe in us? This car was one of the first steps toward that. Also, I have not forgotten that you can't drive, which is why we have our own driver.

"What I want from you all is to be proud that you are in the Howlers gang. This isn't any kiddie crap any more . . . But our leader needs to stay under the radar. We're starting off with one car today, but we'll have a fleet soon."

Gary was taking in everything that Kai had said. He was right about it all. He had been thinking about using the money for his own benefit, yet as a sixteen-year-old teenager, he couldn't help wishing he could lead a normal life . . . even though he knew that as someone who had already killed, it would be impossible.

Just then, the car drove past the convenience store where Tyler worked. For a brief moment, Gary saw him through the window staring at their car. Then again, nearly everyone on the street was doing the same. All of the pedestrians had stopped for a moment, not used to such a sight.

The windows were tinted so no one could see who was inside, which felt strange. Off in the distance Gary could see the area where his apartment block was, and it made him think of his landlord.

"Kai . . . since we have enough money to buy this car . . . can we buy the apartment blocks where I live? Also the shops we just went by," Gary asked hesitantly.

Innu was also thinking about using the money to help out the orphanage. Perhaps they could purchase it and then upgrade it, so that Suzan would no longer have to worry.

There was a silence before Kai answered with a surprising no.

"Gary, we might have a lot of cash on our hands, but at the same time we don't have an unlimited amount. We aren't a charity, either. Do you really think those places make that much profit? They would be more trouble than they're worth.

"Since you're the boss, and I know you well enough to know you wouldn't ask if you didn't have your reasons, there is one major problem that I think you're overlooking. That shop and those apartments are in the Underdogs territory. To put it simply, they're not for sale.

"We should also not try to expand outward just yet. That's asking for a war that we're not ready for."

The answer upset Gary, but it reaffirmed his goal of wanting to get rid of the Underdogs.

"By the way, your suit is in the trunk. I chose you the best of the best, and Gio here is going to give you a lift to your girlfriend's place. Make a good impression and woo her off her feet." Kai grinned as he threw over a small box. "Also, I wasn't sure you had protection, so I picked you some up."

"How do you . . ." Gary looked to his right, and Innu was trying to look away even harder. "You told him!"

At the same time, on the other side of town, Xin had just told her family about a guest who was soon to arrive.

Hopefully, you picked something fancy, streaker boy. Jayden smiled, as he was actually looking forward to tonight's dinner.

CHAPTER 69

CLACK CLACK

Ever since Stacy had stopped coming to school, it had been impossible for Amy to enjoy her school life. To keep her mind occupied, she had focused even more on her studies, which was about the only good thing to come out of it.

During the lunch break was when it always hit the hardest. Just a few days ago, she had still blamed Stacy for transferring away, believing that her best friend had done so to avoid her. However, after learning that she had died, Amy couldn't help but be depressed that their last shared memory had been of Stacy walking out on her.

Seeing her alone, some girls from her class did invite her over to come eat with them. In fact, even though Gary had prepared her a homemade lunch because it was cheaper, today Gary had left money on the table so she could go to the canteen. Amy understood this to be his attempt to cheer her up.

But she declined the girls' invitation. Although she did crave companionship during such a hard time, she also felt guilty about accepting an invitation out of pity.

It's times like these, that I wish I went to the same school as Gary . . . at least then I would have someone I know, and I could talk to. Should I go and visit Mom again, after school?

She thought back to Gary's smile at the pool club. Her brother seemed to be unaware of it, but he smiled so wide when he was lying that his eyes became upside-down crescent moons. Amy was sure he was only trying to look out for her, but it still hurt knowing that he wanted to do everything on his own.

If only I hadn't accompanied Stacy that day, then I wouldn't have to worry about a gang being after Gary now . . . Who knows what would have happened to her if she had gone on her own . . . Oh, just why did you have to agree to that day in the first place, Stacy?

Gary doesn't seem to be too worried about it, though. Did he meet all those people so they could protect him? Did he have some type of deal with them? But then I can't figure it out . . . why did she call him boss?

Amy was scribbling in a notebook, writing down all the clues she had gathered so far and making a spider diagram connecting all the points she had in her head. Of course, she didn't write down exactly what they meant, in case anyone ever found her notebook.

Amy used acronyms and doodles so that it looked like nothing in particular. "BC," which stood for "bloody clothes," was connected to a doodle of a bird, representing Hawk, accompanied by a question mark. That one was also linked to a doodle of a music note, which symbolized the karaoke club, as well as GE for the Gray Elephants.

She wasn't sure about it, but then there was also Stacy's death, shortly after they had confessed. *Was that the Gray Elephants' doing? If so, could they be after me next? But why would they go so far? They already have Gary's information, and they know what school he goes to Do they know what he looks like? They never asked me anything like that.*

But then . . . what did Gary do that day after he found out about Stacy, coming back with his clothes full of blood again . . . is it all linked? Maybe I should pay a visit to Stacy's new school and find an answer there.

Since Gary wasn't going to give her a clear answer, she was going to track down the information herself. Amy was worried that if she could figure everything out, there was a good chance the police might be able to as well.

It was the end of the school day, and Amy stood frozen by the exit, about forty yards from the gate. For some reason, her body wasn't listening to her and was refusing to move forward.

What is happening to me? I know I had trouble after the attack, but I was able to walk home on my own plenty of times even after Stacy had transferred. Why can't I move now?

After thinking about it, she concluded that there was one major difference. Stacy had died, and it didn't seem to be a coincidence. The longer Amy waited, the more students would leave the school, meaning she would be on her own if she continued to hesitate.

Soon she realized that her breathing was getting deeper. Her surroundings were darkening. She wrapped her arms around herself and rubbed her shoulders.

I don't understand what's happening to me! Should I call Gary, ask him to pick me up? she thought, but instead she started taking deep breaths, one after the other, and eventually she started to feel better. She didn't want to bother him with something like this.

When she looked up, only a few students were left.

How long . . . was I like that for?

Amy's sense of time was off; even after thirty minutes there would still be students hanging around the front gates. Still, she couldn't stay here forever, and she eventually started walking. Taking a taxi wasn't an option for two reasons: taxis were expensive, and they weren't exactly safe. More and more horror stories were coming out, and Amy believed that getting in a taxi would be an easy way for her to get captured again.

As she exited the gates, Amy felt somewhat relieved. It might have been a small thing, but for some reason she felt like she had just climbed a mountain.

Still, she walked briskly, looking around constantly, keeping close to the buildings and away from the curb. Unfortunately, every time she heard a car driving past, she froze up, stopping in her tracks, her heart thumping, and she was prepared to run at any second.

Come on, I'm not that far from home. She was now on a more pedestrian street. There were fewer cars here, so she was a little less panicked, but even then a car had come down this street and Amy stopped. But she also noticed something else.

clack, clack

Amy looked around but couldn't see where the sound had come from. Thinking it must have just been her imagination, she continued on. At a traffic light, she stopped to tie her shoes, but then she suddenly heard it again.

clack, clack

This time Amy was sure that her ears weren't playing a trick on her. Worst of all, whatever was making the sound seemed to be nearby.

CHAPTER 70

PROTECTORS

Amy could tell that she was being followed.

If I turn around now, they'll know that I know that I'm being followed . . . please just let me be overly paranoid, but I need to make sure.

At the moment, she was on a quiet street. it was a residential area rather than the main street, but she saw a family at a crossing not too far away. Hurrying herself but not making it too obvious, she eventually found herself waiting at the crossing with them.

When the light turned green, she crossed the road, and while looking left and right for a second, she glimpsed someone who wasn't too far behind her.

This is too much of a coincidence that they crossed with us at the same time. They have to be following me, but why? Don't they already know where I live? Do they plan to kidnap me again, to get Gary to come to them?

The family she was following lived in the same apartment block; she had seen them before. Normally this would be a good thing, but she would be leading her pursuer right where they wanted to go.

Looking around, she checked for others, but didn't see any.

Shit . . . if I stay on this route, they'll follow me home . . . so what do I do?

Amy decided to try to shake them off. Maybe she was being paranoid, but she went to the next crossing and waited.

We're still on the same street, so if I cross from one side of the road to another, and they do the same, then they're definitely following me . . .

In the middle of her walk across the street, she could hear the clacking behind her, and the fear was getting to her. She could no longer contain it, and her legs started to move on their own.

She was sprinting across the street, and when she made it to the other side and glanced back, she saw a man in a suit running as well.

No, no, no!

Amy ran for her life, as fast as she could, not worrying about whether she would get too tired. She wanted to reach for her phone, but she was afraid taking it out would only slow her down.

Run, I have to run, my legs need to move faster! These thoughts were repeating in her head, and she couldn't think straight. However, her mind was clear enough to remember one thing: to not run toward her home.

Still, as she continued to run, not knowing where she was going and refusing to go down an alleyway to make it easier for an attacker to catch her in a secret place, she realized that she was slowing down.

I have to call someone . . . the police, but they won't know where I am . . . Gary . . . I promised him I would let him know whenever I was in trouble!

Her legs were hurting and so was her side, and finally the man had come to a stop. With her lungs heaving, she took out her phone and looked behind her . . . but no one was there.

What the . . . was I imagining things?

Not too far from Amy's position, down one of the many alleys she had run past, a man in a suit lay on the ground. His lip was busted and bleeding, and there was fear in his eyes as two people approached him.

"You know, when I was given this job, I was sure it would just be a waste of time. 'Who would be interested in such an innocent-looking girl? Surely nothing will happen.' However, I'm not exactly in a position where I can just let things play out . . ." The woman spoke as she dug her high heel into the chest of the man on the ground.

The poor man started screaming in pain, as the woman started twisting and turning it, but the next second, he was gagged by two other men, while a third one was blocking the alleyway.

"I thought about it . . . if they asked me to look after that girl, then she must be important, and unfortunately for you, I decided to come myself. So now tell me two things, what gang do you belong to . . . and why were you following her? It's your choice if you want to make this nice and easy . . . or if you want us to convince you to talk. Feel free to choose the latter, but I guarantee you, the latter option will make death seem like your only escape," Olivia said with a big smile.

Still worried about his sister, Gary had asked Kai to make sure she would be protected, just in case. Since Kai had been busy today, he had delegated this task to their newly recruited reinforcement. However, even he hadn't expected the former boss to go out personally.

They had been staying away from her, thinking nothing would happen. After all, they didn't know who this girl was, or her relation to the Howlers gang, yet Olivia had been told that this was an order from Gary. So she told herself that she had to give it her best.

Muffled grunts and screams filled the alleyway as Olivia and her men did their work, and eventually she had gotten every single bit of information she could from the man. Unfortunately, it turned out that he was as clueless as they were. Cleaning the blood from her hands, the woman looked off into the distance, down the street.

So the Gray Elephants hired this guy; the question is, why would a big-time gang be after a girl like her? And what does this all have to do with the Howlers?

On top of that, if they wanted to do something, they could have done it themselves. They've gone to a lot of trouble to hire someone else to do their dirty work . . . You Howlers seem to already have your share of trouble with you. I guess this might be exciting after all.

Meanwhile, a man wearing a leather jacket and sunglasses strolled down the same street, smiling away and looking straight ahead.

So they have protection on the girl, and if my eyes aren't deceiving me, that woman was Olivia Pearl, the leader of the Pincers . . . although according to the rumors she is the former leader. Seeing how she has come out personally, there must be some truth behind it all.

Now, why have the Howlers gone through all this trouble to hire guards to protect this girl? That is interesting. Very interesting. Raven smiled.

CHAPTER 71

MEETING THE PARENTS

The meeting time was upon them, and it was finally time for Gary to leave the Wolf's Pool Club. As he walked up the stairs from the basement wearing his new suit, he adjusted his cuffs a bit.

"So . . . how do I look?" Gary asked, looking for the opinions of his fellow gang members.

Each of them couldn't help but stare at Gary; the suit was almost a perfect fit, as if it had been tailor-made. It was a standard suit, black with a white shirt and a black tie, and they had never seen Gary look more presentable than at this moment.

"You look like a damn mob boss!" Innu blurted out excitedly.

Gary didn't know whether to take that as a compliment. After all, he was trying to make a good impression on Xin's parents, not other gangsters.

I knew it, it's the hair, but I can't change anything about the damn color, Gary thought, but with nothing else to do, he walked outside, where the car was waiting for him along with his driver. Interestingly, Kai had come along as well, saying that he had some things to talk with him about.

"So why is Gary all dressed up? Does he have a date or something?" Marie asked.

Innu, who was closest to her, just gave her a look but didn't say a word otherwise. He still remembered what had happened last time. He had no desire to end up as a punching bag. Unfortunately, Innu's silence was just as telling . . .

"Who is she?" Marie demanded to know.

Outside, Kai held the car door for Gary as he sheepishly made a grand bow, making him look like a butler. The green-haired teenager didn't know how to react to this, but with bigger problems to worry about, he just ignored his friend's behavior. Kai followed right after and pressed a button to raise the divider between the passengers and the driver, ensuring their privacy.

"I can see you're nervous about this whole thing, and I don't want to add to your worries, but there is something you should know," Kai revealed. "It's about Xin's father. I need you to be careful about what exactly you tell him today. And I don't mean that just because he's the mayor."

"I understand." Gary let out a sigh. "I'm already aware that her father seems to have connections to one of the gangs, so I won't say anything about the Howlers. Anyway, I'm just going there today as the potential boyfriend of his daughter."

Kai gave Gary a wry smile, contemplating whether he should tell him that he had found documents with Ben Clove's name on them. Ultimately, he decided against it. It seemed better to let his friend continue to believe that the mayor's involvement with the underworld was limited to just that.

"You still have my gift?" Kai asked. Immediately, Gary went to pat his inner pocket. He could feel the ring of the outer packaging.

"Sometimes I don't know if you're brave or stupid." Kai shook his head. In the first place, it was meant to just be a little joke. "It's your first date with the girl, and you're going to her parents' house, yet you actually bring them along."

Gary started to scratch the back of his head.

"Kai, sometimes it's really hard to tell if you're joking or not. You always have the same expression on your face. You would be really good at poker."

"So I've been told."

Suddenly the car came to a halt. The divider was rolled down and so was the driver's window. The driver and what looked like a guard talked for a while, before the gates were eventually opened for them.

A few minutes later, they approached the house, and Gary saw Xin and Jayden standing at the top of the steps, waiting for him.

"Oh, that's quite a nice car. I guess he's really pulling out all the stops. Do you know what his parents do to be able to afford a car like that?" Jayden asked his sister, who had not been paying attention.

Xin was too excited for someone to be coming over to their home for the first time, especially in such a grand manner. Initially, her parents had rejected her suggestion: one, because Gary was a boy, and two, because they knew nothing about him.

Fortunately, Jayden had been there to convince their parents, saying that the boy had really helped out with looking for Xin. When their mother heard that, her opinion of Gary had instantly improved; she believed that he truly cared about her daughter. Although Ben Clove had remained reluctant, the others had managed to make him agree eventually.

When Jayden repeated his question, Xin realized that she didn't have an answer. What did she even know about Gary? What did his parents do, who was he, and why was he riding in a car like that? Gary got out of the car, all dressed up in the suit and clearly nervous; he thanked his friend before he walked up the stairs.

"Just give me a call when you need to be picked up again. I wish you good luck, Gary." Kai gave him a thumbs-up. As the car prepared to drive away, Jayden's and Kai's eyes met for a second. Neither broke contact.

"Gary, I'm glad you made it, and you look great. I'm sorry for the short notice, but thank you so much for coming today." Xin greeted him with a smile. It was the first time Gary had seen her in something other than her school uniform, not counting the time at the karate club. She was wearing a long blue dress, and he could hear her heart beating as quickly as his. It seemed like she didn't know whether to hug him, shake his hand, or just let him in.

"Thank you," Gary said. "And Xin, you look . . . even better than I imagined."

The words had trouble leaving his mouth, and both teenagers became red-faced.

"Ah jeez, am I a ghost or something?" Jayden asked, scratching the back of his head. "Food thief, please remember that this is a family dinner, not a real dinner date. Still, I'm also happy to meet you again. I hope you don't have any plans afterward, since I have a lot of questions that I want to ask you, and I'm sure Xin has a lot to tell you as well."

Questions? Gary wondered what type of questions the Altered might have for him. Would he question him about the red color gang that day? Why the two of them fought, or something else, which was even more worrying? Suddenly it felt as if meeting the parents would be the easy part of this evening, yet he had his own agenda for being here.

Whether it was the right thing to do on their first meeting or not, Gary had made his decision. He was going to at least try to convince her parents to keep her in school. He wasn't the type of person to run away from things.

"Come on, let us show you to the living room. Dinner will be ready in a bit," Jayden said as he walked inside. Gary couldn't help but admire the large house, imagining how much it must have cost. He didn't know the exact numbers, but he didn't believe that a mayor would receive a generous enough wage to be able to afford such a luxury home, not in a Tier 3 town like Slough, at least. It was clear that their level of wealth was influenced by something else, which made him think about Kai's words.

It looked like he wanted to say something else back there, Gary thought.

He suddenly felt a hand on his chest. He had only taken one step into the house.

"I'm sorry, but we need to frisk every person who enters the house, even if you're today's guest of honor," one of the guards explained, and before Gary could say a word, another had already started to pat him down from head to toe . . . until the man started to pat his breast pocket, and he heard a crumpling sound.

Huh? . . . Oh shit, I completely forgot about that!

The next second the man reached into the pocket and pulled out a square packet.

CHAPTER 72

THE CLOVE FAMILY

*What the f*ck is that guard doing holding that thing like he's at a show and tell?* was Gary's first thought. He could tell by the look of shock on Xin's and Jayden's faces that they had clearly recognized the item for what it was.

"Er . . . er . . ." Xin was fuming, unable to find the right words, while Gary had yet to decide whether he should just snatch it out of the man's hand or pretend like it wasn't his.

"Hey, calm down, it's not like a condom is going to be used as a weapon," Jayden said as he walked forward. "Actually, on second thought, you could probably suffocate someone with one of these things."

The Altered snatched it out of the guard's hand before he could even react. Then he turned to Gary, staring him right in the eyes, an evil smile on his face.

"While I'm happy to see that you care about protection, I really hope you weren't thinking of using this anytime soon, Gary. Otherwise, I might have you assist me in testing out my theory of how lethal a weapon such a thing would make."

All Gary could do was gulp and shake his head, as he quickly opted to use his plan B.

"That's not mine! . . . yeah, you saw my friend in the car earlier, right? It's his suit! He must have left it inside as a prank! I'm sorry, I would never think of doing something like that with your sister."

"Oh!" Jayden gasped theatrically. "So you're saying my sister isn't pretty enough for you now?"

Gary was aware that this was one of those situations where no matter what he said, it was going to be taken the wrong way. Unfortunately, understanding the situation wouldn't help him get out of it. Right now, he wanted to kill Kai for his "gift" . . . even though he knew it was his own fault.

Since a suit didn't have the pocket space, it would have been impossible to take along the whole box. Still, after he had changed, Gary had taken out a single one. He had little hope that anything would happen tonight, yet as the saying went, "better safe than sorry" . . . But now he felt like any second he might see his life flash before his eyes.

Thankfully, Xin came to his rescue by pulling on her brother's ear.

"Stop acting this way toward Gary, you dolt. He just said that it was a prank, so why are you still teasing him about it? Besides, I don't need you deciding things for me!"

A little while later, Gary was escorted to the living room, where Xin had sat down on a single sofa by herself. Meanwhile, her guest was sitting on a sofa next to Jayden, and he was still unable to look either one in the eyes. Since the condom incident, the atmosphere was a little awkward to say the least.

"So, Gary, why don't we use this time to learn a bit more about you? Maybe something that only we would be interested in. Apart from you being a horndog, I mean," Jayden said, breaking the silence. "Not just anyone can take one of my punches. You were clearly more durable than those other guys that day, so I've been wondering where you learned to fight like that? What style are you training in?"

"Wow, it's not often Jayden praises anyone. That sounds like you were a lot better than when you came to the karate club. Be honest, did you hold back in your fight against me that day? Since you're in the rugby club, that means you must have learned outside school, no?" Xin added, and Jayden was paying close attention to the green-haired teenager's answers.

"Ah . . . I'm not in a club or anything like that," Gary replied nervously, still keeping his head down. "I've had an interest in fighting ever since I was young. My dad was actually the one who introduced it to me. Now I watch the Altered Fighting Championship all the time. Those guys are athletes who are meant to be the best of the best.

"I don't even remember when, but at some point I started watching the most skillful fighters who have practiced nothing but punching and kicking, and ways to beat their opponent. Those fights always got me heated up, so I've been studying them a lot . . ."

Gary trailed off. In the world of fighting, just hard work wasn't enough. Everyone worked hard. Unfortunately, the cold hard truth was that while reflexes, flexibility, and strength could be improved, there were things like talent that one couldn't change. And on the world stage, where the best fought against the best, those people had often been born with a natural advantage.

Of course, becoming Altered changed everything even further. He himself knew that best. While becoming a werewolf was surely different, even a fraction of what he was doing these days would have been impossible with his old body.

"Anyway, recently I found someone else who is really interested in it as well. He does a lot of Muay Thai fighting, and the two of us have been practicing quite a lot," Gary continued.

He had learned that the best way to tell a lie was to mix it with part of the truth. That way, he didn't have to make up a lot of stuff. As long as he avoided telling certain bits, the other person would just fill in the blanks.

"I see, so you must be quite the fan of mine, huh? Is that why you chose to get close to Xin? To get to me?" Jayden asked. Just as Gary was about to explain that that wasn't the case, the Altered just waved it off.

"I'm just kidding, I already know that you had no idea. Still, that's actually one of the reasons I wanted to talk to you. My and Xin's relationship, the fact that she is my little sister, is supposed to stay a secret.

"There's more than one reason for it, but I won't bore you with any of the details. If you want what's best for Xin, I ask you to keep it to yourself. Right now, it's even more important than before."

Gary nodded, immediately agreeing; he didn't want to make her life any harder than it was.

"Say, Xin, now that we have time, mind explaining to me what's going to happen to you?" Gary asked. "Why will you no longer be going to Westbridge? Is it because of what happened? And where will you go, since you said you might only come back on the weekends?"

To try to convince her parents, he needed to know why they wanted her gone in the first place.

"Actually it's—"

"Dinner is ready." A beautiful middle-aged woman who was nearly as glowing as Xin opened the door. Her hair was in curls rather than straightened like Xin's, but it was undeniably the same ashen color. To put it simply, Gary could clearly see where she had gotten her good looks.

"Oh!" the woman said as she noticed the boy in the room, and she placed her hands together, smiling at him. "And this young man must be the one joining us today. Sorry I didn't introduce myself. My name is Natalia Clove, but no need to introduce yourself now, you can do that at the dinner table."

After she said these words, Gary noticed that Natalia was staring at him. No, more specifically, she was staring at his hair.

"Ah . . . it's my natural color . . . I can't change it?" Gary blurted out, since this was somewhat the truth now, at least according to the system.

Unsurprisingly, his response earned him a chuckle from everyone in the room. Gary was embarrassed, but he realized that making them laugh might have been a good thing. Following Xin's mother, the three of them finally entered the dining room.

There was a large rectangular table, and each table setting had a place card in front of it. Gary saw that he would be seated next to the mayor, at the head of the table. He gulped hard once again but sat down next to the corpulent man.

Seeing the mayor in person was different from seeing him on TV. There was a certain aura around him, an aura of confidence that Gary had felt around other people before: Damion, Brandon . . . and Kai. The aura of a leader.

I feel like this dinner is going to be a battle itself.

"Welcome to our humble home, Gary Dem," Ben said, offering him a handshake.

CHAPTER 73

THE MEAL (PART 1)

Gary had noticed that the mayor had slightly flinched when he came in. It wasn't hard to guess what had elicited this reaction. Right now, he didn't feel like he had green hair, but rather a giant glowing beacon growing on the top of his head.

Should I have tried to shave it off before coming here, or would it have just grown back?

Since his first impression was already negative, Gary decided to be on his best behavior, so he enthusiastically accepted the handshake. However, it felt as if the mayor was trying to crush his hand. Gary wasn't sure if the mayor simply had a strong grip, or if this was supposed to be some sort of test.

What the hell is this guy doing? Gary thought as he kept up a friendly smile, mimicking Xin's father. Not wanting to come off as weak, the alpha werewolf increased his grip, though he made sure not to injure the man.

"You're quite the strong one," Ben said, seemingly impressed by Gary's strength. He then looked him up and down as if he was inspecting him. "You know, I often tell Xin that she should look for a boy who is at least as strong as her brother here, and you're the first guy who seems decent."

The mayor patted Gary's arm, while Xin turned a few shades of red. Ever since he became a werewolf, the teenager had gained the body of an athlete. Although he knew that his system was responsible for it, and not his own hard work, he didn't mind taking the credit.

Strangely, the mayor continued to stand opposite him. Gary saw that the others were also still standing, so he felt it would be rude if he sat down before the patriarch of the family. Honestly, he just wanted the meal to start, but the mayor continued to wait for something. In the end, Gary just nervously laughed, which seemed to change the mayor's mood in an instant, as his smile disappeared from his face.

"I thought you might have known better after seeing the way you were dressed." Ben sighed. "I'm guessing you brought no gift?"

What? Was I supposed to bring a gift? I thought this was just dinner? I've never gone to anyone's house before, other than Tom's. I never knew that . . . and it's not like I ever had the money to buy a gift for someone else before. Is this something rich people do?

"I'm sorry, I didn't realize . . . I'll be happy to buy you something next time . . . to make up for it," Gary managed to stutter out in a mix of confusion and panic.

"Brave of you to assume there will be a next time," Ben said as he took his seat. With that, everyone else sat down as well. But Xin wasn't pleased by her father's antics.

"Dad, why are you hassling Gary about a gift? He's not one of your guests, but my classmate. Why would he have to bring you a gift, especially since all of this was on such short notice?"

"I know, I know, darling." Ben laughed it off. "I was just teasing the young man. He should be able to take it, don't you think?"

There were a few chuckles around the table, and Gary nervously joined in, but he had a feeling the mayor hadn't been joking. He was also starting to rethink his choice of trying to convince the man.

Fortunately, the food was served just then, giving Gary a welcome reprieve. As much as he wanted to dig in, he waited for Xin's father to take the first bite. Unfortunately, that was where his manners ended. The others couldn't help but stare at him as he quickly took large bites, seemingly afraid that someone might take away his food.

"Whoa, you're acting like you haven't eaten in weeks. Slow down there, buddy," Jayden said. "You seem to be a big eater, like me; no wonder you stole all my food back then."

"He did *what*?" Xin's mother gasped in shock.

"Ah, my bad, I guess 'stole' is the wrong word. The first time I met Gary, I invited him back to my hotel. I told him he could take whatever he wanted, though I didn't expect him to raid my entire fridge."

"Wait, you two met before? When was that?" Xin asked, suddenly very curious. She had never heard her brother mention Gary before.

"Ah, it was when I went to pick you up that one time. However, you texted me that you already had a lift," Jayden explained, knowing he couldn't reveal the full details. "Actually, it's quite the funny story. While I was ready to turn around, my headlights started to shine on this pale white a—"

Suddenly Jayden felt a certain heat radiating from across the table, and a pair of dagger eyes were staring at him. Gary was imperceptibly shaking his head, telling him not to continue that story.

"Never mind, now that I think about it, it's one of those things that is funnier in the moment."

The room went silent once again. After the comment about his table manners, Gary slowed down, making sure to eat at the same pace as the Altered. It was a difficult task, especially since most of the food was a lot yummier than what he would usually eat. He was even tempted to ask for seconds to take home so he could share them with Amy, but he decided against it, afraid that their opinion of him might decrease further.

Is my brother talking about the night we were attacked by those monsters . . . is that the day the two of them met for the first time? Wasn't Tom looking for Gary that day as well? What was he doing in that area then? Xin wondered.

She wanted to ask Jayden more about that night.

CHAPTER 74

THE MEAL (PART 2)

Eventually, everyone had finished their meal. Xin's parents had asked Gary a few more questions. Fortunately, it was just normal small talk about his family and how he was doing in school in general. He was more than happy to tell them about it, especially about being one of the rugby stars of Westbridge, which apparently gained him a bit more favor with the mayor.

"Speaking of school, the reason I'm here is that I heard that you wanted to transfer Xin somewhere else," Gary said, addressing the difficult topic. "If you don't mind, Xin, I wanted to ask you if you could tell me the reason, or at least where you'll be going."

"Don't you think the reason for it is pretty clear?" Xin's father raised an eyebrow. "Your school was attacked by a gang, and my daughter got kidnapped in the aftermath. We were lucky that Jayden happened to be in town, but things could have easily ended up a lot worse.

"If we allow Xin to stay at Westbridge, she will just be targeted again sooner or later. I'm happy that you care for my daughter, Gary, but even as its mayor, I have to admit that Slough is not the safest place. That's why we have decided to transfer her to another school in a Tier 2 city."

It was just as Gary had expected, so he knew it was going to be hard to convince them. Still, it was at least worth a try.

"But is a Tier 2 city really that much safer? I heard that they have even bigger gangs in the Tier 2 and Tier 1 cities. Aren't you afraid that the same thing might happen again? At least here, she would be with her family, not to mention Jayden and your guards. I can't imagine you can be in two places at once."

"Don't worry, we have selected a special boarding academy for her. Her protection is our top priority, so trust me when I say that with how much the tuition costs, their security is top-notch. Also, although they have gangs up there, it's not the same as it is here in Slough.

"As mayor, I am painfully aware of my own town's gang situation. You see, in the bigger cities, the status quo rarely changes. Developments don't just happen suddenly, so even if something were to happen, we could always pull Xin out before chaos breaks out.

"Slough is different. How much do you know about the gang situation in our city?" Ben asked.

"I've heard some bits and pieces," he answered, doing his best not to grin.

The mayor sighed. "I suppose in this day and age it's nothing but wishful thinking on my part to hope that you hadn't. Anyway, Slough isn't safe these days. Even before those ingrates tried to hold your school hostage, there was a wide-scale attack by the color gangs not too long ago.

"That was because the two big-time gangs have been trying to start something. What's more, a new gang has recently risen. As if the situation weren't bad enough already, I suspect these Howlers may make everything even more complicated and dangerous for the average citizen."

Hearing his gang name caused Gary to start coughing. It was the last thing he had expected to hear at this dinner. Nevertheless, for argument's sake, he had to push further.

"But . . . are all gangs bad?" Gary asked.

This question earned him strange glances from the Clove family. Somebody Gary's age usually wouldn't say such a thing . . . unless of course they were thinking about joining a gang in the future.

"That's . . . quite an interesting question. Care to elaborate?" Ben Clove rested his chin on his hand.

Unfortunately, Gary hadn't really thought things through. He had mostly been referring to his own gang. He looked around the table and realized that neither Xin nor Jayden was going to save him from this one.

"Well, I mean . . ." Gary glanced at the guards in the room. "What about your guards? Aren't they from the Rising Dragon gang? Don't you use them to protect yourself and your family? I would say that is a good thing that they're doing.

"I used to hate gangs a lot, but the more I thought about it, the more I started to just see them like any business. In the world that we live in . . . they are like a necessary evil. They might have a different name, but aren't corporations similar to gangs? They tell smaller companies to do their bidding, and if they don't oblige, they get bought out or bullied out of the market. And who's to say that this new gang that has come and taken over isn't better than the old one? Maybe they want to change the status quo for the better?"

Gary realized that he had gone on a bit of a tangent, and he might even have gone one step too far. So he stopped there and waited for a response.

"For a child, your worldview is quite peculiar." Xin's father finally broke the silence. "Still, I agree that they can seem to be a necessary evil. Corporations, and even political parties and campaigns, act like gangs in the ways you've described. I won't deny that some of their tactics may be unethical.

"However, I think you're missing a key difference. Gangs kill, steal, rob, and force others to do things; in short, pretty much everything they do is illegal. Take that new gang as an example. They came in and beat another gang into submission, thereby acquiring their assets. Does that sound fair or legal to you?"

Damn, he's talking about the Howlers and the Pincers; even the mayor knows about that already. That only happened yesterday. How did the news travel so fast? Was it someone from the Rising Dragons who told him?

For some reason, the conversation that Kai had with Gary in the car replayed in his head.

There's something Kai didn't tell me. There's a reason why he told me to be careful.

CHAPTER 75

THE MEAL (PART 3)

Ben Clove continued speaking; he had switched into mayor mode, making Gary realize that arguing with him on this topic wasn't the best idea. This was more a situation for someone like Tom or his sister to deal with.

"As bad as gangs might be, at least there is a status quo between them that the others respect," Xin's father continued. "No matter how noble the intentions of a new gang, their appearance makes everything worse. The whole balance of power gets shifted. I can guarantee you that soon another gang will come in and try to get a piece of the pie.

"But fine, I'll humor you. Suppose these Howlers actually just want the best for the common people; why did they choose to go about it this way? They could have joined the police force or become judges, or politicians like me, something that can benefit our society as a whole while still adhering to its rules."

Gary didn't like the way the mayor had seemingly simplified things. If it were so simple, wouldn't people have done it by now? He was sure that many had tried and failed in changing things the legal way. Heck, wasn't the lawyer he had met yesterday the best example of how easy it was to play the system?

And yet this conversation allowed Gary to examine his own feelings on the topic. When exactly had he come around to the idea of gangs? At least the Howlers' way of doing things seemed to be just . . .

Maybe I've been hanging around Kai too much. Gary smiled at this thought, which didn't go unnoticed by Ben.

"Say, Gary, you seem to know a lot about gangs for someone your age. I doubt many would know that these guards of mine are part of the Rising Dragon gang. Don't tell me you're planning to join one in the future?"

"No, no, not at all." Gary shook his hands to deny it vehemently. "It's just . . . when I was with Jayden I heard that name mentioned. Based on the tattoos your guards have on their necks, I assumed they were gang members. As for what I plan to do in the future . . . I honestly don't know yet. As long as it allows me to look after my family, I'll be happy with pretty much anything, I guess."

When he said these words, the image that appeared in Gary's head wasn't just of his mother and Amy, but also of all his friends at the Wolf's Pool Club, as well as Tom.

The intense conversation about gangs had come to an end, just in time for dessert to be brought out. Chocolate cake. Gary looked at it with mixed feelings. He could only imagine how great it would taste, judging by the quality of food he had enjoyed so far. Ultimately, though, he placed his fork down.

"What's wrong, don't you like chocolate cake?" Xin's mother asked.

"No . . . it's not that . . . unfortunately, I'm allergic to chocolate," Gary answered, letting out a heavy sigh.

"Damn!" Jayden commented. "If I were allergic to chocolate . . . I don't even know what I would do."

Xin started to remember when Gary got sick. It was a distinctive memory, since that was what had started her troubles with Tiffany. There had been that chocolate bar as well as Tom's bag out on the table, which had been seemingly filled with more chocolate at the time.

That explains why he was sick . . . but why would Tom give him any? Didn't they know he was allergic before a few weeks ago? That doesn't make any sense.

Fortunately, it was not much of an issue. Instead of chocolate cake, Gary's dessert became a bowl of vanilla ice cream and afterward, he realized that it was already pretty late.

"I was thinking, does Xin really have to go to another school?" Gary finally asked. "I mean, aren't you afraid that moving all the time will affect her studies? I understand that you're worried about the gangs, but I don't think anything like that will happen again.

"Security has been improved, and there are people like me who can look out for her. Also, now that the gangs know that there is someone like Jayden behind her, I doubt they would try anything. On the other hand, if something like this happens with a gang in a Tier 2 city . . . I don't know if it's true or not, but I've heard someone say that those gangs have their own Altered."

It was the only thing Gary could come up with to try to make them change their mind. Xin looked as if she was in pain. It reassured him that she didn't want to move either.

"Ah, that's very sweet of you, Gary. I'm very happy that my dear Xin managed to make a friend who cares so much about her," Natalia said with her hands together. "However, we have already been over this a few times. Whatever you might say, we have already thought of everything. If you really want to see Xin, she will be able to come back on weekends, so not all will be lost."

"Actually, Mum, I decided I won't be coming back. I'll stay at the academy, I mean," Xin clarified. "Gary, I was going to tell you when we were on our own, but this will probably be the last time we see each other for a while.

"I'm not just moving to any boarding school, but I'll be joining the Altered Fighting Academy. I also want to be serious about this, so I plan to stay in their boarding program and continue their training even on weekends. That's why I invited you over and wanted to speak to you today."

Hearing those words from Xin rather than from her father or mother, Gary realized that this was something Xin had decided on her own. After the meal had finished up, the conversation seemed to lead elsewhere and Gary didn't really know what to do or what to say.

Given the late hour, he eventually bid his goodbyes to the adults, and it was time for him to say goodbye to Xin. They stood by the door; her parents were already gone and just her brother was by her side.

"I'm sorry, Gary, I didn't realize it would upset you so much . . . and sorry for giving you such a crappy first date." Xin apologized as she held Gary's hand. The next second she leaned in, and before he could react, she already had pressed her soft lips on his cheek.

"This is my thank-you present for saving me." She leaned back, her face red, before she suddenly ran off.

Leaving Gary to stroke the side of his face.

"That girl, always trying to do what she wants but never being able to." Jayden sighed. "Come on, let's head outside. You're not completely off the hook yet, streaker boy. It's time for our conversation."

CHAPTER 76

THE AFA

Gary hadn't had a chance to call or text Kai to come and pick him up. Honestly, his mind was still trying to comprehend everything that had happened with Xin, especially the sudden kiss on his cheek at the very end. He was still rubbing his face to the point that it had become even redder than before.

It would definitely become a memory he would never be able to forget. Unfortunately, it seemed destined to become a melancholic one, since he had no idea when he would even be able to see her again. Were they even allowed to keep their phones in the AFC? Were he and Xin actually even a couple, or was it best for him to just forget about her and try to move on?

What was worse, Jayden seemed to insist on having their conversation.

"What exactly do you want to talk about?" Gary asked, since he had no idea. There were so many topics the Altered might have in mind, none of them good . . .

Instead of answering, Jayden walked off to an annex on the property. Another building not too far away. "Come on, you'll find out inside; why don't we finish off what we started."

Gary was a little worried what those words exactly meant. Was the Altered challenging him to another fight? If so, Gary didn't mind too much. He didn't get many chances to fight with someone as great as Jayden.

However, based on the day before yesterday, when he had seen Jayden's anger take hold of him, he was worried that the Altered might just want to get rid of him, especially after the little show of affection from Xin and what had been found in his pocket.

Hang on, Jayden still has that, right?

"Come on!" Jayden said. "I'm not going to kill you, if that's what you're worried about."

Gary gulped, but he sighed the next moment. Xin's brother was right; if he wanted to kill him, he could probably do it. He also would likely avoid doing so on his parents' property.

Besides, Jayden isn't a gangster in the first place. I guess I've just been hanging around dangerous people for too long. Gary shook his head.

Following Jayden into the annex, Gary found himself in what could only be described as a training room. There were mats on the floors, bags on the side, and even a ring on one end of the room. It was a setup that any Altered fighter would have dreamed to have in their own home.

While Gary was still admiring all the training equipment, Jayden threw him a pair of red gloves. "Put them on, and we'll go for a round or two, all right?" Despite his tone, it didn't seem like Gary had much of a choice. The Altered was already wearing a pair of white gloves.

"Wait, are you serious? But we already fought before, and you're . . . well, Jayden Tiger. What chance do I stand against one of our country's top fifty Altered fighters? Fighting you is just asking for a beating," Gary argued. He wanted to fight, but not if Jayden was to go full Altered on him.

"Don't worry, last time I attacked you because I mistook you for one of those goons. It's just a friendly spar, so I won't go all out on you. Since you managed to take a few of my hits, I'm curious to see how good you truly are. You said you like fighting, right? Why not take this as an opportunity to learn. And if you need extra incentive, how about I give you my autograph if you manage to win?"

Hearing this from one of his idols, Gary started to put on the gloves. Since this was just going to be a friendly spar, and he didn't think Jayden would be going at him as aggressively as before, he agreed. The autograph reward was also enticing. He was sure it would be worth a lot of money if he were to sell it. Maybe he could use it as an excuse for moving his family into a different apartment.

I fought the Pincers and my stats have improved since the last time we fought. It might also be a good chance to see whether that one Pawn point toward my next grade gave me any benefits I'm not aware of. Let's check out the gap between the two of us, Gary thought.

Jayden offered Gary a change of clothes, something he would be more comfortable in. After changing, he got into a fighting stance.

Meanwhile, Jayden was standing there relaxed, with no particular form. He was jumping up and down on his toes, seemingly warming up. The sight sent shivers down Gary's spine.

I thought he was going to take it easy on me, so why the hell is he doing what he does in all of his official matches?

Before Jayden was fully warmed up, Gary decided to interrupt him. He moved forward, and then, once he thought he was close enough, he sprinted ahead at full speed. The burst of sudden movement caught Jayden by surprise, which was what Gary had been going for as he threw out his fist.

Jayden lifted his leg and used the werewolf's momentum to kick him in the chin. It was a strong hit; the system told him so.

"Clever, but you should take into account our ranges before throwing out a punch," Jayden said.

–14 HP

My Endurance has increased, and he's not even using his Altered body . . . I can't tell how strong this guy is! Gary thought.

Recovering, he tried to throw another punch, covering himself in case Jayden retaliated further. Gary was able to bear the pain, but for some reason when he did throw a punch it was a little off target and missed his opponent's head completely.

"You should take the time to recover," Jayden advised. "Your sense of balance has shifted. I'm impressed you weren't knocked out by that counter. Even if you can stand up again, it will take a few moments before you're back to normal."

Rather than use the opportunity to punch Gary, Jayden grabbed him by the scruff of his shirt. Immediately, Gary grabbed his arm and used all his strength to rip it off, tearing part of his clothing away.

Shit . . . that thing must have been expensive! Let's hope it's possible to mend it, Gary thought as he delivered a kick.

It was strange because based on Jayden's movements so far, Gary had expected him to avoid the kick. Instead, his arm was already raised to block it.

So you think I'm that weak, huh? Well, you're in for a surprise! Gary thought as he put all of his speed and power into the kick.

Skill activated: Controlled Transformation

His leg slammed into the side of Jayden's arm, and it caused his feet to skid a little. The Altered's arm was throbbing, but before Gary could react, Jayden grabbed onto the leg that had kicked him and used his strength to push Gary off balance.

He hopped on the other leg for a second before a kick suddenly swept it away, causing him to fall on his back. He winced in pain, and the next moment, he saw Jayden's fist coming toward his face.

This is going to hurt, Gary thought as he closed his eyes and braced himself . . . but the punch never connected. Opening his eyes, he saw the fist inches from his face.

"Well, looks like it's my win. If you feel like you can do better, we can go for another round, but I already got what I wanted," Jayden said as he offered Gary a hand.

"Oh, I see, so you were just using me, telling me I could learn something from this. All I learned was you can easily kick my ass," Gary replied in a snarky manner, a little upset that he didn't fare better in the fight. That was the second time he had lost to Jayden now, and he wasn't even sure just how wide the gap between them was.

"So, what exactly did you get out of this? Revenge on me for raiding your fridge?"

Jayden turned around and grinned. "Well, there's that too, I suppose, though after all my teasing during dinner I'd say you're already off the hook. There's no shame in having lost, especially since you lost to one of the best fighters out there.

"Besides, it's hardly a fair fight seeing as I'm older than you and have a lot more experience. Still, for someone your age, you really are a skilled fighter, though I can tell that your fighting style is not exactly orthodox. With more training, I'm sure you could grow up to be an excellent fighter, which brings me to what I wanted to talk with you about.

"You really like my sister, don't you? I mean, not just anyone would have gone up against a color gang to get her back. If you want to chase after Xin . . . how about joining the AFA as well? Like I said, you're talented, and it would be a shame to waste all of that potential.

"Don't you think that would be the perfect place for an Altered like yourself?"

CHAPTER 77

A SPECIAL MEETING

Gary didn't know what to say after Jayden's accusation. So he opted to stay quiet, which in itself was pretty telling to the Altered. Since they seemed to be done with their conversation, Gary texted Kai, who told him that he would pick him up in around ten minutes.

It felt like a small eternity as Gary and Jayden waited together in awkward silence.

How did he find out? The first time we met, I was buck naked . . . and I didn't do anything serious during our fight two days ago, did I? Gary was racking his brain trying to figure out how he had been discovered. They had only fought for brief moments before today. *Was it the kick on the arm? He could have avoided that blow . . . but he took it straight on. Was that the whole reason he wanted to fight? To test me?*

For once, Gary was right on the money with his guess. Jayden had had his suspicions after fighting him two days ago. It just seemed strange for the teenager to be able to perform that well. After all, the Altered had seen that Gary, just like himself, had fought his way through to the cabin, yet he hadn't looked exhausted.

This meant that the green-haired teenager had either the stamina of a top athlete . . . or that of an Altered. He might have believed the former, but streaker boy had looked completely different from when Jayden had first met him. Unless Gary had been using performance-enhancing drugs, which shouldn't be able to change someone that drastically in such a short amount of time, the only other explanation would be that he had become an Altered.

The final nail in the coffin was the kick. Jayden had decided to take the full strength of his attack head on, and that was what had convinced him that Gary wasn't completely human anymore. The real question was, how had the food thief been able to pay for it?

A kid being sponsored who wasn't in the AFA was practically unheard of. It wasn't that no one his age was selected, but whoever sponsored him, would have also paid for his tuition, and of course they would have registered him. Since he wasn't on the register for Altered, it would have had to be an illegal procedure, which would cost even more . . .

"You're not in any trouble. Your secret is safe with me," Jayden said as the car arrived. "I won't pry into your circumstances, but I highly recommend you think my idea over. Even if you hadn't been chasing after my little sis, I would still tell you to go to the AFA. It will completely change your life. You'll be able to move to a high-tier city, and you'll also be able to look after your family."

With that, Jayden headed back inside, while Gary approached the Bersedez Menz. Before entering, though, Gary looked toward the house and saw a curtain drawn and Xin looking out of it.

He gave her a wave, which she returned before closing the curtain, and he was off. Perhaps never coming back to this place ever again. During the car ride, Kai looked at Gary expectantly, waiting for his friend to share the details. Unfortunately, he just stared out the window, seemingly in a world of his own.

"Shall I take it that the date didn't go as well as you would have liked? Is that what's on your mind?" Kai asked eventually.

"No . . . I'm just thinking about everyone and everything," Gary answered, shifting his gaze to Kai. "Do you think we could ever move to a Tier 2 city . . . I mean all of us. Changing schools and everything?"

As he pondered Jayden's suggestion, he saw a few big problems. Gary didn't have a sponsor, so he would have to come up with the funds to join the AFA in the first place. Then there was the fact that it was located in a Tier 2 city.

Joining the AFA would mean leaving everything behind, unless he could take all of it with him. Sure, if he had enough money he could take Amy and his mother when she got better, but what about the gang? On top of that, the money that they had earned wasn't his money. Leader or not, it was primarily the Howlers' money, which was why he asked Kai.

"It should be possible . . . if we're talking down the line," Kai answered after taking some time to think about it. "However, if you mean right now, then I'll have to ask you to forget about it. It's already too late. Since we've taken over the Pincers' area, we're officially one of Slough's small-time gangs.

"At the moment, we are at a crucial phase for the Howlers as a gang. Taking over was just the first step, and we'll definitely have to prepare for the others trying to challenge us for our territory now. Then there are other things we have to do in Slough.

"Still, once we've taken over the town and can guarantee that nobody will try to pry it from our hands, we could talk about it. After all, I have my sights on the higher-tier cities anyway. So if there's something you want in those higher-tier cities, then go for it. Use it as a goal to push you forward even more."

The answer at least gave Gary some hope that maybe one day he would see Xin again, though for now he would have to concentrate on Slough. They needed to deal with everything here, including the Underdogs and the Gray Elephants.

The two started to talk about what went on at Xin's house, and Gary told Kai about the unfortunate events such as the condom incident and the dinner table problems. He even admitted that he was worried he might never see Xin again. Kai responded by trying to hold back his smirk, showing some concern, and lastly pretending to wipe away a tear, much to Gary's annoyance.

"Well, it sounds like it's a good thing that I didn't go into detail about the mayor after all. Otherwise, you might have said something really rude in that heated conversation of yours."

"What do you mean?" Gary asked.

"You already know that the mayor is involved with the gangs in this area. In particular the Rising Dragon, but there is a lot more to that than meets the eye. Tomorrow there will be a meeting between all five of the gangs.

"The invitation was originally sent out to Olivia, but of course with us having taken over the Pincers, we got one addressed to us personally. That means you, as our leader, will have to attend this little meeting and as for the one who called it in the first place . . . well, I think you can guess where I'm going with this."

CHAPTER 78

THE PAST RESURFACES

Inside a dark room where there was very little light, a young teenager sat in a chair. Across from him was a floating head in a glass container filled with a green liquid.

Originally I thought that maybe you would only be gone for a day or two, but you still haven't gotten back, Blake thought. The head in front of him was none other than Billy's. *At least the liquid will keep it from rotting for now.*

Lately, Blake had been visiting the Hunters' base a lot. Usually he only came down with his father, practicing what he needed in the dojo above. However, as the days passed it became apparent that his father wasn't going to come back anytime soon, so he decided to make the most of his time.

At first, he had tried various weapons. Technically, some of them belonged to his father and he shouldn't have used them, but since his last sword had broken, he required replacements.

Still, despite his training, it wasn't like Blake had been rushing out to go hunting, at least not on his own. Today was one of those days when he just didn't feel like training and instead couldn't keep his eyes off Billy's head in front of him.

Something . . . has changed in me ever since that day, Blake thought. *I've always wanted to live an ordinary life, but now . . .*

things that I used to enjoy, like rugby, just seem so boring in comparison.

Blake thought back to when he had helped Gary fight against the red color gang members. A rush had come over him; he didn't just help Gary because he needed to, but because he enjoyed using his skills.

The skills he had practiced over and over for years were finally being put to use, but now he was at a standstill once again. Unable to move forward.

Maybe I could ask Gary to go hunting with me again? See if we can find any Altered? No, that wouldn't work; Gary only hunted Billy because he was dangerous to others. He doesn't have the same view on Altered as we do, and besides I don't think getting close to him is a good idea.

Blake got up and went to the bookshelf, which contained countless books and journals from his ancestors as well as other prominent hunters in the past. Many of the journals had been gathered from different families, not just his, but most of them told the same history. How their group was created to slay the beasts that threatened to take over the land.

The beasts carried something inside them called the shadow. They could infect humans with the shadow as well, making them slowly decay into chaos. It was a bad time for humanity until those who bore the symbol of the red dragon had gathered to smite the beasts, ridding the land of the shadow's presence.

Reading one of the journals again made Blake chuckle. The stories sounded like fairy tales, yet there was some truth to them. After all, fossils of the beasts those hunters used to hunt resurfaced from time to time, and that was how they created Altered in the first place.

The hunters had continued to do the same as the followers of the red dragon, getting rid of those that had been infected with the beasts' power. Although the world might hate them in this era, theirs was a noble quest to make sure the world didn't fall into chaos again.

But I guess Gary is different; he's not a beast, the test said so. We say that Altered go mad as their blood starts to darken, but Gary isn't the same. I wonder if there is anything more about werewolves in these journals? He admitted that he couldn't control himself during the full moon, and the next one isn't that far off.

Maybe one of these books has something that might help him. Otherwise, when my father comes back, we might end up having to hunt him again, which would break my promise. Something is telling me that it would be best that I keep it.

Looking through the journals, Blake skimmed through a lot of information, looking for stories about werewolves. Just as before, though, most of them told tales of the olden days from different viewpoints.

However, he did notice that even when their stories didn't add up to a single truth, a few things that were coherent among them all. One thing that a lot of the journals mentioned was one of the strongest hunters in existence that many of them looked up to.

A passage about him caught Blake's eye. This man was praised by many of the hunters and was seen as an idol. He was hailed by all the sources as a once-in-a-generation genius with the sword.

Many hunters tried to replicate his mastery of the sword, and it was said that he had the ability to know where to strike. The journals claimed that he attributed his gift to an innate ability to see white lines that told him the optimal place to strike. It seemed like an exaggeration, but apparently he hadn't been the only one among the hunters with such ability.

It was impossible to confirm or deny it. Blake only knew that he wasn't one of those people. Still, he was focusing on this person because there were many names for him, but one of the sources had named him *Gary*.

When Blake read that passage, he had to blink twice to make sure his eyes weren't playing tricks on him. It was amusing that his schoolmate had the same name. As he turned the page, though, he spotted a story about this Gary that mentioned werewolves.

The tension between the two alphas had been rising. We had been informed that this would happen. Gary was told to decide what to do next, whether he would be involved in this war and choose to help his friend.

After all, everyone knew there was a saying among all the werewolves: Two alphas could never coexist.

Reading it again, Blake tried to get his head around what it meant. It didn't really shine any light on the situation with Gary, and since he knew nothing about werewolves, the words didn't make sense.

Unfortunately, the other pages were too worn and damaged to make out anything coherent. It was a real disappointment, as he had been hoping to learn what happened next.

I wonder if I should tell Gary about this . . . I guess I should see if there is more first, Blake thought as he continued to dig in to find out what had happened in the past, to know what might happen in the future.

CHAPTER 79

A SPECIAL MISSION

Tier 4 was the second-lowest tier ranking a town or city could get. Nearly all jobs in such a place involved manual labor. If one couldn't work that way, there were other means of making a living, including another type of manual labor.

The jobs in Tier 4 towns were often dangerous, yet they produced items for the higher-ranking towns and cities. They were essentially factories for their respective countries and the whole world. There was always a dark, thick smog over those towns.

The air was polluted, making the people suffer, and it was unfriendly to their bodies just like the people were. These towns also had more gangs than one could count. On top of that, if you weren't in a gang for protection, you would soon find yourself in a bloody mess.

Unlike in a Tier 3 town like Slough, where the gangs worked behind the scenes and skimming money off other companies, in this particular Tier 4 town they didn't shy away from doing things out in the open. Being in no gang was risky because it meant gang members could attack you without fearing any consequences. If you were asked to fight for the gang, even if you weren't a fighter you had better be there.

Of course, some people managed to survive without a gang. They were either too weak to join a gang, addicted to drugs, or reliant on something else such as alcohol to escape reality. It was rare that these types of people could afford to live in a Tier 4 town for long, and usually it was just a matter of time until they ended up having to move to a Tier 5 town.

Then there were those who were just a little too crazy and that needed to be avoided at all costs.

When Ozacas first entered the town of Dreadix, he thought that his stay there would be a short one. Any Altered who came to a Tier 4 town did so only to run away from something. Most likely they had offended someone they couldn't afford to, were on the run from the White Rose agents, or were fleeing for some other messed-up reason.

Whatever the case, the fact that he, a three-star hunter, had been called to assist two others of that rank meant that this mission would be a tough one. Still, the experienced Altered Hunter wasn't afraid. In fact, if he could be the one to bring down this Altered, he would only be one kill away from ranking up into a four-star hunter.

Until he realized that this job was slightly different compared to the ones he was used to.

Walking down a smoggy street, he met up with the other Altered Hunters. The two of them were covered in hoods, since this was a bad part of town, even for a Tier 4 town. As they walked down the road, they saw people who were all skinnier than should be healthy. They were most likely barely able to afford food, making them resemble zombies as they dragged their feet along on their way home.

"Have you considered my offer, Ozacas?" the hunter with orange spiky hair sticking out from his mask asked. His body was slightly larger than the others, but it was top heavy and didn't make him look fat, just muscled.

"I'm still in the middle of training my son," the three-star hunter replied. "However, once he's ready, I'll happily take him along to that Tier 2 city. Unfortunately, he still has a lot to learn.

"As a matter of fact, I hope that we can deal with this matter quickly. I've been here longer than I had anticipated, and as you might know, Slough has had its fair share of problems recently."

Eventually, they arrived in front of a crummy-looking apartment building. Still, it seemed to be in better condition than the surrounding buildings, seeing as all its floors were somewhat intact.

"This should be the right place . . . we just need to find out what is happening here and report back to the association. We need to be quick and not hesitate like last time," the orange-haired man said, since he was the leader of this group.

Rather than entering through the front door, which was closed, they went around the side looking for an opening. Jumping off the side of the other building, the leader used his momentum to grab the ledge of a window on the second floor.

Fortunately, it was already smashed. He pulled himself in, and the others followed his example. Once inside, each of them pulled out their concealed weapons. For Ozacas, it was a single longsword, though it wasn't the same one that he had used when fighting against Billy.

This one was a little more special in design. On its hilt green roots grew upward from the bottom. His colleagues had similar special weapons. The orange-haired leader had two small axes in his hands, while the third member had a chain.

Walking through the hallway, the group had already put on their masks and activated the masks' special function: a heat-searching mechanism that enabled then to see a group of several people that were above them.

However, their heat signals were a little hotter than usual; this was true for all of them.

"It's the same as last time; the reading isn't too high, but it's still above the norm," the leader said. "Remember, they're not regular humans, so don't hesitate this time."

It wasn't the first raid they had been on. After all, they had been in this city a while, but they had a special mission to accomplish, and they wouldn't return home until it was complete.

The leader placed a special device under the door, allowing him to look inside. He saw four people standing around, and with his mask he sensed one more further back in the room. The orange-haired man pointed at Ozacas and his colleague, assigning them their roles.

They counted down from three . . . two . . . one . . . The leader immediately burst into the room, rolling on the floor, and he soon reached one of them. He swung his axe, cleanly chopping off one of the legs of the closest human, causing his top half to fall down.

But as the body fell, one could clearly see that it wasn't human at all. It had what looked like large warts on its body and tusks like a walrus on its face. Immediately the other hunters were alerted.

But before they could act, someone had wrapped a set of chains around another body and pulled it toward them. A kick in the beast's face broke one of the large tusks, causing it to bleed. The blood coming out from the mouth of the suspected Altered was a little darker than it should have been.

As for Ozacas, he had another task to deal with while the others were fighting the four people in the room. He continued to charge forward and burst through another set of doors in the room. Inside were already countless dead bodies, but one person was still alive. He looked just like the others with the large tusks and warts on his face, but more important was what was in his hand.

Ozacas stabbed his sword into the ground; the sword started to glow, and strange roots appeared. They instantly traveled through the air and grabbed the man, wrapping around him and holding him in place. He tried to resist and break through, but the roots were too strong. Ozacas swung his sword, cutting off the man's hand and grabbing what he needed.

The Altered weren't this easy to deal with, and that was because the creatures they were fighting weren't really Altered. None of the kills they made today would go toward their stars. It was why they hesitated in the last raid, but something was up with these people.

So this is what caused all this trouble, Ozacas thought as he lifted the syringe filled with a strange black liquidlike substance.

CHAPTER 80

AN ANNOYING RETURN (PART 1)

School these days seemed pretty pointless to Gary. He listened to the teachers' lectures, but all of it seemed to be going in one ear and out the other. He couldn't help but ask himself what the point of all of this was.

He still had two more years to go until graduation, but could he really continue to live a normal life until then? Or at least keep up this façade? Would his grades now even matter at all, if he were to really transfer to the AFA?

Truth be told, the main thing that was keeping Gary in Westbridge was that he was afraid social services might come to investigate if he stopped coming in. Since not going to school was illegal, it would warrant an investigation.

Gary was afraid that not even Kai would be able to do anything about him and Amy not having an actual guardian, with their mother in the hospital. Still, there was another reason why Gary couldn't quite concentrate, and it wasn't because of the full moon that would arrive in eleven days; it was the report he had gotten yesterday. Just thinking about it made him clench his fists and wish he could just head over to the Gray Elephants gang now and deal with them.

I can't believe those guys are still going after Amy? Is this their way of coming after me? Is this supposed to be just a warning or something? I'm just glad that Olivia was there personally. It seems like the system's rules are really keeping her in place . . . but I can't let this continue.

The Gray Elephants had gone one step too far. In order to stop them from further pursuing his family, Gary had decided that it would be best to get rid of them. Whether he would turn their leaders to force them to follow his rules, as he had done to Olivia, or kill them, he didn't care anymore.

These guys are sick in the head . . . how could they go after a schoolgirl like that? Gary thought. However, the next moment he caught himself. Lately he was thinking about killing far too often, and he noticed that these thoughts tended to pop up more easily when it was close to the full moon. Taking a deep breath, he calmed himself.

Besides, he had something else he needed to worry about today, and that was the special meeting between the small-time gangs in Slough. After what felt like an eternity, the bell finally rang, signaling the end of the school day.

"Hey, so Gary, my dad told me this morning that I got accepted as an intern at the company where he works," Tom told him as they walked out of the school building. "My mom apparently handled Principal Young, and she just texted me that I'll be excused. My parents will come pick me up this evening, and I'll be back some time next week."

At first glance, it seemed preposterous to give any student time off in the middle of a school year; however, there were always exceptions. Unlike Gary, Tom was actually one of Westbridge's smartest students, so he enjoyed certain perks. Besides, in their current year, the school even encouraged the students to pick a couple of weeks to gain work experience, though normally it was supposed to happen in the second half of the school year at a specially designated time.

Gary contemplated whether he should ask the school to sign off on him working at one of the restaurants on Burnham Street for a couple of weeks as well. It would be easy enough to have Olivia write a report about what a great worker Gary had been, and it would give him credit for days of school. Then again, it might be wiser to use that at a later time . . .

"Anyway, you know my parents work in Brocknell, so I won't be able to come back before the internship ends. However, I promise you, I'll ask my dad your question about the beasts and see if I can find out anything about werewolves as well. I just wanted to let you know that I will be back before the next full moon, and while I'm away, I just hope . . . that no more trouble comes your way." Tom smiled.

Smiling back, Gary was reminded that he was really lucky to have one of the most supportive friends. Every time he thought of Tom this way, he felt like he was a little brother that needed protecting just as much as his sister.

One day, Tom, when I don't have to lie to you any more. When the Underdogs are dealt with . . . I'll tell you the truth, Gary thought.

With school over, Gary was happy to see that there was no crowd in front of the school this time. He had strictly warned Kai not to pull such a stunt again, and apparently it had worked. There was no longer any reason for him to head to the Wolf's Pool Club, since they had plenty of workers, including White, so he decided to head home.

Since Amy had nearly been attacked yesterday, Gary wanted to reassure her that everything was all right. The only way he could do that was by spending time with her. Afterward, he would meet Kai at the Wolf's Pool Club, and they could drive to the meeting with the small-time gangs.

On his way home, though, he decided to stop at his go-to convenience store, grabbing his daily food to replenish his Energy. Gary expected to see Tyler there like he did every day, and the cashier was there, only his attention wasn't focused on him.

Instead, it turned out that the drunken man who had thrown a tantrum last Saturday had returned. Only this time he wasn't so drunk. Gary quickly and silently hid between the aisles, wishing to avoid any unnecessary attention. He also didn't want Tyler to get in trouble, but from listening to what was going on, it seemed like it was too late anyway.

"Tyler, you need to apologize to this man immediately. The customer is *always* right! You've disrespected this hardworking man, and you're lucky that he hasn't decided to press charges. Really, I can't believe you would do that, but then again, maybe I shouldn't be surprised, coming from someone who is treating the store like a storage unit and taking expired food from it! You're on your last straw, young man!"

AN ANNOYING RETURN (PART 2)

Gary didn't recognize the other man's voice. It sounded like he was Tyler's boss. As he peeked around the corner, he saw a fat and sweaty man that he had never seen here before. if he hadn't been wearing the uniform and talking down to Tyler, Gary would have thought he was just another customer.

"But, sir, I was only handling the situation according to protocol since his card got declined! Should I have just given him the product?" Tyler argued, while his hands trembled from trying to stay polite. "How can you make me apologize when he nearly assaulted me and even spat in my hair?"

"I had cash on me!" the rude customer insisted. "You youngsters are so rude that you wouldn't even give me the time of day! Don't pretend that you were the victim in all of this! What about your friend, huh? He's the one who *assaulted me*! Yet here you are refusing to give out information on him! If he can't pay me back, then you're leaving me no choice but to ask you to compensate me! As an employee of this shop, you will have to pay for it!"

Now that Gary looked closer, he could see that the man had a bandage on his nose. He couldn't recall if he had hit the man hard enough to break it, but even if he had, the drunkard deserved every-thing that had happened to him that day.

"I've already told you, sir, I don't know his name. And even if I did, company policy forbids me from divulging our other custom-ers' personal data! I really don't approve of your actions that day." Tyler was unwilling to bow down before the troublemaker.

"Fine, then, I guess you don't mind me talking to my friends in the Underdogs about this. If you don't want to compensate me di-rectly, I'm sure they can just do that after increasing your protection fees!" The drunken man pointed at him before turning around with an evil smile.

It was obvious that this man had no connection to the Under-dogs whatsoever. Having worked as their transporter for as long as he had, Gary knew how Damion's group operated. They wouldn't ask, they would force.

If that drunk guy really knew someone from the Underdogs, they would have come to the shop on the same day, teaching Tyler and everyone else involved a lesson. There would be no need for him to make such a show in front of Tyler's superiors. Unfortunately, the fat guy seemed to fall completely for the little trick.

"Hang on! I'm sure we can come to an understanding. There's no need to go that far. Our store will happily pay your medical bills." The manager stopped the man before he could leave. Then he turned to his employee. "Naturally, all of it will be deducted from your wages, Tyler!"

"You can't do that! How am I supposed to pay my rent? Or buy food? That has to be ille—"

The manager slapped Tyler across the face.

"You've already done enough. I will not allow you to put this shop into further jeopardy because of your actions. You will receive no pay this month."

It was clear that Tyler was stunned by the manager's action, while the old man wasn't even trying to hide his enjoyment of the university student's treatment. His shoulders were moving up and down with laughter.

"Sir, I have come on time every day! I have worked overtime whenever you have asked me, and this is how you repay me? You choose to trust this stranger's word over mine? You think just be-cause I need this job, you can treat me like a dog?" Tyler was about to slap the manager back, but he hesitated at the last moment.

The university student was furious, but he was also aware of the harsh reality. If he were to hit his manager, he would lose his job. It was hard to even get a job these days, and if the manager spread rumors about him, it might be impossible to find another one.

While thinking of a way out, Tyler suddenly heard a large whack. The slap vibrated throughout the whole shop as his manager flew headfirst into the cigarettes.

"How the f*ck can you hit your employees like that?" Gary asked, still shaking with anger.

Damn it . . . I let my anger take over again. I only put Tyler in an even worse situation, Gary realized, but Tyler looked ecstatic.

"You . . . i-it's you!" The old man pointed at him, his finger shaking.

Gary took a step forward, but the old man immediately ran out of the shop, afraid for his life. By then, it looked like the manager was coming to. When he stood up, the side of his cheek looked like a giant balloon.

"*Y-you! You're fired, Tyler! As for you, you green-haired punk, you're banned from this shop!*" the manager shouted in fury.

Tyler and Gary left. A little ways down the street they sat down on the curb. Tyler had a couple of cans of pop in his bag and offered Gary one.

"I'm sorry about making you lose your job . . . and causing you so much trouble back there. You're only in trouble because of me," Gary sighed, taking a sip of the drink.

"Nah, it's not your fault. Honestly, I never liked that guy. He was a shitty manager and only came in to bitch about everything. Besides, after what he did, I don't think I could work there again. Also, the boss might fire him if I told him that he banned our most loyal customer. Without you, they'll lose like half of their profits. It might go under without your help."

The two of them laughed, but Gary still felt bad about what had happened, and he was wondering if there was a way he could fix things. When he saw a car drive by, an idea suddenly popped into his head.

"Say, Tyler, can you drive?"

"Yeah. I mean, I don't have a car, but I've got a license," Tyler replied, wondering why Gary had asked him that out of nowhere.

Hearing this, Gary decided to make a quick call. The former cashier was still confused about what was going on, but judging by Gary's grin, it was going to be something good. After a short conversation, Gary hung up and turned to Tyler.

"How would you like to work as a driver?"

CHAPTER 82

THE MEETING (PART 1)

Tyler immediately accepted Gary's offer. Gary didn't even have a chance to go into detail; whether it was because he trusted Gary or he really needed a job, Gary wasn't sure.

During the quick phone call, Gary had asked Kai about their financial details and if doing something like this was okay. When Kai had asked why he wanted to know, Gary had given him a short version of events. He had heard a sigh, but it was followed by "Fine, we can put him on the payroll."

When Tyler asked about the pay, Gary told him that they would pay him the same amount he had received at the convenience store. All he had to do was be ready for a call whenever they required him. The car would be kept at the Wolf's Pool Club anyway, so Tyler would just have to be present in that area during his on-duty hours.

Since it would be his first day as a driver, Tyler excused himself, stating the need to come to work in something more presentable. Gary bid him farewell after giving him the address. After all, he needed to do things himself before the big meeting today.

He ended up spending some time with Amy, eating dinner together and watching a TV show. For a brief moment, it felt as if things had gone back to normal. Gary was even a bit sad when he told his sister that he had to go. Amy didn't say anything, but he noticed that she was sad about it.

"Hey, nice suit, but you don't have to dress that formally." Gary greeted Tyler, surprised to see him at the club already. There was more than half an hour until the agreed-upon time, and Tyler looked like he had been waiting for a while already.

"Hey, I got in because of your recommendation, so I don't want to let you down. I need to make a good impression," Tyler insisted.

Gary felt a bit awkward, because he had yet to tell his driver about their new relationship and that he was actually the one who had hired him. Still, it was good to do something that made him feel nice. For the first time, Gary was able to help someone because of the new situation he had found himself in.

He entered the club, and the others waved hello. Business was as usual, but now rather than just teens they also had a few adults in the place having an early drink and playing pool. However, most of the eyes in the room seemed to be attracted to a certain person. One of the older men seemed so distracted that he even managed to miss the ball completely.

"Is that woman the boss of this place?" Tyler whispered.

The person who drew everyone's attention was none other than Olivia Pearl, who was sitting in the back. Despite her attractiveness, she was giving off vibes such that no one wished to sit next to her. Gary didn't blame Tyler for thinking she was the boss. Her clothes screamed wealth, and she just had this air around her.

She was here today because she would be accompanying them to the gang meeting. Because she was the ex-leader of one of these small-time gangs, Kai had said it would make quite an impression if she was by their side this evening.

"Just wait here and enjoy yourself. Your work will start soon," Gary said as he walked over to Olivia, because there was a problem that he needed to solve. Seeing him do this made the others nervous, and the new customers who had never entered the Wolf's Pool Club before were amazed that someone had the balls to walk up to her.

"I want to make something clear. I don't like you." Gary didn't mince his words.

"Well, please tell me something I didn't know." Olivia rolled her eyes.

"However . . . I'm still thankful that you helped out my little sister. Even if you did it only because you were ordered to . . . you did a good job."

"No problem, boss," Olivia replied, and carried on as she had been doing before.

Gary still hadn't forgotten everything Olivia had done, and he probably never would. Working for him was just a minor punishment, and although she was being obedient for now, if there wasn't a solution or things started to change closer to the full moon, he would not hesitate to get rid of her.

Kai had come up from the basement and was happy to see them. He then called them downstairs because he had prepared something for the two of them. Gary received his replacement uniform, and Olivia also got one of her own.

She looked at it for a while, and for the first time Kai thought he saw a smile on her face. Her outfit was all one piece, with a single zipper from the belly button all the way up to the neck. It was tight-fitting and of course in the Howlers' gang colors.

Gary's was the same as his previous one, but before handing it over, Kai said, "Please don't ruin this one. The material for it isn't cheap, nor is it easy to procure."

As it turned out, Olivia wasn't shy about getting naked, causing the two teenage boys to awkwardly look away. Once all of them were dressed, it was time for them to leave, but before they did, Gary put his black wolf mask on. Surprisingly, Kai also wore a special mask: a golden fox mask with black highlights.

"Well, I can't exactly wear the same mask as our boss, now can I? Besides, all three of us will be at this meeting. They know Olivia's face but not ours, and I would like to keep it that way," Kai explained, noticing Gary's confusion.

At this meeting, each gang leader would be present, and they were only allowed to bring two guards with them. So the others wouldn't be coming with them this time. If any gang didn't follow this rule, the meeting would be rescheduled.

However, according to Kai it would be bad for them if that happened. Although the gangs weren't working together, this meeting did bring some unity between them. It was also how they were able to survive even though there were big gangs around. And with war looming on the horizon, it was important to know what the others planned to do.

They exited the Wolf's Pool Club from the back and headed down the alleyway. This way, the customers wouldn't see them leaving in their uniforms. Gary texted Tyler to meet them out front.

However, when he saw the car, Tyler thought nothing of it and continued to tap his feet waiting for Gary to introduce him. Getting out of the driver's seat was Kai.

"You must be our new driver, right? It's nice to meet you."

"Huh?" Tyler was speechless, but all the masked stranger did was hand him the keys and get into the back of the car. He realized that he probably should have asked for more money. Once he was in the car, he saw a second masked figure in the back, as well as the woman from before.

This just strengthened his earlier assumption that she was the owner and leader. In the rearview mirror, Tyler also saw a bit of green hair sticking out over one of the masks.

Is that? . . . no, it couldn't be . . . if it is . . . just who the hell are you, Gary? Tyler thought, but not wanting to ruin his first day on the job, he kept quiet and followed the directions to their already programmed destination.

It was time for the meeting.

CHAPTER 83

THE MEETING
(PART 2)

The drive to the meeting place had taken a while, Gary noticed, which indicated that it was quite far out of town. There didn't seem to be any way to get to the location other than by car. No train or bus went to the area, and he could count on both hands the number of cars he had seen go by.

Their destination was essentially what one would call a country house, only it really was in the middle of nowhere. It seemed as if someone had randomly decided to plunk the house down here.

It made Gary wonder when the world had become like this. People lived stacked up on top of each other in apartment buildings. The only jobs available were in cities or towns, and here there were just fields of empty land where no one lived.

The car pulled up into a large gravel driveway that looked like it could fit fifteen cars or so. There were already three parked there, all of them brands that were just as expensive as the one they were in, if not more so.

Then there was the house itself. While the Clove family's house was big, what they were looking at now was a true manor. Gary couldn't even guess how many rooms it had. This made it even stranger that a house like this would be in the middle of no-where . . .

"Whoa, what are you guys even doing here? This place is huge . . . I guess you must be some pretty important people," Tyler couldn't help but say as he stared at the manor in amazement.

"Of course you can build things like this in the middle of no-where; the land here is worthless," Olivia replied as she raised her-self to get out of the car.

Tyler realized that he should be doing his job properly, and he rushed out of the car to open the door for her. When they'd all got-ten out, they looked around, trying to see who else had already ar-rived, yet the other cars looked empty. It was impossible to see if anyone was inside, because the windows were all tinted far too dark, like their own.

Just before they headed inside, though, Kai had a few words for their new driver.

"Your name's Tyler, right?" Kai asked, and Tyler nodded. "Well, I'm going to be straight with you. For your own sake, cut the small talk. The less you know, the better, so don't ask us who we are, what we're doing, or anything about this place.

"In fact, just stay in the car, and don't come out unless we're back and we tell you to. Your only job is to be ready to drive us wher-ever we tell you to. Do that, and everything will be okay."

For some reason, Tyler found these words quite heavy, and he couldn't help but wonder what these people were doing here, but he decided to just nod along anyway. When he got back in the car, the group started to walk toward the entrance, their leader natu-rally in the middle.

Damn this is nerve-racking as hell, there's going to be four other gangs the same size as the Pincers here . . . and what will even happen at these meetings anyway? Gary couldn't help but think.

For once even Kai hadn't been too sure about what happened in those types of meetings. According to Olivia, they were rare and were usually only held to discuss certain agendas. If she were to harbor a guess, it would be due to the Howlers taking over the Pincers in the first place. However, the meeting had actually been called before that happened, so there should be more than that being discussed today.

Before they entered, they heard another car pulling up from behind. The group stopped for a second and turned their heads. When the car parked, four figures including the driver exited the vehicle.

One of them stood out more than the others. He had a square-looking nose that stuck out that matched his face, but he also carried himself with a confidence that the others just didn't seem to have.

"Tony freaking Lock. Leader of the Lock gang." Olivia folded her arms as she identified the man to the masked teenagers next to her.

"Is he trouble?" Kai asked, as it appeared that Tony had spotted the three of them. The gang leader smiled as he came their way.

"Trouble? Not really, it's more like he's seriously annoying. Tony and his gang used to visit Burnham Street quite often, and it wasn't because he enjoyed the food there," Olivia explained. "Every chance this guy got, he would try to talk our two sides into working together, but I think rather than getting our two gangs to join up, he was just trying to court me."

"What makes you think that?" Gary asked.

"He proposed to me," Olivia replied matter-of-factly.

Judging by the fact that she didn't have a ring on her finger and the two gangs had never joined up, Gary and Kai could only imagine how it must have gone after turning him down. Considering that gangsters were pretty petty people, Tony might just have a grudge against the Pincers.

"Well, well, well." Tony smiled. "If it isn't Olivia Pearl, alive and well. Here I heard that your gang got taken over. I cried my heart out yesterday, thinking I would never see you again. It made me realize that my feelings for you may not be gone after all.

"It's a real pleasure to see you again today. I guess those rumors were all just false."

"All of it is true," Olivia replied immediately. "This guy here is the new boss."

Tony pulled a face that clearly showed that he wasn't impressed.

"The masked clown? I seriously don't know if you're pulling my leg or what. Either way, Wolfie, don't you think it's rude to not show your face? Trying to keep the Howlers a secret when there's a meeting full of leaders isn't exactly polite."

Tony slowly reached for the werewolf's mask. Gary hesitated. If he stepped back, would it be offensive? Should he grab his hand? But while he was thinking about what to do, Kai acted, sending in a swift kick from the side, knocking Tony's arm away before he could reach the mask. Kai's hands remained casually in his pockets.

The two guards by Tony's side rushed forward.

"Stop!" Tony shouted. "Not here. Now's not the time. Look, I don't know what type of trick you used to pull Olivia to your side, but just see what happens if you pull this crap in there. Once this meeting is over, it's all fair game out here."

Tony and his men walked past the three of them and entered the manor, and the doors quickly closed behind them.

"Word of advice," Kai told Gary once the Lock gang was out of earshot. "Don't take crap from any of them. Don't let them push you around. Think of them as nothing but adult bullies.

"We're the new gang, so they will see us as pushovers in this whole thing, but because we've taken over the Pincers, you've earned a place at their table. Heck, since you took over the Pincers, a gang at the same level as them, it means we are above them.

"We have a goal, and this place is nothing but a stepping-stone. I want you to remember that. We are not at the same level. *They* are the ones *below us!*"

"Strong words," Olivia commented after hearing everything. "I didn't realize that your plans were so lofty, but if they really are set high, then he's right. You're no weak shit, so don't let them treat you like it."

Straightening his clothes and letting out a deep breath, Gary pushed the doors open and the two people at his side followed. There was no one inside to greet them. The entryway looked empty, but there was noisy chatter coming from further inside.

Two people were shouting at the top of their lungs. Others laughed. Following the sound, Gary found himself in a large room with several sofas.

Each gang had taken a sofa as their territory. Gary tried to see if there was anyone he recognized. Of course, other than Tony, and the Rising Dragon gang leader he had met before, none of them had a familiar face.

The others looked back at them, clearly trying to gauge the new leader. It looked like they wanted to say something, but keeping Kai's words in mind, Gary just walked across the room without sparing them so much as another glance.

The room had gone silent, as if they were expecting Gary or someone to say something. Until . . .

"It looks like you all made it here and well. Let's start this meeting right away."

Gary recognized that voice; it belonged to someone he didn't expect to see at the meeting at all.

What is Xin's father doing here?

CHAPTER 84

THE MEETING (PART 3)

After speaking to Kai and seeing how Ben Clove was involved in all of this, Gary had expected the mayor's involvement to be loosely connected. Perhaps in the same way as he was connected to the Rising Dragon gang. The mayor did seem to have a heavy interest in gangs, and it was the first time he had seen one publicly use one for his bodyguards, but there were stranger things that happened in the world.

Now, the fact that he was at this meeting itself meant there was probably more, and Gary carefully watched him walk across the room. The large man was confident in his steps, not even caring or worried in front of all these gang leaders. Even if the Rising Dragon gang was on his side, they couldn't stop all the gangs that were there, which told Gary that something was definitely up.

Does Xin know anything about this? I doubt it. I don't even think the Underdogs or the Gray Elephants know about this, either. Otherwise, the red color gang would have never even tried to target Xin, Gary thought. *If it were a meeting between all significant gangs in Slough, then they would certainly be here. It probably means that the mayor is scared of them. That or the reason for this meeting is something that he doesn't want them to know about.*

"Ladies and gentlemen, I'm glad that all of you were able to make it." Ben started the meeting off and looked around the room at each of them, stopping and looking at the Howlers for a few more seconds before continuing. "All of us are busy people, so I won't waste your precious time. There are two agenda items for this meeting, so let's get the first one out of the way.

"The last time we met, all five gangs agreed to an alliance. It allowed you to continue your work as you wished without disturbing others, while at the same time serving as a guarantee to protect you all, as well as protecting me. I'm glad that you took the time to listen. We had a deal that not only benefited me, but benefited you as well.

"If one of you were to get attacked by the Gray Elephants or the Underdogs, then we agreed to help out each other. Which brings up a problem. Unfortunately, the Pincers have been taken over and replaced in a single day." Ben then looked over to Gary's sofa. "It was too quick for our alliance to even act."

Thoughts started to swirl through Gary's head. What if all of this was a trap? Had the Howlers been invited here so the other gangs could take revenge? Kai had mentioned that possibility to him, which was another reason they had brought Olivia along. Seeing her should cause them to back off a little, but this wasn't why he was worried.

Gary's heart was beating loudly, not because of his words, but because he was worried that his mask wouldn't be enough to disguise him. It had stopped others from recognizing him so far, but this wasn't one of those dumb superhero comics where people couldn't tell the difference between someone with glasses and without.

"The new gang is called the Howlers, if I am not mistaken?" There was a pause as if he was waiting for them to say something, but since Kai stayed silent, Gary did the same. "I see that you have brought along Miss Olivia Pearl. Since she is here, can I take it that what happened was more of an agreement rather than a forceful takeover?"

Once again, the question was met with silence from the trio. Olivia's lack of expression didn't make it easier for any of the others to figure anything out. They only had the rumors to go by.

"Are the Howlers willing to work with the rest of us? The fact that you decided to come here, rather than outright refuse this meeting, must mean you have some interest, no? So what do you say?" the mayor asked with a smile, not letting the silence disturb him.

Seeing this side of Xin's father, along with that smile, made Gary want to run away. Gang members were more predictable than this politician. Who knew what he had planned? Who knew what he had done to get to the position he was in now?

The only thing Gary hoped was that the mayor wasn't as bad as the other gangs himself. Otherwise, he didn't know how he would face Xin next time. Would he be able to keep his lips sealed if her father said something that annoyed him again? If he spoke ill of gangs when he was doing this? The man was a hypocrite and a liar!

"You said there were two agenda items," Kai said, without answering any of the previous questions. Not only was his voice a little muffled through the mask he was wearing, but Gary felt like Kai was trying to slightly change it as well. It made him wonder if he should have been doing the same thing all along as well.

"From what we've been told, this meeting had already been planned before we made the Pincers submit to us. So before we decide anything, we would like to know what the real agenda of this meeting is."

"If you want to be part of our meeting, then take your mask off!" Tony stood up and pointed at Kai. "You think hiding your identity is going to save you after this meeting is over? We know your territory, and we will be happy to force you to comply, just like you did with the Pincers."

Skill activated: Controlled Transformation

"Is that supposed to be a threat?" Gary spoke up for the first time, as he looked toward the gang leader. He had tried to lower his voice, but to make sure he wouldn't be recognized he had also used Controlled Transformation on the area around his throat.

Since Gary hadn't said anything, now that he had revealed such a deep and menacing voice, the other gang members were really taken aback. The unknown person was scaring the other leaders. It was clear from Kai's words earlier that they had beaten the Pincers, just as the rumors had claimed.

The real reason Gary had been unable to hold his tongue any longer was Tony's announcement that he would attack those that worked on Burnham Street. He knew that during a gang war there would be other victims, not just gang members.

"Everyone, may I remind you that we've gathered here simply for a talk?" Ben cleared his throat in an attempt to restore order and cool everyone's head. "Fine, I see no problem with letting you know the details of this meeting, as it is something that concerns everyone, no matter if you wish to join us or not. We can decide that afterward, though it is something that you probably will want to comply with anyway.

"Based on all the information I have gathered, the war between the Gray Elephants and the Underdogs could start any day now. The Gray Elephants look to be making their move, and there is no doubt in my mind that it will be worse than what happened to Chavley during the color gang war."

Gary knew that tensions had to be high between the Gray Elephants and the Underdogs after the attack the other day, but he thought it would still be a while before an attack occurred. Was something pushing one side to act faster than the other?

This war . . . it could be my chance to get rid of the Gray Elephants while they are distracted or weak, Gary thought. He had already planned to get rid of them anyway because of what they had done to his sister, and this might be the perfect opportunity.

"Because of this, they will very likely approach you in the coming days, but if our plan is to succeed, I ask you all to refuse to make an alliance with them. One will take out the other, at which point we will strike together as a group. Then we will be the ones who take over this town!

"The agenda of this meeting was to remind all of you to not get blinded by greed. No matter what either side might offer you, if we don't use the chance to get rid of both gangs once and for all, it will be just a question of time until the winning side will recover and take over Slough as a whole.

"If we don't have an agreement, then we'll *all* have a problem. And that includes you, Howlers!"

Kai had told Gary that this was what the other gangs might do, but he had originally predicted there would be a second war after the first, one between the five small gangs. Yet he had clearly been unaware that those five were already in some type of secret alliance, seemingly organized by the mayor.

Kai might have an answer, but since he didn't speak up, Gary chose to do so. Thinking back to what Kai had told him earlier, this was what the werewolf had to say:

"No! We are going to do what we want and I'm telling you not to get involved."

CHAPTER 85

THE MEETING
(PART 4)

The few words that Gary had spoken boomed out in his deep voice. He hadn't cancelled the Controlled Transformation. Since only a small part of his body was changed, it barely consumed any Energy.

However, unlike before, when Gary's words had sounded quite intimidating, this time they only caused the tensions to rise within the room.

"You no-name piece of shit!" a bald man cursed as he jumped up from his sofa, and two more bald men jumped up from the chairs next to him. The three looked similar, and it was hard to know whether they were triplets or just looked the same. Regardless, they were the heads of the Blood Triangles.

"You come in here, invited when we didn't have to, and you tell us to not get involved?" The triplet in the center spoke. "Do you think everyone in here is a weak piece of crap? That you can just spew your mouth, and we have to listen to you because you took over the Pincers! Those damned masks should have been the first sign that you guys were up to no good."

No one was sticking up for the Howlers, and it was safe to say that most of them were on the side of the Blood Triangles and felt the same way toward the new gang.

"Now let's calm down and give our guests a chance to speak. It's always best to try to settle things with words first," Ben said, looking at Gary. For some reason, the three bald men seemed to listen and got back in their seats. But it was clear that the mayor was on their side as well. After all, he'd basically said that if they couldn't solve the problem with words, they would take action instead.

Gary wondered if he had done the right thing; perhaps backing down was correct, but then what about his sister, and what about the future of Slough? The plans and the future of the Howlers had been set; sooner or later they would be doing this anyway.

"As I said . . ." Gary was adamant. "We will be doing what we want."

Kai added to his leader's declaration: "It sounds like your plans might just mess with ours a little. So take this as our warning to not get in our way."

Some gritted their teeth, others clenched their fists, but most of them looked toward Ben, as if he was the deciding party in all of this.

"Fine, I did my best to stop you from getting hurt." Ben sighed as he shrugged and walked to the other side of the room.

It was the signal for everything to start off; the Blood Triangle trio stood up and the one in front almost dashed across the room, jumping on the table in the center and leaping toward them. The first one to act as if he was expecting it was Kai.

He sprang up from his seat and kicked the bald man in the stomach, using his own momentum against him; the man fell back and crashed into one of the others.

"That fox-masked freak is fast," the triplet said, holding on to his stomach.

Everyone had gotten up from their seats now.

"You attacked us, so all is fair game now," Kai said.

Tony Lock jumped up from his seat, ready to tackle Gary to the ground. Gary was ready and unafraid, of course, but there was no need for him to do anything.

Olivia stepped between them and spun on her back foot, lifting her leg in the air; the heel of her foot met Tony's square nose with a loud crunch. Blood started to pour out of it instantly. Gary knew it was broken, as he had managed to break his nose during rugby training against Blake not too long ago.

While Tony was busy checking his nose, Olivia took out her whip and swung it, wrapping it around Tony's leg and pulling, causing him to fall on his back and hit the ground. Tony was a large man, and even with the whip's extra properties it should have been difficult to do, yet Olivia made it look easy.

She's more useful than I thought, Kai mused.

Seeing what she could do with a whip, the others were hesitant to charge, yet they knew that the numbers advantage was on their side. However, Gary wanted to stop this quickly, as he didn't want to go to war with all these small gangs.

For the longest time, these gangs had never gone against the Underdogs or the Gray Elephants, even with their alliance. In fact, they were still waiting to go after the other one only after they had their war. Which meant as long as they knew there was someone stronger than them, they wouldn't dare to touch them.

A small smirk appeared on Gary's face, peeking out under his mask.

"Stop now, or I'll get rid of you all," Gary growled as he lifted his hand. He had made it transform completely: fur on the outside, his nails elongated to claws. He had only used the Controlled Transformation on his hand, but it was enough to make everyone freeze in place.

The puzzle pieces were starting to come together for the gang leaders.

The Howlers had a frigging Altered as their leader.

That was how they were able to get the Pincers. Why they were confident. It was no wonder Olivia had quickly submitted to them, despite the rumors claiming that theirs had been a small force. Since the Howlers had come seemingly out of nowhere, they likely had a large corporation or another gang completely backing them.

"We gave you a warning, yet you chose to ignore it." Kai scoffed, probing them for a reaction. "This will be your second warning, and I guarantee you won't get a third. As you saw with the Pincers, we're not interested in eliminating you, and Olivia has been able to see the light and join us. As long as you don't get in our way, we won't get in yours either . . ."

None of the gang members moved, and even the mayor seemed worried now. All the gang leaders were in one place; none of their guards or members were with them. They all knew the power of an Altered, and if Gary wished to do so, he could kill all of them. Doing so would outright solve a lot of the Howlers' issues up front . . .

It was something none of them had expected.

"We don't want any trouble; we agree to your terms," one of the men said, and then he stood up and left. Soon after, other gangs who had yet to make their move also left, leaving only the Blood Triangle gang, the Lock gang, and the Rising Dragon gang.

The others helped pick up their injured brethren, but eventually they left as well, leaving only the Rising Dragons; Tony looked back at Olivia for a second before continuing to head out.

"Well, it looks like we have finally reached an understanding. Mr. Mayor, I want you to remember our name. I'm sure you will hear it a lot more often in the future." Kai smiled as the Howlers also prepared to leave. On their way out, Gary stopped and looked at Ben Clove.

"Does your family know your involvement in all of this?" Gary asked. "How do you think they would react if they learned of this alliance? That you, as the mayor who promised to protect the people, were just turning a blind eye to their doings?"

"They know nothing!" Ben replied; for the first time his face changed into something other than that politician's smile. "Leave them out of this, and if you don't and you touch them, I assure you that you will regret it as well."

Ben spoke confidently while also shying away. He was frightened, so it sounded like it was the truth, but perhaps his other words were true as well. With Jayden Tiger in their family, the mayor wouldn't have had to do all this if he could use Jayden to do his bidding.

As Gary left, he thought, *Is a war really starting soon . . . and just how will it start?*

At the same time, two adults were leading a group of children down the sidewalk, while Kevin walked in front; they had eventually arrived outside what looked like a large warehouse. It looked uncomfortable as Kevin surveyed the area they were in. It wasn't the nicest of places, but then again, the same was true for the Black Rock Orphanage.

"I assure you the inside has been renovated to meet your needs." The man smiled. "Once you go in, your lives will change forever."

CHAPTER 86

BECOMING AN ALTERED (PART 1)

In a certain room of the big white house, a stream of banging sounds interspersed with grunts and yells could be heard even with the doors closed, and after a while it stopped.

Slough's mayor stood in the center of his office huffing and panting, his fists bloody. He was out of breath and the room itself had been turned upside down like there had been a robbery.

Papers were strewn all across the floor, along with broken chairs, smashed paintings, ripped books, and more.

"Those damned Howlers . . . why did they have to appear *now*? They could ruin *everything*! Everything I've painstakingly built up! I chose this town carefully. I carefully made all my connections . . . I was so close, and now they're about to ruin it *all*!" Ben clenched his fist and was about to smash his desk when he heard a knock just outside his door.

He straightened out his clothes and opened the door. Standing outside was D, leader of the Rising Dragon gang, who seemed to be spending most of his time at the mayor's.

"The NIRV Corp. representative is here," D explained.

Arriving home after the dreadful meeting, Ben had completely forgotten about his appointment today. On top of that, it was an important one that he couldn't miss.

"Tell him I will be with him in just a minute, and let's move the meeting to the living room; make sure the office doors are locked behind me," Ben ordered.

After a few minutes, Ben went to the living room, where his wife and daughter sat peacefully chatting with his guest, an older gentleman with gray hair and glasses, wearing a lab coat.

These people from NIRV seem to never leave without their coats, Ben thought as he put on a smile and went for a handshake. The representative stood up and shook the mayor's hand, noticing that his hands were bandaged up.

"I didn't expect your profession to cause you to use your hands in such ways." The representative sounded surprised as he pushed his glasses back up onto the top of his head.

Once again, Ben smiled, but it was a forced smile. NIRV was perhaps the biggest corporation in the world. It was the first one to successfully create an Altered. Ever since, it had been leading the way, always coming up with better technologies, making the process safer, and finding a vast amount of ancient beast fossils to be used as Altered.

Of course, this was why Ben had called them, because they were the best of the best, and his daughter only deserved the best in his eyes. However, as the market leader, NIRV had located its headquarters in a Tier 1 city. This house visit alone had cost the Clove family a small fortune.

Most people in Tier 1 cities tended to look down on those who lived in lower tiers. Therefore Ben disliked most of those in the Tier 1 cities, even though he wished to be one of those people one day.

"I just needed to release some anger; it's a stressful job, after all," Ben explained.

The NIRV employee didn't comment any further. Instead, he turned on the large TV in the room. What followed was a presentation of sorts; the employee went through all the benefits and the risks that one had to be aware of when undergoing the Altered process.

In the past, there was a high risk of the person dying, but nowadays NIRV had managed to decrease the fatality chance to around one in a million. However, there were some clear points to take away from the presentation.

Once a person selected a specific type of Altered, there was no way to change into another type of Altered. On top of that, there was also no way to reverse the process once it had been completed. Learning to control the Altered form would differ from person to person.

Interestingly, it was possible to upgrade one's Altered form, though. NIRV occasionally managed to find similar beast fossils. When the procedure was performed on an Altered, they could be strengthened if the fossil turned out to be stronger than the original. If this was the case, NIRV would be happy to upgrade the Altered free of charge.

"Now, as you wished, I've brought along a selection for you to choose from. All this Altered DNA has yet to appear on the market, and not a single person has had access to it. In other words, it will be unique to her . . . unless of course someone manages to find more of that type of fossil," the representative explained.

There was a reason why Ben had asked for this. It would have been a lot cheaper if they had asked for a more common Altered form. Although some of them could climb the ladder of fame with their strength, if they didn't, they would serve as guards to corporations or amount to very little in the world.

On the other hand, a unique Altered would be able to garner a lot of attention from corporations and more. If Xin didn't make it as an Altered fighter like she wished, then her father still wanted his only daughter to have an easy and good life. Even if it was costly, the mayor was sure that it would be worth every penny.

I want my family to be safe . . . even after I leave, Ben thought.

"Since you don't seem to have any questions, shall we proceed?" The employee lifted a small metal briefcase and placed it on the table in front of him. "At NIRV, we strive to perfect the Alterification process. Since you've chosen our top option, we've prepared something special for you. It will be announced at our next press conference, but there's no longer even a need to go to a lab."

As the man explained everything, he opened the metal briefcase, inside there were three syringes that contained a liquid. "Now all that is needed is just a simple injection." He smiled.

CHAPTER 87

BECOMING AN ALTERED (PART 2)

The syringes in the special metallic suitcase were quite large. Each needle was a good three inches long, which didn't exactly make Xin jump for joy when she saw them. However, she had heard that the Altered process in the past had been quite a painful one.

So perhaps this was an easier alternative, which pleased her. Looking at them closely, she saw that the liquid in each syringe was a different color: green, blue, and yellow.

"Of course, there is only so much data that we can gather based on the fossils of the beast we dig up," the NIRV employee continued. "Still, I will do my best to describe the type of beast that each syringe contains to make your choice easier."

The TV screen behind the man changed once again, bringing up a 3D render of the beast. The graphics made it look so real and alive, but the man assured them that it was all simulated by computer graphics.

On screen was a giant serpentlike creature in an empty room. It had long, hard, green scales with no pattern on its body. However, its tail had two spikes sticking out from the end, making it look like a hammer.

"Please bear in mind that we can only portray the appearance of the beast. We are unsure what traits will be passed on from the beast to the Altered. Perhaps they will be minimal, or there may be even something that we've been unable to uncover," the man explained.

Xin knew that, based on her brother's experience. In Jayden's case, his sponsor had believed that he was just consuming a normal beast that looked like a tiger. It came as a shock to everyone and the whole world when it turned out that the fossil had been a special type, a white tiger. There were even more special things that the public didn't know much about.

The video screen moved on to the next beast. The scenery changed, and now there was a body of water with a creature swimming through it. It was hard to tell the size of the creature from the scale, but it looked very elegant.

Similar to the previous creature, it had one long body. Two large fins that were flat and wide were attached to the side of its body, as well as a single long fin that allowed it to cut through the water. It also had a sharp horn on the top of its head.

Before the final creature appeared, the screen went dark. At first Xin thought the video was broken, but a few seconds later she saw an outline of glowing light resembling a large bird.

The shape of the bird was not regular, though. Its wings appeared jagged, as if it was made from pointy rocks, and the same was true for its head. The longer Xin stared at the beast, the more she could make out what it was, which sent shivers through her whole body.

With that, the presentation was over.

"What was with the last one?" Natalia Clove asked.

"Ah, I believe the CGI team must have gotten quite creative with that one. After all, it's quite boring just seeing the beasts in the same room all the time," the man replied with a nervous chuckle.

It was time for Xin to pick, and she intensely looked at all three syringes, thinking back to the videos. The NIRV employee thought he had a pretty good idea which one the girl would pick. Young girls like her usually picked the most elegant creatures, and he had seen her eyes light up when she saw the water beast. After all, the appearance of their Altered form was important to a lot of people.

"I want to go for the one that made the most impact on me. For some reason, I just can't keep forgetting about it. This one," Xin said as she picked up the yellow syringe. "I'm serious about doing well in the AFC, so it has to be this one."

The man was shocked, but he was also happy with her choice. He handed her a pamphlet that explained what they were about to do, how to administer the injection, and details about whom to contact if she experienced any side effects.

"Can't you administer the injection now for us?" Natalia asked.

"Sure, I was going to suggest staying a couple of days to see how she was doing anyway. It would be great to gather some data as well. Why don't you go to your room, Miss Clove, and get ready? I'll be with you in a second," the man said.

Xin and her mother headed upstairs excitedly to wait for the man. As he packed up his suitcase, though, Ben grabbed his hand.

"Wait, since you're already here, and you've brought those syringes with you, how about parting with one more?" Ben asked.

After seeing the beasts on screen, and after what had transpired at the meeting, Xin's father couldn't resist becoming an Altered himself. As the mayor, he never wanted to go through a similar situation again. He hated having to rely on others like D to protect himself and his family, and these syringes could spell the end to that . . .

"According to our records, you have enough money for one syringe, but a second one would bring you close to bankruptcy. NIRV would need some type of collateral if you wish to purchase another one. With all due respect, Mr. Clove, are you sure you wish to do that?" the man asked him.

Ben Clove was a little scared about when and how that company had looked into his finances, but what he was saying was unfortunately the truth. The Clove family could afford one syringe, but that was only because Jayden had given his father a large check, so they could afford the best treatment for Xin.

Their own funds would not suffice to pay for a second syringe ... unless he used other funds.

"There are always other ways to make money, especially as an Altered in a city like this," Ben said.

"Very well, then. NIRV happens to have a contract for such a situation, which I will need you to sign. But for now, please choose whichever one you would like," the man said with a slight smile, opening the suitcase once again.

PRIME SUSPECT

Lately, Anton Millstun had been spending more time in his office than out in the field. Not because there weren't many crimes going on in Slough; it was quite the opposite. Lately a certain case of his had become an obsession. In his office he had made a board with photos from different cases and linked them all together with names written underneath.

"There really haven't been any more killings by a crazed Altered ever since Billy was dealt with." The chief of police talked out loud, as he often did, since it helped him think more clearly.

"All the deaths can be attributed to him, but there are still things that don't make sense. The main one is the blood that was found in the alleyway and at Barry's death scene. Altered Hunters don't go after anyone other than Altered.

"The theory that an Altered Hunter is also an Altered himself doesn't make sense in the case of Barry's death, and what reason would Billy have had to go after him? There was zero connection between the two. Yet with all Billy's other victims, we were able to pinpoint them to those underground fights he had.

"I'm sure of it; although it may not be a mass murderer, another Altered is involved in all of this, one that isn't Billy. But there haven't been any matches for the blood that was found on the scene. On top of that is the case that started this all. Billy's first kill would have had to be his parents. Which means the first case at the building site is unrelated."

Heading to his desk, Anton grabbed another picture and pinned it up on his board. It was a photo of a large student, with the name Gil written underneath it.

"According to the teachers at Westbridge, Gil was Barry's closest friend. However, not long after his death, Gil dropped out of school and no one has been able to get in contact with him. According to his classmates he sometimes claimed that he would just join the gray color gang. However, after an attack they have seemingly disbanded and been absorbed by the red color gang, which means they're no help any more either.

"Could he be the Altered I'm looking for? Regardless, even if he isn't, he might be able to provide me another perspective. Something that I might not be aware of."

Finally, heading back to the table once more, the chief picked up another picture and put a pin in the center. It was a photo of a green-haired boy, which he put next to the picture of a Black boy with blond hair.

"Both of them fought against Billy in those underground matches, and on top of that they go to the same school as Barry and Gil. Somehow, this whole school just seems to be a beacon for trouble. That green-haired kid, in particular . . . I remember him, he was the one who rebelled against the red color gang members."

Taking out a big red marker, Anton wrote *Altered* next to Gary's photo with a question mark.

"In the picture I have of him at the moment, he looks different than when I saw him."

He had found the next person to interrogate, and just then there was a knock on the door. Before Anton could even answer, the door was opened from the other side.

"Now, who's the lucky guy who just volunteered to clean the toilets for the next two weeks?" Anton asked, turning around, but when he saw who it was, he wasn't so surprised any more. Two figures had entered wearing white-colored uniforms.

"We just came to inform you that we will be leaving Slough tomorrow," Sadie declared, looking around at the mess in the room. If she didn't know any better, she would have assumed she'd have stumbled into the lair of a psychopath.

"What about the second Altered killer and what about the Altered Hunters?" Anton raised his eyebrow.

"You mean the ones who dealt with Billy for us? If there had been any news, I'm sure you would have heard about it. Anyway, our superiors have deemed the case closed," Sadie answered. "Of course, we initially came here because of the three gang members' deaths, and although Billy's blood wasn't found at the scene, the markings on their bodies do fit the other deaths."

"That's bullcrap, and you know it!" Anton slammed his hands on the desk. "Altered or not, an attack with bare hands should leave DNA! And what about the one who attacked the high school student? There is still a lot to do."

Sadie folded her arms like she knew that something like this was going to happen, but she couldn't be bothered to explain. Her partner Frank knew that as well. Slough's chief of police wouldn't give up so easily.

"Sorry, Anton, but you know that the power of White Rose agents is limited. Even if we suspect that another Altered killer might be out there, for all we know he might have fled somewhere else. If there is another death, then we will come back as soon as possible, but for now with no leads, there isn't much we can do."

"No leads?" Anton stepped aside to reveal the board he had been working on and pointed toward the two students. "Here's your lead!"

Sadie couldn't help but scoff.

"That just proves you have nothing but assumptions at best, and not even good ones. We already went to the school and tested him. Don't bother reading the report, there was nothing. That kid's blood was as red as can be. Misguided as he might be, we know for sure that he isn't an Altered. Anyway, we have said what we needed to say."

Before Anton could say anything else, Sadie left the room. It was clear Anton was frustrated, but turning around, he grabbed his pen and drew a big red X on Gary's picture.

"If they say he's not an Altered, then they must have tested him; I guess he really isn't one."

Taking the picture off the wall, Anton paused for a second.

"What made them think that he was an Altered in the first place? The two of us came to the same conclusion but . . . why?"

Maybe there was still some hope in this case after all.

After leaving the police station, the two White Rose agents hailed a cab and headed to their hotel room. Sadie was seriously annoyed, and Frank was trying to figure out what to say.

"You know, he's a good police officer. You shouldn't give him such a hard time," Frank said. Letting out a big sigh, Sadie finally unfolded her arms. She then paused for a second before rubbing the area around her ankle.

"I know . . . I'm just frustrated. The wound still hasn't healed from that day, and for some reason it's been starting to itch more and more. On top of that . . . well . . . you know the rest already."

Lately, Sadie had been experiencing some side effects, and from the sounds of it, they were getting worse.

"Don't worry, that's why we're heading back to the White Rose base. The guy from the lab will take a look at you and find out what's wrong with it. You will be okay in no time, don't worry." Frank patted his partner on the shoulder.

CHAPTER 89

THE START OF ALTERED (PART 1)

At the end of the school day, Tom rushed home, unable to contain his excitement any longer. Today he would be leaving Slough. Not forever, of course, but he would spend the next week or so gaining valuable work experience. The best thing about it was that he would be doing so under his parents' supervision.

Tom had always been interested in what exactly his parents were doing. When he asked about it, they would explain a few details here and there, but they seemed to avoid one particular question, always stating that they would tell him once he was older.

This curiosity drove Tom mad, and it had largely contributed to his desire to follow in his parents' footsteps. It seemed like a silly reason, but it was a goal that allowed him to focus on school and not so much on his other passion: playing video games.

Being accepted to work at his parents' workplace meant he was a step closer to his goal.

Outside his house, his parents were already waiting, and they had packed his bags for him as well. The Greens were always in a rush and rarely home as well. This was another reason why Tom wanted to be in the same field as them: just so he could spend more time with them, and not feel so . . . distant.

"We'll be out of town for a full week," James Green said as he was ready to start the car. "You made sure to tell all your friends and teachers, right?"

"Sure did. Mom also had a talk with Principal Young, so I'm all good to go," Tom replied, bouncing up and down in his seat. "Come on, let's go. No time to waste."

The car went out of Slough and onto the highway, and for the first time, Tom saw the sign to Brocknell. During the drive, Tom couldn't help but think about his best friend. Were it not for Gary having turned into a werewolf, he would probably just miss him slightly, but now? Who knew what could happen in the span of a single week?

When they entered the Tier 2 city Tom couldn't help but stare out the window, admiring all the sights. Technically this wasn't the first time he had been here, but the last time he had been a lot younger. His memory of that time was naturally a little fuzzy.

Still, it was just as impressive as he remembered it to be. There were more skyscrapers here; they housed large corporations with offices, or rich people who liked to live at the top and stare out at the city.

Another prominent thing was the advertisements. Digital screens all over the different buildings advertised clothes, restaurants, and luxury items that probably cost more than one month's worth of his parents' wages combined.

The people on the streets wore nice clothes and looked clean cut and presentable. The biggest difference, however, was the fact that nowhere in the city, not even in different regions, did there seem to be any sign of poverty.

There was no graffiti, no litter, no sign of any gangs. Tom was witnessing the difference between a single rank in tiers.

However, seeing all of this just made Tom wonder how great a Tier 1 city would look. That was something he had never experienced before. Those cities were similar to gated communities, and they didn't allow tourism. Those who worked or lived there were given special passes to enter and leave the city.

It truly was a place that was only for the select few . . . in other words, the rich and mighty.

Eventually the car stopped, and Tom's eyes lit up. They hadn't gone to the apartment that his parents stayed in. Instead, they had gone straight to the lab itself.

"Sorry about this, Tom, I know you must be tired after school, but there are just a few things that we need to finish up. I hope you don't mind?" his father asked.

"Of course I don't mind. I wouldn't have been able to sleep today thinking about this anyway. This is much better!" Tom quickly got out of the car, leaving his mother to park it.

The lab was quite large, with an open area for employees and the public to walk on, while the road enclosed the entire block. So there were no other buildings next to it.

The shape of the building itself was quite strange. It was like a teardrop on its side. The higher-tier cities did tend to have more impractical architectural designs, but still. The lab was large and impressive nonetheless.

Eventually, father and son reached the front of the building, and Tom stopped outside for a second. He couldn't move any further as he stared at the letters above the building.

"What is this, Dad?" Tom asked. "I had no idea they had a building in this city! Why did you keep this a secret from me? How could you and Mom never mention this to me?"

Scratching the back of his head, Tom's father was a bit nervous at his son's reaction.

"There are quite a few reasons I didn't tell you, and I never knew it was such a big deal, honestly. It's just our job and what we love to do." His dad smiled.

Tom followed his dad into the building, with the letters *NIRV* high above.

CHAPTER 90

THE START OF ALTERED (PART 2)

Even at this late hour, inside the reception hall Tom saw countless workers in their white lab coats all around the place. It seemed like a building that never went to sleep. Regardless, this was just the reception hall and there was nothing to see here; the interesting stuff was inside.

His father spoke to the receptionist for few moments, and eventually he handed Tom a digital tablet.

"You need to read this and sign here before we can give you a temporary pass for your internship," his father explained.

"An NDA? So I can't talk about anything that I see inside with anyone else outside, is that right?"' Tom asked after skimming over the pages. There were a lot of technical terms, and Tom felt like he would be here for half an hour if he read them all.

"You need to actually read everything written in there, Tom. Don't just click agree like you would on a computer. It's important you understand what you are signing," his father insisted. "I had to really pull some strings to get you in here. A temp intern position didn't even exist last week, but hey, your old man knows a few people," James said, cracking his knuckles, which just embarrassed his son.

Sitting down in the few seats in the lobby, Tom started reading the agreement, and his mother soon joined them. The terms were very strict. It felt like he was about to learn the secrets of the world, and that this legal mumbo jumbo was there for him to prepare for the repercussions.

Now he was starting to understand why his mother and father had only been able to tell him so much. They were just following the rules that had been set out. In the end, Tom signed it. After all, if anything, this level of secrecy only got him more excited about what was hidden inside.

After returning the tablet, Tom was given a pass but no lab coat, which made him feel a little disheartened, but he understood. He was expecting to see some big secrets, but instead what followed were just . . . hallways.

There were countless hallways of people walking past, heading to where they needed to be.

"You look disappointed." His father chuckled. "Unfortunately, we are only allowed to see what we are working on. So our projects remain a secret from each other."

For the first time, Tom also noticed a group of people who weren't wearing lab coats at all. In fact, the way they walked around the place, with their strange clothing and hairstyles, they seemed very out of place. They looked more like gangsters he would expect to find in Slough.

No, that's impossible, there can't be gangsters in a place like this. Even if they owned the place, they would be in a Tier 1 city, not this lab, Tom thought as they took a turn away from them.

Eventually, the three of them stopped outside a large oval door. His father used his pass and the door opened, allowing Tom to lay his eyes on a magnificent, gigantic fossil. The room was lined with giant glass containers containing countless different fossils, with numerous workers around each one.

"Remember when you asked me about beasts before? You can't imagine how nervous I got, afraid that someone had leaked some intel or spread a rumor," James explained while they approached fossil of the beast they were working on.

It was a small one; the bones looked like those of a dog, and his mother was typing away on the computer that was placed just underneath it.

"So, is this where they make the Altered DNA? From the beast fossils? That's so cool!" Tom commented.

"Actually, it's a little more complicated than that, Tom. You see, what I'm about to tell you is something that the public has no idea about with regard to Altered. Of course, I don't have to tell you that all of this information is completely classified."

His father waited until Tom nodded, then continued with his explanation.

"You see, we can't actually extract much at all from these fossils. It's impossible to make Altered from the fossils. Now I know you're going to be confused for a second, so hear me out.

"There is a reason why one fossil can create one Altered, and that's because what we need to do with this fossil is bring it back to life. Now our job is to extract the bones and as much of the original beast as we can from here.

"Then it goes onto another section of the lab. I've never seen it myself, but there they have something they call a nest crystal. From what I gather, it's a special energy generator, though they make it sound like stuff out of fairy tales. I mean, can you imagine a single crystal being able to supply enough energy to run the whole world?

"Anyway, they somehow use their nest crystal on the fossil, and as long as we have done our job properly, it brings the fossil back to life."

Tom needed a few moments to take everything in. It sounded like a rumor he would have heard from the internet, and if anyone but his father were saying these things, he would have called them a liar.

"So are you saying that there are still real beasts in this world?" Tom asked.

"Well, not natural beasts anyway. However, NIRV seems able to bring back the beast to life, though they don't live for long. After a few tests, they are sent to a special team. The group we passed on the way here, the ones without the lab coats, are part of that.

"They kill the beast, and once the beast is dead, they extract special crystals from inside its body. Those crystals are then used to gather the Altered DNA. That is how the world came to create the Altered we know today."

It seemed like Gary was on to something when he had asked his best friend if beasts still existed.

The only question now was what had prompted him to ask that bizarre question in the first place?

CHAPTER 91

UNDERDOGS GIVE UP?

After the trio returned to the Wolf's Pool Club, they sent Tyler home. He was given a burner phone like all the other Howlers and was instructed to answer it as soon as he was called. The job seemed quite easy, and he was pleased with what he needed to do.

Of course, he wanted to ask questions after seeing a group of scary people leaving the place, but he remembered the warning from the blond guy in the fox mask. Surprised that Kai had decided to pay him for the rest of the month up front, he took the hint and left.

I'll just ask Gary about it when I see him, Tyler thought, unaware that Gary had been with him the whole time. Tyler had suspected him to be under the wolf mask; after all, the green hair seemed like a dead giveaway. However, during the car ride back, he had heard him speak a few times. The voice was far too deep to be Gary's, so all of his suspicions were cleared. In fact, Tyler now believed that Gary must have dyed his hair to mimic the gangster boss.

Once again, the masked teenagers chose to enter through the back entrance, so as to not disturb anyone. While Kai went inside, where he was promptly asked to share the details about what had happened during the meeting, Gary stayed outside for a minute. Olivia intended to return to Burnham Street, and the alpha werewolf had a question he hadn't felt comfortable asking her in the car.

"Do you think there will be any problems because of what happened at today's meeting?"

"It depends on what you would consider a problem." Olivia shrugged. "Whatever they might do, it won't be anything I can't handle on my own. However, after your little display, I would be surprised if any of them tried anything. You just worry about what you need to do next." With that, Olivia got into her own car and drove off.

Gary joined the others just in time to see Kai mimicking his speech about the Howlers doing what they wanted and for the other gangs not to get involved. Unfortunately, all he could think about were Olivia's words.

What should he do next? Since the small gangs were no longer going to pose a problem, getting rid of the Gray Elephants and the Underdogs was all that was left.

Before the big war happens, I have to get stronger . . . and I have to level up this system as much as I can. Maybe this is the break period I need. With a war brewing, the Underdogs might have stopped looking for me for now, Gary thought.

That same night, a peculiar trio was walking around Slough. Two large men in suits were accompanied by a teenager whose most prominent feature was the large black hoodie over his head. They stopped outside an apartment building.

"Are you sure this is the right place?" one of the men asked.

"Of course, I'm sure. Heck, it was easy enough to get the information. I didn't have to do much other than a simple phone call, but without a doubt, this should be his home address," the other man replied confidently.

They moved their young hooded companion to the side and knocked at the door.

"Who is it?" A woman's voice came from the other side. She looked through the peephole and saw two figures she didn't recognize at all.

"We are from Westbridge, ma'am. Your son Gary has caused some trouble at school. Do you mind if we come inside to talk about it?" the man asked.

"Gary? I'm sorry, but there is no Gary here, you must have gotten the wrong number." The woman replied and quickly retreated into her apartment.

The two men sighed, looking at each other, before using all their strength to kick in the door. It was a bad neighborhood and the door wasn't exactly strong, making it easy to break into.

The woman inside was shaking, a phone in her hand. The intruders slapped the phone out of her hand and shut the door behind them. They quickly gagged her, and finally the young man took off his hood.

Gil looked around the house for photos or anything like that, and eventually he found some of a male student. However, it didn't look like Gary at all.

"You sure this is the right person?" one of the men asked, no longer so sure.

Gil studied the photo for a while, even though he knew straightaway that it wasn't the right person.

"I'm not sure. This photo might have been taken a while ago, and since he dyed his hair, it's hard to tell," Gil replied, looking away but smiling as he did so. "I think it could be him."

Turning around, the dropout ran over and punched the woman on the right side of her face.

"You know a boy called Gary Dem, don't you?" Gil asked.

"What the f*ck do you think you're doing, kid? You don't have to hit her!" one of the men complained.

"Damion told us to get the information no matter what. She already lied to us . . . so now it's time to get her to tell the truth." Gil countered, not once looking at the other two, but only staring at the poor helpless woman in front of him.

A short while later, the lady was a bloody mess, lying barely conscious on the floor. Gil's knuckles were sore after how much he had used them.

"I found a birth certificate. The names of her and her son don't match up with the one we are looking for," the first man stated. "It looks like someone gave the school a fake address. Either our transporter is smarter than we gave him credit for . . . or somebody is looking out for him."

The other man looked at the woman, thinking about what to do with her. He reached into his coat pocket and placed a thick pile of cash on the floor.

"Don't do anything stupid. If we hear so much as a rumor about you complaining to the police, or telling anyone else that we were here, we'll have to pay you another visit. This is for your troubles. It should cover any medical expenses and then some."

With that, the three left, without getting any closer to their suspect.

"We can't catch them at school or his home address. Damion is going to burst. We have to come up with something else." His partner sighed.

"Don't worry." Gil turned around, droplets of the woman's blood still on his face. He was a frightening figure in the darkness, startling even the two Underdogs members for a second.

"I have a plan . . ." Gil smiled.

A little while later the two men left, and Gil was free to do as he wished, but he quickly turned around and headed back to the same apartment they had left only moments ago.

CHAPTER 92

THE WORST NIGHT

Not counting the meeting, it had been a rather normal day for the Howlers. Since there was school the next day, they didn't stay too long at the pool club, either. Each of them went back home, continuing their ordinary lives. Right now, the gang was on a reaction basis. They would wait to see the moves of the others first before they themselves acted.

However, what none of them could have known was just how special tonight actually was going to be. It certainly wasn't a night where they could have afforded to relax.

What used to be one of the gray color gang bases was currently being used by the Gray Elephants. It had been empty for a while and not even gray color gang members were allowed to return until now. The reason for that had been kept a secret.

Three large delivery trucks were parked outside to the warehouse, around the back. Several gang members were hidden inside, ready to move.

The orphans from the Black Rock Orphanage had just arrived at what was supposed to be their new home. Kevin, as the oldest child, was surveying the area, since it didn't exactly look like your typical orphanage.

I can't look worried in front of everyone. I was the one who convinced Suzan to accept this deal. If this place ends up being worse than the orphanage, it will be my fault, he thought.

All the other kids were looking to him for guidance. After Innu, he had been at the Black Rock Orphanage the longest, so he knew them all and saw the worried looks on their cute faces.

"It will be okay," Kevin reassured them with a smile. The men slid the door open. As soon as the orphans saw the inside of the building, their faces lit up with big smiles.

The warehouse had been completely converted. Warm yellow lights illuminated the inside. The building was furnished with colorful floor mats, play houses, climbing frames, and even charming beds for all of them.

Surprisingly, some other kids around their age were already present.

"Please, make yourselves welcome." The man gestured with his arms open. "These children are orphans just like you. Given the lack of funding for orphanages in the Slough area, our boss had us gather all of them here in an attempt to create a safe haven for them."

The smaller children didn't stay to listen. They were over the moon and had run inside to play with the other kids. Unsurprisingly, they were quickly making new friends, all of them enjoying the shiny new toys that would have been a pipe dream in the old orphanage.

Kevin counted about fifty children. But, the converted large warehouse didn't feel cramped at all.

"There are plenty of staff to cater to all your needs. Just go ahead and have fun," the man prompted those who were still hesitating.

Kevin noticed a few older-looking kids, but just like him, they didn't seem too excited to be here. They sat on their beds being anti-social, while the smaller ones played.

Truth be told, Kevin wanted to do the same, but he was finding the whole situation weird.

There are so many people looking after us? Why would a private corporation invest so much money in multiple orphanages? Maybe the owner used to be an orphan himself? Kevin scratched his head as he thought about it more.

Am I overthinking the situation? No, I'm the responsible one now. I should try to talk with the others and see if they noticed anything strange first.

Walking over to the beds that were stacked on the side, Kevin greeted the kids sitting on their beds with a hesitant wave. A friendly girl with cute bangs and short blond hair waved back. On the bed next to hers, a kid with an Afro signaled for Kevin to sit next to them. They seemed more approachable than the rest.

"Hi, there, my name's Kevin," he said, introducing himself. "I don't want to bother you, it's just . . . you know . . . at my orphanage there isn't really anyone my age. It's kinda nice to see others that kinda understand my situation for a change."

The two smiled and welcomed Kevin, understanding what he meant. Sure, Kevin went to school, but he didn't really associate too much with the others, too afraid of his secret getting out. If anything, he would more likely get bullied for being different.

The three of them got to talking, and Kevin asked them multiple questions, mainly about how long they had been there. Apparently it hadn't been long at all. The girl, whose name was Birdie, had been there for two weeks, whereas the boy had come in one week after her from a different orphanage.

From the sounds of things the people treated them nicely; they were given good food and an allowance when they went out, but there were some strange conditions that Kevin didn't know how to feel about.

For one, all the kids were now being homeschooled. It did explain the educational supplies toward the back of the warehouse. Honestly, Kevin didn't know if this was a good thing or bad thing for him, since school wasn't his favorite place.

I guess this place might be all right, but I still can't shake the feeling that something is off, Kevin thought.

"Don't worry too much," Birdie replied. "This place is fun, even though this area kinda sucks. Honestly, they won't let us go out on our own. We can only go in groups, accompanied by one of the adults, which I guess is a good thing in this sketchy area.

"Still, if you're lucky, you might get adopted quickly. I don't know how they do it, but they seem to have a list of people wishing to adopt. Not counting your group, we were down to half the initial number from when I came here. Sometimes even a bunch of us get adopted at once. It's crazy. I've never seen anything like it before."

Birdie seemed like a nice kid who was all smiles, which was why Kevin didn't want to say anything negative, but the last fact she mentioned was the final nail in the coffin. There was definitely something up with the place, and he needed to find out what it was.

It just wasn't normal. Where were these adopters before? A simple Google search would have shown them all the orphanages they wanted. And why did so many children get adopted and so quickly?

I'm really hoping that I'm wrong about all of this. I might have convinced Suzan to do something terrible and put us all in danger. First . . . let's make sure my imagination is not running wild and find out what exactly is going on here.

At the same time, a large man driving a fancy car was approaching the warehouse. In the passenger seat was his longtime friend, still wearing his sunglasses, although it was already very late.

"Are you ready?" Brandon asked Raven. "Today is the day this whole city falls and breaks into chaos. We both agreed that there is no better time than now . . . don't tell me you're starting to feel guilty now?"

"No." Raven shook his head. "The way I see it, it's either some orphans' lives or ours, and I can't exactly afford to die yet. Not until I find out what happened to my brother."

"Good, then we will get the show on the road. The last group of orphans has arrived. The war will begin tonight."

CHAPTER 93

WHAT WOULD INNU DO?

Although it was late and already dark out, a brave woman wrapped up in a coat was walking the dark streets on her own. The area wasn't the safest, and a woman shouldn't be out and about on her own at this late hour. She knew all of this when she decided to go out walking. However, she just had to.

I just don't feel good about this decision. I miss the kids too much, Suzan thought. *What's the point of having all of this money . . . if I don't feel happy?*

Suzan was walking to the new location of the orphanage. She had promised herself that she wouldn't. She knew that it would only make it harder on them and herself. Nevertheless, she decided that there was something that she could do, something that would fill the hole in her heart.

With all the money, she could now adopt at least one of the children she had grown to love. It would allow her to have a final goodbye with all the kids. Honestly, if she could and the system allowed it, she would have taken them all home. Suzan hated to play favorites, but it was the last good thing she could do for them.

Hoping to catch them just before they went to sleep, she picked up her pace and finally arrived at the address. Surprisingly, the streets were quiet on the way there.

"No one is allowed to enter this area. It has been boarded off to the public. Go home," a man standing outside told her in a gruff voice. There was a metal fence covering the whole area of warehouses, and it looked like this was one of the few entrances.

"I'm sorry that I've come here unannounced. My kids, the ones from the Black Rock Orphanage, should have arrived here today. I used to work there and I just wanted to see them one more time. I was planning on adopting one of them. I'm here for business, I promise." Suzan's voice felt a little shaky. Maybe it was because she had been dealing with kids a lot, but she was finding it hard to talk to the two men in front of her.

With their large bodies and crossed arms, they didn't give off the impression of a welcoming place.

"That so? Too bad, we're closed already. Now leave, or we're going to have to force you to leave. We already said this place is off limits!" the man said threateningly.

Thinking that the men didn't understand, she decided to try to walk past them and find someone else, but they stood in her way and pushed her with such force that she fell to the ground.

"We're not joking! This is your last warning!" the other man shouted at her.

Understanding that there was next to no chance that she would be able to get out of such a place, Suzan left, but not without looking for another way to get in. At the same time, she attempted to call her business partners to complain about their workers.

"The number you have dialed is no longer in service" was all she heard on the other end.

What the— Not in service? That can't be! I just talked with them yesterday, she thought.

Worrying that something was seriously wrong, she did the only thing she could think of to get help, and that was to call the police. Whether they would help or not was another thing altogether.

Ever since the White Rose agents had informed Anton that they would be leaving, he had been working through the night to find some type of lead in the case. Something that would make them stay. If they stayed, the case would be reopened, but without them, not even he could give a good enough reason to his higher-ups to keep it under investigation.

"Roo!" Anton shouted, and the young officer rushed into the room and gave his superior a salute.

"Yes, sir!"

"I keep looking through everything and I feel like I'm just one puzzle piece away from solving everything. I've looked at all the reported deaths, starting with the construction site that day, to see if any of them matched the profile of an Altered killer, but I found nothing." Anton ruffled his hair in frustration.

Roo saw the bags under the chief's eyes and felt like this case was driving him mad.

"Sir, I hate to say it, but maybe that's because there wasn't another killing by that Altered? I'm not saying you're wrong about there being another Altered killer, but perhaps your approach is wrong in looking for that Altered's other victims?"

His words didn't seem to have any effect on his superior, and Anton let out a big sigh.

"Have you looked into missing people?" the young officer specified.

"Missing people?"

"Right, I mean, people go missing all the time. Running away from crimes or possibly something else. Who is to say that we found whoever that other Altered has killed? How about we look at all the people that have been reported missing ever since the construction site incident? We can probably limit the search even further to around the time Billy was killed."

These words lit a spark in Anton. It was something that they should have done, but his mind had been so busy lately with all the things happening around him.

"Sir, there has been a call from a woman," another officer said as she rushed in. "She sounds panicked, and she's in what used to be the gray color gang area. We need your opinion on how to handle this situation!"

Inside the warehouse, after learning of the strange events, Kevin had been looking around to see if he could find anything else strange. He spoke to a few kids as well, but they had only similar stories to Birdie's.

I've noticed one thing; everything feels temporary and rushed, Kevin thought. *These colored mats are great, but they're easy to buy and install. And they say the warehouse has been renovated, but there's no insulation. It still has its metal exterior.*

Instead, they're using a lot of electricity and have spent a fortune on portable heaters. Even if they have a lot of money at their disposal, it should take time for them to renovate the orphanages . . . It's as if they're certain we won't be here for too long.

Kevin eventually found something while searching the place. The metal walls appeared quite damaged, with a few dents here and there, and some panels were temporarily boarded up. However, he noticed a larger panel at the bottom.

It looked crudely made, held together by a few nails here and there. Kevin figured that with a few pulls he might be able to get it undone. Before he attempted to do so, though, he made sure that nobody was paying attention to him. Luckily, the adults seemed to completely ignore the playing children.

He pulled on the wood a few times, and the nails came undone on one side. He lifted it up so it slid upward, at which point he noticed that it was covering a large hole that opened to the outside.

Maybe knowing this will come in handy later. Birdie said that they wouldn't let us out on our own, which is a little strange, Kevin thought.

"All right, everyone!" one of the men shouted. "Orphans from the Black Rock Orphanage, since this is your first day, we'll need to take a photo of each one of you. These will be your profile photos for our clie—your future parents. Everyone, make sure to look your best."

The other kids followed the men outside. Looking at the hole he had just found, Kevin wondered if he should use this opportunity to leave. Something was telling him that if he did go with the others . . . there was a big chance that he wouldn't come back.

In the end, Kevin made his choice . . . and joined up with the other orphans.

Innu would never leave others alone!

CHAPTER 94

NO ESCAPE!

If the men working at the warehouse were doing something strange, then Kevin had to find out what it was before he could tell anyone about it. He understood that the police wouldn't act just because an orphan told them that he was scared in his new surroundings. The police in a Tier 3 town like Slough were usually busy, so they couldn't just answer any call, especially a kid's.

The good news was that at least they were taking out a few orphans at a time, for whatever purposes they had. This made Kevin believe that time was on his side. Time to figure out what was going on . . . or if all of it was just his imagination running wild.

Thinking about this, Kevin went ahead with the rest of the kids from his orphanage. There were twenty-three children in total who came from the Black Rock Orphanage.

Leaving the warehouse, they found themselves in a large white tent that was split up into different sections. Following instructions, the orphans lined up, patiently waiting in one section until they were called into the next section.

"Next!" one of the men called out.

In the other section of the tent, Kevin briefly made out a photographer with the standard equipment used in a photo shoot. However, none of the children returned after having their photo taken, at least not in the line with the others.

Noticing the unrest of the waiting orphans, one of the men explained that after taking the photo they would be asked some questions. That way, they could match up the kids' personalities and wishes to their future parents.

Since when do orphans like us get the luxury to be picky and choose who we want to be with? Kevin didn't trust that explanation one bit.

"Next!" the same man called out after a few minutes.

Finally, it was Kevin's turn. He sat on the chair and the camera went off as normal. Still, he was looking around to see if he could spot anything strange. Perhaps a hint at what they were doing.

After the photo was done, it was time for Kevin to walk into the next section of the tent. As he did, he noticed a large table in front of him, but there was nothing on it. No papers or anything, just a man sitting down on the other side.

Maybe it's like an interview rather than a questionnaire?

Hearing footsteps and sensing someone behind him, Kevin turned around and saw a man behind him holding what looked like a needle. His instincts kicked in and he immediately kicked the man in the family jewels as hard as he could.

The man bent over in pain, letting the needle fall on the ground as he covered his nether regions. Hearing the soul-crushing scream that turned into a whimper, the other man tried to get up from the table, but Kevin was faster. He kicked the side of the table, causing it to bang into the man before he could get up.

I knew something like this was too good to be true. If I hadn't been so suspicious, that guy would have pricked me with that needle! Kevin thought as he rushed out of the tent, but he wasn't safe yet.

Just as he made it outside, he saw several men standing next to large trucks that were mostly blocking the way for him to run anywhere else. The most shocking thing, though, wasn't the number of people, but in their arms was one of the kids from Black Rock Orphanage. The one who had gone just before Kevin.

The boy's body was shaking, but they held on to him strongly and threw him into the back of the truck, treating him no better than a sack of potatoes.

*What the f*ck is going on? What are they doing? . . . Are they kidnapping them? . . . Did they do all of this to sell our organs?* Kevin thought.

All he knew was that these men were up to no good, and he assumed it had something to do with whatever they had intended to inject him with.

"Hey, what's that kid doing?" one of the men shouted as he spotted Kevin. There seemed to be more people outside than inside, and Kevin knew that he had better chances heading back from where he came from.

Entering the tent again, he saw that the second man had gotten up, while his partner was still recovering. Kevin rushed forward to grab the dropped syringe and put it into his pocket, and as he got back up, he saw the man's face in the perfect position, allowing him to kick him perfectly with the heel of his foot, knocking him onto the ground once more.

Not slowing down, Kevin ran into the photography room he was in just seconds ago, where the photographer was taking a photo of what would have been the next victim.

"It's a trap! All of it! They're trying to kidnap us! We need to get out of here, quickly! Let's head to the police station!" Kevin was clearly panicked and frazzled and although the kids didn't understand what was going on, they knew him and they trusted him, especially since they saw his tears running down his face as he informed them.

The kids got into action as they began to scream and run right back into the warehouse. The adults took a moment to understand the situation. Kevin ran inside with the others, and the panic from those in the Black Rock Orphanage spread to the others.

"Kevin!" Birdie called out as she ran up to him. "What's going on? Is everything all right?"

"No, these guys . . . I don't know what they're doing, but they were trying to inject us with some shit! I saw them throwing one of my friends into a truck! We have to get out of here!"

Just as he said those words, the workers had blocked off the exit of the warehouse and closed the doors firmly. One of the kids tried to push one of the adults, but a fist hit the kid right in the face, knocking him onto his back as blood poured from his mouth.

It made the situation that they were all in very clear.

"You little brats, we tried to do this in a peaceful and convenient way! You just had to mess things up, didn't you?" a man shouted from behind, and Kevin saw that one of the kids had been grabbed by the back of his shirt. More men were behind him.

"How . . . how do we get out of this situation?" Birdie asked.

Kevin wanted to fight. Knock the person out and free the kids. Innu had taught him a few things, but he didn't feel confident in his ability to take out adults. Not to mention, a lot of them looked to be well-built. At the same time, there was only one of him and many of them.

"I have to get out of here! I still have the syringe! The police will have to do something if I show it to them!" Kevin clenched his fist and ran as fast as he could to the side of the wall that he had seen before. Birdie was following right behind him.

One of the men saw him running and attempted to grab him, but Kevin slid across the floor as if he was going for home plate and managed to just avoid the man's fingers. Unfortunately Birdie wasn't as lucky.

"*Kevin!*" she screamed as the man tossed her over his shoulder, and the adults were gathering all the children and tying them up.

"I'll come back, I'll get help, I promise!" Kevin shouted back, taking all his will to turn around. He hurried back to the panel, lifted it up quickly crawled through, and was out of the warehouse.

He knew he couldn't stop there, so he kept running. He didn't have a phone with him, so he needed to find someone who did before the men could get to him. Fortunately, no one was following him just yet. They were too busy dealing with all the orphans inside the warehouse.

Eventually, Kevin reached the metal fence. Not seeing an easy way through, he climbed up, sticking his hands and feet into whatever gaps he could find. Reaching the top, he jumped down and continued to run.

How could this happen? . . . we were all happy and then . . . and then I told Suzan . . . I told her to sell the place. Everything that's happening . . . it's all because of me!

Running out of breath, he put his hands on his knees, panting hard, wiping the tears away.

"Kevin, is that you?"

Looking up, he couldn't help but break out in a sobbing mess as he recognized the voice.

"Suzan . . ."

CHAPTER 95

SOMEONE, HELP!

Before explaining the full extent of what had happened to him and the other orphans, Kevin needed to move even farther away from the warehouse. Suzan seemed to understand that something was wrong, and noticing that he seemed exhausted from running, she took off her coat and wrapped it around him. She led him to the main street and they hid between a few darkened shops.

Kevin found it very hard to confess to Suzan what was happening inside the warehouse. After all, he blamed himself. Nevertheless, between heavy sobs he told her everything that he had seen, and immediately Suzan fell to her knees, banging them against the concrete, not caring about the pain.

"I'm sorry, Suzan. I'm so, so sorry. This is all my fault!" Kevin cried out as he knelt down next to her and started to bawl his eyes out once again. Seeing him in that condition, Suzan hugged him tightly, bringing his head close to her chest.

"Shhh, it's not your fault, Kevin. You're just a kid. I'm the adult who signed those papers after they were the ones who pressured me. They are the ones who are doing all those bad things . . . None of it is your fault." Suzan tried to calm him down. "I'm just happy that you are safe. I'm happy that you made it out. And all we can do now is try to help them."

They both understood the seriousness of the situation. Based on what they had observed, it was too dangerous for them to go in by themselves. There were multiple people involved, and the group had money. These people were obviously professional gangsters.

Suzan clicked redial and shared the information with the police. The person on the other end had some good news, telling her that they had already sent someone out. The dispatcher then asked Suzan where she was and what she was wearing. A bit confused, she answered the questions.

A few minutes later, a black SUV pulled up next to them and a young man in a police uniform got out.

"Both of you get in, and we can talk inside," Roo instructed them.

They looked at each other and thought that this was a strange response by the police. When they were told that someone was on the way, they had expected multiple cars, not a lone officer. Seeing their hesitation, Roo showed them his badge, proving he was a real officer. "Look, this area is not safe. Please get inside first, and then we can talk." Roo looked around, as if wondering if someone had followed him.

Unable to trust him, Suzan called a third time, and the dispatcher confirmed that the officer in front of her really was with the police. After all, the last thing she wanted to do was head back with the same dangerous people.

Once they were in the SUV, Roo started driving them away from the warehouse.

"Wait, Officer!" Kevin shouted. "You're driving the wrong way! We have to help the others! They're still in there!" But Roo ignored his pleas and continued to drive. Only after they were out of the area and on the road did he pull over and park the car.

"You really don't understand where you were." Roo sighed, shaking his head. "I'm sorry, you guys must have been scared. We got your report, and they sent me to pick you up and get you out of there. I can take you to the police station or back home, it's up to you."

They couldn't believe it.

"Is that it? That's the only thing the police will do? They're kidnapping children there! They're tossing them in trucks. How can the police ignore this?" Suzan yelled.

Roo looked at the ground; it was hard for him to meet her eyes.

"Look, I'll give you an explanation, but you're not going to like it. This whole area is owned by the Gray Elephants gang. The police force aren't heavy-handed with people. There isn't much we can do. If we want to send a full force in on them and enter private property, we would need a warrant. Sure, we could use what you said, but it would still take time for a judge to clear it, and by then . . . well. The Gray Elephants gang are great at slowing us down whenever we have made requests in the past.

"I'm glad that you managed to escape, but by now they must be cleaning things up. Worst thing is, their victims this time are all orphans. There isn't anyone to report them missing."

Kevin reached into his pocket and pulled out the syringe he had picked up filled with the strange colored liquid.

"What about this? They tried to inject me with this. I'm sure it's some type of illegal substance; can't you use this to go after them?" he asked.

Roo looked at it for a while; he wasn't sure what it was.

"All right, I can take it back to the station and have it inspected. I promise you, I'm just as worried about them as you are. However, there are rules we have to abide by. The best thing we can do now is if you can give me a description of the trucks you saw. Did you happen to see the license plates or any other defining features?

"We will have patrol cars on the lookout for them. Once they spot the trucks, we'll attempt to pull them over. We'll just make up some reason to search their vehicle, and if we find the kids you're looking for, that's when we can act . . . That's all I can do for now," Roo explained.

While Roo headed back to the police station, Kevin explained what the trucks looked like. He told him everything he could remember, but he wasn't sure how much help it would be. There was no telling if the trucks would move today, or if there might be others.

And the more he thought about it, the more Kevin believed that Roo was just saying things to get him off his back. Could the police force really afford to use so many vehicles to search for the trucks?

They might just send out a memo to their current officers to see if they spotted any trucks, but that was probably it.

At the police station, Roo parked the SUV and went inside, leaving Suzan and Kevin outside the entrance.

"If the police don't act, they might get hurt. What do we do now?" Kevin asked.

Suzan looked like her mind was about to collapse in on her. She had the same fears as Kevin. The way the police talked, the Gray Elephants were just too big a problem, especially inside their territory, whatever that meant.

"I—I . . . I don't know," Suzan mumbled, defeated.

Kevin decided to do what he would did when he found himself in a tough situation, which often helped him come up with a solution . . . even though it usually ended up being the opposite.

"Why don't we contact Innu? You can call him, right? You have his number. Tell him what happened!" Kevin said.

"Innu? Are you sure? He's just a kid. It might be better not to drag him into any of this." Suzan was hesitant.

"He's not a child any more!" Kevin shot back immediately. "He looks after us all just as much as you do, Suzan. I know . . . I know he might not be able to help, and it's a long shot . . . but I think we should tell him. Who knows . . . what if he has an idea? Please . . . he looked after all of us at the orphanage every day, even after he left!"

Suzan thought back to the last time she had seen Innu. He certainly did seem more dependable. In the end, in the desperate situation they were in, she decided to give Innu a call. She didn't know what exactly she was expecting, but she decided to trust Kevin's opinion.

"Hello, Suzan, I'm surprised you called me so late." Kevin could hear Innu's voice on the other end of the phone. "I'm sorry I've been unable to make it lately. I'll be sure to visit you soon."

Suzan was finding it hard to tell him what had happened. Taking a long deep breath, she finally let it out.

"The kids at the Black Rock Orphanage, they're in trouble."

Sitting in his bedroom in the crummy apartment where his foster parents lived, Innu had just gotten off the phone. He placed it down slowly and thought about what to do.

"The Gray Elephants . . . and trucks. I don't have a clue what they are up to, but it will be hard to find them. I'll need all the help I can get," Innu said as he picked up his phone.

He was hesitant as he was about to make the call.

"No, I have to ask, they're like family to me. They're the only ones who might be able to help now!"

Eventually, after a few rings, the person on the other end picked up.

"Gary, I need your help . . . I need the Howlers' help."

There was only a slight pause before his friend answered.

"Of course I'll help!"

CHAPTER 96

THE START OF IT ALL

When Innu had joined the Howlers, he had done so mostly on a whim. Kai's approach to recruiting had intrigued him, and unlike the other recruiters, Kai had exuded a very confident aura. On top of that, they had made a deal, and Innu wasn't one to break his word.

Still, he could leave at any point if need be. It wasn't like they were forcing him to stay, nor did he owe any of them a debt. However, for some reason, he had chosen to stay.

His partner Green Fang's performance had also done its job to intrigue him. As long as he could make money, then he would be happy. Originally he had planned to join one of the smaller gangs to earn some money while using his fists, legs, knees, and elbows. It was the only thing he was good at.

At the same time, he wasn't really old enough to earn money legally, yet he required money to help those he cared about now. Perhaps the reason he stayed was the amount of money he could earn compared to others, but when he thought about it more, that wasn't it.

What he had never expected was to feel so closely connected to his fellow gang members. Gary had come to his old school and fought off Billy, which was the point in time that he had really earned Innu's respect. From that day onward, events had kept happening around the gang leader that had only elevated his position in Innu's esteem.

He didn't know what had happened, but Innu had decided that not only was Gary the right leader for him to follow, but he was truly part of the gang. This was also the reason he had called him first, over Kai.

Gary was a person who he could trust, and who would return to him the same level of trust.

When Innu was in trouble, the first person he thought of was not only Gary as his leader, but more so his friend. However, he was in for another surprise; the green-haired teenager didn't even need to hear what exactly he needed help with, already agreeing.

I knew that Gary, and this whole gang was the right gang to follow, Innu thought.

He quickly gave him a brief summary over the phone, everything that Kevin had told him. Gary hung up even more determined than before to help his friend out.

It was also the first time Innu had told Gary that he used to be an orphan. Innu felt like he needed to give a reason why he wanted to help them so much, so he couldn't be shy about his background or past. Now it made sense why Gary and Blake had seen him in front of the orphanage that day.

Fortunately for him, the duo had been there and defeated the omega werewolf; otherwise . . . Gary didn't even want to finish that thought.

Those Gray Elephants gang members are scum . . . they were the ones who were part of that color gang attack that put Mom in the hospital. They kidnapped Amy, and won't stop harassing her, and now they are even doing things like this . . . hurting people who are close to Innu.

Maybe this is a sign . . . that they need to be dealt with, Gary thought.

Heading into his wardrobe, Gary grabbed a bag and started unpacking. It was the new uniform he had received from Kai. It looked similar to his old one, nearly identical, but there was one drastic change.

Where the sleeves of the blazer would be, they were stretched more and had a slit going down to the elbows. It wasn't the best for keeping warm because of this design, but Gary had figured out why Kai had done this.

"Probably doesn't want me ruining any more of the gang's clothes," Gary chuckled to himself.

Getting on his phone, Gary asked everyone to meet at the Wolf's Pool Club and to do so quickly. Meanwhile, Innu would update everyone on the way there about what was going on. The message was also sent out Olivia.

The main goal was to get the kids back from Innu's orphanage, but doing so would mean they were going up against the Gray Elephants. If this was an important operation for the gang, then they would do anything to stop others from intervening, meaning they needed all the help they could get.

"Amy!" Gary shouted as he was about to open the door. "I'm going out, one of my friends needs some help. Can you do me a favor? . . . Make sure to stay inside today, no matter what."

Gary didn't stay to listen to Amy's answer, and he had closed the door, before she could ask any more questions. His sister hardly ever went out on her own at night, especially after what had happened to her lately.

She hadn't talked about the mysterious man who had been following her; for some reason she had kept it a secret from Gary, even though he knew who it was. Perhaps she thought it was all in her head, but Gary knew that it wasn't. For now, though, he would keep it to himself; there was no need for him to worry his sister.

A short while later, the car had picked up Gary with Tyler at the wheel. He had picked up a few of the others as the rest had made their way to the pool club. All of the main members of the Howlers, along with Olivia, Suzan, and Kevin, were in the club, which now had a *CLOSED* sign on the door. Gary noticed that White was also present. Marie and her mother had taken her in and were looking after her for the time being.

"Innu, who are all these people?" Kevin whispered.

As he watched the others talking with concerned looks on their faces, taking the issue seriously, Innu couldn't help but smile. He was so happy that he had people he could rely on who would go this far for him.

"They're my friends, and they're going to help us," Innu replied.

"What could the Gray Elephants want with a bunch of orphans?" Marie asked, as she couldn't quite believe that even a gang would go that low.

"There are plenty of reasons. Harvesting them for organs, trafficking, making certain types of videos. The world isn't as sweet as you think it is. As long as their people need and want certain things, they will deliver," Olivia answered casually, reminding them that while they had just dipped their toes into the underworld, she was fully in it.

"All right, at the moment, we have Austin and his followers on their motorbikes searching around town to see if they can spot any of those trucks," Kai reported. "Olivia, you also have your people searching for the vehicles. Once we get information, we will move out and try to stop them."

"Stop them?" Suzan exclaimed, jumping out of her seat. "Don't you mean call the police? How will you stop them? Kevin said there were large men who weren't scared to use their fists, and not even the police sounded like they wanted to deal with them!"

"Exactly." Kai scoffed. "The police don't want to get involved in any of this, so what would calling them accomplish? We just have to take matters into our own hands."

Suzan and Kevin didn't understand. Where was the group's

confidence coming from? Neither one of them had heard Innu mention anything about them, so why were they so willing to help him? Innu was doing up the wraps that covered his hands; he also looked like he was ready to personally get involved.

Austin was the first to get a call from his side. One of his people had spotted one of the trucks and was following it.

"How many trucks are there?" Austin asked.

"We spotted two, but they split up, and now we're following both of them!" his friend shouted over the sound of his motorbike.

"Ask him what area they are heading to," Kai said, as he had a bad feeling about this.

Olivia got a call at the same time, reporting two trucks that matched the description, but they were both going in different directions.

"Gary, did you hear?" Kai asked.

Gary nodded; he had heard the names of the four areas and wondered why Kai looked so panicked, but then it hit him.

"All the areas . . . are owned by the Underdogs." Gary gulped down hard.

A smile appeared on Olivia's face.

"I don't know what they're going to use those orphans for, but whatever it is, this has to be their way of declaring the start of the war . . ."

CHAPTER 97

EVERYONE INVOLVED

The Pincers gang members, as well as Austin's schoolmates, were told to follow the trucks for now. They had spotted four so far. However, since all four of the trucks were heading to different locations, the Howlers had to decide what to do.

In the first place, they were unsure what had happened to the rest of the children; perhaps they were still at the warehouse, but it was unlikely.

Chavley is my home area, while Cipen is the main area where the Underdogs' businesses are. If this is an attack, the largest attack force will be in that area, Gary concluded. I don't know what to do . . . but I don't think splitting up will be our best choice. One, I can't protect everyone else if they're not close to me, and two, I think this war is going to be tough on all of us.

"Olivia, head out and check on your two groups. We'll trust your judgment, but please keep us updated on what you plan to do," Kai ordered. With that, Olivia was ready to leave, but Gary had one more thing to say to her.

"Olivia . . . if it's possible, prioritize saving . . . but if you have to engage the Gray Elephants members, don't hold back. Do whatever you need to take them out," Gary ordered as he clenched his fists. He was beyond annoyed at the predicament that the Gray Elephants had put him in. These people would continue to act this way unless they were dead.

The color gang war had already devastated a single area, but this attack could very well implicate the whole town. He could only place his trust in the beta werewolf and pray that she would keep the Bronton and Kidminstin areas safe.

"Gary, it's your call about where we go next. I think you know it's best if we stay together. The Gray Elephants are a big gang, after all, so choose one place." Kai let him have the last say.

"Amy should be safe, and I have a mark on her to know how she is doing. The apartment is locked up, and she should stay indoors. Mom got hurt last time because she was working. They should have no interest in the residents of the area . . . right?"

"We need to finish this once and for all; we will finish it today. We'll head to Cipen," Gary decided.

The reason for his choice was that Cipen was also where the nightclub that served as the base for Damion and the Underdogs was. If things went well, Gary could get both threats off his back today.

The two groups continued to follow the large trucks. Knowing what territory they were headed for, one would think that they would stop outside some of the establishments they owned. However, this wasn't the case at all.

Instead, they had surprisingly stopped at the busiest places in each location, the ends of the main streets where restaurants, bars, and shops were located. They stopped dead in the middle.

"Hey, report this to Austin," said Bo.

The next second, they saw the driver leaving the vehicle, and strangely he seemed to be fleeing. He didn't look left or right, but only at the parked truck, before he took off.

"Hey . . . you don't think they planted a bomb in that thing, did they?" Felix suggested, judging by the way the man was escaping the area. However, since they were on motorbikes, they believed themselves to be relatively safe.

Once the man was far enough away from the vehicle, he pressed a button on a device and the back slowly started to open.

"Can you hear that?" Alfie asked.

Carefully listening, they could make out growls and snarls, which also caught the attention of someone on the main street. He appeared to be drunk as he wobbled over to the vehicle. Eventually, the door fully opened, and a small creature leapt out of it, pinning the drunkard to the ground.

"*Argh!* Someone help me! It's a monster! A monster is trying to eat me!" the man shouted in his panic.

The boys laughed at the sight. They didn't take him seriously, believing him to just be delusional, but eventually his cries for help stopped. They stood up and saw that the creature had let him go, and he wasn't moving at all.

The creature's nails looked like sharp pencils, and something was dripping off them. Then more of them left the vehicle and ran down the street, jumping on whoever they found and clawing at them.

The first creature turned around and looked at the teenagers, smiling at them with a face full of blood. What they were looking at now really was a monster.

The same scene was happening all over the area. Each truck would open and about a dozen little monsters would file out, killing whoever happened to be unlucky enough to be out on the street. Each one looked slightly different, but all of them shared traits that no normal human would possess: teeth strong enough to crush bones, melted mouths, elongated nails, and so on.

The town fell into chaos. Panic quickly spread, with murders happening left and right.

A few minutes later, television reports were coming out to everyone in Slough. It was no longer an issue just for the Howlers.

"There have been reports of mass killings going on in at least four areas of Slough. The attackers seem to be modified in some way . . . similar to Altered. Yet it is clear that their minds are not there. Slough police have advised everyone to stay indoors.

"I repeat, everyone who is out and about should head home and stay indoors until the matter is resolved."

As Amy watched everything that was happening on TV, she became worried for her brother.

Wait, didn't Gary tell me to stay indoors as well? Don't tell me he's involved in this!

Underneath his house, Blake looked at the set of weapons on the wall. He quickly picked a blade from them while packing his things and getting dressed.

I don't know what's going on, but the reporter said it themself. Those things aren't human, which means I have a job to do. It's what Dad would do.

Rushing out from their hotel room, wearing their gray uniforms, were a couple who didn't look pleased at all.

"Get in contact with Anton and tell him to update us on everything that is happening," Sadie ordered an assistant who was following along at their side—the liaison who would talk to the police and the White Rose base.

"Get Anton to barricade the entirety of Slough! Not a single person is to leave this town. We can't let those crazed Altered out of here."

"This is unheard of! Do you not think we should make a personal report to White Rose HQ ourselves to call for more backup?" Frank asked.

"What's the point? We both know backup won't arrive in time. We're the only Altered here, so we have to act now! The only thing we can do is put some trust in this town's people."

People are dying left and right? This world really has gone crazy. I'm happy that my little sis is going to be leaving this place, but if I have the power to help, I should, Jayden thought while he looked through his cupboard for a disguise.

After all, a superstar like him getting involved like this would be big news, which he would rather avoid. Eventually, he pulled out a scarf and a wig that he used for photo shoots.

Well, it's not as fancy as streaker boy's, but it will have to do.

CHAPTER 98

YOU CAN'T DIE

The news spread quickly throughout Slough, and the public rushed into their homes. Some took the news seriously, while others thought that the police were exaggerating or that this was just a made-up story to get people off the streets.

Whatever the case, the Gray Elephants didn't care because their aim was to get another group's attention, and that they certainly did.

"Boss!" One of the men in suits came running into Damion's office, only to see that he was already standing, surrounded by some of his most trusted men.

"Speak!" Damion shouted at the man who had just entered.

"We keep getting calls from all our businesses in all of the areas! It's definitely a targeted attack!" the man explained. Damion turned around, picked up something off the desk, and spun back, throwing a knife and hitting the man in the forehead, killing him on the spot.

"That's wasting my time with information I already know!" Damion scoffed. "We knew the Gray Elephants were going to attack us, but those weasels can't even bother to do it themselves. For now, forget about all the other areas. We will protect Cipen and get rid of all of the attackers here.

"After today, businesses will have no other choice anyway. Once we're the only ones in town, they will come and go when this all blows over, and we will just take them back. You, tell me, have we heard any news from Kirk and the Cheetah Squad?" Damion asked.

The man gulped before answering. "Yes, one of his men reported that he has almost annihilated the entirety of the Gray Elephants gang that was at their warehouse. However, none of their leaders were present."

Hearing this news, the Underdogs, gang leader smiled.

"Good, that means that their leaders are somewhere else and will be personally coming over. The only question is who the f*ck is pulling their strings? . . . Ah, it doesn't matter, I'll find out soon enough, once I skin all their members alive. Tell Kirk to head to the other areas to clear them out as he makes his way back here."

He walked to the wall at the back of the room and looked up at a pair of small red axes. They looked like decorations, and Damion's men wondered why their boss would grab them now, of all times. They didn't look normal; their handles were covered in scales and their heads were white, as if made of bone.

Damion's weapon of choice had always been a pair of small axes—perhaps because when he used them, there was a mess, instilling fear in those who followed him, making them think twice about ever crossing him. And this pair was certainly quite special.

"I was hoping to solve the damned package situation before this, but these Gray Elephants just couldn't cherish their last days on earth. Pulling this stunt could get us all killed. Well, I'll at least make sure they'll die before us!" Damion murmured, as he walked out the door.

He kicked the office door open and entered the nightclub, which had been open for a couple of hours. The customers were frightened and shaking; they had run inside to escape the monsters.

Damion strode through with his men behind him, some carrying conventional weapons, and some carrying none. He walked up the stairs to the street and kicked that door open as well to see the chaos unfolding.

People were screaming and running in every direction. However, there didn't seem to be any gang members on the streets, at least not yet.

Damion gave his orders. "Send out the small-timers to the ends of the streets. Tell them to stay there and kill anyone who isn't a panicked civilian. I doubt this will be the full attack, so if I were them, I would be waiting for us to get tired."

The newbies and some of the younger members ran out to either side. One of those "lucky" enough to help protect Cipen was Gil. However, he and his group didn't get far before they encountered the beings the people were running from.

They looked like children, only clearly deformed, resembling strange beasts more than human beings. The main thing, though, was that they were covered in blood and the street behind them was strewn with bodies.

An Underdogs gang member pulled out his knife, and one of the creatures ran toward him. The man slashed his knife, cutting deep into the beast's hand; however, it used its other hand with its pencil-like nails, similar to long mini drills, to repeatedly stab the gangster in the side of the neck, and he dropped dead.

Watching this, Gil panicked. He had a baseball bat, so he mustered all his strength and swung from below, hitting the creature in the ribs and sending him off in the other direction. However, the other gang members, despite outnumbering the creatures three to one, were having trouble dealing with them, and Gil heard growls near him. Looking up, he saw that the creature he had swatted away was up again. He was sure he had broken its ribs, yet the only sign of damage was black blood seeping out from its mouth as it stared at him.

Shit, I'm going to die here! Gil thought as refreshed his grip and prepared to swing his bat once again at the creature's head. But it was prepared for him. At the last moment it stepped back, making him miss completely and leaving him open to attack. The beast was ready to pierce its claws right through Gil's body.

Having overswung the bat, Gil had no way out . . .

When he closed his eyes, readying for the pain, he heard a scream. He opened his eyes again to see a red axe chopping the beast's arms off. The next second, Damion used the other axe to slice the beast's head off, killing it on the spot.

"You . . . you're the one who claimed to know where Greeny was, right?" Damion asked. "I'll have you accompany me. It's too early for you to die."

CHAPTER 99

THE UNDERDOGS' STRONGEST SQUAD

The Underdogs had known that the Gray Elephants gang had been planning something. In fact, they had been tipped off that it was to start today. However, Brandon had been smart enough to keep the plans of what exactly would happen between himself and Raven.

With both gangs as big as they were, it was impossible to guarantee that there were no moles. In fact, Raven had gone one step further and had advised his friend to tell the teams only the area they would drive to. That way the Underdogs would be in for a surprise.

Nevertheless, armed with the knowledge that something was going down, Damion had sent out Kirk, along with the five-member Cheetah Squad, to the Gray Elephants' factory ahead of the attack. This was his number one squad and his most trusted as well.

The factory wasn't just any regular factory; it was the source of the Gray Elephants' main income, and it was also rumored to be where the leaders often met.

The Cheetah Squad was the strongest group in the Underdogs. They had never failed to complete a job before, and that was mainly because their leader was an Altered. Today was no different.

Kirk stood in the center of the factory, which manufactured car parts, but right now it was no longer operating. The machines had stopped and it was a bloody mess. A worker's face had been shoved into the assembly line and was bleeding.

The group didn't care whether the workers were part of the Gray Elephants; all of them were to be punished and dealt with. It was the risk they took when deciding who they would be paying to protect them.

Countless gang members had been defeated all around, and the Cheetah Squad's clothes were no longer black, but glistening with red. Placing his phone back in his pocket, Kirk took a big breath.

"All right, everyone, it looks like we had a busy day today. We were a little too late, and the Gray Elephants seem to have already started attacking all over the place." Kirk sighed. "We need to get moving, but before we go, we have one more order: to make sure this place won't be in operating condition for a while. If we can't beat them head-on in this war, or they continue to run away from us, that's fine. We'll just hit them in their finances and force them to come out eventually."

A few minutes later the group left the factory with explosions going off in the background. The whole factory would have to be rebuilt, and the people inside probably would never be able to walk again.

Two vehicles waited for them outside, ready to take them to the area closest to the attacks. In the lead car, Kirk leaned forward, resting his head against the seat in front of him.

"How many were in that factory?" Kirk asked.

"About twenty, sir," the man next to him answered.

"Add that to my list, and make sure it's updated," Kirk ordered while clenching his fist. The others in the car stayed silent.

How long will I have to keep doing this, and . . . will all my sins be forgiven? Kirk wondered. *The only way I can stay sane is to make up for all those I have hurt and use my strength to save others.*

The occupants of the car remained silent until they reached the next area and heard screaming.

"We are finally here, sir. According to the news we have received, they seem to be crazed Altered who have been taken over by their other side," the man said as he got out of the car and opened the door for Kirk.

The group had stopped on the other side of a bridge that led to a local cluster of bars owned by the Underdogs. It was popular for night drinking and pub crawls, in which people would stop at all the bars in the area before heading home. The Underdogs had made it their place of business because of the nice profits it returned. They dealt with other gang members as well as drunken customers who liked to cause trouble. It was one of the few areas that welcomed the Underdogs and their business, as it allowed them to run more smoothly.

Today, though, the customers weren't happy; instead there was fear in their eyes.

As he ran over the bridge, Kirk saw a young man and a young woman trying to escape from the creatures. She was struggling to run in her high heels, and suddenly one of her heels snapped off and she fell to the ground.

The man stopped to help his partner but saw that the creatures chasing them weren't too far behind.

"I'm . . . I'm sorry!" the man shouted as he turned around and ran, abandoning her.

"You bastard!" the woman cursed as she threw her shoes away and attempted to get up, but a creature was closing in on her. The next second, though, she looked up and saw a man with yellow skin and spots all over his body.

The creature lay a short distance away, its face mangled, and the man standing over her had a bloody fist.

CHAPTER 100

CLASH OF THE BEASTS

"Hey, folks, I'm right here in Kidminstin! Did you guys all see that just now?" A young university student wearing a puffy oversized coat and chains around his neck was filming the event on his phone.

He wasn't just a regular student, though. Scotty was a popular livestreamer who happened to be in the area, rating different bars and their best drinks. When the attacks started, he continued to film the whole thing, and the reason was simple.

The number of his viewers had skyrocketed!

Rather than being overwhelmed with fear, Scotty had seen an opportunity. He had managed to gather over two hundred viewers after livestreaming for a couple of months, but right now, his viewership was in the thousands! People not only from Slough were watching what was going on, but from other cities as well, as they had never seen such Altered before.

Is this real, or are they promoting some type of movie?

Yeah, I've never even heard or seen this many crazy Altered in the same place before.

I heard some rumors on the dark web. They say that there are large numbers of Altered in the lower-tier towns that have gone crazy.

But that doesn't make any sense. I thought there weren't any Altered in the lower-tier towns?

Which is why it doesn't make any sense and this person is just talking out of his ass.

Don't believe everything you see on the internet.

"Did you all see that just now? That man suddenly transformed his arms and legs and burst across to save that woman right now, yo!" Scotty commented. "It's an Altered. I can't believe there is an Altered in Slough, here to help the people!"

Soon, though, one of Scotty's viewers recognized the man as Kirk Summerfield.

Hey, that's not just any Altered, that's Kirk Summerfield! The rookie AFC guy, the Cheetah Altered.

Yeah, it is him! I guess he couldn't just stand back and watch what was happening in his town, so he had to get involved.

Whoa, does that mean this whole thing is real?

I dunno. Might just be some promo for the AFC. Maybe they will reveal this as some new type of match style?

"It's not a setup, guys," Scotty said after checking in with his live feed. He wasn't happy that his viewers were doubting the seriousness of this situation. "I couldn't get a good shot because I wasn't ready for what happened, but when I was leaving the place I saw real blood. I saw the look in the girl's eyes before she . . . died."

Have you ever heard of paid actors before, Scotty, or are you really that naive?

F in the chat for the poor woman, people.

"Remember to add her to the list," Kirk shouted as he continued to advance. Only one creature had followed this group, but Kirk was sure that more were nearby.

However, Kirk noticed that he had merely injured the beast. It stood up and opened its mouth, stretching the skin until it bled from the sides, and let out a nasty growl.

It's so small; is it really an Altered? . . . Guess it has to be. There's no way a normal human could have survived my hit when I didn't hold back, Kirk thought.

This time, instead of using his fists, Kirk grew out his sharp nails and dashed forward again. The creature was fast, but Kirk was faster, and his nails pierced right through its head.

Does that mean the Gray Elephants have turned children into Altered? Just how did they get their hands on so much Altered DNA? There's something else going on here. Things seem to have gone berserk with the rest of them. Damion could be in more trouble if I don't hurry up.

"I'm sorry, once you've been turned into a crazed Altered, there's no coming back from it. I'm sorry for what they did to you," Kirk apologized as he let go of the corpse.

Leaving the body on the ground, he continued to the source of the screams. He entered the main road, where some cars had been flipped and others destroyed. Countless dead Underdogs lay on the ground. He was a little proud that they had at least stayed to try to fight, rather than running away.

People huddled inside the establishments with the doors locked, staring outside, but it was quite calm, because standing in the middle of the street was a man facing the creatures on his own.

Scotty had followed Kirk and the others and zoomed in on the lone man.

"Look at this, it looks like a regular person is taking on the monsters," Scotty commented.

On camera, viewers saw a man wearing a sports shirt, a scarf around his neck, and a cap on his head. He dodged two of the creatures' attacks and grabbed the backs of their heads, slamming them into the ground.

Damn . . . this is harder than I thought without transforming any of my body, Jayden thought.

While he was catching his breath, another beast that he thought he had dealt with had gotten back up, thrusting its hand forward. Still, Jayden was ready, waiting for the right time to kick it in its head.

When he lifted his foot off the ground, though, he sensed something else approaching from the front and punched it in the side of its face instead.

"These guys are tougher than you think," Kirk said to the apparent stranger.

CHAPTER 101

ANTIHERO

The police had been quick to respond, which was a little strange even for them. However, they had managed to go to most of the areas where the current troubles were occurring. Still, many of the people who had been walking by questioned their tactics.

In one area, the police had surrounded the main street with cars at all exits, in a circle. Simply put, they weren't letting the creatures escape, hoping to minimize the damage outside the barrier, yet none of the police had entered the place themselves.

On the edge of the road, where the police cars had blocked it, a large van marked with the words *Channel 5 News* pulled up. A cameraman and a female reporter with short hair, wearing diamond earrings and a light blue suit, got out.

Of course, like most TV presenters, she was quite the looker. The news always earned better ratings when Kate Dar was on the scene. Immediately, the camera started rolling with its red dot lit and she got out her microphone, pointing it toward one of the officers.

"Officer, I'm Kate Dar from Channel Five News. I've come here hoping that you would be able to answer some of the public's questions." Immediately the police officer looked nervous, and the other officers standing nearby wondered what to do.

The problem was that they were already having trouble trying to stop the general public from entering. Many people were still holed up inside the buildings, and their family members had started arriving, hoping to get them out of danger.

"Many videos of the strange creatures that are assumed to be crazed Altered have appeared online, but our viewers want to know what is your plan to get the civilians out of these areas." The reporter pushed on. "As far as we know, none of the police have acted, and seeing the situation, it seems to be true. What do you have to say to that?"

As Kate asked her questions, screams could still be heard behind her. The camera zoomed in on countless dead bodies, mainly those of men in suits who looked to have been trying to protect the people.

However, the men were unable to put up much of a fight against the creatures, and now it looked like the crazed Altered were going for their next target. They were bashing themselves against the doors and windows of the shops, trying to break them.

"Help them, please!" the watchers were shouting as Kate shoved the microphone into the officer's face.

"Look, we are here to contain the damage," the officer replied. "And stop people like you from getting inside. This is the best option. If we go in and end up losing our lives, then these creatures will kill all of you as well!"

Some officers shook their heads at the comment. They had been trained how to deal with reporters in tense situations, but they understood. The pressure was getting to them. They had been watching the creatures fight against what they assumed were gangsters.

But although the gangsters had the same weapons as the police, better skills in using them, and more fighters in their ranks, they were still getting killed. Furthermore, the creatures seemed to be attracted to whatever human was closest to them. If the police went in, they would be sacrificing themselves for no reason.

At least they could get in their cars and create a barrier of some sort until they thought of a solution.

"Are you saying that the police are incompetent to solve this situation? If the police can't solve it, then who can?" Kate asked.

A hooded figure was slowly pushing people out of his way as he walked through the crowd. His head was down and he was dressed in all black. Eventually, he got to the front and approached the reporter and police officer.

"Step back, this is a restricted area, no one is allowed past this point!" the police officer shouted, but the stranger did not stop.

Kate pointed her cameraman toward the commotion; she had a feeling that something was about to happen.

"Let me through," the hooded man said. His voice was slightly altered, and when the man lifted his head, the police officer recognized him straightaway. He started to yell, but before he could, the man covered his mouth with a hand, kneed him in the stomach, and threw him aside.

Two more officers stood in the hooded man's way, pulling out their batons. The first officer swung his weapon, but the hooded man easily avoided it and quickly kicked the back of his leg, making him fall, before spinning and kicking the back of his head.

The second officer tried to attack as well, but the hooded man grabbed his wrist and twisted it before kicking him hard in the stomach as well.

"Get out of my way, you guys aren't the ones that I'm here for," the man said as he advanced.

Seeing an opportunity, Kate and her cameraman ran through the gap as they continued to film the stranger. The rest of the police quickly regrouped, stopping the rest of the people from getting closer.

But the hooded man pulled out two swords, ready to charge.

"It's an Altered Hunter," Kate gasped.

CHAPTER 102

ANTIHERO (PART 2)

When Blake first heard the news of the crazed Altered attacking the people in Slough, his first instinct was to go out to help. After all, despite being shunned by the public, the reason Altered Hunters operated was to save people from a situation just like this one.

However, part of Blake knew that he wasn't going out just to help the people. Part of him relished this situation, as it would justify him doing what he'd wanted to do ever since killing Billy. Right now, he was excited to be fighting Altered; however, he noticed one thing when he arrived on the scene.

These Altered are so small . . . and the clothes they are wearing look so shabby. Are they . . . homeless kids? Did someone turn kids into Altered?

It seemed impossible that someone would use the conventional way to turn so many children. After all, those who were turned into Altered were meant to be humans in peak condition, usually between sixteen and twenty-five years old.

Then again, that only applied for those who needed to be sponsored. With enough money, one could be as old as one wanted . . .

As Blake approached, the attention of some of the crazed Altered that had been stabbing holes through doors and windows just seconds ago shifted toward him. Two in particular looked his way.

They screeched and snarled at him; it was a strange sound, between a growl and a scream, but that didn't matter. Blake had to make sure he had the resolve to kill these Altered.

He glanced at the corpses on the ground. Some of them looked like gang members, but there were also civilians among them. Regular people who were simply at the wrong place at the wrong time.

They seem to attack humans on sight, just like the beasts the books described. If these Altered are allowed to live, they will continue to cause more chaos, Blake reasoned.

Both of the creatures leapt toward him at the same time. He swung his father's swords in a half arc, bashing them against the Altered's hard claws. The swords weren't light by any means, and the armor Blake wore gave him a boost in strength when he attacked.

Suddenly, a third Altered approached Blake, and as it thrust its hands forward, Blake rolled onto the ground, narrowly avoiding the attack. When he lifted his head, though, he saw a fourth Altered and quickly raised a sword to knock its claws away, then got back on his feet.

The people watching as they hid inside cars and buildings felt like they were witnessing a scene out of an action movie. They were amazed at the skill the young Altered Hunter was displaying, and they were rooting for him as he might be their only chance to get out alive.

The public knew how strong the Altered were; when they latched on to someone, it was impossible to throw them off, with their sharp claws and lightning reflexes. Still, this lone person was able to block and avoid them and match their strength.

But the beasts were starting to overwhelm him. The lone figure had quickly turned from a hero to someone who was barely surviving. Blake was able to block the attacks, yet he lacked the opportunity to deal any of the creatures a devastating blow.

This is why Altered Hunters are supposed to fight in pairs! Blake thought. *Since they're smaller than regular Altered, I thought I might fare better, but this is proving difficult. As soon as I find an opening to attack one of them, the others back him up.*

The young Altered Hunter felt his stamina disappearing. If he didn't do something soon, there would be serious trouble. Finally, his movements were a little too slow as one of the creatures got behind him and stabbed repeatedly toward Blake's back.

Everyone thought it was the end of the brave warrior who had come to help them, but just then Blake spun around, swinging his sword with his full strength, and sliced the neck of the creature, cutting its head off.

He looked at his armor and saw a few scratches on it, but it had withstood most of the attack. *Looks like that answers my question of whether they can get through this armor, although I didn't want to test that. I guess they're not as scary as a werewolf!* Blake thought, a little more confident.

More help had arrived, in the form of two figures that landed in the center of the street. They flapped their large, powerful wings, knocking several creatures away. Then the female dug her claw into the shoulder of the next closest creature. It dripped blood as she threw it to the ground.

"It looks like we hit the jackpot," Sadie said with a smile. "Who would have thought that we would have all of these Altered and an Altered Hunter right here in front of us?"

Everyone recognized the new arrivals as White Rose agents.

"Frank, take care of these little ones, and I'll go after this one!" Sadie ordered, as she dashed forward to strike with her claw. Blake lifted his sword to counter the claw, but Sadie pushed back with her greater strength.

Instead of meeting her next attack head on, he rolled to the side.

"What is White Rose doing?" someone shouted. "Why are they attacking him when he was trying to kill the beasts?"

"I heard them call him an Altered Hunter."

"Who cares about that? They're the ones who were too slow to respond! If it weren't for him, we might be dead!"

The watchers started to complain and boo the White Rose agents. Frank was also having a hard time, facing off against nine crazed Altered, who proved to be quite resilient.

"Ah, Sadie, maybe we should call a truce for a second," Frank suggested.

However, the look on Sadie's face was a clear no. She never cared about public opinion. They had PR teams for that sort of nonsense. Just as she was ready to charge forward again, though, the back of her foot started to throb in pain. The next second something had wrapped around her arm and she was being pulled back.

Whatever had wrapped around her arm quickly unwrapped. The weapon had cut the White Rose agent's forearm. Sadie turned and saw a woman dressed in black and gold, holding a whip.

"I really never liked you police in the first place," Olivia said.

CHAPTER 103

A TRUCE?

The reporter Kate Dar was continuing to film the events that were unfolding. She and her cameraman quickly moved to a safe spot outside one of the shops where many people were holed up watching what was going on.

The White Rose agents being here will be a huge scoop, Kate thought. *This may be one of the biggest events to happen this year. Who would have thought this small town had an Altered Hunter as well?*

It was a question on a lot of people's minds: What was going on right now with Slough? Ever since the brutal death of some gangsters at a construction site around a month ago, this Tier 3 town had managed to make the news rather frequently.

Altered killings even reached a nationwide broadcast level, and it was the same with Billy. His face was plastered all over the country. Yet this story right in front of them would be broadcast for months.

The camera zoomed in on one of the crazed beasts. It looked like an Altered, but it was too small to be an adult. What's more, when had anyone ever seen so many of them in one place? A group of vicious crazed Altered was sure to rouse the Anti-Altered movement, a group that seemed to be growing by the day as more cases popped up.

"Is a corporation secretly using Slough as a testing base?" Kate whispered as she continued to report, not wanting to catch the attention of any of the Altered.

It was then that the battle had started between the Altered Hunter and the White Rose agents. The people watching from the shops were clearly frustrated about what White Rose were doing; many of them saw White Rose as being on the same side as the police force. Then a new individual with a whip had entered the fray.

It was a strange standoff, as there were two White Rose agents, the Altered Hunter, and now seemingly another.

"Is it another Altered Hunter? No, that makes no sense; she's not bothering to cover up her face," Kate said for the benefit of her viewers. "Just who is this stunning person?"

Sadie looked at her now bleeding forearm. A whip was a fast weapon, but as an Altered she should have been able to avoid it. This whip was far faster than a regular one, and the pain in her arm was also greater than it should have been.

That weapon . . . I don't think it's an ordinary whip. Is it a Anti-Altered weapon? Sadie thought.

Anti-Altered weapons, or Anti weapons for short, had been discovered rather recently. The fossils of ancient creatures had been found buried deep in mountains, under the sea, in caves, and elsewhere. They were used for the Alterification process, but every so often archaeologists uncovered special weapons that had hardly deteriorated.

They seemed to have been made from the ancient beasts themselves, which was why they were so special. The public wasn't privy to this information, mostly because these weapons were a rarity. Sometimes rich people bought them as a status symbol, believing that they were nothing but relics of the past, unaware of how much power they actually held.

However, another group of people besides the Altered Hunters seemed to be using more of these weapons recently, and that was powerful gangs. It was an alternative to increasing one's strength, which was quite a bit cheaper than becoming an Altered.

So Sadie had an idea about what type of person this woman in front of her was.

I don't know this woman with the whip, but as long as she's not trying to fight me and is keeping that crazy woman off my back, I should be good, Blake thought, wondering if he should make a run for it. However, if he did, who would take care of the crazed Altered? *She might keep up with one White Rose agent, but she will have no chance if I don't engage the man. They're strong . . . perhaps too strong even for me to handle.*

Blake wasn't used to being the decision maker in tough situations like this; he had always relied on his father.

Then one of the little Altered creatures leapt toward Olivia. Spinning out of the way, she wrapped the whip around its arms, tying it up, and then lifted it into the air and slammed it into the ground.

Her reflexes were fast, and her strength was greater than before. Even Olivia was surprised at how well her body was reacting.

That kid . . . has given me quite a gift. Olivia smiled to herself.

"My boss has given me permission to go all out against the Gray Elephants, but I'm sure he won't mind if I include you in that list as well," Olivia said as she swung her whip again, striking the ground just in front from another crazed Altered coming toward her.

As the whip cracked against the ground, it became clear that either the weapon was extraordinary, or she had abnormal strength. While Sadie stared the woman down, she wondered what to do.

Frank had leapt back between the two groups. He had taken out another of the Altered creatures; his arm was bloody and his wings scratched up with a few puncture wounds. He had been dealing with most of the crazed Altered while his partner was having a field day.

"I can't take it any more!" Frank shouted. "That's it, I'm calling a truce, I don't care what you say, Sadie. Hey, you, Altered Hunter guy, whip lady, how about it? You won't attack us, we won't attack you. Let's just get rid of these crazed Altered."

Seeing how much trouble her partner was in, and how difficult these two people in front of her would be, Sadie bit her tongue and took it.

"Fine."

Immediately, turning toward the others, Sadie threw out one of her feathers, hitting one of the crazed Altered in the forehead. It was bleeding, but the projectile hadn't managed to pierce hard enough to kill it.

Damn it, either these little guys are tough or I'm still having problems, Sadie thought as the back of her leg throbbed.

The people's hopes had now risen, seeing that all four of them had started to fight off the group of crazed Altered together.

Blake was more than happy to agree to a truce, as he could finally focus on taking on these creatures. Meanwhile, Olivia was testing the limits of her new body against some worthy foes. She felt as if she could draw more power from her weapon now than when she had been a human.

Only about ten creatures remained, and after a short while the four fighters managed to beat them all. Sadie had simply destroyed the arms and legs of the last one rather than outright killing it. She was sure White Rose would be interested in having a live sample to find out what exactly these creatures were. Perhaps it was because they were children or weak beings that had been turned into Altered, but none of them were as strong as real Altered.

The people inside the shops waited for a while, unsure if everything was over. Nobody wanted to risk going out, in case there might be more creatures around. However, although they couldn't see or hear any more creatures, they saw another threat approaching and decided to stay indoors.

A menacing group of people, carrying assorted weapons, were walking down the street. About fifteen had come out from each side, surrounding the four fighters.

"These aren't Altered," Blake said; he could tell straightaway from the energy readings. Their temperatures were all normal.

"Nope, they're not." Olivia smiled. "They're gangsters, but they are scum nonetheless."

CHAPTER 104

A TRUCE (PART 2)

Olivia recognized them as members of the Gray Elephants. Perhaps the little monsters they had created were just the initial attack. If they couldn't deal with the Underdogs members, then the Gray Elephants would come in next, either destroying their businesses, or getting rid of every Underdogs member.

In a gang war between two large gangs, one would have to either take the leader out, which was nearly impossible, or wipe out the gang completely, and it looked like the Gray Elephants were now going for the latter.

"It's okay, though, I have my own help for this," Olivia said.

Behind them, another group of people charged at the gangsters. Olivia didn't hold back in helping them, because after all, she didn't want to lose any of her own people.

I don't usually fight humans, but I guess I owe her a favor, Blake thought as he charged in as well. Still, the young Altered Hunter had put away his weapons, opting to incapacitate them with his fists.

The two White Rose agents were simply annoyed that these random people had tried to attack them, so another fight had broken out. The Gray Elephants members must have believed that their opponents would be tired after seeing them fighting just moments ago.

However, even if they were, their strength was enough to deal with normal humans, especially with the help of the former Pincers members. The Gray Elephants were taken care of rather quickly and lay unconscious on the ground.

"What are you waiting for? Arrest these idiots!" Sadie shouted at the police officers, who had yet to come forward from behind their barricade of cars.

"I hope you are not including my people in this?" Olivia looked the White Rose agent in the eyes before turning to the police. "After all, these guys are just concerned citizens who were protecting themselves. They did nothing wrong. However, if you feel differently, we are going to have some serious trouble between us!"

The gang members who now technically belonged to the Howlers certainly didn't look like regular citizens, from the clothes they were wearing to the weapons they had brought along, and especially the familiarity with which they used them.

"I think it's best we just leave it for now," Frank whispered to his partner. "Something's going on; the police reported that the same thing is happening in other areas. We don't have time to deal with them, and besides, we really don't have much on them apart from them using weapons, but they could argue that it was self-defense and if they're connected to some big names you know it will be a tough battle with so little to bring them in on."

Looking out of the corner of his eye, Frank also spotted the camera and the woman who was already running toward them for a few words.

"Besides, we have a lot of eyes on us at the moment," he said, knowing full well how big a story this would be, and perhaps the whole country would be watching.

It was true; not only the camera but a lot of the public were watching, and although Sadie didn't care what the people thought, she couldn't deny that because of Olivia's people, lives might have been saved today.

What's more, neither the woman, her people, nor the Altered Hunter had done much more than incapacitate the Gray Elephants members. It was as if they already knew that they could have been taken in for excessive force otherwise. They really had little to bring them in on.

"Patch yourself up, and once you're healed and back at a hundred percent, we'll move to the next area where reports are coming in. I don't want you to die from this mess in this no-name town." Sadie sighed.

As she walked away, the female White Rose agent touched her foot a couple of times and looked at the strange woman. For some reason, the wound on her leg had been hurting ever since she had arrived.

This can't be a coincidence . . . Am I really doing the right thing in letting her get away? Sadie wondered.

Just then, several cell phones started ringing. The sounds were coming from some of the dead bodies. Not the dead bodies of the public or those of the Gray Elephants.

No, they were coming from the bodies of the other gang members. The ones who had perished before any of the others could arrive. The Underdogs. Usually the police wouldn't answer such calls, but the phones hadn't stopped ringing. Something was clearly up.

After putting on a pair of gloves, Sadie fished out a phone and answered the call.

"This is an emergency!" the man on the other end shouted. "The Cipen area is under attack. We are in serious trouble! We need help from all areas immediately. Head to Cipen, that's an order now!"

The man didn't even confirm who had answered the phone, clearly in distress and worried.

"Well, it looks like we know what area we need to head to next," Sadie said.

At the same time, the reporter had also caught wind of the phone call, and she wasn't the only one.

Are there even more of those crazed Altered there? Maybe even stronger ones? Blake thought. *But is it really wise to test my luck if the White Rose agents are heading there as well? They will need to prepare before they go, so maybe I can get a head start.*

With that, Blake was on his way but not before taking a second look at the woman who had helped him. Her temperature had risen occasionally during the fight, but no more than for anyone else. Still, he chose to ignore it as he was in a rush.

Cipen? I should report to that brat just in case he went to that area, Olivia thought.

CHAPTER 105

THE RED BLOOD STREET

Everyone knew that Damion Hawk was the leader of the Underdogs gang. His purple suit had already become iconic, though he spent most of his time in the nightclub called the Basement.

They were such a large gang and a prominent force that they didn't worry about the fact that their leader was known to all in Slough, possibly making them an easy target.

They were also known to be the only gang in Slough that had an Altered.

How someone like Kirk was working for Damion was anyone's best guess, and it was kept a secret even from those in the Underdogs. All they knew was that he was loyal till the very end.

Regardless, everyone believed that Damion, the leader, wasn't the strongest or best when it came to fighting. After all, they never saw him in action or taking the helm in a fight.

They knew and had heard of his cruel nature, but as a fighter?

This was in contrast to the Gray Elephants, who were known for using their fists. So although their leader wasn't seen a lot, if anyone were to try to control them, the leader of the Gray Elephants would have to be a strong fighter to earn the respect of the others.

This difference between the two gangs was why people believed that Damion was a leader because of his decision making. However, as Damion's men watched him fight, Gil stayed by his side through this mess. They immediately knew that all those rumors were false; they were utterly wrong.

To allow ease of movement, Damion had taken off his purple suit.

Or more accurately speaking, he had timed it as one of the crazed Altered came toward him; he threw the suit, covering its face, then threw one of his unique axes at it. The two landed on the floor, and dark blood soaked through the purple suit before Damion picked it up from the ground. The buttons on his white shirt, which was also soaked in dark blood, were torn off, revealing his dark tan skin and his well-developed muscles underneath.

It was safe to say that ordinary gang members could not take on the crazed Altered, even though they were skilled in fighting. No matter how much they hit, slashed, or whacked the crazed Altered with their weapons, the Altered got back up again.

Just then, one of the gang members side-kicked one of the crazed Altered away, knocking it to the floor, but its claws had stabbed his leg in the process. The gang member was worried that it would soon get back up, but before it did, Damion was there swinging both of his axes right toward its head.

He had a smile on his face as the blades of the axes plunged into the skull, and the creature stopped moving.

"You guys keep doing what you're doing. I'll finish them off," Damion ordered with a sinister smile.

Not too far from where they stood, opposite where the night-club would be, was a black of apartments on top of the restaurants. Brandon and Raven stood on the rooftop watching the scene unfold in front of them.

"He's quite the monster, that's for sure," Raven commented. "Most people nowadays seem to have forgotten that the Underdogs rose to their position before the famous Kirk joined them."

"Yes, and that only increased the gang's position in this town. I tried to convince Kirk to come to our side many times, but he would never budge or take the bite. I wonder how he managed to wrap someone like Damion that tightly around his finger." Brandon let out a big sigh. He could now see that, primarily because of Damion, the crazed Altered were at their end.

"They did their job well, didn't they?" Brandon asked. "I don't know if this is what Sin wanted us to use his solution for, but if we can get rid of all the Underdogs, then that will be perfect."

"The reports we have gotten back have been good," Raven replied. "In each area, all the Underdogs have been dealt with. Although it's the same for our crazed Altered, not that we intended to keep them after this anyway."

Just then, Damion swung his special axes, sending the last crazed Altered to the ground, no longer moving. Many of the Underdogs had died, leaving only ten alive.

Damion and Gil had made it, so their numbers were now twelve.

Honestly, seeing them like this, Brandon thought he could have gone down there with the rest of the Gray Elephants members and finished them off himself. However, to be sure, they would stick to the plan.

Moments later, two more trucks appeared on both sides of the street. It wasn't the end for Damion and the others.

The back doors of the trucks opened, ten crazed Altered stormed out of each one, doubling their strength. After a tough battle, they would have to go through it again. Only this time, it would be more problematic.

"It was a good thing we did all that testing." Brandon smiled.

They had been given only one syringe of liquid, but by using small amounts and realizing they could dilute the substance, they had discovered many of its effects: How much was required to turn someone? If diluted, how long it would take someone to turn? And so on. All of these tests allowed them to plan everything out and to time it perfectly—and the mastermind behind all of it was Raven.

It was possible that Damion and the other outside help would arrive to deal with the crazed Altered in other areas, but really they were sent only to delay and stop the Gray Elephants from coming back in the first place.

"Boss, what do we do?" one of the men asked.

"Isn't it obvious? Fight for your lives, so we can get out of this situation!" he shouted back.

The crazed Altered charged in, running past the shops and clubs that had people inside them, scared to come out. They were heading toward the town center as if they were attracted by something, like sharks attracted to the scent of blood.

However, a few got a whiff of something else: the people who were bleeding inside the shops. They turned their heads and started to claw at the shop doors and windows, attempting to get inside.

A little ways away, the Channel Five van had arrived. They had spotted one of the trucks on their way here and noticed the same abandoned truck just moments ago. Kate had a hunch that it was important.

She just didn't realize how significant it was when several of the creatures had come out from the back of the trucks. She left the van with her trusty cameraman and continued to film.

Only this time, she wasn't so quick to storm the busy street.

Did the police not reach this area yet? Are there not enough of them? This area has more of those monsters than the last area did. If White Rose doesn't get here soon . . . Kate thought. Still, it was strange because, unlike the place they had just left, there wasn't a single police officer to be seen.

No patrol cars, nothing. This was why Kate didn't enter the street, even though most of it was clear. Still, she saw a few stray Altered attacking the windows, and she sure didn't want to grab their attention.

The camera zoomed in on the worried people's faces, and eventually, one of the Altered smashed through the strong glass. Immediately, it pulled a person out of the shop, dragged the person to the center of the street, and dug its mouth into the person's body.

With the Altered busy eating one of its victims and the shop no longer safe, the door opened and about thirty people stormed toward Kate, knocking her and her cameraman over. It was like a stampede, but she couldn't blame them, and honestly, she felt like she should run away as well.

When Kate and her cameraman regained their footing, they looked back on the street. They thought they would see dead people or the creature chasing after the others, but instead they saw a man in a black-and-gold blazer.

He was lifting the creature by its throat, its arms no longer attached to its body, having fallen to the ground; he was surrounded by others wearing the same black-and-gold uniform.

"Who are these people who have just arrived, and how were they able to take down that crazed Altered?" Kate reported. "The uniform and their colors are the same as those of the woman who helped that Altered Hunter! Are they part of the same group?"

Zooming in to the man holding the creature up, the camera revealed a black-and-gold wolf mask and red glowing eyes underneath.

CHAPTER 106

TWO ALTERED CLASH

Although many people were busy watching Kate's news report on television, some youngsters were getting their updates about the situation in Slough through other sources. One of those was Scotty, the livestreamer, who was becoming more famous by the second.

This is it, I've found my calling! People are eating this crap up. All I need to do is keep searching for big events like this, follow them, and people will keep following me. Scotty was already picturing the good life as he held his phone as still as possible for the others to see what was going on right now.

Kirk and his Cheetah Squad had come into the middle of the street, which naturally wasn't being used right now, since many cars had been toppled over and crushed. The Altered was impressive as he continued to fight off the crazed beasts one by one, mainly using his speed and forward punches.

Someone else was catching the eyes of the others even more: the stranger whose face was hidden. He wore his cap quite low, while his scarf covered everything below his eyes.

Who is that guy? I mean, Kirk is an Altered and transformed, but this guy looks and acts like a ninja!
He has to be an Altered as well! There's no way a non-Altered can do that much!

Just as the viewers were talking about Jayden, he jumped on the shoulders of one of the creatures, pushing it back, then kicked another one in the face. When a third swiped toward him, he did a backflip and kicked it on the chin.

Damn, I haven't fought like this in a long time. Jayden grinned underneath his disguise. *But it's also nice to just use my strength to beat them sometimes.*

Given his unique Altered form, he couldn't afford to transform; that would be a dead giveaway as to who he was. He needed to be more creative with the way he fought, bringing him back to his school days. This fighting style was what was getting the attention of all the others.

Soon, with the two of them on the job, the crazed Altered in the area had been defeated. It was nice, quick, and easy. Slowly, the people who had been hiding in the restaurants and bars came out, and so did the few who had stayed in their cars.

Immediately they started clapping for their two saviors.

"Thank you! Thank you for saving us!" they cheered. Some people got closer to personally thank them.

Meanwhile, the shop owners mainly stayed back. They knew that the ones who had protected them were gang members, because of the clothing they were wearing, and they often had to deal with the Underdogs. They were grateful now, but many struggled to stay open because of the high prices they had to pay the Underdogs for protection. Not only that, but they felt like the Underdogs had just done what they were obligated to do.

With the dangerous creatures defeated, Scotty felt like he should take this chance to interview the two heroes. His viewers certainly demanded it, and if he managed to do that he could upload the interview to PouTube, increasing his own fame even more.

He immediately ran out and joined the crowd, but before any of them could approach the two, Kirk had spun around and pounced on the strange masked man. It looked like he hadn't aimed to injure him, merely going for his hat, yet before the Cheetah Altered could reach him, the man knocked his hand away.

Jayden jumped back a few steps. "Hey, man, what was that for? We helped each other, and now you attack me?" he asked, surprised by Kirk, and he wasn't the only one. The confused crowd stopped moving forward.

I thought they were on the same side and knew each other. Why are they fighting?

Actually, I think he went for his hat. Maybe he's as curious as we are about the identity of whoever is under that disguise.

I wish he had succeeded. I'll bet whoever it is, is really handsome!

More like hideous! Why else would someone who's going to save people cover up what they look like? Probably doesn't want anyone hating on him.

"There is only one Altered in this town, and that's me . . . so who are you and who are you working for?" Kirk asked the stranger.

He charged him again. This time seemed faster than before, but Jayden avoided the attack, moving his head to the side. He grabbed Kirk and, with the momentum of his own body, threw him forward to the ground.

"Hey, I really don't want to fight, and besides, aren't you supposed to buy me dinner before you start asking me all those questions?" Jayden asked teasingly, making sure to change his voice.

The Underdogs members couldn't believe what they were seeing. Kirk was faster than any of them; he was also a rookie champion in the AFC. Yet a person who looked like a regular human had just thrown him to the ground.

Am I dreaming? Did he really just do that to Kirk Summerfield? Only if we're dreaming the same thing. That guy is seriously skilled. He has to be a professionally trained fighter!

There's no way that guy isn't an Altered! Just how strong is he, if he's managing that much before even transforming!

As Kirk quickly got up off the ground, he was having similar thoughts; the other person's movements were clearly not those of an amateur. Now that Kirk was taking things a bit more seriously, his body started to change more; his teeth started to elongate, giving him larger canines, and his eyes narrowed.

Damn, this is bad, Jayden thought. *If I transform, everyone will know who I am, and that I'm staying in this town. Reporters will be all over me, and I just don't want to deal with this crap. This guy clearly is misunderstanding something.*

"Hey, cheetah dude, we'll meet again some other day. There are other areas in this city that need help—"

Just as Jayden was about to finish his sentence, Kirk's trouser leg expanded in size. His large leg muscles came into view, and he leapt straight across, trying to swipe a claw toward Jayden's face. As his claw was swung down for a brief second, Kirk saw a white glowing aura.

"His eyes . . . so he really is an Altered," Kirk realized as Jayden parried his hands to the side.

"That crap will only get you so far," Jayden lectured him. "Your fighting is no better than a kid's. I can clearly see where you're aiming. You're still an amateur to me."

With that he threw a punch of his own, stopping just short of hitting Kirk, yet the Cheetah Altered could feel that something had hit him, even though the fist had yet to touch his body.

Although the force wasn't strong, it conveyed to Kirk that whoever was under that disguise could beat him anytime he wanted.

"I already said I don't want to fight. I just happened to be in this town at this time, so I decided to help." With that explanation, Jayden moved his hand away.

The fighting seemed to be over between the two, and Kirk had even canceled his partial transformation. The people who had been watching were satisfied by this outcome. They were thankful to both fighters for saving their lives, and the last thing they wanted was for either one to injure the other.

"Sir!" one of the Underdogs members shouted, having just gotten off the phone. "The boss seems to be in trouble. We're to head to Cipen straightaway!"

Jayden thought that was good news. *If that guy heads to Cipen, the people there should be okay. I heard that one of the reported areas was Chavley, so I'll head over there and make sure all the creatures there are dealt with.*

"Hey, good luck," Jayden called after Kirk as he left. "Also, if you think you're the only Altered in town, you're in for a big surprise. Maybe don't go all crazy on them from the get-go like you did me!"

Other Altered? Kirk wondered.

CHAPTER 107

WE CAN'T HELP

The event in Slough had been going on for a little over an hour, which was enough time for Channel Five to attract attention not just around Slough but around the whole country.

The video was being viewed live by everyone, with a bit of a delay, allowing the gruesome scenes to be blurred out. The plus side was that it was late, so the news channels were able to show more.

Still, many people saw the mystery man in his black-and-gold outfit holding up one of the Altered like it was a child. Even with its small figure, not many of them felt sorry for it.

Even now, they could see that the Altered was trying to bite at the man holding it up with its deformed mouth, swinging its legs as it tried to kill its opponent.

Somewhere in a dark room at the Lock gang's base, a large man was sitting comfortably drinking a dark liquid.

"That damned wolfman!" Tony shouted at his TV screen. "They are getting involved in this war, aren't they?"

"Well, they could just be concerned citizens," his right-hand man replied.

Tony scoffed and finished his drink in one gulp.

They weren't the only gang watching for today's outcome. Many of the other gangs were also carefully watching, waiting to see if they had done the right thing at the meeting or if they had made a mistake. When it was all over, they would decide their next move.

Inside his repaired office, the mayor watched the TV along with the Rising Dragon leader, D.

"It looks like they weren't lying when they said they would get involved in this war," D commented.

"It's surprising how much power the Gray Elephants have. I was certain that the Underdogs would come out the winner in this war, but now with this third intervention, depending on what happens today, we will have to change our plans," Ben Clove said as he looked at his hands, closing and opening them slowly, smiling to himself.

At the same time, two people in particular were watching what had happened live.

"Who are they?" Brandon shouted.

As the crowd was running away, they saw a person walking through, calmly passing everyone. One of the Altered had leapt toward a civilian, with its hand seconds away from digging into a woman.

At that moment, Gary had transformed his hands and sliced right through the tiny limbs of the Crazed Altered, then lifted it into the air.

"He has to be an Altered, to be able to deal with someone like that so quickly," Raven said. "It's the only thing that makes sense. Their arrival could ruin everything!"

"You believe that?" Brandon said. "We still have our gang members; it just means we might have to make our move sooner."

He walked off the rooftop, leaving Raven to watch how things would play out.

Back on the ground floor, not only all the regular Howlers members had appeared, but also Innu, and Suzan and Kevin with him as well. They saw the child that Gary held in his hands, and those who were taking down the Underdogs members behind him.

They fell to their knees, their limbs numb.

"That was Tommy's favorite shirt!" Suzan said, her eyes full of tears.

"And there is little Bobo!" Kevin cried, holding on to Suzan as well; the two of them had gone into complete shock.

"*Gary!*" Innu shouted. "*Put him down!*"

Gary turned his head toward Innu. Although Innu hadn't fallen to his knees and hadn't turned around to look at the others, he was sniffling. Not just because of the children from his orphanage, but the others as well. The ones he had promised to go back to save had already been turned and were lying dead on the ground.

"Innu," Gary replied. "Are these . . . the orphans that you were looking for?"

Innu nodded in response. Gary looked behind him to see if any crazed Altered were nearby, but the others seemed to be still fighting the Underdogs members.

Gary placed the crazed Altered on the ground but kept a firm grip with one hand on its head and kicked its legs so it was down on its knees, allowing everyone to get a clear look at what he was holding.

"I'm sorry, Innu, I know you knew them . . . but what do you want me to do?" Gary asked. "I want to help, but they're like the twins were before. I know it, and you know it. If I hadn't stopped him, he would have killed the woman running away. If I let him go now, everyone in this town will be in danger.

"I can tell right now that if I let this fake Altered go, he would rip out your throats without a second thought."

It was true that these were Gary's thoughts, but there was more than just what he believed to be the case; the system had also told him it would be the case.

New Quest received
Save the town of Slough
Someone has created fake Altered and let them loose.
Save the town by getting rid of them
30/64 Infected Altered have been killed
Quest reward: Will depend on your contribution to ridding the
town of the Infected Altered

The four areas of Slough that the Underdogs owned had ten crazed Altered each attacking them, and now Cipen was under a second wave more significant than the other attacks. It was clear now, after seeing Innu, that every single orphan had already been turned into these Crazed Altered.

"He's right, Innu," Marie said as she approached him and placed her hand on his shoulder. "You remember those twins? These guys look similar to them. The best thing we can do is put them out of their misery. Do you think your friends and the orphans would have liked to hurt people like this?"

Innu didn't know how to answer, and he didn't turn around either, still worried about what type of faces the others would show. He felt like he had given them false hope.

"I . . . I . . ." Innu sniffled. "I joined this gang . . . I got into underground fighting all because of them. I did everything I could to save them . . . so what do I do now?"

"Innu!" Suzan shouted; after the sadness, now that she understood the situation, another emotion followed. "Your friend, I can tell he's special, right? You knew he could help us because he's unique! You asked what to do now; I'll tell you what to do.

"He's right. Help them, free them from this pain, and then after that . . . make sure the people that put you through this suffer even worse than they did!"

Kevin was surprised by Suzan's words; she had never asked Innu to do anything, and she had never condoned violence, but seeing the kids she raised in this state must have snapped something inside her.

"I . . . I want them all to pay!" Suzan screamed.

It was an emotional scene that played out on camera, so much so that Kate hadn't even said a word as she filmed it. The group that had suddenly appeared seemed to have answers that they were missing.

Innu wiped his tears away with his sleeve and nodded toward Gary.

"Okay, let's do this, and I promise if you help me get what I want, if you help me get revenge against the people that did this to my family, I will follow you forever!" Innu shouted at the top of his lungs.

Looking down at the crazed Altered, Gary braced himself. The killing was happening more often, and killing things that didn't seem human felt similar to hurting an animal; but Gary knew who these creatures were, so as he used Controlled Transformation on his fingernails and stabbed the crazed Altered in the chest, killing it on the spot, he asked himself a question.

Why is it so easy to do now? he thought as he let go of the body, allowing it to fall to the ground, and turned toward the rest of the Underdogs gang in front of him.

CHAPTER 108

THE FINAL MARK

With everything going on, and since there was nothing they could do to help out, Suzan took Kevin back to their car, which was parked at the end of the main street. The group had split up between cars, one driven by Marie's mother, and the other by the gang's newest employee, Tyler.

Tyler couldn't believe everything that was happening, and he was starting to wonder what type of group he and Gary were involved in. However, while he had been waiting in the car, he decided to tune in to the news on his phone, and he was able to hear what was being said.

Gary had altered his voice, and he was trying to make it a habit whenever he donned the mask. Given his hair color, it was the least he could do to make people doubt him being the same guy who was the leader of the Howlers. Similarly, Kai had also decided to wear his fox mask to cover his face, while the others were okay with their faces showing.

Tyler felt like he was with the good guys after hearing the dreaded tale of what these Altered really were. A red banner popped up on his phone's screen:

Could the crazed Altered really be orphans that have been experimented on?

Man . . . how many times have I been called on today already? First I thought driving a car like this was a dream come true. But if I'd known my job was going to be this hard, I would have asked for more cash, Tyler thought.

Opening the car door and getting in, Kevin and Suzan felt a bit safer from all the chaos, but they noticed that Tyler was watching the TV reports on his phone.

"Can you please turn the video up?" Suzan politely asked, and Tyler quickly complied and tilted the phone so they could watch with him.

"Do you think Innu will be okay?" Kevin asked as they listened to the reporter.

"Of course. Didn't you say it yourself, he's an adult now, someone that we can rely on. He will be okay." Suzan said, rubbing the top of the young teenager's head as all three continued to watch the news channel to find out just how this chaos would unfold and end.

"When this is over . . . I'll take you both in myself."

With no more distractions, it was time for the Howlers to make their move, but they were concerned about one thing. They saw the Underdogs fighting against the crazed Altered, but the Gray Elephants were nowhere to be seen.

"They should be somewhere nearby. If the Underdogs manage to survive this, they'll surely try to finish them off," Kai said, as if he could read Gary's mind. "If we get involved now, we'll just be helping the Underdogs. That being said, this could also be our perfect chance to attack."

"Look, there's Damion!"

Gary had noticed that Kai's heartbeat increased dramatically when he mentioned the leader. He also didn't miss how much spite Kai felt when uttering his name.

I don't know why, but he seems to hate Damion as much as I do . . . No, that's not right. To me, he's just someone I have to get rid of in order to protect my family, but there seems to be something personal going on between them. Was that also the reason he founded the Howlers?

Make sure to kill him. Don't do whatever you did to Olivia. It's too dangerous to keep him alive; he would just find a way to backstab us. We have to take him out here and now!

While Gary was thinking about what to do and how to tackle the situation, he heard people screaming.

"What are you doing? Get away from the door!" a woman shouted from one of the shops. But it wasn't just one of the shops, it was all of them. Large groups of people were forcing their way outside.

Dressed in all types of clothing, they filled the street, and now they blocked the entrances from both main streets.

"These guys are trouble," Austin said, as he noticed one of them pulling a small blade from his pocket.

"You're saying they're gangsters, right?" Marie asked. "If that's the case, then why didn't they come to help out before?"

"You seem to be misunderstanding something, Marie. They're not part of the Underdogs. Those should be the Gray Elephants members who have been here in plain sight from the beginning, watching everything carefully," Kai answered.

From the elated looks on their faces about the sorry state of the Underdogs, Kai's explanation was spot on. Their numbers were large, and Cipen was full of large fancy restaurant-bars and clubs and hotels. There was already a large population on this one street alone. It was easy for them to hide among the people, and that was exactly what they had done.

Now Gary and the others were surrounded by a hundred or so gang members. They had not charged in where the Underdogs were just yet, and they even took a step back as if they knew how close they could get to the crazed Altered before they would be attacked.

One of the Gray Elephants members looked toward the Howlers group.

"We have orders to get rid of the new troublemakers that have decided to get in—" Halfway through his speech, a gang member came running out toward him. Innu jumped up and kneed the man right in the face, knocking him to the ground.

"I'll kill every one of you bastards!" Innu shouted as he quickly kicked another gangster in the arm. But a third one was getting ready to punch Innu to get him off his colleague.

Just before he could, though, a fist came down, knuckle on knuckle, but it was clearly stronger as the attacker's fist was pushed back with a loud crack.

"Hey, don't hog them all to yourself. Let us take some of them out as well," Austin declared.

"Gary, you take care of the Altered, and Damion, find an opening; this might be your only chance," Kai told him. "Don't forget what I said."

The fox-masked teenager joined the others, making sure that Marie stayed close by his side. The group were fighting in a circle, trying their best against the gang members, who had the advantage in numbers.

Gary hesitated, since there were far more of the Gray Elephants members than had been the case with the Pincers. Even if this was his only chance to go after Damion, he didn't want to sacrifice any of his friends.

I can't leave them; I need to help as well. Getting rid of the Gray Elephants is just as important, Gary thought as he prepared to run forward. He saw someone approaching Marie from behind, sneaking up on her.

A second later, though, the man's body started to shake violently, as if he was being electrocuted. When he fell to the ground, a man stood over him in a black robe and wearing a black mask.

"Bl—"

"No!" the Altered Hunter shouted back. "I am here to deal with the people who caused all of this mess, and I will try my best to make sure no one gets hurt because of these guys."

Gary was wondering how Blake knew it was him, but it must have been his special mask, or perhaps because Gary's hand was still transformed. At the same time, Gary had worn those clothes before. He also understood that this was Blake's way of saying he would protect them without actually saying that.

On top of that, Gary could tell that another person was close by, one who soon would be able to provide support as well.

I never thought I would be relying on her so much, but if they are here, then the Howlers can deal with this! Gary thought.

He broke off from the rest, and the first thing he did was get behind one of the crazed Altered and pull its arms, breaking one apart. The next moment, he stabbed his claw into the back of its neck.

+400 Exp

Gary realized that because the amount of Exp he would earn for each kill was large during this quest, it was his chance to level up. Jumping into the fray, Gary also saw the hunting target he had made a long time ago among the Underdogs members.

However, right now, Damion was the biggest priority. Swinging his axes like a madman, he was defeating a lot of the crazed Altered. Unfortunately, his gang members were unable to keep up, and out of the dozen who had survived the first wave, fewer than half were alive.

Seeing this, one of the Gray Elephants members tried to charge in, but one of the crazed Altered quickly turned around and leapt toward him, killing him instantly.

This caused the other Gray Elephants members to pile on and attempt to take out the crazed Altered as quickly as possible. They eventually killed it, but their buddy was still dead.

They really can't control it, Gary thought.

In the end, the second wave of crazed Altered had ended. All twenty had been killed, and Gary had finished off five of them. They were far easier to deal with than the twins. Whether it was because he had gotten stronger or they had gotten weaker, he was unsure. Perhaps it was a bit of both.

Congratulations, you have now reached: Level 17
A stat point has been granted
Exp 452/3245

Still, the fight wasn't over, as it now allowed the other Gray Elephants gang members to get involved. Before that, though, Gary turned around and looked at Damion, who was out of breath. The gang leader looked quite strong with his two axes, though he had still taken a few scratches here and there.

He doesn't look so scary anymore . . . if I get rid of him, half of my problems will be over, Gary thought, and seeing Gil at his side, he made a decision.

Bloodlust has been detected
Forced Bond has been activated
7/8 Marks have been assigned

CHAPTER 109

UNDERDOGS VS. HOWLERS

With all the crazed Altered dead and out of the fight, Gary and Damion took a second to catch their breath, along with the other Underdogs members. The Gray Elephants didn't charge in just yet because they were a little in disbelief, having seen what looked like a human chopping the monsters down limb from limb using his two axes, and on the other side, what was clearly an Altered in front of them.

Quest complete
The infected Altered have been dealt with, and you have played your part in saving the town
Quest reward: Because of your contribution, you have received a Pawn point!

Although Gary was happy and the quest reward was unexpected, he had to quickly wipe the screens away because he had something else he needed to deal with. His eyes and Damion's eyes met, and Damion saw the narrow red eyes staring at him.

"Oh, and here I thought that I was going to thank you for helping me out, but it looks like that's not the case after all." Damion smiled. "Tell me what I did? Did I get rid of your gang, kill someone dear to you?"

These words just made Gary angrier; Damion had never done that to him, but during his time at the Underdogs, he had undoubtedly done so with others. That was why Gary had to do all of this in the first place.

"Get them both!" one of the senior Gray Elephants members ordered, and they charged in from both sides. Almost immediately, Damion swung his axes, hitting the first one in the head and finishing him straightaway, then continued for the next one.

A few had gone toward Gary; he dodged a baseball bat that was swung at him and hit the ground, then threw a fist of his own, hitting the man right in the face. The next second, what looked like a chain was wrapped around his arm.

Skill Activated: Controlled Transformation

Gary activated his skill, bulging his muscles and pulling on the chain, causing his attacker to fall to the floor and be dragged along. As the next one approached, Gary grabbed his neck and kneed him in the stomach before throwing him toward several people trying to attack him from behind. He never looked away from Damion as he dealt with each new threat.

"Wait!" the senior Gray Elephants member shouted; he had noticed something. "Pull back."

The gang members obeyed, and some dragged their injured friends away from the fighting.

"You—you're not after us, are you? You're here for him?" the senior Gray Elephant said.

In fact, Gary was there for both of them; he just never expected Damion to be in such a vulnerable situation. But perhaps he could use it to his advantage.

"Go ahead, then; if you manage to beat him, it will only help us. We'll make sure he doesn't run away," the senior Gray Elephant said, putting his hand up, signaling to the others to stay where they were. It was clear that the Gray Elephants just wanted Gary and Damion to fight each other.

"Are you going to listen to what these guys have to say?" Damion shouted. "Haha, look at how weak you all are. Rather than just face me head-on, you planned to attack with these monsters, and now you have come out only when another attacks us, and you Gray Elephants are standing back and allowing this to happen! Fine, whatever it takes. Make sure you really kill me because I will make sure that each one of you pays for this tenfold!"

"Damion," Gary finally said. "Whether it's now or later . . . you were going to die anyway."

The senior Gray Elephants member started to smile, as it seemed like his guest had agreed to the condition.

On the outer edge of the main street, where Tyler and the others were waiting as they watched the fight, the police force finally arrived at the scene. Several cars pulled up, and Anton, along with his partner Roo, got out of one of them.

I knew I was right. There are more than just Billy and Kirk in this town who are Altered. It looks like one of these guys here is our suspect, Anton thought.

At the same time, the two White Rose agents emerged from one of the other vehicles. Frank's injuries had healed, thanks to his unique body and a little first aid. It was the reason why they were late.

"Well, would you look at that, our little Altered Hunter arrived here before us, and now he's hurting civilians," Sadie said.

"Well, perhaps he's trapped. All of the crazed Altered have been dealt with," Frank replied. "What should we do? Should we go in?"

"No," Sadie said, and Anton turned his head. "You understand right, Chief." She smiled. "We came here because of an Altered problem. That problem no longer exists. What we are witnessing right now is just a gang war. "Just patiently wait for all of them to take out each other, and then we will come in and pick up all the scraps."

Although the method seemed underhanded, Anton agreed and radioed in to the police force on the other side, giving them the order not to engage. To not even let civilians out, because the Gray Elephants had dressed in civilian clothes, so for now, they would just capture everyone they could.

After making the call, Anton started to watch what was going on.

"That looks like Damon, so the Underdogs and the Gray Elephants have finally had a go at each other, but who are the ones in the black and gold?"

It was clear that these were a separate group because most of them were busy fighting off the Gray Elephants, but the one with the strange mask was going up against the leader of the Underdogs.

I have a feeling this whole thing is going to be troublesome, Anton thought.

Kate and her cameraman had entered one of the buildings and were now on the rooftop, allowing them to film everything from above.

Gary and Damion were about to engage in combat in the middle of the street, but the Gray Elephants members who had surrounded them moved out of the way to let a large man through.

"Well, now this is certainly interesting, isn't it," Brandon said with a smile.

CHAPTER 110

THREE-WAY GANG WAR

Gary recognized the large man immediately. How could he forget him, when only a few days ago that person had nonchalantly killed Riv right in front of him?

I won't let you get away, either, Gary thought.

Bloodlust has been detected
Forced Bond has been activated
8/8 Marks have been assigned

With that, all three of Gary's hunting targets were in the same area. Although his system had told him he wouldn't get any more stat points for eating people, he wasn't sure if he might get still some from hunting down his targets.

However, even if that turned out not to be the case, he had to get rid of them. With Damion and Brandon gone, he wouldn't have to worry about his and his family's safety. As for Gil, Gary had special plans for him. The mark of his former schoolmate had been close to where his mother had gotten hurt, so there were some questions that he needed to ask.

Is that big guy going to join in the fight, or is he just here to watch? Gary remained cautious. Werewolf or not, he wasn't keen on turning his back to an enemy.

Brandon smiled at the wolf-masked teenager, seemingly understanding his dilemma.

"Please go ahead, I don't want to interrupt. Do what you have to," the Gray Elephants leader said, putting his hands up and even backing off a few steps. "None of you are to interfere in that guy's fight!"

Hearing him shout those instructions at his men, Gary charged in again. Damion tsked; he'd hoped to be able to play those two against each other. Unfortunately, the other gang leader proved to be more than just a musclehead. Having no other choice, Damion swung an axe. Leaning back, Gary avoided it, but only just.

He's faster than I was expecting. Could he be an Altered who was hiding it? Gary wondered.

Damion's next axe was already swinging from above, and Gary stepped to the side and kicked the head of the axe into the ground. The pavement was solid, but it stood no chance against the blade of the axe, which cut deep easily.

Seeing an opportunity, Gary took a swipe toward his opponent. His nails dug into Damion's side and blood splattered onto the ground. Quickly Damion grabbed Gary's arm and swung his other axe toward him.

The werewolf tried to break free, but he was surprised to find himself unable to do so. Damion had an unnaturally tight grip on him.

Altered or not, this guy isn't normal! he thought in a slight panic.

2 Points have been allocated into Strength
Your base Strength is now at 20

With his increased Strength, Gary was finally able to pull his claws out of Damion's body. He lifted his forearm and transformed it fully just as the axe went deep into his flesh, stopping short of the bone.

"*Arghhh!*" Gary screamed in agony.

You have been inflicted with a grave injury
–16 HP
84/100 HP
You are heavily bleeding, –4 HP for every minute that has passed

During the fight, the werewolf had managed to avoid getting injured. It was the first time in a while, but even with his Endurance the axe was a deadly weapon, and with Damion's strength he could understand why it would cause so much damage.

Gary pulled his arm away and quickly retreated a good distance, waiting for his emergency healing to do its job. However, if his Energy got too low, then emergency healing would be unable to do its job. If that were to happen, then Gary had a glimpse of how long he could survive, since 4 HP per minute was deadly.

"Pah, here I was worried about you, but you seem to be just a new Altered who's grown too big for your britches! Just because you gained new power and managed to overtake the Pincers, you thought you could rule this town," Damion said, ridiculing him. "Are you some type of child? And as for you f*ckers!" Damion pointed his axe toward Brandon. "Once I'm done with him, I'll hunt down every single one of you!"

The axes were so effective because Damion had bought them at one of the Dark Guild's auctions. They were made from the very beasts that Altered had come from, making them the perfect anti-Altered weapons. They were also the crux of his power and why Damion was way stronger than the average person.

Gary was happy for Damion's little speech, because it bought his arm enough time to fully heal. Seeing this, Damion's eyes widened. He knew that many Altered healed faster than usual, but this speed was just nonsensical.

I can take his hits as long as he doesn't strike anything vital. I have to beat him here! Gary thought, encouraging himself as he charged in again, still having plenty of tricks up his sleeve.

Meanwhile, the other Howlers were fighting those around them. Their formation of protecting each other's backs had been working to a degree.

Marie, with her two blades, proved skillful enough to not allow them to get close. Innu, filled with rage, was kicking and punching harder than usual, and Austin was a strong wall of muscle as always. However, one person in the group was, oddly, slowing them down.

One of the Gray Elephants charged in and Kai went for a kick . . . and missed. His opponent rugby-tackled him to the ground, pinning him down. Before he could do anything else, though, the helper in the black mask kicked the man in the ribs, pushing him off the fox-masked teenager.

"Stay focused!" Blake shouted. Luckily, he was covering for the mistakes Kai had been making.

"This guy is good. Maybe we should invite him into the Howlers?" Austin asked.

"You do know what that black mask is, right? And the weapons he's using? Which means he's probably a . . ." Marie didn't finish her sentence, realizing the others would then know, but she thought inviting an Altered Hunter into their group would be impossible, since Gary was their leader.

Meanwhile, Austin was worried.

What's wrong with Kai? he wondered. *These guys might be stronger than the Pincers, but his performance is horrible today. He's talented, maybe more so than the rest of us, so why does he seem so distracted? Is he worried about Gary? He keeps staring at him, but he's never been worried about him before.* Something was clearly up.

Just then a large bat crashed against Austin's forearms as he raised them in front of his face. His block was successful, but his arms were now throbbing with pain. The others were sustaining more and more injuries as well.

"There are just too many of them this time; we need to do something else!" Austin shouted. *If only we weren't so weak. It's starting to feel like we're always dragging Gary down!* he thought.

At that moment, though, he heard the Gray Elephants groaning, followed by several bangs.

Up above, Kate had heard the noise and turned her camera toward it. *I knew she must have been involved with them somehow.* She smiled.

"The mysterious woman with the whip has now arrived in Cipen. She appears to belong to the third group that arrived earlier today," Kate reported.

Olivia stood there, gasping for breath. "You guys are useless."

But she had brought backup along with her. With more men on their side, a true gang war was taking place.

"Go help the boss," Kai told her as he applied pressure to the wound on his arm, a deep cut that had happened during the fight when he hadn't been paying attention.

"Don't worry, I was already planning to. I feel this need to help him," Olivia said, and she wasn't lying.

Kate quickly moved the camera back to the others, as she knew that seeing an Altered fight was guaranteed to get more attention for the news channel. Just in time, too, as the Altered furiously attacked the man with the axes.

Gary had charged in bravely, grabbing the axes by the handle just below the head. He kicked Damion hard in the stomach with all his strength, and again in the ribs, intensifying his wounds.

During the fight, Damion had gotten a few good hits in, but Gary was starting to feel the difference between the two. Unlike his opponent, the werewolf was able to heal his wounds, and his stamina was extraordinary, giving him the advantage over the Underdogs leader, who was already exhausted.

Charging in again, Gary lifted his claw, ready to swipe it toward his opponent's neck, but like a bullet someone bulldozed through the crowd, hitting Gary in the ribs and sending him flying across the ground.

"Sorry I'm late, boss," Kirk apologized.

CHAPTER 111

BIG CAT FIGHT

The first thing that Gary did, before even lifting his head off the ground, was to check whether his mask was still firmly on his face. Fortunately, everything seemed to still be in order in that department. At the same time, he noticed that none of the Gray Elephants members had attacked him, even though he was only a foot away from them.

They must really be loyal to their leader, Gary thought.

Then he heard the voice.

"Sorry I'm late, boss."

He wondered who had come out of nowhere and attacked him from behind. He might have been too focused on attacking Damion, but still, Gary was sure he would have noticed if anyone came to interfere.

Damn it! Gary thought, clenching his fist. *I should have known he would show up.*

Turning his head, he looked up through the mask at Kirk. The cheetah's skin was yellow with black spots, showing that he had partly transformed already. Now it all made sense.

One of the fastest Altered was looking right at the werewolf, yet it was obvious that he didn't recognize him.

You were the only one from the Underdogs I didn't want to fight, Kirk. Why did you have to come now . . . why is someone like you protecting that bastard?

Memories of his time as a transporter flashed in front of Gary's eyes. When he first joined, he had naturally felt frightened and lost, yet Kirk had noticed it. He had slapped Gary on the back, telling him he had to do a good job.

It had been a rather strange encounter, especially since Gary had stuttered out Kirk's name when he recognized one of his idols. He never knew why, but for whatever reason the Altered hadn't seemed to mind spending some of his free time talking to him, something Gary had never seen him do with other transporters.

They had built up quite a bond because of it. Even before meeting Kirk, Gary had watched some of his fights, and his admiration of him as a supporter as well as a friend had grown from there.

The last time he had seen him, Kirk had taught Gary how to throw a punch, which might well have saved his life from the gangsters that fateful day.

Getting up from the ground, Gary looked toward Damion. Kirk stood in front of him, and the rest of the Cheetah Squad had caught up. Their body language was telling him that if he wanted to get to their boss, he would have to get through them first.

Shit. I . . . I need to finish him off here. They already know what school I go to, and I know they will do whatever it takes to find that package. I'm sorry, Kirk, but if you stand in the way . . . then I will have to deal with you as well. You were someone I looked up to, someone I looked forward to seeing every day and talking to; you were like a . . . father . . . to me . . . but I have a real family I need to protect.

Gary clenched his fist. The Howlers might have started out as a way for Kai and Gary to cut ties with the Underdogs, but part of him had always known that in the underworld it would be impossible to have a peaceful separation.

The werewolf had been hoping to take care of Damion without Kirk around. That might have been the only way to avoid that confrontation. Alas, it was too late now.

The masked teenager sprinted back to Damion, though three of the Cheetah Squad members attempted to intercept him with a kick, two of them up high. Immediately, Gary covered his head and blocked the two high kicks.

However, the third one hit him right in the stomach, and it wasn't a soft blow either.

−4 HP

48/100 HP

After Damion's axe attacks and Kirk's surprise attack, Gary was now down to less than half his Health. What's more, the kicks of the Underdog elite group were as strong as they were fast.

They may not be Altered, but they are strong. Figures, since their job is to support Kirk without slowing him down. How am I supposed to get to Damion? Should I just grab a bite and recover my Health? . . . maybe I should keep that a secret unless necessary and use Claw Drain instead?

While Gary thought about what to do, the Cheetah Squad wasn't messing around; they surrounded their masked foe, ready to attack. But Kirk himself had yet to move, perhaps because of all the Gray Elephants members who might go for their boss at any second.

When the first one got close, a strong force whacked him in the stomach, sending one of the elite gang members to the ground.

"And here I thought you were some type of invincible monster." A voice spoke behind him. At the same time, the Gray Elephants members were being roughed up and beaten. No longer were they just patiently waiting off to the side as they turned to see what was happening. The next second they were fighting once again, defending themselves.

Kate, seeing the chaos from above, understood everything clearly. Everything had changed when that woman arrived. She and her people were changing the balance, and along with the other black-and-gold gang members, they pushed through, becoming a strong force to deal with the Gray Elephants members.

The whip in her hands was a force to be reckoned with, just as much as Damion with his axes.

Now, coming through the fallen, seemingly untouched and unhurt, was Olivia Pearl.

"Why don't you just pull the same crap as you did with me?" she asked the alpha werewolf with a smile.

It hadn't been long since her arrival, yet all the Gray Elephants members on one side of the streets had been defeated by the Pincers, the Howlers, and the help they had received from the Altered Hunter. Given their reinforcements, Blake was starting to wonder whether his involvement now was too much. It had been necessary when Gary's friends were on their own, but now he wondered whether he should stay any longer.

I wish it were that easy. She really has no idea how close I came to death with Last Stand, Gary thought, not giving her an answer.

Seeing what was happening, Damion smiled and turned the other way, throwing his axe down at the Gray Elephants member and killing him on the spot.

"Haha, Kirk, you take care of these guys, I'm going after that big fat lump!" Damion ordered.

The next second, the chaos shifted.

The Pincers gang had already clashed with the remaining Gray Elephants. Gary was losing sight of Damion, who seemed to be running somewhere. Fortunately, he had marked him earlier, allowing him to see that Damion was heading toward another mark.

Is Damion chasing after the Gray Elephants leader? Gary wondered. *Does he want to fight him, or is he going to flee? I can't tell.*

Either way, Kirk was standing between them.

"You're not going to let me pass unless I beat you, are you?" Gary asked, while Olivia had already started dealing with five members of the Cheetah Squad.

"Seeing that you want my boss dead, no way," Kirk replied, transforming further.

It looks like that man from before was right . . . there really are others in Slough, Gary thought.

At the same time, the very man that Kirk was thinking about had cleared all the Altered in the Chavley area. Just in case there was more to deal with, he decided to check the news on his phone.

That was when he laid eyes on the fight that was about to take place.

Kudos to you, streaker boy, protecting the neighborhood . . . but is it really wise for you to do it so publicly? Jayden immediately recognized the mask from the day the two of them fought. It was without a doubt Gary.

However, another familiar face appeared on the screen.

Damn it, just what did you do to provoke that cat, dude?

CHAPTER 112

KING OF THE JUNGLE

Although deep down, Gary had known this fight would come one day, he could never visualize it in his head. Fighting against Kirk, of course, he would never be able to win against the rookie champion.

However, right now he had no choice.

New Quest received
King of the Jungle
Defeat the Altered in front of you
Quest reward: ???
Optional Quest received
Waste not, want not
Consume the Altered
Quest reward: Additional stat points

Whenever he ended up in a tough situation, the Werewolf System encourage him to find a way out of his situation by granting him a quest. In this case, it seemed to be confident enough in the teenager that it gave him two.

I've been conserving my Energy in the fight so far because of how many of them are around me, but I can't afford to go easy on him, Gary thought as he used Controlled Transformation on his legs, transforming them fully to benefit from the increased power.

However, he avoided changing his feet for fear that his toenails would go through his shoes. He also used the skill on his arms, hands, and chest without holding back.

Right now Gary's body was close to being fully transformed, but not quite. Even if Gary used Controlled Transformation on most of his body, it still lacked some power compared to Full Transformation. The form would use up a lot of energy, but it was better than losing, since losing would most likely mean death, and not just for him either.

"A wolf-type Altered! I guess it makes sense with the mask," Kirk shouted as he got into a sprinter's stance.

I've seen this before, in some of his Altered fights! the werewolf thought, but before he could act, the Cheetah Altered had crossed the distance between the two in an instant. Gary reached out and grabbed the fist coming toward him. His feet skidded across the ground as he was pushed back.

I just increased my Strength stat going up against Damion, and it's still not enough!

Gary pushed off with his feet, hoping to gain traction, and saw that Kirk was baring his teeth, tightening the muscles in his neck as he shoved Gary forward.

He's really going all out against me . . . I'm not just a kid . . . I have people relying on me. I can do this. No, I HAVE to do this! Gary thought. He readjusted his hands so they were positioned better around Kirk's fist.

Skill activated: Claw Drain
−15 Energy
180/300

After activating the skill, Gary dug his nails into Kirk.

+2 HP
+2 HP
52/100 HP

It wasn't a big boost to his Health, since the damage dealt to the Altered was minimal, but it was at least something. Somewhat in pain, Kirk gritted his teeth and held on tightly to his opponent's arms before lifting Gary's body off the ground and aiming a kick toward his face.

It hit Gary's chin, causing him to let go, and strangely Kirk quickly took off his shoes and transformed his feet. His toes appeared more like those of a cheetah, allowing him to contact more surface area as he pounced toward Gary.

At the same time, he swiped his clawed hands at Gary. Lifting his arms, Gary blocked the blow, but Kirk's claws pierced his skin.

–3 HP

And that wasn't the end of it; as soon as Kirk landed on the ground, he jumped up again and took another swipe.

–3 HP

He continued to swipe side to side, so fast that Gary didn't know what to do. All he could do was keep his arms up, preventing Kirk from dealing him a potentially fatal blow.

Having watched all of his fights, I was sure I'd have an advantage over him, but his current fighting style is nothing like what he uses in the ring! I have to do something, I can't just stand here and turtle up. My Energy will drain way faster than his stamina will. At that moment, after Gary saw that his HP had fallen below one third, he decided to take a wild swing.

Alas, his desperate attempt ended up hitting nothing but air, and his opponent used the chance to claw his chest.

–6 HP
27/100 HP

My Health is getting lower by the second! If this continues, Kirk really is going to kill me!

Just then, for the first time in the fight, Gary was no longer being attacked, and he could not see the system notifications showing his reduced HP.

Did he run out of steam? Gary wondered, and he opened his arms, ready to attack, ready to unleash his own power, which he had yet to use so far.

He could only think that Kirk had gotten tired; there had been no pause in his attacks. After all, Gary's stats were better than some Altered, and he couldn't imagine himself attacking constantly for so long.

"Thanks, I was waiting for you to do that," Kirk said, as a fist came up and hit Gary in the chin as hard as possible. Kirk had pounced off the ground using the power of his strong legs to deliver one of his strongest blows. Gary was airborne for a few seconds before he plummeted to the ground.

His endurance is crazy after all those attacks and still not falling down! There are guys in the AFC who couldn't take that much, Kirk thought as he fought to get his wind back.

−10 HP
17/100 HP

Seeing how low his Health was, Gary knew he had to change tactics, but first he felt his injured jaw, and that was when he realized something.

My mask! It must have been knocked off during the hit. He looked up and saw his mask lying on the ground. Quickly, he crawled toward it, but a hand had picked it up before he could reach it.

"Gary . . ." the person uttered in disbelief.

Of all people, it just had to be Gil holding his wolf mask. Now his hunting target had seen his face, revealing that he was a member of the Howlers. The person that the Underdogs had been looking for was right here in front of them.

Screw this. Gary decided to go all out since his identity was already compromised.

Skill activated: Full Transformation

CHAPTER 113

THE ALPHA HOWL

For most of the fight, Gil had been out of his depth. This was nothing like the color gang war he had participated in. The gang members here were using deadly weapons, and Gil had seen several people chopped down in front of him by the Underdogs leader.

The dropout had thought he was tough enough to handle it, especially after Damion had killed off those who had refused to swear their allegiance to him; he thought he would never see a day bloodier than that, yet it turned out that it might just have been wishful thinking on his part. Gil realized that today when he saw how easily the adults were losing their lives against the crazed Altered.

I don't really care who wins this stupid war. If the Gray Elephants win, I'm just gonna tell them that I was captured during the color gang war and was forced to join the Underdogs. If they somehow win this, nothing changes much. So it's better if I just do nothing anyway, Gil thought, happy that the Underdogs leader had told him to stay out of the fights, which he had intended to do since the beginning.

The fight between the two apparent Altered was catching the attention of everyone who wasn't busy fighting, and even some who were. Although they seemed evenly matched, the fight between the two gangs seemed to be lessening as more and more gang members became unable to continue to fight.

One could only take so many beatings.

In some ways it felt like the lower-ranked gang members had reached a truce. They had exchanged fists, exchanged wounds and blood, but all of them understood that their fighting was pointless in the grand scheme of things.

Whichever side's Altered won would have the power to punish the weaker side.

Still there were those who were fighting hard, who knew they could make a difference, such as the newly arrived Cheetah Squad and Olivia Pearl.

As for the rest, even if they were lying injured on the ground, they were watching the Altered fight, and that was when the mask had dropped at Gil's feet. He didn't think much of it, but when he picked it up, he looked toward the wolf-type Altered, though it was the last person he would have suspected to see.

Gary? . . . What is that dweeb doing in a place like this? Why is he in the middle of a gang war, and since when is he an Altered? Gil's jaw dropped wide open, as nothing seemed to make sense anymore.

However, things were starting to click in his head. Gil had had no idea that the transporter the Underdogs had been looking for was Gary. He had only bluffed, seeing it as nothing but a means to get some revenge. After all, their descriptions did match.

There was no way someone like Gary would be sponsored by a corporation and turned into Altered DNA. However, what if whatever was inside that package had turned Gary into what he was seeing right now? What if his shot in the dark actually hit the bull's-eye?

A smile appeared on Gil's face, but that smile just as quickly disappeared. The next second, Gary's face started to change before anyone else could see it. Fur grew out of his face, his nose elongated, and his skin began to peel off, replaced with a tough hide.

The werewolf's skin became thicker, his teeth became sharper, and his whole body became larger. The seams of his blazer didn't rip this time, thanks to the adjustments that Kai had made, but the same couldn't be said for his trouser legs or his shoes.

Now everyone saw Gary fully transformed into a full wolf-like Altered and his darting red eyes staring at them all.

Those red eyes met Gil's, and flashbacks appeared in his head.

No . . . no . . . it can't be! I remember that day. The day I got attacked on my first run with the gray color gang . . . it was him. It was this piece of shit! He was the one who attacked me!

Gil had never understood why he had been attacked that day. The best explanation he could come up with was that it had been some vigilante who had seen too many superhero movies. However, now that he knew who it was, he understood why Gary had come after him.

He remembered what he had done. Gil had attacked Gary's scrawny little boyfriend. Of course, with this newfound power it was only natural that he would come after him for revenge.

Everything was telling Gil to run, and that was exactly what he did as he headed back into the Basement nightclub.

At the same time, Gil wasn't the only one who could see what Gary had become. No one else had seen his face without the mask. However, because of his uniform, even the most ignorant of the Howlers now knew for certain that Gary was an Altered.

As they looked at Gary's full form, a memory resurfaced in their heads; for Innu, it was one that he would never forget.

"Was he the one that who trying to kill us that time?" Innu blurted out. "We were in the woods looking for him!"

The others understood Innu's concern, and it also answered a lot of their questions about how Gary was able to do such things, and on top of that how he was able to defeat the twins. He wasn't just an Altered, he was a menacing, vicious one.

"You're wrong!" Kai corrected him. "Look at him. There were two of them that day. We were attacked by a black one, and a brown one saved us." This was merely Kai's own conclusion; Gary had admitted being an Altered, but Kai hadn't asked him too much about it. However, given his fur color it was a good bet, and it would coincide with Tom's actions.

Seeing this new larger form, Kirk still had to be fearless; he knew that if he hesitated, it would only hamper him and his skills. Once again, he got into a sprinting stance, his hands touching the ground.

"A full transformation isn't necessarily a good thing. I've taken down guys bigger than you!" Kirk shouted as he sprang off the ground, even slightly faster than last time.

Aware that Gary would expect him to do the same thing again, the Cheetah Altered ran across the ground, and at the last second he spun his body to add extra power to his fist. With the weight and momentum of his entire body, Kirk crashed into Gary, pushing the werewolf away . . . but merely by a few inches.

Gary's toes had dug into the ground, breaking it open, while his solid wall of muscle and weight was able to withstand the blow a lot more this time. He lifted Kirk by his arms and slammed his body into the concrete.

The next moment, Gary looked up at the moon and felt an instinct inside him take over. Following it, he let out a loud howl.

Ahh-wooo!

The alpha werewolf felt the howl reverberate at the top of his lungs. It didn't sound like a normal wolf's howl; this one was far deeper, and those around him felt the vibrations in their own bodies.

At the same time, not too far away, Olivia sensed it as well, feeling a slight desire to join in.

The beta werewolf's eyes glowed blue as she felt her strength rising.

"I'm really starting to like this feeling." She smiled, getting her whip ready for more action.

CHAPTER 114

WEAPON DUEL

A little before Gary went into his Full Transformation, the rest of the Howlers had been dealing with another problem. Despite having the larger force, the Gray Elephants were losing, now that Olivia had arrived with her Pincers gang members.

If it had been just the Pincers against the Gray Elephants, the small-time gang would have lost. Fortunately, the Howlers had quality members to help, and then there was Olivia herself. If she had been someone to fear before, there was even more reason now.

On top of that, the Cheetah Squad, who were part of the Underdogs, were also dealing with the Gray Elephants. In the end, it was almost as if the Gray Elephants were being pressured by two strong forces, and with their leader having run off somewhere, the morale of the group wasn't particularly high.

This had led most of the Gray Elephants to admit defeat, knowing full what the outcome would be. Now, though, the Cheetah Squad were facing off against Olivia and the rest of the Howlers.

"We have to be careful!" Kai shouted. "Those guys are skilled enough to not drag down an Altered, so don't think of them as just another one of those regular Joes!"

With Kai, Innu, Austin, Marie, and Olivia, there were five of them to go up against the five elite gang members, and everyone was ready for a clash.

"Hey, you seriously want me to take out one of them on my own?" Marie shouted, but the others were too preoccupied to reply; all of them were engaged in their own combat.

One of the Cheetah Squad members, a bald man with scars all over his face, looked toward Marie. Her hands were shaking a little as she held her blades. She had been doing okay so far, and the real-life situations had allowed her to improve quickly. Still, there was a vast difference between what she was about to do and what she had been doing so far.

During the fight, she had simply been trying to survive. Injuring those close to her, stalling until someone else could deal with her opponent, but now she had a one-on-one situation. It wasn't possible for her to do things this way.

Damn it, how could the others forget about me? Marie thought, on the verge of tears. *Damn you, Kyle, ever since you saw that bastard, it's like your mind is too busy to notice the things right in front of you!*

"I see you are a person who uses weapons as well," the bald man said with a smile. He flicked his arms out and two pocket blades appeared. They were smaller than what Marie used, but the man's confidence made her even more afraid, and it was her first time going up against someone who was using weapons like hers.

The bald man didn't hesitate as he thrust the blades toward her. Quickly, Marie stepped back, avoiding his first attack. However, he didn't stop there. Having noticed her lack of confidence, he tried to stab her again. She continued to back away, not seeing any chance to retaliate.

He's slower than Kyle's kicks; maybe I can do something, she thought as she went in to slash toward his arm, but at the last second she pulled back.

What . . . what is wrong with me . . . I hesitated. Her hands were shaking, and she realized why she was so frightened. An important lesson had been ingrained into her. It had served her well so far, but now that she faced someone who was using a blade and didn't care about killing her, her legs went weak.

The best time to attack was when someone was attacking her; the timing had been off just a little. An image of the blade piercing her stomach and her life flashing before her eyes appeared in her head.

Once again, while Marie was distracted, the bald man thrust the two little knives, one after the other. And Marie avoided each strike, one after the other. It was all she could do.

Am I imagining things, or is he getting faster? Marie thought in a panic.

Unfortunately, it was not just in her head. The man was indeed getting faster, having treated the earlier attacks as a warm-up. While avoiding his blows, Marie felt something against her back leg, but it was too late, and she tripped over one of the many dead bodies on the ground.

With nowhere to run, it looked like the images in her head were going to come true. She swung her blade, hoping it would either hit the man or parry his blade, but he pulled back, avoiding her slash, and continued his attack.

"Don't worry, I won't make it painful!" the man promised her. But the next second, his body seemed to light up slightly; it shook out of control and the weapons dropped from his hand. Something whacked him twice on the back of the head, and he collapsed to the ground.

Marie thought Kai had come to his senses and helped her out, but instead she saw the stranger in his full black mask.

The Altered Hunter! Didn't he leave? Marie felt that she should say something.

"Th-thank you for saving me."

The truth was, Blake had indeed decided to leave the fight. It wasn't his fight to get involved in, and even though there was at least one Altered present, it wasn't the right time to hunt Kirk with so many people around. It wasn't how Altered Hunters were trained to do things.

Regardless, Blake did want to stay and watch how everything played out, and he saw that Marie, whom he recognized from school, was in trouble. In the end, he couldn't help getting involved once again.

Once he saw that she was fine, the Altered Hunter ran off again, and Marie went to see how the others were doing. Her fellow Howlers members were pretty banged up. Austin sat on the ground, bleeding from the top of his head, but he had no opponent in front of him.

Innu was in slightly better condition, but he was so unsteady on his feet that he had collapsed. The adrenaline that had kept him in the fight so far had escaped his body.

Then there was Kai. He was standing, but he looked like he was barely holding on. Even from behind, she could tell that his body was badly hurt. He resembled a boxer on wobbly legs, swaying as he stepped forward. The fox mask was still on his face, but part of it had cracked.

Is Kyle losing? I have to help! Marie thought, since she saw that the others were in no condition to fight.

Just as she got up, though, Gary let out a loud howl and everyone turned their attention to the large brown-furred wolf.

Olivia paused in her fight with her opponent and smiled.

This strength . . . I've never felt like this before. She threw out her whip, wrapping it around the man's leg, and pulled, trying to make him fall. But he had let the momentum take him in, and he jumped into a spin while delivering a kick. It was then that Olivia knew she had gotten stronger.

Grabbing his leg, she squeezed it hard, making the Cheetah Squad member scream in pain. She then threw him to the ground and stepped on his chest, swinging her whip at him mercilessly.

Seeing his friend getting beaten, Kai's opponent decided to help. Olivia stopped her attack, charged forward, and avoided his punch before grabbing his face and slamming it onto the ground.

She had the power of the Anti-Altered weapon on top of her natural increased strength from being a werewolf, and now she was receiving another boost, thanks to Gary.

She looked up toward Kai and gave him a condescending smile.

She's become so strong . . . Gary, what did you do to her? Did you turn her, like in those books? If that's the case . . . can you do the same to me? Kai thought as he looked at Gary's full werewolf form.

CHAPTER 115

ONE DOWN

As soon as Kirk and his Cheetah Squad arrived, a strange new confidence had risen in Damion. It was as if he believed that now that they were here, the group would not lose this war.

So instead of concentrating on the Altered that was in front of him, he went after the closest Gray Elephants member. Damion knew that this would ignite the fighting between everyone once again.

No longer was it a safe duel that everyone could just watch and the sense of danger would kick into them all. Leaving the Altered to Kirk, Damion continued to swing his axes toward Brandon and the rest of the Gray Elephants.

His movements were faster, and his strength was beyond what his opponents could handle. Each swing hit its mark before they could touch him, killing them or chopping off their limbs in one go. He looked like a robot that was possessed.

That was when Brandon, the titan of a force that the Gray Elephants knew him as, did something that they never expected him to do . . . He ran away.

The large man made a beeline through the crowd of his own people, roughly shoving them out of the way, without so much as looking back.

"What's this?" Damion chortled. "The mighty Gray Elephants leader is running away? Do you not dare to fight me after all you've done? If I had known your muscles were just for show, I would have gotten rid of you a long time ago!"

Damion threw one of his axes, but a body got in the way. The Underdogs leader ran forward and pulled the axe from the body, not losing his momentum.

With all of the Gray Elephants in his way, Damion was forced to slow down, allowing Brandon to increase the distance. For a large person, he was surprisingly fast.

Kicking a man to the ground, Damion continued to chase Brandon, leaving the Gray Elephants wondering what to do. In the end, they didn't follow him, because they had their own problem to solve.

"Don't worry, I'm sure Brandon has a plan," one of the Gray Elephants said.

As Brandon ran down the street, he saw that the police had boarded up the area. If he continued in the same direction, he would be easily stopped, and so would the person who was following him.

Turning right, he went through a narrow alleyway, where a couple of policemen stood guard at the other end. However, when he approached them, they stepped to the side, allowing both him and Damion to get through with no harm.

Strange, I'm sure one of the others was supposed to be the brains behind it all. I guess that guy isn't all muscles, Damion thought. Suddenly, he stopped, turned around, and headed toward the two policemen, throwing his axe straight at them. It sliced halfway through one officer's neck.

"You scum who have been paid off, you should just do your jobs. At least I know what I am." Damion cursed as he kicked the other man to the ground. He pulled the axe out of the deceased man's neck before using it to kill the other officer as well.

Returning to the chase and following Brandon's trail, Damion soon found himself in an underground parking garage. It was dark inside, with a few lights here and there. It looked like it was under-going a refurb.

"Come on! You took me down here for a reason, right?" Damion shouted, holding his side, which still hurt from being attacked by Gary.

I hope Kirk brings him back alive; that way I can really bring him pain when he needs it.

An object flew toward Damion, but he slashed it in half. Some-one kicked him in the ribs, directly over his wound. Bearing the pain and gritting his teeth, he swung his axe and hit something solid, and a man screamed.

"One down . . . no matter how many you have brought with you, they will all fall!" Damion shouted.

He looked around and saw five more men, as well as Brandon, who now had a large smile on his face.

"You know, they say I'm the strongest of the Gray Elephants, but that's just because whoever I fight, I make sure they never live to tell the tale," Brandon boasted while holding a riot shield with the words *POLICE FORCE* on it.

As Damion had suspected, the Gray Elephants had bought off some people in the police force, which had allowed them to get away with a lot. They charged, but Damion gripped his axes tightly, ready to give it his all.

He ran forward, ignoring the onslaught; he leapt into the air with the two axes behind his head, swinging them to give himself the most momentum.

Brandon was confident as he lifted his riot shield to block the attack.

Haha, what an idiot, now we'll all be able to get him at once after this attack, the Gray Elephants leader thought.

When the axes slammed down, they tore right through the riot shield and Brandon's head; he fell to the ground, dead in an instant. Seconds later, the others charged in, kicking and hitting Damion as much as they could, but just as he had claimed, he took them out one by one.

Tsk, that bastard made this too easy. What was he thinking, trying to use a normal shield to block these two demons? They really were worth every single penny.

In his injured state, Damion slowly walked out of the parking garage. Half a minute later, a man in a black leather jacket emerged from a corner, walked over to Brandon's dead body, and stared at it in silence.

That's why I told you to just lure him in, but no, you just had to try to take him out yourself, Raven thought. *I warned you repeatedly that Damion Hawk is a dangerous man. I have no idea how he does it, whether it's sheer luck, perseverance, or something else, but somehow he always manages to catch a second wind when he's on his last legs.*

First Yoven, now you, Brandon. I guess that's it for the Gray Elephants, then. Well, I'll just have to see the upside in all of this. I won't have to worry about Sin, and now I have all the time I need to finish off my personal vendettas.

A clang rang out, and still on edge, Raven turned his head, afraid that Damion had returned. Fortunately, it was only a young student. Raven let out a big sigh.

"Too bad, kiddo, but I can't afford any witnesses." The last remaining Gray Elephants leader pulled out a knife and ran toward the student who had stumbled in. The young man quickly held up his hands.

"Wait, I can help you!" He spoke quickly as he backed off. "I was part of the gray color gang and I got kidnapped by the Underdogs! I can help you get what they want! They're looking for a boy . . . a boy who stole a package from them . . . his name is Gary . . . Gary Dem!"

Raven stopped immediately, because he had heard that name once before, but he had never expected to hear it here, of all places.

CHAPTER 116

A TRUE LAST STAND

When Gary had evolved and chosen the Warrior Class, the main advantage was the fact that his Energy pool had tripled. He thought at first that this was best because when he unlocked more skills he would be able to use them more.

However, recently he hadn't been able to access as many skills as he had initially thought. Still, this was because of all these crazy situations happening so soon and one after another.

The idea of using more skills was to allow him to become more versatile when fighting. However, one more thing had improved. With over 110 Energy left to spare, Gary wouldn't have to worry about running out during Full Transformation for a while, which was a great thing, seeing as it was his strongest form.

Nevertheless, he also couldn't afford to drag things out, but it would hopefully be enough for him to do what needed to be done. Gary looked at Kirk, who was on the ground, and sliced down at him with his claws, which were slightly larger in this form.

Kirk rolled out of the way and stood up, using his strong legs to leap back into the air, with one arm was over his ribs. He had been badly injured from a single throw, and pieces of the ground itself had been partly destroyed, indicating the power that he had endured.

Gary's claws hit the ground, scratching the surface of the stone pavement and leaving deep claw marks. Looking up toward Kirk and seeing him injured, he decided to continue the chase.

Damn it, what's up with this guy? He was already strong, but now he'll be even stronger. And what happened to his injuries from before? It's as if I never hit him at all. Kirk was worried.

He pounced back as the werewolf charged him again. Those who were on the ground or close to the fight got out of the way. Although many had seen Altered on TV, Gary's current appearance was terrifying to them all.

The second the werewolf got close enough, Kirk jumped back, his feet pressing on a building's window. As he pushed off, the glass broke behind him, but it was enough to propel him forward like a spear.

Kirk's nails pierced deep into Gary's chest, but the hide proved too thick for the Cheetah Altered to reach his opponent's organs. Still, when Kirk's feet touched the ground, he dragged his hand as hard as he could, allowing for his nails to rip through the hide, creating a large wound directly across his body.

-6 HP

11/100 HP

In this form my Endurance is even higher, so the attacks might look bad, but they don't do as much damage. Still, with this low Health I have to be careful, Gary thought.

The werewolf swiped toward Kirk again, but missed. Next he tried to kick; instead of swinging wildly he was resorting to the moves he had practiced. Kirk anticipated this and lifted his arm, shifting his whole body to the side so that he almost fell over.

His arm felt like it might break at any second.

That power is crazy . . . even if I can see the attack coming my way, I have to avoid it, Kirk thought.

Seeing another punch instead of a claw, Kirk realized that the Altered was fighting rather than giving in to his inner beast, but

Kirk had experience in how to combat using both. Accepting one's beast side was part of becoming an Altered, and combining the two was how one should fight. Using one or the other wasn't going to cut it.

Kirk pounced back, avoiding the blow, and quickly used his powerful legs to come in again. He gave two quick swipes to the werewolf's upper arms, scratching them and causing them to bleed.

–1 HP
–1 HP
9/100 HP

The damage wasn't great, but Gary wasn't in the best condition either.

Skill activated: Claw Drain
–15 Energy

I need to get some of my Health back! Gary thought.

Pushing off with his muscular legs, Gary boosted himself forward as fast as he could; as long as he hit Kirk, he would get some Health back. However, there was no such luck, as Kirk moved to the side, continuing to evade him.

Unfortunately, Claw Drain lasted only two seconds at its current level. Trying desperately to get to Kirk left Gary open, an opportunity that the Cheetah Altered quickly used to swipe at him two more times.

–1 HP
–1 HP
7/100 HP

I . . . I . . . I can't catch him . . . if I can't catch him, I can't heal . . . fighting a trained Altered like him seems to be too much for the current me, even fully transformed.

Gary was starting to panic. He spun around, but the more erratic his movements became, the easier it was for his opponent to see where he was aiming his attack. Once again, Kirk leapt toward his back, this time wrapping his legs around the werewolf's waist. Quickly, he dug both his hands into the top of Gary's neck, before leaping off again.

–3 HP
–3 HP
1/100 HP

Holy shit, this is getting too close! My eyesight is getting blurry . . . If I get hit again . . ."
Turning around, Gary saw the two claws near him, leaving him with no other choice.

Skill activated: Last Stand

As the claws scratched his face, one went through his eye, but the other missed, hitting his cheek. The pain was really going through Gary's body.

–4 HP
1/100 HP
Last Stand is activated (59 seconds remaining)

He saw the number, but he knew that he would be safe for the next minute, no matter how much damage he took.

"You've lost a lot of blood, and you're still standing. I admire your will to keep fighting!" Kirk said, praising Gary, surprised he hadn't reacted despite losing an eye. Since his technique of jumping in and out was working, he wasn't going to change it.

However, Gary's mind was at a loss. Using Full Transformation had already been a desperate move on his part, yet Kirk had forced him to activate his secret ability Last Stand as well. That skill didn't make him invincible, only temporarily unkillable, yet what use was it when he couldn't hit his opponent, much less finish him off?

The pouncing in and out continued, and Gary continued to swing wildly, but nothing was working. More blood, more wounds, more pain that Gary had to suffer through.

"*Don't give up!*" Kai shouted at the top of his lungs. The side of his head was bleeding from his earlier fight, and it was starting to stain his mask red. Yet he still stood as confidently as possible while yelling, "You need to keep living!"

Gary knew that Kai was right. Although he still hadn't figured out what to do, all he could do was try his best. He watched Kirk's body coming toward him and readied for another attack.

He twisted his body and threw his hand out from underneath. It was similar to an uppercut, but instead of going for Kirk's head, Gary was aiming for his stomach. Kirk's claws were about to reach him, but Gary thought he would be able to deal him a significant blow just before jumping away.

Last Stand duration has elapsed

No . . . if I get hit by this . . . I'll die!

Something wrapped around Kirk's leg and pulled him back ever so slightly.

"*Arghhh!*" Gary screamed.

His fist not only smashed into Kirk's stomach but pierced right through his body, and Gary could see his bestial hand in front of him.

CHAPTER 117

THE WINNERS

Gary was unsure what would happen once his HP reached 0—whether he would just faint and lose consciousness or if his system would really kill him off—but he sure as hell wasn't willing to find out. It was a test that he might not come back from. He was certain that no matter the consequence, if not for his Last Stand skill, he would have surely died as a result of Kirk's attacks. Driven by his fear of death, the werewolf had put his all into that last punch.

His survival instinct had kicked in him, making him use every ounce of strength in his body. He had completely ignored who his opponent was and his personal relationship to him; it had merely become a fight to the death, in which the only options were to kill or be killed.

His feet and hips twisted just the right way, directing the power from his whole body into the punch. Unbeknownst to Gary, he was delivering a textbook blow.

His furry hand was covered in blood, and Kirk's body was limp. Even through his hand, he could feel his heartbeat. It was slowing down, and the light in Kirk's eyes was starting to fade out. Blood dripped from the open wound, painting Gary's hand and the ground red.

"Did Kirk actually lose to the wolf Altered? But how?" The surviving Underdogs members couldn't believe what had happened, and neither could the Cheetah Squad. Although the Howlers had beaten them, the teenagers weren't murderers, and they didn't plan to change that if it could be helped.

Surprisingly, even Olivia had been somewhat tame with her opponents, even though the pain of being whipped with her special weapon had made some of them think they might have been better off dead.

"He . . . he actually managed to beat Kirk, the rookie champion," Kai uttered in disbelief. It was then that Olivia snapped the whip back to herself and wrapped it around her arm.

That boy . . . I could tell he was on his last legs, she thought. *It was almost as if my body chose to do whatever it could to save him. Was that because he turned me into a werewolf? Would I have been free if I hadn't intervened and Kirk would have finished him off? . . . Either way, this result should be more beneficial to me.*

I thought this group of kids would stay back and only come in after the fight between the two, like the other smaller gangs had planned, but that's not the case at all. It's only a matter of time until news spreads that there is a new Altered in town who's stronger than Kirk. They shouldn't be planning to make their move any time soon.

A wide smile appeared on Olivia's face. She had grand aspirations to move up, but she had always been careful. It was hard for any gang to rise up, since those in power would do everything to keep the status quo.

The Lady Boss had been biding her time, hoping to gather support from her clients until everything was perfect, yet the Howlers had come and taken over. However, given today's performance, she felt like they would amount to great things in the end. It was possible this gang would achieve what she always wanted, and if she stayed by the alpha werewolf's side she would reap the benefits.

Clenching her hand, she wondered what she was starting to become.

You have defeated your first Altered
Quest reward: 2 Pawn points have been granted due to the diffi-
culty of the quest
Additional rewards: Instant Level Up
Skill selection
Congratulations, you have now reached: Level 18
A stat point has been granted
Optional Quest (Waste not want not) is still in progress
Consume the body of the Altered for additional stat points

Right now, Gary didn't care what the system was showing him.

"Kirk!" the alpha werewolf growled out through his large snout. "Kirk!"

It was clear that Gary was trying to communicate with his defeated opponent, but the onlookers wondered why. Getting no response, and seeing that he couldn't keep up his form for much longer, the teenager did something surprising.

Pulling out his hand, Gary caught Kirk before he fell to the ground and leapt to the side of the building, digging his claws into the walls. He leapt up again, digging his hand in. The werewolf was jumping up the wall while carrying Kirk away. After he reached the rooftop, he ran off into the distance.

The others watched in amazement, not quite sure what to do now. All the gangs' leaders were now gone, with only the Howlers having someone who could take charge. Kate, was on the rooftop, had lost sight of the two Altered and had no way to follow them.

However, the crowds on the ground remained. Hearing someone beginning to speak, Kate asked her cameraman to swiftly zoom in.

"Listen up!" Kai shouted as he confidently walked into the center of the street, where Gary and Kirk had been fighting just seconds ago, pools of blood all around.

"This war is over!" Kai declared. "Everyone, remember our name! We Howlers are the ones who punished the Gray Elephants who created and unleashed these monsters in the town of Slough, and our leader was the one who defeated the Underdogs' Altered. From this day on, you all better be careful because we will take over everything the Gray Elephants and the Underdogs own! Should any of you try to stop us . . . then I welcome it!"

His words were loud and clear for everyone to hear, and all the gang members on the ground had no case to argue. Where were their strong leaders? They were nowhere to be seen.

However, the Howlers wouldn't be able to take over today, not yet, and Kai knew that; his declaration was mainly aimed at the other small-time gangs, because he was sure that there was a group of people waiting to make their move, and he was right.

At either end of the street, the police had come out of their cars with their megaphones ready.

"Everyone, please stay indoors for a little while longer. It is still not safe to come out. I repeat, please stay indoors for a little longer. It is not safe to come out," Anton announced over the megaphone.

"Erghh, what does he mean it's not safe to come out?" Marie asked, worried that this meant something else was about to happen.

"No, they can't be. We freaking defeated those monsters, and fought off all these gang members!" Innu shouted. "They can't be thinking of . . ."

"All right, everyone!" Sadie the White Rose agent shouted out. "Go and bring them all in!"

Alas, Innu's guess was spot on.

CHAPTER 118

ESCAPE

The police were already on the move once they saw that the fighting had started to settle down. They had been waiting for the moment when one of the Altered would finish the other off.

No matter what state they were in, Altered were dangerous. There was no point in losing police officers' lives over the current incident, and Sadie was being cautious for other reasons.

When that wolf Altered howled, my foot started to hurt again. Was he the one who bit me? But according to the gathered DNA it was the deceased Billy Bruntin . . . not to mention, his fur color was different.

Since when are there so many Altered in this shitty Tier 3 town? We will have to make a report to stay here longer after this, Sadie thought.

"Are you sure you want to do this?" Anton asked one more time before giving the order to his men. "You know that reporter from Channel Five is filming everything, right? If we do this, we will look like the bad guys."

Sadie laughed at his comment.

"I don't care about the public's opinion," she replied. "Whether we are the bad guys or not, we are simply doing our job. Besides, do you really think these people came here to protect the innocent?

"No, this whole war started because of the gangs in the first place. Those Howlers must have seen an opportunity and decided to take advantage of it. No one cares for the people but us. They seem to forget, because your men wear uniforms, but they have lives too. They have families they need to go home to."

It was then that the unexpected had occurred: the fight was over, but the wolf Altered had taken both of them out of the area. He was most likely the gang leader, so Sadie had been sure he would stay back and protect his fellow gang members.

However, Gary had not simply left the scene, but he had taken Kirk's body with him. Because of this, she needed to act fast. In her Altered form, she should be able to catch up to him and arrest him while he was still weakened.

The next second, a single wing sprouted from her back.

"What the—? What is wrong with me?" Sadie was confused at her body not listening to her.

"Don't worry about them, let's just deal with those in front of us. Let's protect the people like you said," Frank said, attempting to cheer his partner up.

The single wing retracted back into her body, to her dismay.

The police started to charge in from both sides. If the injured Howlers were to fight their way out of this, it would be difficult.

"Come on! We won't be able to convince them to get you out of this one; we have to go!" Olivia shouted. She wasn't sure if it was her own desire or her just adhering to the pack rules, but she felt compelled to help the little rascals.

In her own group, they wouldn't be punished too much, not unless the police had proof that they had murdered some of those who were dead, but most of that had been done by Damion.

The others got up, staying close behind her. They ran forward and saw that the police had covered even the narrow streets on the other side. So instead, she threw her whip toward the door of one of the shops, wrapping it around the handle. She pulled the handle completely off and flung it to the side, throwing it toward the police.

"She's really good with that whip, huh? I mean she's doing things that are impossible, right?" Marie asked.

The others didn't think about it much, but Marie was right. A special trait of the whip was that as long as Olivia could picture what she wanted to do with it, the whip would do exactly that. It would follow the image in her mind, giving her perfect control.

With her added strength and speed, it had made her a lot stronger than before. The group thought that they might have to barge through the crowd of people inside, but as they entered everyone stepped out of their way.

"There's a door in the back!"

"Come this way, we'll try to hold off the police for you."

It looked like they had gained the public's trust for getting involved and dealing with those creatures, more so than the police. Immediately after the Howlers had entered, they stood in front of the door, trying to slow down the police however they could.

They followed the owner of the shop to the back door; he was drastically trying to find the key among the dozens on his key ring.

"It's okay, old man, thanks for the help so far!" Olivia shouted as she booted the door open. They were now on the other side of the street.

She ran out, and the others quickly followed behind her.

"We'll send someone to pay for the door, I promise," Kai said as he ran past with the rest.

They were finally on the other side, but the others would soon catch up with them. If the police sent a car after them or someone spotted them, they would be in trouble.

Just then a car came screeching around the corner. It stopped in front of the gang members, and Kevin opened the door from the inside.

"Get in, quick!"

They jumped into the car, squashing into the back, while Olivia calmly opened the front passenger door and got in. It was a bit of a squeeze, but that didn't matter right now.

The next second, the car was driving off away from the scene.

"Whoa . . . man, my hands are shaking," Tyler confessed behind the wheel.

"You've certainly earned your keep. Remind me to give you a bonus once we make it out safely," Kai said.

"How did you know . . . how?" Innu asked.

"You guys were all over the news. We were watching what was going on, and when we saw the police making their move, we knew we had to do something," Suzan explained.

"But what about the wolf mask boy, should we drive around and try to find him?" Tyler asked.

"He's okay," Olivia answered. "Trust me."

At that moment, Gary didn't know where he was, but he had been leaping across shop and apartment rooftops, getting away from the area as much as he could. Eventually he could no longer hear the sounds of fighting.

He stayed where he was, on an empty rooftop, just a few clothes-lines full of laundry that people had not taken in even though it was now nighttime. Gary carefully placed Kirk on the floor and inspected the wound in his body.

Kirk's eyes were still working as they looked toward him.

"What . . . are you doing?" Kirk finally managed to say.

Gary was still unrecognizable in his werewolf form, but as he canceled his Full Transformation, his face started to revert, tears flowing down his face.

"I'm sorry . . . I'm so sorry."

As the fur disappeared and the face went back to normal, Kirk could see who he was.

"Greeny?"

STAY WITH ME

Gary was just far too upset to care about whether Kirk recognized him. In fact, in some way he felt that he needed Kirk to know who had been the one to fight and defeat him, and how much Gary regretted it.

He had decided to agree to Kai's plan, yet when he had killed all those orphans, it had felt like the only way to save them; but this . . . this seemed liked a complete waste, a misunderstanding that could have somehow been avoided . . .

Aware of the kind of injury he had dealt the Altered, Gary had felt as if someone had plunged a knife into his heart, but now, seeing the way Kirk looked at him, with just a tiny smirk on his face, yet without any blame in his eyes, it felt like someone had twisted it.

"I—I didn't mean to, Kirk . . . I didn't mean for a-any of this to happen!" Gary sniffled between his words, tears rolling down his face and landing on the Altered. "E-everything started going wrong that d-day when I was supposed to d-deliver that package. I—I didn't steal it, I swear!

"Instead of the c-client, there were those gangsters who attacked me . . . and I—I somehow turned into this. Wh-whatever was in the package did th-this to me, but it was impossible to explain. D-Damion would have killed me for sure! Th-there was nothing left in the suitcase and the g-gangsters, they were . . . they were . . . so I went into hiding . . ." After telling his part of the tale, Gary started to trail off.

He didn't know why, but the werewolf felt compelled to explain to the Altered how everything came to be, and how they ended up in this situation. Gary felt extremely guilty about how things had turned out. While he was speaking, though, he realized it meant nothing. All of those things that happened to him . . . why did it mean Kirk had to end up this way?

"I understand, Greeny," Kirk eventually said. "I've seen people change after becoming an Altered, but you never seemed the type to hurt anyone because you wanted to. I've also heard rumors about how the Pincers let half of their working staff go, and I bet that you had a hand in that now that I know who you are. Even I thought those rumors had to be false.

"I could feel your desperate punch at the end; everything you have done so far seems to have been for the sake of survival." After finishing his sentence, Kirk coughed, and a little blood escaped from his mouth.

"Don't speak!" Gary shouted. "I'm going to save you!"

Checking the system, Gary looked through the skills he had. There was the Alpha Bite; if he attempted to bite Kirk now, he could turn him into a werewolf. If that was the case, then perhaps eating some flesh would allow Kirk to heal just like him.

Although Kirk was the enemy, he would be able to follow Gary.

Skill activated: Alpha Bite

At that moment, Gary's eyes glowed red, his canines lengthened, and he looked at Kirk's other arm, which was mostly intact, and lifted it up. Without hesitation this time, he bit into it.

"Argh! You're trying to kill me quicker!" Kirk let out a dry joke. "I'm kidding, I barely even feel it any more."

Error: Alpha Bite cannot be used

"What do you mean Error, you shitty system? Explain to me! Don't give me a skill and then tell me that there is an Error in the skill!" Gary lifted Kirk's arm and bit into it again in another spot.

Error: Alpha Bite only works on human targets!

Seeing the message twice, Gary let go of the arm and allowed it to drop to the ground. He was at a loss as to what to do, and the second time he had bitten into Kirk, the Altered didn't even make a sound. The werewolf looked at his idol and saw that his eyes had blurred even more.

"Gary, are you still there?" Kirk asked, even though the teenager's face was right in front of him. "I want to tell you something . . . I never wanted to do this. You know . . . I'm glad that I'm the one who ended up like this and not you.

"I had always planned to let you go. The only reason I was looking for you was so I could hide you from Damion. You're a good kid who was just unlucky to be born into this kind of world. You know . . . I saw you one day . . . when you left the hospital . . . I'm sorry I didn't arrive earlier . . . hope your mother recovers . . ."

"Stop speaking, Kirk, you have to survive! I'll take you to a hospital, I can run really fast, and they can save you!" Gary shouted back.

The truth was Gary was low on Energy, and on top of that, even if there were hospitals that could treat a wound like Kirk's, it would be in one of the high-tier cities, not Slough. The Altered was lucky that he had managed to survive until now, and be able to still speak.

"I wish . . . never became . . . Altered . . . too much . . ." Kirk said, yet his voice became weaker until it drifted off completely.

Gary hadn't even heard why he had decided to follow a scumbag like Damion, why he had worked so hard for that bastard, and now he had no breath at all. His heartbeat had already stopped completely.

"No, Kirk, no!" Gary shouted again, as he started to push on Kirk's chest, up and down. Honestly, Gary didn't know what he was doing, he was just trying to get his heart to beat again. As he was pushing, he thought back on all his interactions with Kirk; why was he so close to this man, who was mostly a stranger to him?

However, eventually Gary stopped because he knew it was useless. He knew that Kirk was dead.

Optional Quest (Waste not want not) is still in progress

The quest screen came up as he looked over his idol's body. Could he really eat someone he cared so much about?

If I leave his body here, what will happen? Who will it go to? Although I've seen him fighting so many times, I've never heard him say anything about his family . . .

There was something in his head, something prompting him to eat the body. When Gary thought about it more, he thought back to some of his lessons. How animals eat their prey fully, as a sign of respect after fighting. However, he wasn't the brightest person, so maybe he had this confused with something else. Still, when people went hunting, it was rude to leave the dead bodies after killing them.

Kirk, I'm going to take a part of you; I'm going to take your body to make me stronger. That way, wherever I go, part of you will be with me. I promise I'll use the strength your body gives me to kill the person who was the cause of all of this! Gary silently swore as he took his first bite.

CHAPTER 120

BODY OF AN ALTERED

The Channel Five broadcast had come to an end; at least the filming of the fight between Gary and Kirk couldn't be continued. Kate would have loved to follow behind the duo, but finding the Altered who had disappeared into the distance seemed like a lost cause. Instead, the reporter went down and attempted to interview the police, yet every single one of them refused to comment on the matter.

Damn, it's clear they were instructed to say that. They must be aware how bad this whole thing is going to make them look. An entire gang war happened right under their noses, despite agents from White Rose having been present. It seems like they might have had some idea of these strange Altered in the first place, Kate thought.

She changed her target and attempted to interview the people who had been in the area, who proved to be far more talkative. She asked them about how frightened they were, when the strange creatures had started to appear, and whether they had heard anything said from below. After all, the cameraman's microphone could only pick up so much from the rooftop.

The only thing that was clear was the name of the mysterious group that had been dressed in black and gold. The Howlers. This name was repeated several times, and it was obvious that the public was on their side.

The consensus was that the Gray Elephants must have had something to do with the strange creatures' appearance; most people guessed that it was a ploy to be used against the Underdogs, who weren't well respected even on this street.

Normally, people hid their dislike for the Underdogs, particularly the shopkeepers, but they spoke freely about them today.

One person who had finished watching the video couldn't believe it.

Cat dude . . . I'm not even sure I would be able to come back from that one, Jayden thought. *That was a strong blow . . . but what is streaker boy doing caught up in all of this? . . . It seems for the best that Xin is leaving Slough, after all . . .*

Now it started to make sense how Gary had been able to locate his sister. Typically, Jayden would have an immediate dislike for anyone remotely connected to any gang, but somehow he still had a soft spot for the werewolf, perhaps because he had tried to save his sister in the first place.

It's a relief that that dominatrix got involved; if she hadn't . . . streaker boy would have undoubtedly been the one to die, Jayden concluded. *Before I leave Slough, I should pay him one more visit and let him explain himself, and find out what's his plan in all of this.*

When Gary had eaten Hawk and friends—and Billy—fear, anger, worry, regret, and all sorts of emotions had come over the werewolf as he got on with the grueling task. Eventually, it reached the point where some type of instinct, something deep within him, would take over.

The first few bites were always the hardest to swallow, and he needed to convince himself to think of them as oversized critters, until this other part came over him. However, for the first time, Gary remained fully conscious throughout the process.

He ate Kirk in tears. The werewolf somehow managed to suppress his instinct, going through this as a way not to hide from anything, to remember every bit of what he did, to remember every-thing that he was doing.

It was tough, but he considered this his own punishment.

Another reason for him not allowing his instinct to take over was so that there would be some parts of Kirk left. He avoided eating the Altered's bones, at least as best he could, but most importantly, he left his head intact.

Most of his flesh was gone, and his clothes were laid out on top of his bones, somewhat covering him. But there was no need to do anything else, according to the system at least.

Optional Quest has been completed
The following stats have been awarded
+3 Strength
+6 Dexterity
+2 Endurance

If it had been any other time, then perhaps Gary would have been amazed at how many stat points he had gained. Each level up only granted him a single one after all, yet now he was gaining several. On top of that, the Dexterity stat, in which he had been severely lacking in the past, had increased the most.

It made sense, seeing as Kirk had been an Altered who had heavily relied on his speed, but right now, Gary wasn't in the mood to think about these types of things. He didn't want to think about eating other Altered or beasts, as the system claimed he would need to do in order to level up.

Congratulations, you have gained 1 Knight point
1 Knight point = 5 Pawn points

At the moment, Gary had three Pawn points saved up, and he had already used one to try to upgrade himself to the next grade. With this he would have surpassed it; however, before he tried to mess around with the system, he needed to do something with the body.

He went to one of the nearby clotheslines, on which a large bed-sheet had been hung out.

"Sorry," Gary said as he pulled it off the line and put the rest of Kirk's body on it. After eating the Altered, Gary had regained nearly all of his Energy; he was just twenty points shy, and he had regained all of his Health as well, with the passive healing. Clearly there were many benefits to consuming an Altered.

It seemed like Altered did indeed count as beasts to the system, but beings like the twins or the orphans didn't.

Bringing the corners of the sheet together, Gary tied it up and chucked it over his shoulder. He knew it was somewhat disrespect-ful, but he wasn't in a situation where he could afford to consider alternatives.

There's a lot of blood still on the rooftop, but I guess there really isn't much I can do about it, but what do I do with the bones?

Gary looked at the markings in the air, his hunting targets. Two of them were active, and the third had disappeared.

So it looks like the Gray Elephants leader kicked the bucket in the end, Gary thought. *But that means that Damion and Gil are still alive.*

Not knowing quite what to do, he did what he usually did in this situation; he made a call to a certain person. But only now that he'd had time to think about it did he realize in what sort of situation he had left his friend, making him wonder if he was okay. He could tell that Olivia was fine, and his current Bond Marks were active, so he at least knew that most of them weren't dead.

Unfortunately, he was unable to connect. Kai had immediately hung up, not allowing the call to go through. Just in case, Gary tried again, but this time . . .

The person you have dialed is currently not available.

Rather than ringing, it hung up immediately; either Kai had switched off his phone or something was wrong.

What is going on? Gary wondered.

CHAPTER 121

THE WHOLE WORLD KNOWS

The Channel Five team was local to Slough. Because of the sudden emergence of the crazed Altered, the studio had sent an emergency broadcast to all of the town's citizens, informing them about what was happening over their phones. With the number of areas that had been attacked at once and with how many had died, they had to notify as many citizens as possible; otherwise more lives would have been lost.

However, now that the interviews were complete, it was time for Kate's higher-ups to decide what to do with her footage. Would it stay local news or be shared with the world? Kate Dar didn't have much hope, feeling that whoever was behind this type of experiment surely would have a large enough backing to shut it down.

Some small articles had been published by indie news reporters and journalists that weren't too flattering for those in the higher-tier cities. As a consequence, they had straight-up been told to delete the whole thing, often followed by a "correction," or the news outlets would start to suppress them to the point where they became forgotten. It wasn't rare for journalists to leave their line of work altogether, after realizing that their dream work wasn't as rosy as they had originally believed it to be.

The only silver lining about this event was that Kate had heard that a local livestreamer by the name of Scotty had recorded the events and that his channel had exploded. His livestream had been accessed by many people outside Slough. What's more, some citizens of Slough had also made videos and taken pictures, which they had started sharing online.

As quickly as one video could be taken down, more were uploaded, and the netizens who saw them made sure to make copies. This event started to grow into a matter that the whole world was going to see. Kate's higher-ups seemed to have come to the same conclusion—that it would be impossible to suppress it—so the station opted to capitalize on the event by sending their footage to stations in all the different-tier cities.

Footage spread across the country not only of the strange crazed Altered but also the fight between Kirk, an up-and-coming star in the AFC, and a wolf Altered.

A red-haired man sat in a sauna room that was far too hot for a regular human. He had no clothes on and simply stared at the ceiling. His body wasn't sweating one bit, despite the extreme heat. The water vapor in the air sizzled the moment it touched him, as if his body were made out of hot coals.

Well, I never expected them to use the test syringe in such a manner, Sin thought. *They should have just used the entire thing on one person. Honestly, I don't know whether to call this development a good or bad thing.*

At least I won't have to go to that shithole again, but who knows what development this might bring . . . Will the status finally shift? Sin smiled.

Sin wasn't the only King in charge of a Tier 1 city who had seen the video. Inside a white lab, where several workers were pacing up and down, a woman stood on a balcony staring down at all her workers.

I can't believe our package never made it out of that place, she thought. *Worse yet, it looks like someone has already gotten their hands on it. How did they know? . . . No, that doesn't matter; the problem is that they all know now! It looks like we might have a little rat in our group.*

Before we continue on with the development, we have to find out who it was!

The situation attracted attention from outside the country as well. However, the public wasn't too invested in the news. Most people didn't care about what was happening in a foreign land, and they thought of it as nothing but an experiment that had gone too far in the race to create superior Altered. Similar things had occurred in their countries before, leading to far deadlier outcomes.

After all, each country had their own government-funded institutions as well as private ones working around the clock to deliver the next generation of Altered. Since the passage of the worldwide No Lethal Weapons Act, the Altered were now the way of showing off their country's strength.

The number of Altered a country had was important, but their individual strength was even more so. If anything, the only debate other countries had surrounding the event was just how strong was this wolf Altered that they had seen.

And yet one person had been watching the news and saw something he had never expected to see. His hands clenched the armrests of the chair he was sitting in, so tightly that the wood fibers inside started to snap.

"What on earth is happening? What the hell are these people doing?" the man screamed at the top of his voice, his eyes glowing red in the darkness; standing next to him was a person with blue eyes.

"There must have been another bloodline still alive; it's the only thing that makes sense based on what we are seeing right now," the blue-eyed man answered.

"Another bloodline should be impossible!" the red-eyed man yelled, so loudly that the TV fell over backward off its stand and broke.

"If there is another one, you know what this means and has always meant," the blue-eyed man said.

"We'll start searching for him. I can only hope we'll find him before it's too late."

CHAPTER 122

THE START
OF THE END

It had been a tough night for the Howlers gang, and more than that, it was another large turning point for them. Who would have thought that a group of teenagers could impact their small town so much?

After Tyler drove them a short distance, Olivia left the car; it had thankfully left plenty of space for the others. Marie was sure she had been touched in strange places multiple times and couldn't even yell at the boys because she had no clue who had been responsible, not that she believed they were doing it on purpose in the first place.

Olivia had called one of her men to pick her up and said she would be waiting to hear what they were to do next. At the same time, the Lady Boss knew she would be busy, trying to get her men who had been arrested tonight out of a cell.

Still, she knew that this period of time was crucial. If they wanted to take advantage of the situation that had been created between the two biggest gangs, they would have to act soon. However, Kai had only given her a lackluster response, telling her he would inform her soon.

Tyler kept driving, listening in on his passengers' talk about what had happened. He honestly couldn't believe it; never in his wildest dreams did he imagine something like this would happen in Slough, much less his involvement in it, albeit passively.

Sometimes he thought about quitting his new job. It seemed far too dangerous, but today he felt like he had done some good, and he was getting addicted to this feeling, addicted to the excitement.

Marie talked about how she had been saved by the Altered Hunter, wondering what the man looked like underneath his mask. Austin noted that his fists and punches were getting stronger. None of them seemed willing to address the topic of Gary being a confirmed Altered, but perhaps they wanted to hear an explanation from their boss himself.

As for Innu, Kevin, and Suzan, none of them were in any mood to talk, despite how excited the others were, but no one could blame them.

"I can't believe they were all turned by the Gray Elephants," Innu eventually said.

"I got an update from that young police officer from before. They managed to get a warrant and search the warehouse, but as expected they found nothing," Suzan informed him, but the truth was they already knew what happened with those orphans. The fact that they found nothing in the place that was meant to be the new orphanage said a lot in itself.

In the end, Suzan and Kevin couldn't hold back their sadness anymore; as they sobbed, the car continued on. That was when Innu asked Tyler to drop them off at a certain destination.

"Kai, we are going to find out who was responsible for all of this, right? We're going to take down the Gray Elephants and find out who is behind them, right? It can't just be some small-time gang in Slough!" Innu asked the fox-masked teenager.

"Huh, what? Erghh, yeah, sure . . ." Kai replied, once again not saying much else, not even caring that Innu had blown his cover by calling out his name.

Austin looked at the blond teenager, wondering if he had been hit too hard on the head or something, but it was clear that anything they talked about with him today wouldn't quite go through.

"We're here," Tyler announced.

The place they had stopped at was none other than the Black Rock Orphanage. The trio stepped out of the car and said their goodbyes. A few minutes later, the vehicle stopped once more, letting Austin out, leaving only Marie, Kai, and Tyler inside.

However, Kai continued being aloof, just blankly looking at his phone every once in a while.

"You know, you're close, so you don't have to go, right?" Marie finally said.

"No," Kai replied instantly. "I have to go *because* we are so close. I can't afford to mess anything up at this point."

The car had stopped at the location Kai had requested. He opened the trunk and took out a bag that he had prepared from the beginning. Taking off his mask and changing into more casual clothes, he closed the trunk and signaled for Tyler to take Marie home.

It was quite a walk, and during it Kai tried to fix himself up as much as he could, but the bruises on his face made it clear he had been fighting. Eventually, the high schooler found himself at a quiet little stream.

It wasn't wide, and there was a downward hill on both sides that created a pathway for cyclists and joggers. Kai felt a vibration in his trouser pocket; after pulling out his phone and looking at who it was, he pressed the red end call button.

I should switch off my phone for now, Kai thought, and he did just that.

Walking down the hill, now on the pathway, he soon found himself walking toward the underside of a bridge. Up ahead were several men in suits. Some of them appeared injured, as if they had just gotten out of a fight, while others looked completely fine.

There were even a few members of the Cheetah Squad who had apparently made it out without arrest. However, Kai wasn't scared, because this meeting was for those in the Underdogs, and since he was technically a member he had been called in as well.

There was a sofa up against the wall that linked to the bridge above, and next to it were two flaming barrels fueled by paper and wood.

"This should be everyone!" A loud voice came from the person on the sofa. Damion sat there relaxed, seemingly in a good mood. "I called you all here because I got rid of that damned Gray Elephants leader, and we need to plan what to do next . . . Hang on, where's Kirk?"

Of course, Damion hadn't bothered to watch any of the news channels, having just made it out, and nobody wanted to be the bearer of bad news. However, one person answered as he stepped forward through the crowd.

"Kirk is dead . . . or at least I think he's dead. It was all over the news," Kai informed the Underdogs leader.

"Dead? Did that damn wolf-masked freak really kill him?" Damion stood up and kicked one of the burning barrels. "How? How is that possible? Kirk wasn't just anyone, he was the goddamn rookie champion!

"Do you know what kind of favor I had to call in to get someone of his caliber to work for me?"

Damion strode over toward Kai, the axes still in his hands. Knowing their leader's temper, the others stepped back, but the blond teenager didn't flinch, because he knew he would be safe.

"It's the truth, and we need to know what to do next," Kai answered, as Damion stopped right in front of him.

Damion lifted Kai's hair and looked at the bruise on his head.

"While the rest of us were fighting, you were having scraps with other kids, how cute," Damion commented, dropping one of the axes on the ground between the two of them. He then ruffled his hair and pushed his head to the side.

"Take it, that's yours now. With the situation we're in now, we are going to need every bit of help we can get, even from someone like you. Use it well, otherwise I'll use it on you," Damion threatened, sitting back down.

Kai looked at the axe for a short while before picking it up off the ground, holding it firmly in his hand. He inspected it carefully, having expected something like a surge of power in his body, but there was nothing. If he didn't know any better, he would think this was just a sharp, ornate axe.

"It's not every day that I give out a present; how about some f*cking gratitude?" Damion shouted at him.

Feeling that the tensions were settled, the others started to walk back in, closer to Kai. Gripping the handle tightly, he thought of all the others, so he put on a fake smile and bowed.

"Thank you . . . Father. I will make sure to put it to good use!"

ABOUT THE AUTHOR

JKSManga is the pen name of UK-based, *New York Times*–bestselling LitRPG author Kawin Jack Sherwin, whose series include My Vampire System, My Dragon System, and My Werewolf System. His works have sold fifteen million copies worldwide, and several have been adapted into comic books.

9 781039 454415